BLOODED ON ARACHNE IS . . .

BLOODED ON ARACHNE

MICHAEL BISHOP

A TIMESCAPE BOOK
PUBLISHED BY POCKET BOOKS NEW YORK

ACKNOWLEDGMENTS

"Among the Hominids at Olduvai," copyright © 1978 by TASP Press/Robert Frazier for *The Anthology of Speculative Poetry*.

"Blooded on Arachne," copyright © 1975 by Robert Silverberg and Roger Elwood for *Epoch*.

"For the Lady of a Physicist," copyright © 1978 by Michael Bishop for *Black Holes*.

"The House of Compassionate Sharers," copyright © 1977 by Baronet Publishing Company for *Cosmos*.

"In Chinistrex Fortronza the People Are Machines," copyright © 1976 by Thomas M. Disch and Charles Naylor for *New Constellations*.

"On the Street of the Serpents," copyright © 1974 by David Gerrold for *Science Fiction Emphasis I*.

"Piñon Fall," copyright © 1970 by UPD Publishing Corporation for *Galaxy*.

"Rogue Tomato," coypright © 1975 by Robert Silverberg for *New Dimensions 5*.

"Spacemen and Gypsies," "The White Otters of Childhood," "Cathadonian Odyssey," "Leaps of Faith," and "Effigies," copyright © 1971, 1973, 1974, 1977, and 1978 by Mercury Press, Inc. for *The Magazine of Fantasy and Science Fiction*.

 A Timescape Book published by
POCKET BOOKS, a Simon & Schuster division of
GULF & WESTERN CORPORATION
1230 Avenue of the Americas, New York, N.Y. 10020

For Ursula K. Le Guin

CONTENTS

PREFACE

AFTER nearly eleven years of writing and selling stories marketed as either science fiction or fantasy, if not both together, I am pleased to have Arkham House publish this hardcover edition of my first collection. *Blooded on Arachne* contains eleven stories and two poems, all possessing many of the recognizable attributes of science fiction. The earliest story is "Piñon Fall," the most recent "Leaps of Faith," and the differences between their approaches and emphases are telling. A subsequent volume from Arkham House will feature material that deliberately smudges the borderline between fantasy and reality. Here, however, the stress is on the *palpability* of the disorienting tomorrows, the unfamiliar landscapes, the strange beings, and the occasionally unprecedented conflicts that suggested themselves to me.

The British writer Ian Watson has called me an "exoticist," and I have myself written about the importance of otherworldly "local color" in the works of fantasists and science fictioneers. Therefore, if you do not find yourself *living* in these exotic worlds, experiencing them as a vivid if outlandish species of reality, then I have failed in my intent. Some people, I realize, resist this kind of writing because it unabashedly embraces the unreal, the never-was, the hasn't-been-yet, the speculative, and the altogether unlikely—but the business of writers like Poe, Wells, Bradbury, and Le Guin is to establish the legitimacy of their worlds through the force of their idiosyncratic visions and the rightness of their distinctive prose styles. In these stories, then, I have often had such writers before me as models, pathfinders in the terra incognita of the imagination, and I have tried to trample out and mark with colorful flags a few unusual pathways of my own. How well I have succeeded is not for me to hazard, and how often I have failed is not a topic I want to dwell on.

Some general observations about the stories:

I wrote "Blooded on Arachne" while living in a small drafty house in Athens, Georgia. My central concept—self-aware spiders drifting in lofty squall lines of silk over a rugged sandstone landscape—may have arisen as a wish-fulfillment fantasy. Because I was employed as an instructor of freshman English at the University of Georgia, self-awareness in any guise was attractive to me, and my family and I used to take long, sanity-preserving cruises in the country. This was before the traumatic squeeze of the energy crunch.

"Cathadonian Odyssey" dates from the same period. Its exotic landscape, its gutsy heroine, and its dependence on such venerable sf conceits as downed spacefarers, mysterious aliens, and telekinesis—well, these are flourishes that still occasionally appeal to me. I had just desultorily read a book entitled *Psychic Discoveries Behind the Iron Curtain* because it seemed to me at the time that an aspiring sf writer ought to know about such things.

Damon Knight declined to use the original version of "Effigies" in his *Orbit* anthology series, but expressed a qualified fondness for the notion of growing people from seeds, calling it "spooky." Cadmus, the founder of Thebes, is reputed to have grown an army of mindless warriors from dragon's teeth (it might not be inappropriate to call these warriors dragoons), but I do not think I can cite a classical impetus for "Effigies." About the time I wrote the story I had been doing a lot of gardening, and the vaguely erotic contours of my squash and okra mounds may have led me to devise a metaphor linking human and vegetable generative forces. (Or maybe not.) Some people have complained about this story's "bleakness," but my gardens never turned out very well, either.

"The House of Compassionate Sharers" is another story that Damon Knight saw in a flatulent early version. (Bless the man's heart. Years after those annoying rejections I begin to appreciate a little of what *he* suffered at my hands.) I later completely rewrote the story, shortening it by almost a third, and resubmitted it to Damon with an epigraph from his fine 1968 short story "Masks." For perfectly good reasons—nor am I being coy—he declined this version, too, and it subsequently appeared as the lead story in the first issue of the regrettably short-lived magazine *Cosmos,* edited by David G. Hartwell. Soon thereafter Terry Carr, Gardner Dozois, and Donald A. Wollheim acquired reprint rights for their respective best-of-the-year anthologies. My first, and so far only, hat trick.

Thomas M. Disch and Charles Naylor provided the incentive for writing "In Chinistrex Fortronza the People Are Machines." They were compiling an anthology of original stories based on cagey recastings of myths, legends, and fairy tales (whether ancient or contemporary); and my jumping-off place was "The Nightingale" by Hans Christian Andersen. Andersen's version begins, "In China, you know of course, the emperor is Chinese, and everyone he has around him is Chinese too." The charm of the original tale lies in its simplicity; whereas the chief shortcoming of my far-future adaptation, as Richard Delap once correctly pointed out, is its infernal *busyness*. Still, I am fool enough to think that a second perusal—I know, *I know*—may well reward the patient reader: "Zizizi, click, rescan."

"Leaps of Faith" probably represents one of the few *serious* sf tales—if not the only one—about fleas. My, ahem, hard scientific information came from an article entitled "The Flying Leap of the Flea" in *Scientific American.* The incidents structuring the narrative, meanwhile, had some odd, even perplexing, parallels in my own experience. In 1977 Ursula K. Le Guin recommended "Leaps of Faith" for a Nebula Award in the short story category, but with the exception of Edward L. Ferman at *Fantasy and Science Fiction,* who first published it, no one else seems to have noticed this off-trail little narrative.

I remain grateful to David Gerrold for buying "On the Street of the Serpents" for his anthology *Science Fiction Emphasis* when I was still a very new, and very uncertain, young writer. His enthusiasm for this effort, and later his and Betty Ballantine's joint encouragement, led me to write my first novel. Although "Serpents" by no means pleases everyone, I am proud to have written it. It recalls for me my senior year of high school in Seville, Spain; the birth of my first child; my ambivalent feelings about teaching English to Air Force Academy candidates during the dark mid-tunnel days of the Vietnam War; and my doubts about my ability to succeed as a writer.

"Piñon Fall" was my first fiction sale. (Earlier I had placed a poem, rather Keatsian in style and subject matter, with the *Georgia Review*.) Ejler Jakobsson at *Galaxy* purchased it in the spring of 1970 for a C-note. Not long after its publication there appeared in *If, Galaxy's* sister magazine, this enthusiastic response from Mrs. Charles E. Willis of Albany, Georgia: "The delicately haunting theme of this story remained with me long after I had finished reading it—not a commonplace occurrence. The writer shows a sensitivity of expression and a talent for original description not frequently encountered. . . . I look forward to reading more by Mr. Bishop." She probably wanted a letter. Mrs. Charles E. Willis of Albany, Georgia, is my mother.

"Rogue Tomato," a finalist for the 1976 Hugo Award in the short story category, deserves neither exegesis nor defense. It is a shameless piece of work. I love it.

In a cover letter to Ed Ferman I described "Spacemen and Gypsies" as a "parable about the conflict between technology and art" (I was twenty-five), to which highfalutin characterization Ed responded, "I don't want *parables;* I want *stories.*" But he bought it anyway. The astronauts in the story hijacked my imagination by way of television coverage of the Apollo moon missions, while my East European vagabonds held me at knife point via a magical painting by Henri Rousseau entitled *The Sleeping Gypsy.* Looking back, then, I can see that the conflict was not so much between technology and art—which, after all, need not be in conflict—as between the cool black-and-white of our most popular electronic medium and the fresh technicolor palette of an eccentric French primitive. I am not antiastronaut, merely propolychrome.

I wrote "The White Otters of Childhood" before the publication of either Peter Benchley's extravagantly popular novel *Jaws* or Edward Bryant's moderately well known story "Shark." My wife—who seems to think that, given half a chance, I would rewrite the children's classics of A. A. Milne to inflict an accidental poisoning on Pooh Bear and a grief-stricken suicide on Piglet—*likes* this story, the nearest thing to headlong melodrama I have probably ever written. Well, it remains a favorite of mine, too. Influences include four of the five writers whose names appear after the story's epigraphs. Moreover, the notion of the poet-protagonist probably derives from Roger Zelazny's "Rose for Ecclesiastes," which I had first read in one of Judith Merril's definitive annual anthologies. "White Otters" and another long story of mine were finalists for both the Hugo and the Nebula Awards in the novella categories in 1974, but neither of them won. I consoled myself by buying a bowling shirt.

This collection also contains two poems, "Among the Hominids at Olduvai" and "For the Lady of a Physicist." The former first appeared in Robert Frazier's *Anthology of Speculative Poetry*, with a subsequent appearance in a special "Perceptions of Science Fiction" issue of *Pacific Quarterly Moana*. The latter poem was published in Jerry Pournelle's anthology *Black Holes*. It eventually won the 1979 Rhysling Award, long-poem category, given by the Science Fiction Poetry Association. Had there been an awards ceremony, I would have thanked, among others, Andrew Marvell and Stephen Hawking.

The stories and poems follow, and I had best stand back and let you read them.

AMONG THE HOMINIDS
AT OLDUVAI

1.

Their mothers drop them in the dust of unnamed
    basins.
Their sires rove like jackals on the periphery of
    extinction.
How I came to be among them is anybody's guess.

II.

Their sun is a gazelle's heart held throbbingly aloft.
They are learning how to pick apart its ventricles.
Scavengers, they speak to me only of their appetites.

III.

Heedless, I ask them of Pangaea and its postmitotic
    progeny.
Laurasia and Gondwanaland are orphans to their
    understanding.
The incontinence of Africa sculpts them to its needs.

IV.

Language begins to sprout in the left brains of the
    females.
The males poach dextrous insights from the dead
    savannahs.
Birth remains a labor insusceptible to practical
    division.

V.

The tools they make resemble plectra for uninvented
lutes.
My pocketknife is a triumph no less complex than
television.
What percussive music rings above the barren of
this watercourse.

VI.

My awe goes ghosting at their austere commensal
feasts.
Together they break crayfish and suck the slip of
birds' eggs.
Their most lovely artifact is a fragile group
compassion.

VII.

What they make of me is what the millennia have
made.
My sophistication seems a fossil from the future's
coldest stratum.
Am I the last anachronism of what they move
toward?

BLOODED ON ARACHNE

ETHAN Dedicos stood at the turnstile in the sapphirine depot with the other disembarked passengers of the *Dawn Rite*. Outside, the wind blew and the world fell away. Among the dronings of people sounds, it was his turn.

"I've come to be blooded," he told the man at the stile. Because of the noise, he had to repeat himself, shouting.

"Go the H'Sej," the stile-tender said out of a skinned-looking face.

Ethan glanced around: bodies, polarized glass, a series of plastic domes, red sandstone beyond, a pinprick sun. "I don't—"

"There, by the footslide. That one, boy. The hag-sage with the spider crown. Move on, Ethan Dedicos, you make us lag."

He went through. Bodies pressed behind him, angry of elbow, flashing-loud of teeth. Hands shoved at him, hands pushed him this way and that. By the footslide the H'Sej was staring at him, a man maybe old, with skin the color of burgundy wine and brown satchel clothes that swallowed him. The spider crown was made of blue metal, and the tips of its eight legs seemed to grow into the hag-sage's narrow skull.

"I'm Ethan Dedicos," the boy said. "I've come to be blooded."

"Who sends you, Ethan?"

"The Martial Arm. I'm to be a star-bearer, an officer of the Arm. Isn't that why you're here, H'Sej? Didn't you come to meet me?"

3

"I know you, Ethan Dedicos. But I have to know if you know what you want. Now you can come with me."

The hag-sage turned, ignoring the crowd in Scarlet Sky Depot, and maneuvered agilely onto the footslide. How old, the boy wondered, how old the H'Sej assigned me? He followed the burgundy man.

"Can you tell me your name?" he shouted.

"Integrity Swain, Child of Learned Artifice," the maybe-old man said, grabbing Ethan's arm and pulling him alongside. The name was a genealogy, not solely a descriptive designation. Learned Artifice had been this hag-sage's father, and their people lived in the salt gardens on the margin of Arachne's desolate sea bottoms. That was where you went when you were blooded, and that was all you knew until the H'Sej made you aware of more. "Sej, only Sej, is what the outli people call me, boy."

Then they were out of Scarlet Sky Depot, on the precipice-stair that fell into the basin where Port Eggerton lay: white larvae nestled plastically against the red sandstone. Other people went quickly into air tunnels that led down to the administrative complex.

The wind blew. The pinprick sun hurled glitterings across the sky, and even here the noise of a world continuously eroding and reshaping itself made real talk impossible. Dizzied, Ethan put an arm over his eyes to block the blowing sand, the scathing light, the fear of falling.

"Sej!" he shouted. "The tubes! Can't we take the tubes down?"

"We aren't going into Port Eggerton, lamb's eyes."

"I must report to the Martial Arm!"

"You report afterward!"

And the maybe-old blooder of boys led him away from the drop-tube terminals, away from the precipice-stair, across an expanse of plateau. They fought the wind to a chimney of rocks beyond Scarlet Sky Depot, now a shimmering bubble-within-a-bubble-within-a-bubble at their backs, and plunged down the wide abrasive chimney into silence.

On a ledge they halted, and Ethan Dedicos could see nothing but the dark-red rocks surrounding them. Above, maybe the sky. Below, faceted cliffs without bottom. In the wide stone chimney he trembled with a calmness as eerie as drugsleep.

"What do we—?"

"We wait, Ethan Dedicos."

"Why do we wait here, Sej?"

"For transport and because you aren't to see a friend-face until the blooding's done. You aren't to think of Earth or probeship voyagings. We provide now, my people of the salt gardens."

"And the blooding—what must I do?"

"Survive, of course." The hag-sage chuckled. "We play old games on Arachne."

And the maybe-old blooder of boys squatted on the ledge so that his brown vestments billowed around him and his burgundy hands hung over his knees like the bodies of skinned rabbits. He stopped talking, and darkness began climbing up the faceted cliffs below. Ethan leaned on the cold rocks, studied Sej's spider crown, and waited.

And stiffened with his aloneness.

On the other side of the plateau, down in the red basin, there were people just like him. Not just wind-burned hag-sages; not just the promise of cranky spidherds, arrogant in their gardens of salt and sandstone.

Impatience burned in Ethan Dedicos like a secret fuse.

Then from deep in the chimney of rock a golden spheroid rose toward them, a ring of luminous orange coursing about its circumference. The coursing ring emitted a hum more musical than a siren's song. The entire canyon glowed with the spheroid's ascent.

"Sej!"

"The nucleoscaphe from Garden Home. Our transportation."

"Such a vehicle! I didn't think—"

"The spidherds of Garden Home aren't barbarians, un-blooded one."

Humming, the nucleoscaphe hovered beside them. The brilliant-orange ring swept upward and became a halo over the spheroid rather than a belt at its middle. A door appeared, and a ramp reached out to them like a silver tongue. The H'Sej, ignoring the chasm that fell away beneath the ramp, entered the nucleoscaphe. Reluctantly Ethan Dedicos followed, his eyes fixed on the darkness inside the humming spheroid.

Then he was inside, and the howling ruggedness of Arachne seemed light-years away. Beside the maybe-old blooder of boys he found himself in a deep leather chair the color of Mediterranean grapes. The chair swiveled, but

the curved walls of the nucleoscaphe bore nothing upon
them but silken draperies. Directly overhead, there was a
stylized insignia depicting a spider as drawn from the top.

When the nucleoscaphe's ramp retracted and its door
sealed shut, man and boy could not see out. Alone, in a
gargantuan atom.

Soon they began to move. Unearthly music droned in
their ears.

"Sej, this is a wonderful thing, this vehicle. Couldn't you
have had it come to Scarlet Sky Depot? Did you have to
make me climb down a hundred rocks to hitch a ride to
Garden Home?"

"The nucleoscaphe belongs to the spidherds, boy, not to
your outli folk in Port Eggerton. A long-ago gift of Glaktik
Komm and the Martial Arm. You don't like climbing, heh?"

Ethan said, "Will it take us to Garden Home?"

"Close, close. We'll have to walk a few last kilometers,
down from the perimeter cliffs." The H'Sej laughed. "But
only because I like to climb, to walk, to hike. And your
feet, lamb's eyes, how will they fare?"

Ethan was silent.

In only a few minutes, it seemed, the nucleoscaphe had
stopped. It hovered, hummed insanely, and ran out its ramp
for the maybe-old man and the boy to disembark upon.
They went out into the night and the chill, onto a brutal
ledge. The nucleoscaphe closed up behind them and
dropped goldenly into the abyss, disappearing like a coin
sinking through water. Overhead, the stars mocked.

"Come with me, Ethan Dedicos."

Along the ledges, down the uneven sandstone steps, the
H'Sej and the boy struggled. At last they came upon a salt
plain and left the escarpments behind. In the starlight, monstrously alone again, they walked across an empty whiteness. They walked all night. When dawn began reddening
the yardangs that had at last begun to appear in the desert
(grotesque, plastically shaped rocks suggesting the work of
a demented sculptor), they finally sighted Garden Home.

"There," Sej said. "Punish your feet some more, darling
Ethan."

In the morning's attenuated light Ethan Dedicos saw the
salt towers surrounding the central butte of Garden Home:
Garden Home, an assemblage of yellow syntheskin tents
huddled in a cove beneath the encircling pillars of white.
Forty or fifty such tents, all of them large. The encircling

pillars, larger yet, pitted with arabesque holes by Arachne's winds. It was a dream city, but as cruel and as real as eroded rock.

"How can you live out here?" Ethan asked.

"Nowhere else is so dear. For three hundred years there have been spidherds in Garden Home, supported at first by Glaktik Komm but living here now like even our own arachnids. And each year the Martial Arm sends us its stringclinging neostarbs to be blooded. Such as you, lamb's eyes."

"Why was Glaktik Komm a patron, Sej? In the beginning?"

"Someone must care for the spiders, they said. Must keep them away from the new depot. In their saliva is a terrible virus that can affect almost any kind of living cell, a virus to which the arachnids themselves are evolutionarily immune. We must study the Stalking Widows, they said, we must have people who will watch them and destroy their poisons. The first scientists who watched them invented the symbodies you carry in your veins, Ethan Dedicos, to keep your blood lucid starwhen and starwhere. The spidherds of Garden Home are the children of the makers of the symbody, the children of the outli folk who killed disease, for always."

They were close enough to see people among the yellow tents.

"Why must you stay here now?" Ethan asked. "Why must anyone remain in this angry desert of salt?"

"To call the spiderlings home, boy, to sing them back to Garden Home when they have gone ballooning."

Ethan remembered something vague. "Isn't that but once a year?"

"Aye. But we love our leggy beasts. They are as thoughtbright as you or any stringclinging manbud in the Martial Arm. We stay because we belong to them, because we talk the spidherd–Stalking-Widow talk."

"You talk to them? And understand their talk?"

"Talk to them, croon to them, pipe to our spiderlings the homing call of Garden Home. The Stalking Widows are a people, too, unblooded Dedicos."

Ethan said nothing. They strode into a crowd of burgundy people who moved among the plastic buildings. A few of these people hailed the H'Sej wordlessly by dancing their fingers like spider legs. The sun was now full up. Its strange light glittered on people, tents, and stones alike.

Ethan felt lost, alone in the long shadows that rippled from the fanciful salt pillars: lovely, sensuous, weird.

They were in front of a tent. A piece of plastic facing unzipped, and a woman darker than the red wines of Jerez stepped from behind the yellow flap into their paths.

The boy saw that she was not a maybe-old woman, she was antiquity given flesh. Her hair was stringy magenta. Her albino eyes stared out of the crimson-brown stain of a face rivuleted with time webs. She wore brown sacks. A witch for really real, the boy thought. And the witch twisted her head upward in order to see him from her stoop.

"Allo, N'tee Swain," she said to the H'Sej. (A voice like the high notes of an aeolectic flute.) "Is this the boy you bring us to put out for the blooding?"

"Ethan Dedicos he is," Integrity Swain said. And then the blooder of boys added, "This is the Widows' Dreadwife, Ethan. Embrace her well."

The neophyte star-bearer embraced her. Surprisingly, she had no smell, even though her face flesh was against him close. Then she drew back. Albino eyes stooped to see him and crinkled in their mask.

"Come inside, unblooded one. Breakfast for you. Then to the top of Garden Home to see the Stalking Widows and their chirren."

They entered the large tent and ate sand locust from earthen bowls. Ethan noticed a vacuum well in the center of the tent—a sparkling chrome mechanism that could tap water from deep within any planet's crust. Odd to see it in the hands of this semiprimi people. The Widows' Dreadwife fetched him a bowl of water, and her fluty voice echoed in the big syntheskin canopy.

"It never rains on Garden Home, nor on the sea bottoms beyond. We spidherds'd die if Glaktik Komm took back our well."

"True it is," Sej said. "The Stalking Widows and the sand locust have their own ways to water, but the vacuum well is ours. Blood our boys and keep our well, they say."

"And you eat only the sand locust?"

"No, no," the Dreadwife said. "Dull eatings, if so. Also eaten are murdered husbands of the spider people, egg sacs, sea-bottom merkumoles, and our own dead when such dyings come." The Dreadwife laughed, a falsetto piping. "I am soon to be eaten, I think."

Unblooded Dedicos asked no more about the spidherds' diet.

They went out into the hot bright morning—Dreadwife, hag-sage, and boy. Through the paths among the yellow tents they ambled, to a natural stairway leading through salt glens to the roof of Garden Home. This wide, uneven roof overlooked the sea bottoms, which were hidden from the city in the cove by the enclosing pillars themselves.

Before they reached the high place, they stopped beside several valleys in the rock where spidherds tended their charges and sang to the Stalking Widows out of dutiful throats.

"Look upon them with your lamb's eyes, boy." Sej pointed. "Down there you'll see the people who go eight-legged and wraithly in our hearts."

And so he looked down into a bleached, grassless glen and saw a burgundy boy of his own age singing in the lovely patois of Garden Home to a horde of ghostly, stilt-standing mistresses. Fifty or sixty Stalking Widows—tall white ladies whose bodies were almost transparent—moved jauntily about the glen, and the spider-boy moved among them. Ethan could not believe it. They were as tall as elephants.

The burgundy boy stooped now and again to stroke the colorless hair on his ladies' bellies, sometimes even blowing voluptuously on the wind-sensitive trichobothria furring their legs. When he did this, his ladies reared up, waved their foremost limbs, and opened their jaws—but more from pleasurable excitation than from fear or anger. The boy's song, the boy's breath, worked on them almost sexually, but without the end result by which they divorce themselves forever from their spider husbands. The boy was not eaten.

"Can they hear his singing?" Ethan asked. "I didn't think some spiders could hear."

"On Arachne," the Dreadwife said, "they hear, they hear."

The spectacle hypnotized Ethan Dedicos. The wind in his own hair prompted pointless stirrings in his loins. Then the burgundy boy in the glen saw the three of them looking down and waved his loose fingers at them in the character-istic greeting of the spidherds.

"Threnody Hold," the Dreadwife said. "A masterful touchsinger."

They went on. They looked down into other valleys, saw other spidherds touchsinging, watched the stilt-legged giantesses dance. And Ethan Dedicos felt the planet's heat in him like unrequited desire.

They reached the roof of Garden Home and stood looking across the sea bottoms stretching endlessly away to the horizon. And beyond, Ethan thought. The wind blew blastingly here, but not as hard as it had on the plateau outside Scarlet Sky Depot. They did not have to shout to make themselves heard.

"We drop you in the bottoms on the morry," the Dreadwife said.

"What?" Ethan looked down at her sharp profile.

"That's where your blooding begins, as you know," Sej said. "But we begin tomorrow."

"What do I do out there?"

"Come back to us, sweetling," the Widows' Dreadwife piped. "Come back to us with blood on your hands—all bedighted in a grown-up's skin."

"Allo, Baby Tranchlu!" Sej suddenly shouted. He hailed a girl of seven or eight who had just appeared at the top of the path on the other side of the butte and who was walking across its wind-pitted surface toward them.

The girl had a wide Oriental face stained a tentative mauve. She drove before her a group of spiderlings so colorless they seemed to be made of glass. They were a third of the size of the prancing ladies they had seen in the salt glens, but still as tall as Baby Tranchlu herself. Mere babies, they moved on splinter-thin legs, as clumsy as newborn colts. Only the scopulae on the pads of their feet kept Arachne's winds from blowing them away.

Ethan stepped back as the little girl and her spiderlings approached. He wanted to fall into the planet's sky. And drown.

"Come here, Tranchlu. Say allo to this summer's neostarb, here to be blooded."

"Allo," Tranchlu said.

Her spiderlings, nine or ten in all, tottered about the four human beings and ruminantly waggled their mouth parts. Pedipalpi. A combination of hands and soft teeth, these mouth parts; a strange melding. Baby Tranchlu stared at Ethan.

The Dreadwife asked her, "Have you brought these chirren for the wind, small girl?"

"These be firsties," Tranchlu said. "More on the morry. Goose summer we have. They go fly."

"It's gossamer time," Sej translated. "The spiderlings disperse. These that Tranchlu has attempt the wind today, but tomorrow thousands will go ballooning. Many will die. Every year a thousand spidikins fly, and one boy is blooded."

"Go on," the Dreadwife said. "Put them about it, pert smirl."

Baby Tranchlu did a gangly little dance and sang to her babies in the lilting patois that Ethan couldn't understand. She turned, and pirouetted, and danced along the butte to a place where several salt spires thrust up into the sky. The spiderlings followed, stilt-legging in her wake and flashing glassily in the sun.

"Watch how it is," Sej told Ethan.

The spiderlings, as if on the pert smirl's commands, climbed the pitted rocks and fought both wind and gravity with sticky feet. Ethan lifted his head to watch. Clinging precariously to the spires as they moved, the spiderlings turned in slow circles and ejected strands of silk, which floated on the wind. Their underslung spinnerets paid out more and more glistening thread, more and more. And more and more.

The sky was a pale crimson suspended in a crystalline net, a color captured in webs.

"There they go, Tranchlu!" Sej shouted.

And the leggy babies, still clinging to their skyey umbilicals, lifted from the rocks. Upward they were dragged like parachutists jumping backward for the door of an invisible aircraft. Ethan felt as if he were watching a film being run the wrong way. Up, up, up, the spiderlings floated.

"But where are they going?" Ethan asked. "Out there are the sea bottoms—nothing else."

"Out there is all of Arachne," the maybe-old man said.

"What happens to them?"

"Some of them die, some of them come back. None of the people of the Stalking Widows live anywhere but here at Garden Home."

"Then why should these little ones go out at all? Why disperse, if only to die or come back?"

"Goose summer it is, lamb's eyes," the H'Sej said. "They go out."

And when Baby Tranchlu's babies were lost in the webby welkin, the hag-sage, the Dreadwife, and Ethan Dedicos descended the paths of the salt-garden butte to the yellow tents in the cove.

The winds died, the afternoon trekked by, and night came out like a dark maiden wearing candles. There was food, and talk. Then Ethan laid himself down among the bodies of murmuring spidherds, closed his eyes, and slept his first sleep on Arachne. While he slept, the maybe-old man touched his face and whispered, "I love the boys I blood. Remember that, lamb's eyes." Ethan heard an orange humming. Groggy, he rolled over.

And woke up on the sea bottoms.

He got to his feet. The sun was already up. He turned around. In every direction, whiteness whiteness whiteness whiteness.

"Sej!"

There was not even an echo. Only a dead word falling from his mouth, and a hint of wind. The desert air smothered the word, and he wondered if he had shouted anything at all. The sun glowered.

"*SEJ!*"

Again and again he turned around. It was impossible to be this alone. How could they have done this to him? With the nucleoscaphe only. He remembered its humming. *Be sure, be sure.* Kneeling, he looked at the floor of the sea bottom and saw no tracks, no footprints, no telltale striations on its hard white surface. He stood up. He turned around again. There were no landmarks anywhere. Where was his hag-sage?

"*SEJ, YOU BURGUNDY BASTARD!*"

This was his blooding. Drugsleep they had hyped him with in Garden Home and put him out to cope. The Widows' Dreadwife had told him how it would be. Sej had said, "Survive. We play old games on Arachne."

Ethan Dedicos was a neostarb of the Martial Arm, and neostarbs were blooded. So be it. He would play. He would think, and grapple, and run. Very well. What had they given him to play with? What survival pieces had he at hand?

Ethan Dedicos looked at himself and enumerated:

—The silver-blue, seemingly seamless uniform in which he had come to Arachne: light, indestructible, proof against weathers.

—A curved knife; heavy, elaborate of haft, hurtful.

—Two narrow cylinders of water fitted like cartridges into the belt on which he had found the knife; a maybe-supply for two days.

—Nothing else but his wits.

"Sej!" he shouted. "Sej, how are you blooder of boys when you leave your charge to blood himself?"

Irony of name-making. Cruelty of trust. Ethan Dedicos, doubting his neostarb's soul, turned around and around on the salt sea bottom and cursed the probeship fathers, every one. In his head his blood beat loud. And Arachne ached around him like a whitened world wound.

Knowing no directions, Ethan struck out toward the mid-morning sun. He walked and walked. The horizons remained ever distant, ever smooth, annoyingly undisturbed. He looked behind him to see his own footprints, and saw none. He walked some more.

In the midday heat he uncapped a cylinder and drank his first drink: one, two, three drops on the tongue. And walked toward the place where the sun no longer was. And took his second drink: four, five, six drops moistening a cob-webbed mouth.

Then knelt in the middle of nowhere and shut his mind off, *click*. His gut, rumbling, would not so obligingly click off.

Thoughtless, he squatted.

His eyes saw a little hole on the sea bottom, a crumbly place in the whiteness. Ethan Dedicos told his mind to come on. *Click,* it did. Then he dug at the hole and pulled away salt shards and stabbed down with his knife. Scrabbling with his hands, he caught a stunned merkumole and pulled it free of its burrow: an ugly beastie with a hair-horn nose and spatulate feet. In the hot sun Ethan slew it and ate it, sucking the sinewy flesh as if it were candy, crunching the mush-marrowed bones. He drank off his first cylinder of water. The skin and hair horn of the merkumole he thrust back into the caved-in hole contemptuously.

Then shut down his mind, *click*. And walked on the feet of his own shadow, offmindedly trying to step on the shadow's elusive gray head—a bobbing, shadowboxing shadow's head.

His mind would not stay off. What he saw was too strange to look at out of dreamily dead eyes. He halted and

gawked at the horizon, the horizon before him. Pale light
pinked its curving edge, but higher up, the sky was streaming with movement.

It was raining there.

"No," Ethan said aloud. "It doesn't rain on the sea
bottoms."

But what he saw *resembled* rain—even though the only
clouds in sight were three or four miles up, and as feathery
as goose down. Didn't the distant sky glitter with columns
of down-pouring moisture? Didn't the density and height
of those columns verify a desert squall? An advancing
shower?

"It's not supposed to rain out here!" He shook his fist at
the translucent columns for trying to deceive him. He
wanted a rain, but dared not hope. Looking at the lofty
cirrus he thought: As feathery as goose down.

Analogy into equation:

Goose down: goose summer: gossamer.

And suddenly he knew that he was looking at neither a
mirage nor an on-sweeping squall. "Spiderlings coming to
see me!" he shouted. "Tranchlu's ballooning babies and all
their thousand cousins!"

The wind in his mouth, he sprinted toward the arachnid
aviators on their glistening silken tethers—a shower of
blowing cobwebs. If they were coming toward him, then
Garden Home must lie behind their filamentous squall
line. All he need do was walk in that direction, and he
would survive his blooding. His time in the wilderness
would be successfully won through. Thinking that, Ethan
Dedicos let out a joyous yelp. He was sixteen.

But not stupid. He halted again and reconsidered. He
had only one remaining cylinder of water. What were his
chances of stumbling on the burrow of another merkumole? The spidherds of Garden Home had said farewell to
their tottering glass babies early that morning, had watched
them fly off, most likely, right after sunrise. How far might
the spiderlings have ballooned in twelve hours' time? Maybe, Ethan decided, as many as two hundred kilometers,
conservative estimate.

"Sej, you burgundy bastard," he hissed. "Glaktik Komm,
child murderers, and sadists. Venerable starbs of the Arm,
go to Vile Sty."

He hoped these maledictions covered everyone. He would
not be able to walk two hundred kilometers, or more, before

his water ran out and he fell over from the heat. Doornail
Dedicos.

Standing there with the sun at his back and before him
curtains of proteid thread catching the sun's last light, he
peeled a strip of dead flesh from his nose, crisped it between his fingers, and thought. Glaktik Komm, the Martial
Arm, and Integrity Swain were indeed child murderers;
they murdered the child so that a man might move in and
reanimate the vacated corpse. Absolutely. There had to be
a way out of the sea bottoms. The Martial Arm did have
probeship officers, after all, and every one of them had
been blooded.

About a kilometer away Ethan caught sight of a single
drifting spiderling. Sunlight ricocheted off its body and
twinkled from the five or six incredibly lengthy threads
streaming from its spinnerets. Cephalothorax down, the
spider floated toward him. In less than five minutes, as best
as Ethan could judge, it would sweep right by him. Then
the others, the hundreds of others who were still together,
would come ballooning past, too.

"You're my way out," Ethan said. "I'll board you."

But the first balloonist drifted by overhead, out of reach.

Ethan Dedicos waited. In another ten minutes six more
of the advance guard had floated by, all of them either too
high or too far to his left or right to permit a hijacking. He
left off waiting and once again sprinted forward.

On Arachne the afternoon was deepening inexorably into
twilight. The air seemed to be laden with melancholy music
played upon countless strings.

Ethan, still running, was surrounded by showers of
gauze. At last he caught the forelegs of one of the airborne
spiderlings and attempted to hoist himself over its outraged
eyes into the saddle between its abdomen and cephalothorax. For a moment his feet were off the ground, pedal-
ing air. Then several of the spider's leg joints broke off in
his hands, and he crashed back down on the sea bottom,
still holding severed leg pieces. He got up and cast them
aside. Rocking back and forth, the maimed spiderling
floated on.

Half-panicked, Ethan turned in rapid circles in the eye
of the silk storm. His hands felt sticky. He stopped turning
and looked at them. A viscous goo—the colorless blood of
the spider people—adhered to his palms.

As he watched, this goo began taking on a faint pinkish

cast; in another moment it had turned the brilliant burgundy that was the hallmark of the Garden Home spidherds. Contact with air. A chemical reaction. Ethan realized suddenly that he had been blooded. Symbolically blooded. Now all he had to do was survive the very real ordeal of getting back to Garden Home—the part of the blooding that counted.

He wiped his hands on his uniform. "I'll board one of you!" he shouted. "I'll outlive all of you!" He was sixteen.

But he was crying. He wept for himself and the spider whose legs he had pulled away. Sej had as much as told Ethan that the Stalking Widows were intelligent creatures, sentient in the manner of man—or in a manner totally their own, at least. And he, Ethan Dedicos, had cruelly hurt one of their people.

It was not to weep about. He had to try again. Most of the ballooning arachnids were too high to reach, much too high to reach, and the sun had already set; soon they would be flown into starlit darkness. He pulled his belt tight and ran forward, his eyes half misted shut and the immense desertscape glinting with buoyant silk.

Ethan leaped. He caught a spiderling about its thin middle and desperately hung on.

For a moment he feared that the strands supporting it would crumble beneath his additional weight and come cascading down around both of them. He lifted his knees beneath him. The floating spider dipped, then dipped again. Ethan's toes dragged the hard sea bottom, slowing their progress. He lifted his knees again and curled his toes away from the earth. Come on, he thought, come on.

They were up, the spiderling and he—up in the pearly evening sky among hundreds of other airborne travelers, an assault force with no one to make war against. Ethan shut his eyes completely and stretched his legs out. They hung free now, just as he hung free. And the wind washed around his dangling body as if he had been submerged in a beautiful giddy-making tonic.

Finally Ethan opened his eyes and found himself in a jungle of writhing legs. His head was pressed against the spider's belly. He pulled himself up, squeezing his way between two of the creature's hind legs to its chitinous back. He straddled the spiderling, facing rearward, and grasped two of the threads that emerged from its spinnerets. He leaned forward and hung on. After a while his unwilling mount ceased to struggle.

Over one shoulder, Ethan could see the white sea bottoms receding beneath them. The planet's horizons broadened, and broadened, and broadened even more. But only the sea bottoms filled this broadening expanse. Where were they flying off to?

Ethan locked his legs together, tested his grip on the silken cords, and was soon rocked to sleep—deep adolescent sleep, womb-warm slumber. He dreamed that he was piloting the *Dawn Rite* through the surreal glooms of id-space, lost in a comforting nightmare of power.

He woke once, remembering where he was almost immediately. Since it was too dark to see the ground, he closed his dreaming eyes again. The air seemed refreshingly cool, not at all cold. He let the wind sail him back to sleep.

When Ethan Dedicos next woke up, he did so because his spiderling was twisting about in a determined way, as if hoping to dislodge him. He hung on with locked legs and aching hands. It was light. Sort of. He could see neither ground nor sky. The two of them were drifting in a luminous fog, insulated from the outside world. Tatters of insubstantial silver-gray floated past Ethan's face, but the spider's persistent twisting kept him from enjoying the scenery. A cloud bank they were in—a fog of turbulent wispy batting. Where were the other balloonists?

"Stop it!" Ethan shouted. "Damn you, you . . ." He promptly christened the spiderling Bucephalus. "Damn you, Bucephalus!" His voice was muffled by the fog, smothered in moistness.

Bucephalus continued to writhe and sway. The boy wondered how far he would fall if the creature did dislodge him. Several times he felt himself slipping, but gathered his strength and clung like a cat on a bedspread. Shortly he was hanging head-down, while Bucephalus faced skyward and used its forelegs to hoist itself up the silken threads creasing its belly and disappearing into the moving clouds high above.

"What are you doing?" Ethan shouted. "You can't climb up your own balloon wires, you leggy spidikin!"

Then the beast ceased climbing; it left off torquing about. Their frail airship achieved a kind of rocky equilibrium. Looking over his shoulder, upward, Ethan saw Bucephalus joggle several drops of condensed moisture down the flowing silk into its pedipalpi: a drink in flight. Better than Ethan himself could manage.

They floated on for a time, through the silver-gray fog, and then the spider abruptly released its grip on its balloon wires and dropped until joltingly caught up at its own spinnerets. Ethan screamed but held on. When the beast at last stopped bucking, the boy was head-up again.

"You damn near did me that time, Bucie. You damn near did."

They rose through the mist, at last breaking through into painful sunshine. Beneath them their cloud bank undulated like a wide living fleece; above them the sky was the thin Arachnean scarlet that Ethan had almost forgotten. At unhailable distances Ethan saw several other ballooning spiders. He counted nearly forty, whereas before there had been hundreds. The dispersal, he supposed, was progressing as a dispersal ought.

"But to no point," Ethan said aloud. "You either die or return to Garden Home. I hope you're a returnee, Bucephalus. I don't like cloud-walking, it's not first on my list of career priorities."

Through a break in the cloud bank the boy saw that they were over water, water of multicolored blue. The waves sparkled, but it was impossible to judge how high he and his spiderling were. When the clouds at last thinned to mere ghostly wisps, nothing but ocean lay beneath them.

For two or three hours they sailed casually over water. Twice Ethan Dedicos looked on in amazement as companion balloonists reeled in a bit of thread and slowly tailspun into the sea, suiciding. After collapsing upon them, the downed flyers' webs bobbed in random patterns on the bright surface. It was not until these odd self-drownings that Ethan realized his own spiderling might have some control over where they were going.

"Say, Bucie Belle, are you my pilot?"

Ethan looked up at the wind-weaving threads bearing them aloft and tried to discover where the threads ended. He could not. The sun made him squint. Was Bucephalus manufacturing more proteid secretion and silently paying it out? Was it reeling some in, his pilot? Had this been going on all along?

"I wish I knew your talk, Bucie. What kind of blooder of boys fails to teach his neostarb the spidikin lingo?"

Sej, he thought, Sej, you treacherous spidherd.

Far away he saw red cliffs rimming the sea. Their airship drifted in that direction. Eighteen or twenty balloonists still accompanied them, that Ethan could actually see and count. The remainder were gone now, having either plunged into the water or shrunk to invisibility with distance.

Ethan was hungry. Maybe Bucephalus could survive on a drop or two of water every morning, but Ethan wanted food. The taste of yesterday's merkumole was still acrid in his mouth; nevertheless, his stomach made noises as if he had not eaten for a week. But for the moment the boy satisfied himself with a careful sip from the cylinder that Sej and the Dreadwife had provided him.

He looked down and saw earth instead of water, intricate topography instead of the sea's smoothness. Infertile and brownish-red, all of it. Fit country only for predatory arachnids. Why had Glaktik Komm come here? Was it solely to blood probeship captains for the Martial Arm?

No, not solely.

Once, many many years ago, scientists had ogled through microscopes the virulent, shape-changing virus in the saliva of the Stalking Widows. They had done so in order to devise a plastic, semiliving symbody, an adaptable counter to almost any antigen that might enter the bloodstream. Ethan carried these artificial counters in his own blood, while the spidherds of Garden Home had long since developed natural immunity to the arachnid virus.

"How about that, Bucie? You got a mouth full of hungry germs?"

Later Arachne had become an administrative and commercial center, a seedy port. A number of those who came to Arachne were touri-tramps, rugged crazies who sometimes ventured out to Garden Home or even into the dead sea bottoms.

"Not much to see in them, though," Ethan Dedicos told his pilot. "Except the silk storms—and they happen only once a year. Right?"

Bucephalus, the spiderling, kept its own counsel.

They passed over cliff after cliff of creviced sandstone. The entire planet now seemed to be made of lusterless copper. First, white desert. Then, ocean. Now, sandstone.

Shortly it was night again. As myriad stars commenced to burn, the earth blanked out.

Weakened by a night and day aloft, Ethan Dedicos hung on to Bucephalus lethargically. Now another night lay ahead. He uncapped his second cylinder and emptied it in a single breathless gulp. Then the cylinder fell from his fingers and tumbled into darkness. He had eaten nothing all day. His stomach lurched painfully with each new gust of wind. His lips were chapped, his cheeks and forehead blast-burned. And if he went to sleep again, how could he be sure that Bucie would not suicide during the night, plummeting them both to destruction?

He could not. That was the answer: he could not. Knowing the answer too well, he slumped across the spiderling's upturned rear, gripped the threads emerging from its spinnerets, and went to sleep.

When he awoke, only ten other arachnid aviators remained in sight, all a good ways in front of them and conspicuously higher. In the dawn glow over the land Ethan saw a vista depressingly similar to yesterday's endless sandstone. Except that now there were canyons in the rock— monstrous canyons, labyrinthine and cruel. The canyons were new.

Ethan remembered climbing with the H'Sej from Scarlet Sky Depot into a crevice like the mighty ones below. He remembered the nucleoscaphe. Might not these canyons be tributaries to the one he and Sej had traveled in? Did Port Eggerton lie near? Did Garden Home lie near? Probably not, Ethan thought. We have crossed an ocean.

His speculations ceased when Bucephalus began writhing its legs and threatening to topple him into skyey space. Time for a morning drink. Midnight moisture on the balloon wires. Symbolically blooded Dedicos prepared for the spider's topsy-turvy toast to dawn. Inebriate of dew, he silently cursed. Drunken whoreson!

And he was suddenly upside down, admiring red rock.

Then, moments later, he was traumatically upright again, wind whirling blue in his mouth, sun stitching his eyes into a squint.

That day was a dull one. Several times he thought about trying to control the direction of their travel himself—either by cutting a silk strand free or by attempting to pull more thread from one or two of the spinnerets. But he was afraid to experiment. And if he could control their climb and descent, where would he take them? Enigmatic Arachne gave few topographical clues, all of them dreary-dull. As this marvelous floating was finally dull.

Ethan's hunger grew. His weakness, he realized, would

soon be an obstacle to his survival. Faint, fatigued, feverish, he would be bucked into free-falling anonymous death
by bronco Bucephalus's next dipsomaniacal quest for water.
And he would die. It was as simple as that. He—Ethan
Dedicos, neostarb of the elitist Martial Arm—would die,
his body burst upon abrasive rock or abusive sea, his grave
a canyon or a watery grotto. Just another abortive blooding.

Die.

And so, as the afternoon wore on, Ethan made up his
mind to kill the spiderling. He didn't want to. He had to.
To be successfully blooded, one had to survive. That meant
that Bucephalus would have to die.

"I'm sorry," Ethan Dedicos said, meaning it. "I'm sorry
to have to do this."

He removed the knife from his belt, locked his legs
farther down the creature's cephalothorax than usual, and
reached his arms around the abdomen in order to find the
soft membrane where its legs joined its body. Only here
could his knife penetrate the horny skeleton. Bucephalus,
exasperated, languorously waved its legs, but Ethan found
the spot anyway.

And stabbed. And jerked the blade sideways. And
stabbed again.

The spiderling spasmed. Its body hiccupped violently.
Lame, its legs thrashed. Overhead, silken streamers buckled
in the wind, buckled and fluttered. But, forearmed and
resolute, the boy survived these gimpy aerial throes. He
hung on for drear death—the spiderling's, not his own.

Its spasming done, they floated on almost as before.

When Ethan next looked at his hands, they were covered
with clear viscous fluid. He watched as the discharge turned
bright burgundy. This new stain overlapped the old—from
his palms and knuckles, all the way up his wrists. He felt a
murderer, a Jacobean villain, a deranged hero. Oh, blood,
blood, blood, he thought.

And put the thought out of his mind, *click.* So that he
could ensure his own survival. Pilotless now, he had to
hurry. An hour or so ought to suffice, time in which to eat
and plan a second hijacking. If he remained too long aboard
Bucephalus's dead husk, the winds might eventually send
him flailing into nowhere. Only living spiders made it back
to Garden Home. He needed a pilot.

Ethan Dedicos, hanging on with one hand, used his knife

to crack open the chitinous back of the spiderling. Imagine it's lobster, he told himself. Same phylum, after all. Arthropoda. This knowledge proved uncheering.

Deliberately, Ethan ate of the clear tubular heart, squeezing it section by section through the hole he had punctured in Bucephalus's back. He ate until he could eat no more. The taste was vile. His uniform was blotched with wine-colored stains on his chest, and on his thighs, where he had wiped his hands. Again and again he willed himself not to vomit. When he could force no more down, he pulled out still more of the heart and cut loose a large section to hang from his belt. For tomorrow, he told himself. Imagine it's lobster.

By this time, the spiderling's translucent body, open to the air, was shot through with marblings of deepest ruby. To lighten the load that the balloon threads had to bear, Ethan methodically cut away each one of the corpse's legs. He dragged out reddening entrails and heaved them into the wind. They dwindled slimily in the late-afternoon sunlight, spiraling downward in dreamy slow motion.

And as he had hoped, his pilotless airship began to rise.

Four balloonists floated above him now. No more. He had not seen any of the other six spiders plunge into the knife-edged canyons that day; they had simply sailed off. These four remaining ones were his last hope. He had to board one of them before the twilight deepened into night, before night scattered his last hope beyond the prospect of capture. He had to maneuver his fragile craft by body shifts and tuggings of line—expertly, as if he had flown on streaming silk his entire life.

Clumsily, Ethan Dedicos managed. Seldom looking down, he leaned and yanked his way alongside the slowest of the four spiderlings—the slowest and the heaviest. Even so, it bobbed several meters out of reach, to his left and above him. A chasm of air intervened, a frightening chasm of air.

Ethan hacked away portions of Bucephalus's body until he had almost nothing to cling to. Using the toe of one foot against the heel of the other, he pulled his boots free and kicked them into the dropping sun, where they seemed to catch fire and disintegrate. Very little time remained. It was like his last evening on the sea bottoms all over again —but more urgent, more insanely desperate.

Ethan leaned and yanked on the tethers, shifted his

weight, and muttered incoherently into the wind. He looked up and saw that Bucephalus's threads were weaving themselves among those of the spider that he hoped to board. Indifferently, the beast watched him approach. He could almost touch its dangling forelegs, almost look into its mouth. But he wasn't rising anymore. An unbridgeable gap existed, a chasm.

Not knowing what else to do, Ethan unfastened the belt the spidherds had given him and let it drop. Food supply and all: Bucephalus's tubular heart.

Like a buccaneer, he held his knife between clenched teeth. Come on, he thought. Come on. Maybe coincidentally, maybe because of his action, his craft bobbed higher. Then higher again.

And instantly Ethan Dedicos jumped.

He was conscious of his knife slicing his mouth, spinning silverly away. He was conscious of rocking impact and blurred, out-of-kilter horizons. Then he felt his newly filled stomach plummeting canyonward, and his body irresistibly following.

A tailspin. Silk tearing on the sky. This is it, Ethan said to himself. This is it.

At which point he was yanked up by the gossamer canopy pouting from the spiderling's tail, and the world snapped back into place with a *pop*. Miraculously, he was still astride his hijacked arachnid, but now he could see their elongated twilight shadow on a wall of rock below. How far they had fallen! His entire body trembled, his blotched, clinging hands most of all.

Far, far above them the mutilated corpse of Bucephalus rode the gusts ever upward. Ethan felt empty, alone.

"I'm not going to name you," he told his new pilot. "I promise you that: I won't give you a name."

By the time it was completely dark, his heart had stopped its riotous beating, and they had gained a bit of altitude again. Both relieved and exhausted, Ethan pressed his body against his host's, tightened his grip on the silks, and, for the third time in as many nights, went to sleep as if in a treetop cradle. He slept the big drugsleep, he bobbed on the lullaby winds. And dreamed of solid ground grown over with lovely grass.

In the middle of the cool night he opened his eyes and thought he heard the distant sloshing of waves. He did not look down. Soon he was asleep again, dreaming of clip-on epaulets and probeship glory. A venerable starber was he in his sleep rhythms.

The following morning he survived the spiderling's flip-over for water, and, head-down, got a good view of the sea. The same sea as before, or a new one? Multicolored and sparkly, it looked just like the other, but there was no way for Ethan to be sure. White froth and indigo; cream combers and lilac—but not a seacoast or sailing vessel in sight.

Not even in the air was there a sailing vessel. Rightside-up again, he quickly determined that they were alone. The last three balloonists had skyed away during the night, or maybe crumpled down in the dark, to drown. Not again would he be able to switch corpses in midscream (a thought not hateful, so breathstopping had his jump been). Nor could he kill off his current mount for food—but for desperation, but for sheer desperation.

"You're my ticket, trick, and trump," the boy whispered. "You're it, beastie."

Then Ethan himself shook water down the silks, and drank. He was not desperate. Not yet. And all that day they floated where the wind and the spiderling willed—over bright ocean. Until the late afternoon brought land into view once more, a whiteness punctuated with bizarre yardangs; then the red rocks again. A maybe-new continent. He couldn't tell for certain.

Then, at eventide, he suddenly saw Port Eggerton!

And the sapphirine bubble-within-a-bubble-within-a-bubble of Scarlet Sky Depot, high on a cliff above the nestling city!

"We've circled around!" Ethan shouted. "You've brought us back!"

He thought about trying to wrench the airship to earth, about crash-landing on the plateau by the depot. Maybe these bubbles and domes signaled his last chance to look upon the work of man. It would be dark soon, his fourth night aloft. But the Widows' Dreadwife had said, "Come back to us, sweetling. Come back to us with blood on your hands." He had to trust in his spidikin pilot, he had to go cruising craftily back to Garden Home. Otherwise the blooding would be blotted, an all-for-naught mistake. What, what should he do?

With poignant regret Ethan Dedicos watched Port Eggerton slip away beneath them. An opportunity lost. After which, remorseless night fell.

But this night Ethan could not sleep. He made no attempt to sleep. To sleep would be madness. This night, he felt sure, they would balloon their way to the salt escarpments above the spidherds' cove of yellow tents. His journey would be over, his blooding complete. The petty demands of the body—hunger, thirst, weariness—could not eclipse the importance of such a fulfillment.

Adrenaline flowed in the boy, a tiny glandwind raging where Arachne's winds could never roar.

The passing hours, the turning stars, mocked his excitement. He and the spiderling drifted in darkness. Nothing happened. Nothing at all. Had the winds changed again? Would morning again find them over water?

"Weave a spell for us, hag-sage. Burnish your spider crown, Sej, and lift lovely Garden Home out of the desert. Put it anywhere you like, but put it close. Put it goddamn close."

To no avail, this plea. They dipped, and rose, and stuttered in nearly utter blackness, only the stars gleaming. Ethan began to despair. He thought of another day aloft, of his wind-scorched lips and his knotted sinews and the idea of dying at sixteen.

Why not simply slide backward off the arachnid's stupid snout and let whatever lay beneath snuff out his life? In that thought was some sweetness, a temptation like young girls' bodies. It seduced him, almost.

A thin singing saved him, a fluty piping on the wind.

Through the tall darkness, Ethan Dedicos heard this music, and the child of the Stalking Widows heard it too. Instantly they dropped several meters. Ethan's stomach told him that they had dropped. He gripped the silks and pulled himself up a little, so that in a moment he saw far in front of them two tiny flames, like matches burning, and the slowly emerging silhouette of a jagged landform.

It was the roof of Garden Home!

Or was it a dream, a cruel deception?

"No, no," Ethan said. "It's the spidherds' fortress, the Stalking Widows' roost. Home in on that singing, Widows' babe. Home in on it, I tell you!"

They homed. The silver singing, as unearthly as everything else he had encountered on Arachne, led them in.

As they approached the great butte of the Stalking Widows, he could see that the match flames were torches. The dark, milling forms of many people crowded the opening between two salt spires, an opening toward which his pilot was apparently navigating.

And around them, around them in the dark, he somehow knew there were other balloonists sailing in. A very few at a time. Homing in on the eerie song that they had all heard from afar, picking it up long before he himself had heard it. The survivors of goose-summer madness, riding their gossamer tides back home.

And he, Ethan Dedicos, among them. Decorously blooded.

They swept toward the gap in the rock. Torchlight illuminated the strange upturned faces of a hundred burgundy spidherds. He heard cheering, cheering that overrode the ghostly song of the Widows' Dreadwife, for it was she who had sung them in. As they gusted in, he thought he saw her albino eyes flashing out of a fire-tattered face. She was apart from the others, standing on a high ledge. Singing.

The spiderling and boy swept through the gap. Hands caught at him, friendly hands—the hands of spidherds. The cheering swelled until he thought it would rupture the very darkness and spill daylight over all Arachne. Hands clutched at him. Hands held him upright. The press of celebrating bodies bore him staggering, grinning, away from his glassy beast, along a narrow path. Faces among the hands, Baby Tranchlu's and Threnody Hold's. Torches bobbingly accompanied them.

Solid ground, Ethan thought. I'm on solid ground.

And then their procession of faces and hands abruptly halted. And numbly turning up his eyes, Ethan saw a burgundy-dark, maybe-old man in the path in front of them. A hag-sage wearing loose brown sacks and a glinty-blue spider crown. The H'Sej, flickering brightly there.

"Oh, what a man you are now," Sej said. "You're stained and smeared and shredded, just like a spidherd. Just like a spidherd, lovely one."

For a moment Ethan Dedicos stared uncomprehendingly. Then grinned. Then felt a cold, violent ache in his heart. Then crumpled in the hands of the gentle rowdies who had led him to his blooder.

Just like a spidherd Ethan looked, just like a spidherd. Now the Martial Arm would let him drop probeships into id-space. Why did his gut hurt so? His heart, too?

Lurching forward on his knees against the many friendly

hands, he heaved up undigested bits of something saddening. Spittle dripped from his lips and chin. Then he heaved up air, only air. Then he threw back his sweaty face and looked at the imperceptibly lightening sky, where winked a thousand scornful stars.

Just before he passed out, Ethan whispered the word "Bucephalus." No one heard him. No one knew his hurt.

CATHADONIAN ODYSSEY

CATHAY. Caledonia. Put the words together: Cathadonia. That was what the namer of the planet, a murderer with the sensitivity of a poet, had done. He had put the two exotic words together—Cathay and Caledonia—so that the place they designated might have a name worthy of its own bewitching beauty. Cathadonia. Exotic, far-off, bewitching, incomprehensible. A world of numberless pools. A world of bizarrely constituted "orchards," a world with one great, gong-tormented sea.

Cathadonia.

And the first thing that men had done there, down on the surface, was kill as many of the exotic little tripodal natives as their laser pistols could dispatch.

Squiddles, the men off the merchantship had called them. They called them other fanciful names, too, perhaps inspired by the sensitive murderer who had coined the planet's name. *Treefish. Porpurls. Fintails. Willowpusses. Tridderlings. Devil apes.*

The names didn't matter. The men killed the creatures wantonly, brutally, laughingly. For sport. For nothing but sport. They were off the merchantship *Golden* heading homeward from a colonized region of the galactic arm. They made planetfall because no one had really noticed Cathadonia before and because they were ready for a rest. Down on the surface, for relaxation's sake, they killed the ridiculous-looking squiddles. Or treefish. Or porpurls. Or willowpusses. Take your choice of names. The names didn't matter.

Once home, the captain of the *Golden* reported a new

planet to the authorities. He used the name Cathadonia, the murderer's coinage, and Cathadonia was the name that went into the books. The captain said nothing about his crewmen's sanguinary recreation on the planet. How could he? Instead, he gave coordinates, reported that the air was breathable, and volunteered the information that Cathadonia was beautiful. "Just beautiful, really just beautiful."

The men of the *Golden,* after all, were not savages. Hadn't one of them let the word Cathadonia roll off his lips in a moment of slaughterous ecstasy? Didn't the universe forgive its poets, its name-givers?

Later, Earth sent the survey probeship *Nobel,* on its way to the virgin milkiness of the Magellanic Clouds, in the direction of Cathadonia. The *Nobel,* in passing, dropped a descentcraft toward the planet's great ocean. The three scientists aboard that descentcraft were to establish a floating station whose purpose would be to determine the likelihood of encountering life on Cathadonia. The captain of the *Golden* had not mentioned life. The scientists did not know it existed there. Preliminary sensor scans from the *Nobel* suggested the presence of botanicals and the possibility of some sort of inchoate aquatic life. Nothing sentient, surely.

Whatever the situation down there, the scientists aboard the floating station would unravel it.

Unfortunately, something happened to the descentcraft on its way down, something that never happened to survey descentcraft and therefore something the *Nobel*'s crew had made no provision for. In fact, the *Nobel,* as was usual in these cases, went on without confirming touchdown; it went on toward the Magellanic Clouds. And some odd, anomalous force wrenched the controls of the descentcraft out of the hands of its pilots and hurled it planetward thousands of kilometers from the great ocean.

It fell to the surface beside a sentinel willow on the banks of one of Cathadonia's multitudinous pools. There it crumpled, sighed, ticked with alien heat.

This, then, becomes the story of a survivor—the story of Maria Jill Ian, a woman downed on an out-of-the-way world with no hope of immediate rescue, with no companions to share her agony, with no goal but the irrational desire to reach Cathadonia's ocean. A woman who did not wholly understand what had happened to her. A woman

betrayed by her own kind and ambivalently championed
by a creature carrying out a larger betrayal.
　—For Cathadonia.

*I am standing on Cathadonia, first planet from an ugly
little star that Arthur called Ogre's Heart. I am writing in
a logbook that is all I have left of the materials in our descentcraft. God knows why I am writing.*

Arthur is dead. Fischelson is dead. The Nobel *is on its
way to the Magellanic Clouds. It will be back in three
months. Small comfort. I will be dead, too. Why am I not
dead now?*

*The "landscape" about me is dotted with a thousand
small pools. Over each pool a single willowlike tree droops
its head. The pools are clear, I have drunk from them.
And the long slender leaves of the willows—or at least of
this willow—contain a kind of pulp that I have eaten. Trees
at nearby pools appear to bear fruit.*

*But drinking and eating are painful exercises now, and
I don't know why I do it. Arthur and Fischelson are dead.*

*The light from Ogre's Heart sits on the faces of a thou-
sand pools as if they were mirrors. Mirrors. Mirrors wherein
I might drown and rediscover the painlessness of who I was
before . . .*

Maria Jill Ian did not die. She slept by the wreck of the
descentcraft. She slept two of Cathadonia's days, then part
of a third. The silver lacery of the pulpwillow shaded her
during the day, kept off the rains at night.

When she finally woke and began to live again, she
"buried" Arthur and Fischelson by tying pieces of the
descentcraft's wreckage to their mangled bodies and dragging them to the edge of the pool. Then she waded into
the mirror surface and felt the slick pool weeds insinuate
themselves between her toes. A strong woman well into
middle age, she sank first Fischelson's body and then that
of Arthur, her husband. She held the men under and
maneuvered the weights on their corpses so that neither
of them would float up again. She was oblivious to the
smell of their decaying bodies; she knew only that it would
be very easy to tie a weight about her own waist and then
walk deeper into the pool.

The day after accomplishing these burials, Maria Jill
Ian looked away to the western horizon and began walking

toward the pools that glimmered there. Just as she had not known why she bothered to eat and drink, she did not now understand why the horizon should draw her implacably toward the twilight baths of Ogre's Heart.

Later she would rediscover her reasons, but now she simply did what she must.

Today I walked a distance I can't accurately determine. My feet fell on the pliant verges of at least a hundred ponds.

A small thing has happened to keep me going.

The trees over the pools have begun to change. Although their long branches still waterfall to the pools' surfaces, not all these trees are the pulpwillows that stand sentinel in the region where Arthur, Fischelson, and I crashed. Some have brilliant scarlet blossoms; some have trunks that grow in gnarled configurations right out of the pools' centers; some are heavy with globular fruit; some are naked of all adornment and trail their boughs in the water like skeletal hands.

But I've eaten of the trees that bear fruit, and this fruit has been sweet and bursting with flavor, invariably. It's strange that I don't really care for any of it. Still, it's nourishment.

The sky turns first blazing white at twilight, then yellow like lemons, then a brutal pink. And at night the trees stand in stark tableaux that hail me onward.

I still hurt. I still hurt terribly, from the crash, from my loss—but I'm beginning to heal. After sleeping, I'll continue to walk away from Arthur and Fischelson—in the direction of falling, ever-falling Ogre's Heart. . . .

One morning Maria Jill Ian came to a pond beside which grew a huge umbrellalike tree of gold and scarlet. The tree bore a kind of large thick-shelled mahogany-colored nut rather than the commonplace varieties of fruit she had been living on for the past two or three days.

She decided to stop and eat.

The nuts, however, hung high in the branches of the tree. Its twisted bole looked as if it might allow her to climb to the higher entanglements where she could gather food as she liked. Her simple foil jumpsuit did not impede her climbing. Leaves rustled and flashed. She gained a place where she could rest, and stopped.

All about her the pools of Cathadonia lay brilliant and blinding beneath their long-fingered sentinel trees.

Ogre's Heart was moving up the sky.

Maria Jill Ian turned her head to follow the sun's squat ascent. In the whiteness cascading through the branches overhead, she saw a shape—a shape at least as large as a small man, a form swaying over her, eclipsing the falling light, a thing more frightening than the realization that she was light-years from Earth, stranded.

Not thinking, merely reacting, she stepped to the branch below her and then swung out from the willow. She landed on the marshy ground beside the pond, caught herself up, and scrabbled away.

Something vaguely tentacular plunged from the scarlet-and-gold umbrella of the tree and disappeared noiselessly into the pool.

Maria Jill Ian began to run. She ran westward, inevitably toward another pool, struggling in ground that squelched around her boots, looking back now and again in an effort to see the thing that had plunged.

She saw the silver water pearl-up, part, and stream down the creature's narrow head. It was going to pursue her, she knew. Although it came on comically, it flailed with a deftness that demolished the impulse to laugh. Maria Jill Ian did not look back again.

All of Cathadonia breathed with her as, desperately, she ran.

I call him Bracero. It's a joke. He has no arms; he swims like the much-maligned "wetbacks" of another time. I don't know what sort of creature he is.

A description?

Very well. To begin: Bracero has no arms, but in other respects he resembles a man-sized spider monkey—except his body is absolutely hairless, smooth as the side of a porpoise, a whitish-blue like the surfaces of Cathadonia's pools.

To continue: He is arboreal and aquatic at once. He uses his feet and his sleek prehensile tail to climb to the uppermost branches of any poolside willow. Conversely, his armlessness has streamlined his upper torso to such an extent that he can slide through the water like a cephalopod. Indeed, he moves with the liquid grace of an octopus, although one who is five times over an amputee.

To conclude: What disarms even me is Bracero's face.

*It is small, expressive, curious, and winning. The eyes are
an old man's (sometimes), the mouth a baby's, the ears a
young girl's. The trauma of our first meeting has slipped out
of our memories, just as Ogre's Heart plunges deathward
at twilight.*

We are friends, Bracero and I.

The creature had caught up with her when she could run
no more. Halfway between two of the planet's glimmering
pools Maria Jill Ian collapsed and waited for the thing to
fall upon her.

Instead, it stopped at a small distance and regarded her
almost sympathetically, she thought. Its body put her in
mind of a small boy sitting on a three-legged stool, his
arms clasped behind his back as if desirous of looking
penitent. She lay unmoving on the marshy earth, staring
at the creature over one muddied forearm.

Blinking occasionally, it stared back.

Finally she got up and went on to the next pool, where
she leaned against the trunk of an especially blasted-look-
ing tree. The naked creature with two supple legs and a
lithe tail—or another leg—followed her, almost casually.
It made a wide arc away from Maria Jill Ian and came in
behind the willow she was leaning upon. Stoic now, she
didn't even look to see what it was doing.

To join Arthur, to join Fischelson, to join the centuries'
countless dead, would not be unpleasant, she thought.

The eel-beast hoisted itself into the willow and climbed
silently to the highest branches. Then it hung there, looking
down at her like a suddenly sullen child swinging by his
knees.

That evening, her fear gone, she named the creature
Bracero. On the second day beside this pond she saw how
it fed.

Ogre's Heart gave them a characteristically magnesium-
bright dawn. Sentinel trees cast shadows like carefully
penned lines of indigo ink. A thousand mirror pools turned
from slate to silver. Lying on her back, Maria opened her
eyes and witnessed something she didn't entirely believe.

Bracero was still high in the tree. He clutched a narrow
branch with his "tail" and both "feet," his head and torso
swaying gently, freely, like a live pendulum.

Clusters of mahogany-colored nuts swayed, too, in the
dawn wind.

Then, looking up, Maria Jill Ian saw one of the over-sized nuts snap away from the others and float directly up to the creature that had pursued her. Bracero took one foot away from the limb, grasped the willownut, expertly shelled it, and fed himself.

Several times he repeated this procedure, on each occasion the willownut floating within his reach seemingly of its own volition.

The Earth woman stood up and watched in astonishment. Bracero paid her no mind until she moved as if to obtain her own breakfast. Then he shifted in the uppermost branches, descended a little, and made *screeing* noises with his teeth. Maria decided not to go after the mahogany-colored shells that split, so easily it seemed, into meat-filled hemispheres. Did Bracero intend to deny her access to food? Would she have to fight?

Then a willownut fell toward her. But it broke its own fall in midair, bobbed sideways, and floated just beyond her startled hands—a miniature planet, brown and crustily wrinkled, halted in its orbit just at eye level. Bracero had stopped making *screeing* sounds.

Maria Jill Ian looked up. Then she gratefully took the gift and ate.

For the next several weeks she did not have to clamber into a tree again to obtain her food, nor search among the sodden grasses where the fruits and nuts sometimes fell. Bracero saw to her wants. When these were filled, he plunged out of the sentinel willows and rippled the mirror pools. Blithely he swam—until the woman made a move to continue her odyssey westward. Then he again followed.

Maria supposed that the only payment Bracero wanted for serving her was the pleasure of her company. She didn't mind, but she couldn't stay her urge to march relentlessly on Cathadonia's western horizon. Something there pulled her, compelled her onward.

Bracero has telekinetic abilities. He's been with me for almost twelve days now, as best as I'm able to reckon days—and I've been trying very hard to mark the successive risings and settings of Ogre's Heart since it is impossible to determine time by distances covered or landmarks passed.

But for slight variations in the willows, the terrain of Cathadonia is beautifully self-repeating. Looking at it, I can't understand why Bracero is the only native of the

*planet I have so far encountered; he is so meticulously
adapted to this environment that there must be others like
him. Can it be that the men of the Golden were unfortunate
enough to miss seeing even one creature like Bracero?*

*A word about telekinesis, Bracero's uncanny skill at ma-
nipulating objects at a distance.*

*He does it for me every day, several times a day, and
does so for himself as well; afterward, he appears no worse
for this not inconsiderable psychic strain than during times
of simple physical activity. His mind is as sleek as his body.*

*Just today, for instance, I have seen him move the
casabalike melons of an unusual willow that we passed this
morning. He moved them, in fact, all the way to the pool
where we're now loitering. This is no mean distance. It
indicates that Bracero can extend his psychic aura to far
locations, fix upon a specific object, and draw it toward
him at will. Without noticeable aftereffects.*

*Ordinarily, though, he puts under his influence only those
foodstuffs in the trees by which we stop. The casabas (if I
can call them that) were a rare exception, a treat that he
lovingly tendered to both of us. And although I seldom
think about what I eat, I enjoyed these melons, and Bracero seemed to appreciate the delight I took in them.*

*He has an intelligence that is both animal and human. I
have begun to talk to him as if he were a close friend, or
a small child, or (I hesitate to write this) a new incarnation
of Arthur. Bracero watches me when I talk, and listens—
truly listens.*

But I'm off the subject.

*I'm still amazed at the placidity with which Bracero ac-
complishes his psychokinetic feats, the childish nonchalance
of this supranormal juggling. Does it cost him nothing?*

*Aboard the Nobel, of course, we have two PK mediums:
Langland Smart and Margaret Riva. Langland is the older,
and his abilities are more fully developed than Margaret's.
In free-fall he can maneuver an unresisting hypnotized subject in any direction he wants, can make the subject raise
an arm and scratch his nose, can settle him gently into a
padded lift-seat.*

*But afterward, and even during, Langland pays. He loses
weight, suffers dizziness, has nightmares and insomnia
later—and his heartbeat does not fall back into a steady,
safe rhythm for hours, sometimes two or three days, after
such activity.*

It's the same with Margaret, although she can move only small objects and these only across relatively smooth surfaces. She has no ability to levitate things, as do Langland and, more impressively, Bracero. And only Bracero does not pay for the mental forces that he so astonishingly commands over the inert.

The Nobel, meanwhile, expected us to find this watery orchard of a planet uninhabited. Did the men off that merchantship see only pools and trees when they set down here? Arthur and I talked to its captain before we left. He was a nervous ferret of a man. . . .

Ogre's Heart has set. I'm going to stop writing. In the morning we'll be off again. I wonder how much longer it will be before we're there. The willows to the west, the pools limning the horizon—these things call me.

But for tonight it would be nice if Cathadonia had a moon. . . .

For the next two days Maria Jill Ian kept up her compulsive journeying, through terrain that did not alter.

She began to suspect that Bracero was observing her for others of his own kind, that he followed her and fed her not merely to enjoy her company but to maintain a keen and critical surveillance of her movements. She was not an unintelligent woman, by any means, and she was as susceptible to doubts as any healthy paranoid human being.

She believed that she had evidence of Bracero's communicating telepathically with other members of his species. Her evidence consisted of the fact that she still hadn't stumbled across a single one of Bracero's brethren. Before the two of them approached each new willow, each new pool, her sleek friend undoubtedly "wired" ahead an imperative to stay out of sight. The recipient of this communication undoubtedly dove into the water and remained there, nearly insensate, until they departed. Undoubtedly.

That was what Maria Jill Ian believed, and once, as they approached, she saw rings on the surface of a pool. Bracero had been careless, she surmised, and wired his warning later than usual. The slowly fading rings on the surface of the pond corroborated her suspicions. But, of course, she saw nothing but the tree and the water when they had fully arrived. Little corroboration, very little indeed.

Her affection for Bracero did not dwindle because of these suspicions; surely, he did only what he must. Also, none of his brethren had made any hostile move against her. There had been no assaults on her person, nor even any attempts to impede their trek westward.

Maybe Bracero's people had decided jointly to save both her and them the confusion, the upheaval, of further contact. Because he'd seen her first, Bracero had necessarily assumed the combined role of his people's roving watchman and Maria Jill Ian's solicitous escort. She was sure that he returned at least a small portion of the affection she felt for him. His attitude, his expressive face, conveyed as much.

One evening (the evening after she had written the last log entry) they stopped for the night, and Bracero moved as if to clamber up into the inevitable willow. Involuntarily, Maria held up her hand.

"Don't go up there," she said. "There'll be plenty of time to eat. Stay down here." She patted the ground beside her. "We'll talk."

Bracero responded as if he understood her.

His bluish porpoise's skin gleaming in the twilight, he faced her and assumed his comical tripod stance about two meters away. He appeared quite ready to converse—as clinically receptive, Maria thought, as a probeship psychiatrist. His smooth brow was slightly wrinkled, his eyes looked upon her with the estranging narrowness of a devilfish's eyes. Still, his posture suggested no hostility.

Maria Jill Ian talked: "I'm not a dependent woman, Bracero. I know what I'm about. Even now I realize that what draws me on isn't entirely rational. Maybe not rational at all. I know that my loss of Arthur and my idea of home may not be redeemed by following Ogre's Heart to the horizon every day—but because I understand my irrationality, I know what I'm doing. Do you see that, Bracero? One day I'll explain myself to you with more certainty, much more."

Bracero shifted his position. His expression allowed her to think that he did see her point, intuitively.

"Arthur and I used to talk, Bracero. Sometimes without words. Neither of us was dependent on the other, though we were somehow wordlessly interdependent. I know. That sounds like a contradiction—but it's not, not really.

"We had an affinity—a love, you have to call it—that synchronized our feelings and moods in a way not at all mechanical, a spiritual meshing. This was our interdependence, Bracero.

"But we could function with the same rigorous smoothness while apart. He worked his work, I mine; and our shared independence only bound us that much more closely in our love. I miss him, Bracero, I wish he were here beside me now—so that we could talk again, even wordlessly. As before."

She paused. The far ponds twinkled with the day's last light.

"Did you know that I didn't even weep when I buried Fischelson and my husband, when I sank them to the bottom of the pool two weeks behind us? I still can't weep, Bracero. The memory of Arthur's total *aliveness* is still too powerful.

"So different from other men," she concluded. "So different from the cruel ones, the petty ones, the men with stupid hates and overbearing passions. Fischelson, too. Both of them so different."

Maria Jill Ian fell silent. It had done her good to talk, especially to a listener who seemed so congenial. She wished that Bracero could talk. Since he couldn't, she said, "I think Arthur would approve of what we're doing."

A moment later she said, "You don't have to sit there anymore, Bracero. You can climb up into the willow if you like."

Bracero didn't move immediately. He waited as if refraining from the subtle rudeness of leaving too quickly. Then he gracefully swung himself aloft. He hung by his tail from a low limb.

More than on any other similar occasion, Maria Jill Ian was grateful for the Cathadonian's seemingly intentional courtesy. If he were deceiving her, she didn't care.

My hands are trembling almost too violently to write this.
The night before last, I engaged in a long monologue and made Bracero listen to me hold forth on independence, communication, spiritual meshing, love, et cetera.
We haven't moved from this pool, this willow, since that night. The reasons are astounding, they're out of the pale of credibility—but my heart, my head, my trembling hands, all attest to their realness. I have to put it down here. I have to set it down as everything happened—even if my scrawl is ultimately illegible even to me.

*On the morning after our "conversation," I awoke and
looked up to find Bracero. He was there, his legs and tail
wrapped around a branch. When I stood, I could almost
look him squarely in his topsy-turvy eyes, eyes that were
open but glazed over as if with cataracts.*

"Wake up," I said.

*He didn't move. His cephalopod's clouded eyes looked as
removed from me as two useless, tarnished Earth coins.*

"It's morning, it's time to get going again, Bracero."

*He didn't move, still didn't move, and a kind of subdued
panic gripped me. I thought that I would try a feint, a bluff,
to see if that wouldn't set the good warm blood circulating
through him again.*

"I'm going," I said. "You can join me if you like."

*That said, I set off briskly and had slogged through
a good half a kilometer of unending marshland before I actually convinced myself that Bracero wasn't going to follow
and that it was wrong to leave him there: a sort of Cathadonian possum who had never before put on the stiff,
frightening mask of Death.*

I went back.

*Bracero wasn't dead. I could tell that by putting my hand
against his gimlet-hole nostrils and feeling the rapid but
quiet warmth of his breathing. He was in a trance, a coma,
a state of suspended animation—but not really any of these
things, though, because his breathing was hurried, his sleek
body feverish, his pulse (which I found in his throat) tele-
graphically insistent. Only in his relation to the ground was
Bracero suspended; otherwise, his stupor—though deep—
was very animate.*

*I felt I had to stay by him even if it meant losing a day
to our assault on the horizon; I was morally obligated.
Morally obligated. Too, my affection for Bracero has
deepened to a point that embarrasses me. Even the horrible
manner in which he chose to demonstrate his feeling for me
has not turned me against him—though my hands shake,
my head swims.*

*All of yesterday I stayed by him. Bracero didn't improve;
his condition altered not at all.*

*Occasionally I fetched water in a bag made of my over-
tunic and then moistened Bracero's face. I tried to put food
in his mouth—pulp from the willow's leaves, some nutmeat
I had saved, a piece of fruit—but his mouth wouldn't accept these gifts; they dribbled from his lips.*

I went to sleep when Ogre's Heart set. I had nightmares. Shapes moved, voices sang, eerie winds hissed. The awful clamminess of Cathadonia seeped into my bones.

Then, before this ugly little sun had come up again, in the haggard predawn glimmering of the pool, I saw a shape of genuine substance. A shape that wasn't Bracero. A shape floating over the pool.

It was a medieval vision, a fever picture out of Dante.

I screamed into the haggard silence. Inside, I am still screaming; the horrible no-sound of this inward screaming deafens my mind to my heart. Otherwise I couldn't even write this down.

Over the pool, stretched out there as if asleep on his back, a piece of our mangled descentcraft pulling his left leg down into the water, floated Arthur's corpse—horrible, horrible, horrible.

Mercilessly, Ogre's Heart came up to light this fever picture. And nothing I could do would stay its coming.

Maria Jill Ian calmed herself. For the second time in two weeks she waded into one of Cathadonia's pools and laid her husband to rest. She caught Arthur's beautiful, hideous body in her arms. The force that had been holding him in state above the water flicked off and shifted Arthur's melancholy weight entirely to her.

A strong woman, Maria Jill Ian accepted this weight. She lowered her no-longer-human, plundered-of-dignity husband gently into the pool. The anchor she had tied to him two weeks ago pulled him down, but she refused to let him sink away. She supported him. Strangely, it seemed that invisible hands in the water helped her steady Arthur's body and slide him with precision into the silt below.

But Bracero still hung from the branch where he had remained during the whole of his "illness." Weeping quietly, Maria waded toward him.

"You did that for me, didn't you, Bracero? You brought me my husband because I said I wanted him beside me again."

A bitter gift. Over an incredible distance, a distance that it had taken them fourteen of Cathadonia's days to walk, Bracero had exerted his will upon the dead Arthur Ian and reeled him in with his mind—in the space of two nights and one waking period.

The Earth woman could not bring herself to condemn

the eel-beast, the agent of her horror. Although her heart still beat savagely, and her eyes were raw with the sting of salt, she couldn't condemn him.

"No matter what I wish about my husband now, Bracero, let him sleep in peace," she said. "But understand me now: I can respect you for this, I can respect you for your sacrifice."

And Bracero was looking at her again, she saw, with eyes more like a feeble old man's than a devilfish's. His breathing had slowed, too. His limbs and tail appeared less rigid. Three hours later he rippled out of the tree's golden umbrella and took up his expectant tripod stance only a meter away from her.

The Earth woman pulled on her boots and looked back toward the east, at Ogre's Heart climbing the pale yellow sky.

"You're right," she said. "It's time to go again. We've got to forget this place. Arthur wouldn't want us to linger here."

They ate—Bracero ravenously, she only a little—and set off again. Toward the horizon, the western horizon.

We were able to walk, to slog westward, only a half day today—because of Bracero's most recent telekinetic exploit and its aftermath. I've resolved never to think of Arthur as I saw him this morning, but to remember him as he was when I met him, and as he grew to be over the years of our marriage.

I don't know why, but I haven't written here how wearying it is to trek across Cathadonia. The ground sucks at your feet, the marshy soil betrays your sense of balance, the lack of firmness tortures your knees. The muscles in my calves have become extremely hard, my upper thighs like supple marble. Even so, it's sometimes difficult to keep going.

Today, amazingly, I kept going by talking to Bracero. (I still haven't learned my lesson.) I told him everything I could remember about Arthur. Even quotes.

"I'm as hardy as you are," I told Bracero. "Men are hardy creatures. Arthur used to say, 'Men are the ultimate vermin, Maria, as indefatigable as cockroaches, capable of outlasting the universe.' I guess that's why I can keep up with you—go beyond you even."

Even though I can't really go beyond Bracero.

He doesn't have the same trouble with Cathadonia's marshiness that I do. His body is less heavy; his slender limbs are capable of skimming the ground almost without touching it. Usually he swims each of the pools that we come to and reemerges at the western shore, where he lets me catch up with him. But this afternoon, seeing that I wanted to talk, he stayed beside me every step and listened to my schoolgirl's chatter, my woman's wisdom, with the diplomacy of a probeship captain.

Once or twice he immersed himself in a pond, but he always came back, his glistening face radiating a depth of awareness about me, Maria Jill Ian, that I've seen before only in Arthur's face. And so I talked to him of Arthur, fed on Bracero's sympathy, and didn't tire—even though so much talking ought to have made me short of breath.

Once, when we rested and ate, I told him how important it was that we continue pursuing the horizon. I even recited to him from Arthur's favorite poem. And Bracero seemed to respond to the lines as if he understood and even approved the sentiment.

Though much is taken, much abides; and though
We are not now that strength which in old days
Moved earth and heaven, that which we are, we are—
One equal temper of heroic hearts,
Made weak by time and fate, but strong in will
To strive, to seek, to find, and not to yield.

More than I ever thought I could lose has been taken from me, but Bracero's companionship and my own strength remain. These things abide. They make it possible to go on with free hearts, free foreheads, toward the westering sun of Cathadonia.

So be it, Arthur, so be it. . . .

And so they went on, day after day, seeing no one, encountering terrain that repeated itself over and over again—though the fact that they now and again came across a tree that bore different kinds of fruit, or blossoms, or nut capsules, convinced Maria Jill Ian that they were actually making progress.

At last Maria remembered that Cathadonia had an ocean, that eventually these endlessly recurring pools would send out tentacles, link arms, and spill into one another like countless telepathic beings sharing a single liquid mind.

Fischelson, Arthur, and she had made one complete orbit of the planet in their descentcraft before attempting to land, and, she remembered, they had seen the great ocean from the air. How had they fallen so short of their goal? Indeed, what force had so cruelly wrenched the descentcraft from them and sped it raging planetward?

Such things never happened.

Now all Maria Jill Ian had to live for was her march upon that ocean. The ocean. The Sea of Stagnation, Fischelson had suggested before something unprecedented wiped out the two men's lives and her own memory. But now, but now, it couldn't be far, that ocean.

Day by day, Bracero kept pace with her—loping, swimming, outdistancing her when he wished, sometimes lagging playfully behind.

Then he began to lag behind more often, and there was nothing playful in it. Frequently Maria had to call him, almost scold, in order to summon him on.

He came, but he came reluctantly. At each new pool he plunged in and made her wait while he swam five or six more turns than he had taken in the early days of their journeying.

But Maria Jill Ian always waited for him. To leave Bracero now would be to default on a trust. The two of them, after all, still belonged together. Despite his now chronic straggling, even Bracero seemed to recognize this.

One evening, as they prepared for sleep, Maria looked out over their pond and was struck by its size. It was several times larger than the one beside which their descentcraft had crashed. In fact, it had the dimensions of a small lake.

The sentinel tree that bordered this pool trailed its long leaves only in the shallows of the pool's margin, not out over the center.

Why hadn't she noticed before? All of the pools they had passed recently were at least of this size, the trees all as proportionately dwindled in stature as the one she leaned against now. Looking westward, she saw the silhouettes of far fewer trees etched into the lavender sky, than she had seen at twilight only a few days past. The change had occurred so gradually, so imperceptibly, that it was only now apparent to her.

"Bracero!" she called.

The lithe Cathadonian, who had long since learned his name, dropped gracefully from the tree and sat inches away from her.

"We're approaching the ocean, aren't we? Is that why you've been lagging? Does that have something to do with it?"

Bracero looked at her. His stare attempted both to answer her and to comprehend whatever it was compelling her toward the sea. Maria Jill Ian could read these things in the creature's face.

"Let me try to explain," she said. "I'm going toward your great ocean because Arthur, Nathan Fischelson, and I were trying to reach it when something happened to us. Second, I'm going there because all life on Earth, my own planet, arose in the seas. Do you understand, Bracero? That cellular memory is all I have left of home, a little planet in this spiral arm, ninety light-years distant.

"To me, your ocean represents ours.

"That must be how it is. And our oceans whisper to me across the light-years—with the surf noises of Earth, the seething of our species's spawning place."

Maria Jill Ian put her hand to her face. What she had just spoken filled her with an indefinable fear of the cosmos—of its infinite capacity to awe, to stagger, to overwhelm.

"And third," she said finally, "your ocean draws me on because it lies there, to the west. . . ."

I'm afraid. This time is like the other, when I awoke and saw Arthur floating above the dawnlit pool.

But it isn't dawn, it's late afternoon, and in our slender willow Bracero hangs suspended with the glazed look and the catatonic rigidity of that last time. But this, this is the fifth day, and he hasn't eaten or drunk since this violent trance began. His body is incredibly hot.

I'm afraid because the planet seems to be in sympathy with Bracero's efforts, whatever they are.

Two days ago I deserted Bracero and began walking again, in hopes that he would come out of his trance and follow. Instead, when I reached the one semifirm passageway between the two lakes west of here, their surfaces were suddenly riven with roaring waterspouts that reared up taller than the sentinel willows on their banks. The water-

*spouts rained torrents on the isthmus where I hoped to
pass.*

*I had to turn back. When I reached Bracero, he was
swinging more violently than ever, rocking feverishly.*

*I'm afraid because even though he calmed a little after
my departure-and-return, all of Cathadonia still seems a
part of his effort.*

*Several times a day a waterspout forms on this lake and
on all the lakes that I can see from here. These funnels
snarl and pirouette, flashing light and color like giant prisms.*

*I think perhaps Bracero has enlisted, telepathically, the
aid of all his people. From all their individual pools they
strain with him in his new enterprise, working through
Bracero as if he were the principal unit in their mind link.*

*I'm afraid because the skies have several times clouded
over during the middle of the day, eclipsing Ogre's Heart
and suffusing the world in indigo blackness.*

Then the rains fall.

*The the clouds strip themselves away, as in time-lapse
sequences, and shred themselves into thin wisps that let the
glaring light of Ogre's Heart pour down again.*

*Even now I can feel the wind rising, the planet trembling.
Bracero seems vexed to nightmare by his own rocking,
metronomic ecstasy. I'm afraid, I'm afraid. . . .*

On the sixth day the wind was of hurricane force, and
Maria Jill Ian heard the voices of Cathadonia's great ocean
calling to her through the gale. She could scarcely hear
herself think, but she heard these phantom voices as if they
were siren-crooning from the inside of her head.

Astonishingly, Bracero clung with uncanny strength to
his branch. Although his head and torso lifted and fell with
every gust, it seemed that nothing could shake him loose.

Maria held on to the bole of their willow and kept her
eyes closed. Was the world ending? At last she risked
being blown to her death; she let go of the tree, pulled off
her foil overtunic, stripped it into ragged pieces. With these,
she lashed herself to the willow and waited for the storm
to end, or for her life to go out of her.

All that day and all that night Cathadonia was riven by
merciless tempests.

The great ocean to the west sang hauntingly. Maria Jill
Ian had fever visions of gigantic creatures several times
Bracero's size, but otherwise just like him, boiling the seas

with their prodigious minds and feeding limitless power into the receptacle and conductor that Bracero had become.

A psychic umbilical from the seas fed the poor creature, kept him alive, channeled energy into his every brain cell.

And all through the sixth day and night the voices persisted.

The seventh day broke clear and cold. Ogre's Heart showed its wan, sickly crest on the eastern horizon, and the lake surfaces twinkled with muted light.

Maria unlashed herself and slid down the tree to the wet ground. She slept. She awoke to find Bracero in her lap, the first time he had permitted her to touch him— although he had often come achingly close. His body was rubbery and frail. His eyes were narrow and strange. Nothing about him seemed familiar. Still, she stroked his dry flesh and spoke to him a string of soothing nonsense words. Together they waited.

At last, far away to the west, she saw a rounded shape rising over the horizon, looming up as if to intercept Ogre's Heart on its afternoon descent. The shape, a planet, cleared Cathadonia's edge and floated up into the sky like a brown and crustily wrinkled balloon.

It was Earth.

She knew at once it was Earth. She knew despite the fact that its atmosphere had been heated up, boiled off, and ripped away in the colossal psychokinetic furnace of Bracero's people's minds. It was a lifeless, battered shell that floated out there now, not an ocean upon it.

Maybe they had brought it to her in hopes that she would rest satisfied with the gift and leave off her assault on the great ocean. They had dislodged Earth from its orbit, hurled it into the continuum of probeships and nothingness, and drawn it through that surreal vacancy to Cathadonia.

Now, for the first time since the creation of its solar system, Cathadonia had a moon.

Bracero is dead. He brought me my planet out of love, I'm sure of it. How do I bear up under this guilt?

Tomorrow I walk west again. . . .

Love or vengeance. Which of these prompted Bracero to carry out the will of his people? Maria Jill Ian felt sure it was love. But we, you and I, aware of more substantive factors than this poor Earth woman had at hand, you and I may reach a different conclusion.

The answer, of course, is implicit in the story. Perhaps I ought to stop. Imprudently, I choose to add a sort of epilogue. All stories have sequels, written or unwritten, and I don't want you going away from this one believing it solely a love story with a monstrously ironic conclusion. I'm interested in human as well as alien motivation, and you don't want to believe that all of humankind died as the result of an incomprehensible force, a force superior in kind and in quality to our own technological achievements.

Very well. It wasn't so.

Although Earth was still officially the homeworld of our species, men had not lived there in great numbers for several centuries. The entire planet had become a sanctuary, a preserve seeded back into wilderness, and perhaps only a thousand human beings lived there as wardens, keepers, physicians, gardeners, biologists, ecological experts. Men and women of goodwill.

All of them died, every one of them. Nearly twice as many human beings as (if you'll pardon the expression) squiddles who were slaughtered by the crewmen of the *Golden.*

It didn't take men long to discover what had happened to their world, the home of the primeval oceans in which we had spawned. The probeship *Nobel* returned from the Magellanic Clouds and found a double planet where there had once been only Cathadonia. They attempted radio contact with Fischelson and the Ians. Nothing. Well away from this puzzling twin system they hovered, mulling over ludicrous stratagems. After a time, they left.

In other vessels men came back.

They bombarded Cathadonia with nukes of every variety, concentrating on "The Sea of Stagnation." Then they swept the atmosphere clean of radiation and permitted men to go down to the surface.

Of course, they never found Maria Jill Ian, nor the apocryphal log from which you have just read.

How could they? Cathadonia now had tides—colossal, remorseless tides—that swept back and forth across her watery surface with cruel, eroding regularity. To find Maria would have required a miracle. But a legend grew up around her and the two men aboard her descentcraft, the legend you have just read, and almost everyone believed this legend to be true.

Worldshapers came.

In a hundred years they turned our runaway Earth into a paradise; restored to it an atmosphere, mountains, streams, lakes, greenery, everything but oceans; stocked it with every manner of beautiful and awesome beasts from the colony worlds. Cathadonia and Earth, the most breathtaking double planet in the universe. When visitors began coming, hotels were built amid the landscaped gardens of our erstwhile spawning place, and people rose early in the morning to watch Ogre's Heart turn the seas of Cathadonia—across three hundred thousand kilometers of space—into mother-of-pearl mirrors.

Eventually, on Cathadonia, the downed descentcraft was recovered.

Men speculated. The legend surrounding Fischelson and the Ians took on a mystical quality.

This could not last.

Someone, some enterprising soul developed the idea of retracing the route Maria Jill Ian had traversed during her abortive "odyssey" and of flying tourists over it in a skimmercraft piloted by a glib well-briefed guide. The idea caught on. Recorded voices now detailed every step of Maria and her Cathadonian sidekick.

" *'Men are hardy creatures,'* " the recordings mimicked in their never-varying commentary. " *'Men are the ultimate vermin, Maria, as indefatigable as cockroaches.'* "

Everyone aboard the skimmercrafts nodded sagely at the profundity of these observations.

No one ever asked for his money back.

EFFIGIES

BAREFOOTED, trailing her spear, Theleh crosses the gorge bottom. A rag at the point of her spear, blue and tatter-tipped, whips about in the wind like a sliced iguabi tongue. There are fewer iguabi on Hond than there used to be, and Theleh drags her spear because she has no real expectation of a sighting. Neither does she wish to take herself terribly far from the cliffs, where, at least, water and food are available, and she may benefit from the comforting presence—if not the company—of her few remaining fellows.

Then, a hundred strides from her across the crazed red surface of the gorge, Theleh sees a vigorously growing effigy of Verlis. Stunned, she halts and shields her eyes.

Verlis the Maker has been dead nine turnings of Hond, three sheddings. A long time, it seems. His effigy makes a rustling sound and waves about dryly in the wind, a stalk of stubborn vegetation where vegetation ought not to be. Theleh drops her hand. She resumes walking, a hundred swift thoughtful strides. Then she stops in front of this crippled parody of her mentor and stares at its familiar mummy face. In the lovelorn desert wind the face nods at her blankly, wholly unaware of the cruelty of its imperfection. What do Verlis's quirkish efforts to save them mean to this memento of his failure?

Theleh refrains from moving. Almost hypnotized, she casts back to the Maker's lifetime. She allows the sun, like a bludgeon of air, to beat down upon her in rhythm with her pulsebeats. . . .

*   *   *

The glistening structures on the Adiro Cliffs were labyrinths set inside the wind-eroded rock formations surmount-
ing the escarpment; they were set in the rock in the same
way that a lustrous cloth is sometimes used to line a coarser
one. Where the formations broke apart, a polychrome
tower might emerge or a fragile-seeming, spun-metal bridge
jump the chasm between rock spire and rock spire. A be-
queathment.

When Verlis was alive, most of Theleh's people lived
beside the labyrinth-riddled formations in brushwood lean-
tos or stone hovels of no more architectural genius than
a rubble heap. Ever contrary, Verlis himself lived *inside*
the polychrome structures bequeathed the Dying People by
ancestors long dead. Outside the labyrinths, against the
strictures of custom, he cloaked himself in an old shedding
and strode about the others' lean-to and rock encampments
with a purpose all his own. He was the only one of their
number who knew how to navigate the sheath inside the
rocks without a firebrand fisted above his head, and they
saw to it that he now and again had meat only because of
his great age and their unsuppressible awe of him. Evmauna,
chief among the people's hunters, had told everyone that
Verlis knew the secrets of the power sources inside the
labyrinths, that he had access to all the light that anyone
might require. . . .

But Theleh wasn't at this time worried about the old
man. She paid him little heed. Her immediate concerns
were the girl Atmega and the hook-footed boy called Hrul
with whom she had been grouped for hunting expeditions
and procreative affection. Evmauna, playing no favorites,
had made the groupings, and it was unfortunate that Theleh
had only contempt for Hrul—who was cynical to the
point of nihilism and so insensitive as to be an unmeaning
buffoon even in the most "redemptive" of all acts. When
he lay with either Atmega or Theleh, as he must by decree
on alternate risings of the sun, he sang aloud his doubts
and lamentations as they coupled. Then, standing, he would
turn his head to spit a glitter of saliva upon the ground.

"If by sun-high that has become a diamond," Hrul would
say, "then surely you will bear our child."

Atmega gave Theleh further cause for despair because
she thought the boy's ritual crudities amusing, if not always
funny enough for strong laughter. The only ways that
Theleh could express her disapproval, then, were by forcibly

covering Hrul's mouth during the act, feigning a passion she did not feel, and then afterward seeking to convince Atmega of the boy's monstrousness. If the Dying People died in spirit before they died in fact, she argued, their dying would be all the more meaningless; they would rot into Hond like the fibrous guts of broken sanli gourds, whose decay is of no more use to the soil than are the cries of migrating night birds. In this way Theleh sought to win over her friend, her spouse, and her sister.

"You must laugh at Hrul," Atmega would say, "or his mockings *will* come to have meaning. They will kill *your* spirit, Theleh."

"Yes, and I hate him for the murder he moves toward."

"Don't," Atmega advised. "You wrong him. As for me, I love Hrul for the idiocy of his despair. Nothing he turns his hand to has ever succeeded, and all he has ever wanted is to leave some testament to the Night."

"For this you love him?"

Atmega laughed. "I speak to the ideal." An emendation that gave the girls cause to join arms and laugh together— but it didn't truly console, this brief sharing. It was a short-lived respite, and nothing more.

Later Theleh reflected that whatever Hrul left behind him as testament would have to be as twisted as himself. The Night would cover it without favor or discrimination, and the stars encircling Hond would throb like unhealed wounds, pinpricks of bleeding mercury. Why, then, even on Evmauna's order, should one seek to be the vessel of Hrul's impotent seed?

He doesn't believe, Theleh told herself. Therefore, why should I? Why should any of us?

Not long after she had made her groupings of the people at Adiro, Evmauna came before them in open assembly and announced that they would tomorrow descend into the gorge for the hunt. She spoke in firelight. She said that the iguabi had returned from their wintering and were filtering back into the gorge like ghosts. She had seen one herself that afternoon. They were nimble monsters, creatures that at noonday lengthened to many-legged needles but at nightfall flattened like fire-marbled cheeses in a skillet. They were meat, and if you could find them dancing across the gorge bottom, they were easily speared. This turning, they had wintered longer than they ordinarily did.

"But now," Evmauna told the people on the Adiro Cliffs, "they are back. I have seen one."

Verlis appeared from the shadow of the metal structure in the rocks. There was no glow behind him, no intimation of light in the tunnels he alone inhabited. Theleh caught wind of him as a dusty odor on the night, then saw his reedy form beyond the fire tongues licking skyward: an apparition at Evmauna's back, a blackness against the blackness of the cliffs. And it seemed to Theleh, even though she could not see the old man's eyes, that he was looking across the fire directly at her. Seeking reassurance, the girl scooted forward on her buttocks and put a hand on Atmega's ankle.

"And how long must we be gone?" the man Ebeth asked from another part of their circle.

"Until each of us has an iguabi hide to hang from his belt," Evmauna responded. Her face was already marked for the hunt, and the belt at her waist was a belt of iguabi hide.

Theleh watched Verlis emerge from the night, and she tightened her grip on her sister's ankle—for the old man's stare proved to be turned on no one but her, the stare of weak but uncompromising eyes from a cage of bone. For so old a man Verlis was remarkably erect, and when he stopped at the edge of their assembly, everyone but Evmauna had finally seen him.

"Evmauna," he said.

Startled, the woman turned.

"Who are you taking with you tomorrow?" he asked.

"Why? Do you wish to go?"

Verlis chuckled mirthlessly. "I? Not I, Evmauna. Not yet. I wish one of you to remain."

That said, he pointed a single gnarled finger at Evmauna and then swung it toward Theleh. Of all the Dying People on the Adiro Cliffs, Theleh was chosen. The girl tightened her fingers again around Atmega's ankle.

"Do you wish to amputate my foot?" Atmega whispered.

Theleh released the girl's leg, and Hrul, sitting to Atmega's right, smiled at her nastily.

"What do you want her for?" Evmauna was asking Verlis.

"For the most redemptive of acts," Hrul whispered. "And if anything comes of it, the sun will stop and the stars wink out."

"To aid me," Verlis answered Evmauna.

"To aid me," Hrul mocked the old man.

"Hush," Theleh commanded the boy, her brother, her husband.

"It could not be any worse with him than it is with this one," Atmega whispered. "I would wager that the old man doesn't sing."

"Not so well as I," Hrul said. "Like a dying iguabi."

This whispered banter was intolerable. Theleh wanted to hear what Verlis and Evmauna were saying; she wanted the eyes of Ebeth, Denlot, Pelsu, Thami, and all the others turned away from her companions and herself to the unexpected matter at hand. "Swallow your words," she told Atmega and Hrul. "If you reverence me at all, swallow your words." And she clasped her knees and put her chin atop them, Verlis regarding her all the while. She looked at a reddish star above the old man's head and felt her heart send tremulous shudders through her chest.

"I ask her aid," Verlis was saying. "As an age-right. I am more sheddings myself than she and the two you have grouped her with."

"Very well, Verlis. She remains with you."

In the morning the others descended to the gorge with their slings, spears, and knives. A hot wind blew. Theleh watched them work their way down through the rocks; on the gorge bottom they spread out in a line twenty-three abreast. Other Dying People lived to the south, two or three more "tribes" of them—but the twenty-three people in the gorge, and Verlis with her on the escarpment, were the ones who comprised her world. That Verlis had suddenly asserted his place in this world the girl found mystifying and threatening.

On the floor of the gorge the shadows of the moving hunters made a weird black picketing, and it was impossible to tell who was who.

"I have spared you Hrul's company," Verlis said.

"How did you know I didn't care for it?" Theleh refused to look at the old man; she watched the hunters' slow progress through the dawn.

"I stroll about. I eavesdrop."

"You're shameless, then."

"Not so shameless as the old people of *my* youth, Theleh. It was their custom to pretend to omniscience."

What answer could she give the old man? The impertinences of the aged were unanswerable; so, too, their witticisms. Perhaps Hrul's embraces were not to be despised if to avoid them she must keep company with Verlis.

The old man sauntered away from her, erect but still vaguely shambling. He was going toward the labyrinth in the rocks; and when she cast a glance over her shoulder at the man, the dazzle from a polychrome spire erupting from the outcropping there almost blinded her. She put up a hand and saw him gazing at her with a look of benign expectation.

"Come," he said.

"I don't wish to go in there."

"I go in, I come out. There's no harm in it, Theleh, and very little mystery."

"I ask that you not make me enter."

"I am too old to coerce you, Theleh."

To her own embarrassment she responded, "And too old to ravish me, as well."

"Yes. Were I of a meaner spirit, I would regret that. I must confess that I *do* regret it."

"I'm sorry, Verlis," Theleh said, truly contrite. "In any case, our coupling would be to no purpose but an empty pleasure."

"Not even to that, young woman—I am impotent." He crossed to the tunnel entrance and halted there. He was visible to the girl as a lean grayish figure peering into a forever-departed yesterday.

Theleh followed.

"I purposely did not ask you to enter at night," Verlis told her, and he led the way through the smooth silver-black casing of the tunnel to a right-angle turning and a cold steady shimmer of light. "Do you ever at night feel the earth moving?" he asked her as they walked. "Do you ever think that Hond contains colonies of buzzing, burrowing animals just beneath your sleeping head?"

"Never. But Evmauna thinks me unimaginative."

"Ah." Was there disappointment in this sigh? Theleh couldn't tell. "Well, young woman, these sensations you have *not* experienced are evidence of the generators below us in the cliffs. Adiro will have the potential for life long after the Dying People have squandered theirs."

She said nothing. The tunnel debouched on a room containing counters, glassware, beds, apparatus of arcane design and function, double-plated doorways into further chambers or corridors, and an astringent smell unlike any Theleh had ever encountered before. Huge metal shields hung at intervals on the walls, and each one had been engraved with a series of looping symbols or pictograms that she found altogether uninterpretable.

Between these diamond-shaped shields—pinned to the wall in the same way that children had once affixed the wings of pocsit flies to scraps of bark—were Verlis's previous skins. Seven of them. Twenty-one turnings of Hond about its livid primary. The eighth skin he wore on his back like a cloak, and the ninth he still inhabited. Even though he sinned against custom in his open display of his old incarnations, in the unfamiliarity of this rockbound room Theleh found the skins a profound comfort—a ligature to the life she knew. She waited for Verlis to speak.

"Are you frightened?" he finally asked her.

"Yes."

"Why? The strangeness?"

"The strangeness," she acknowledged.

"Does it frighten you that we are dying?"

"It saddens me."

"It's a melancholy thing, Theleh. Not even rollicking song and the besottedness that kia brings are proof against it."

But the music in the old man's words played against the melancholy of their sense, and Theleh was alert to the music. "Have you found something that *is* proof?" she asked him. "What am I to aid you with? Why did you keep me from hunting with the others?"

"Come here, Theleh." He had gone to the other side of the room and placed himself behind one of the four parallel counters, marbled tabletops on thick transparent supports, dividing the room into work areas. The floor was of the same beautifully veined substance as the counter tops, and Theleh approached Verlis silently over its intricate veining.

When she reached the old man, he opened a transparent drawer beneath the counter and extracted several pungent-smelling plants. He thrust them within a hand's breadth of her face.

"Do you know what these are?"

"Weed-wheat stalks, I believe." Theleh took one from Verlis. Holding it, she reflected that Verlis had lived through the ill-remembered Seasons of Rain. A time when meal had been made from weed-wheat; a time when the iguabi had mated before the people's eyes and then melted like miniature rainbows into the crevices of Hond. A time, the girl told herself, that a person had had some hope—

Verlis chuckled. "I thought you too young to remember." He laid the stalks he was holding on the counter, amid some glassware of incredibly sinuous design, and opened another drawer. "But look here, too."

A yellow tray, its cover indented slightly at the forward edge. Verlis placed the tray on the counter, put a finger in the indentation, and slipped its cover off. Theleh saw four rows of black batting in the tray, but little else. Verlis was blocking her view, leaning over the counter with a pair of tiny stainless-steel tweezers. With this instrument he lifted something from one of the rows of batting and held it toward Theleh as he had just done the weed-wheat stalks.

"What is it?" the girl asked.

"A seed."

Of course it was a seed. But when Theleh asked the logical question—"Is it weed-wheat, then?"—the old man placed it carefully back in its tray and showed her an unhealed scraping on the heel of his hand. The wound was sticky looking, with a fluid the color of derva sap, and the skin beneath the fluid was as cracked as the gorge bottom. The wound's ugliness stifled Theleh's sympathetic feelings, and her annoyance with Verlis for ignoring her question came to the fore.

"That must be very painful," she said dutifully.

"I do not heal so well as I used to," Verlis said. "I am a victim, it seems, of entropy." He caught the girl's wrist, but was careful not to let his wound touch her. "I am speaking to the point in showing you this."

Theleh stared.

"Look at the seeds in my tray."

She looked. It was difficult to see the seeds against their black background, for they were also black. Once examined, however, they proved large and ugly, hard and mutedly shiny—as if each kernel had been embossed with a rune of rock and then fired in a kiln. Was that what weed-wheat seeds looked like? Theleh couldn't remember.

"Do you know what I wish to grow with these?" Verlis asked.

The girl shook her head.

"People, Theleh. I wish to grow people."

By working with the genetic material encoded in weed-wheat seeds and using too the cell matter scraped from the heel of his hand, Verlis had sought to program the "seeds" in his tray with all the many and variable characteristics of sentient life. As soon as he had told the girl what he was attempting, Theleh knew him to be mad. She stared at the containers and brines around her, the burners and pipettes, the calibrating mechanisms and syringes, the cryptic formulae on the walls, and she wondered at the magnitude of the man's insanity. At the same time she felt an illogical hope in it. There were forty seeds in the old man's tray, each one painfully engineered through the agencies of sweat and serendipity; and if these seeds grew, the population at Adiro would very nearly be doubled. The Dying People might yet beat back the Night.

Somehow, in the old man's presence, deep within the labyrinth bequeathed him by the dead, this did not seem such an outlandish hope.

"But how can I aid you?" Theleh asked Verlis. "It seems that the greatest part of the work is done."

"We must sow."

"Never in my life have I planted anything, Verlis. But, if you show me how, I will undertake to plant every seed myself."

"No. This isn't something I can let you do alone. If the others are not involved in the midwifing of these lives, Theleh, they will utterly reject them. In their jealousy of me and the people I have conjured from the labyrinth, they will turn their hands to—to who knows what?"

"Then you wish the others to aid us in the planting?"

"I do, Theleh. And the aid I want from you is your support. This has been a lonely triple-turning. I will also entrust to you the nutrients that will see these seeds through germination to adulthood."

"And the seeds themselves?"

"Those, Theleh, *I* must carry."

At sunfall, Theleh and the old man left Adiro's enigmatic fortress and climbed down through knife-edged shadows to the gorge. The girl bore on her back for Verlis's "babies" a heavy packet of food and water crystals, while the invaluable seeds—all forty of them—rode in a bag of grainy reptile hide on the old man's hip. The girl used her spear as a staff and supported Verlis when the footing was most treacherous.

In the gorge itself, however, he walked with a surprising disregard for fatigue; and because the night was not cold enough to send them scurrying for warmth and shelter, Theleh found that all her thoughts were racing ahead to her reunion with the hunters, to the inevitable drama of Verlis's revelation to them of a new but bewildering hope. How would Evmauna respond to the disruption of her hunt? What of Atmega's unbounded enthusiasm and Hrul's inelegant despair?

The world was about to be changed, and Verlis had seen fit to make Theleh a party to its transfiguration. That was not all—he had had the foresight and good sense to think to include *all* the Dying People in this imminent rebirth!

Theleh's heart welled with good feeling. "Verlis," she said as they walked, "you have a canny wisdom, and in judging you harshly from afar I have erred."

"And, Theleh, you have an awesome stride. My 'canny wisdom' has not prevented me from trying to keep pace with it."

They laughed, sharing the star-flecked indigo communion of the sky—but afterward Theleh was careful not to tempt the old man to outdistance himself.

As it was, they reached the hunters' encampment, a group of ledges and rock awnings beneath the cliffs to the gorge's east, well before the sun was out of bed. Three fires burned on the hard, cracked ground, with spits set above them, and the sound of carefree singing drifted to them on the wind as tantalizingly as the fragrance of roasting iguabi. Apparently the festivities of the successful hunt had gone on all night, and were even now continuing, and Theleh and Verlis were swept into them before they had the chance to explain the significance of their arrival.

"Come," Atmega said, gripping Theleh's arm and pulling her to the largest of the fires. "You must have some meat. You also, Verlis. Sit down with us and eat. There's more than enough."

Evmauna, whose hunt-marked face looked both joyful and haggard, greeted the newcomers. Hrul uttered a nit-witticism about Theleh's not wishing to forfeit even one morning's attempt at "redemption" and earned a burst of good-natured and spontaneous laughter. Theleh, however, could feel an angry heat rising through her body—not because she was embarrassed but because Hrul was so conspicuously ignorant of any but the sexual meaning of the word he was playing with.

"Your mind is as small as a pocsit ball," she blurted. "Its wings have never beaten against a liberating breeze—perhaps your mind is wingless!"

"My mind?" said Hrul, feigning amazement. "Impossible. What has inspired this ungrateful attack?"

"Your stupid banter and your empty soul. Redemption, you say. But do you know who it is who will ultimately redeem us, Hrul? *This* man." She took Verlis's hand and lifted it to her shoulder. "Verlis the Maker."

"Despite my 'stupid banter' of a night ago," Hrul responded, his tone parodying an elder's condescension, "I must tell you, Theleh, that it has been many turnings since Verlis has been able to redeem anyone. And now you tell me that he is going to redeem us all. Has he discovered an elixir? A secret potion? A diet unknown to the rest of us? I fear that—"

Laughter filtered through the pauses in Hrul's speech, but now it was nervous and uncertain. It halted altogether when Evmauna barked, "That's enough! You go beyond the limits, Hrul!" Then, still sitting, she asked Verlis to explain Theleh's remark about the redemption of the Dying People. Her inflection made it clear that she was not speaking in a sexual sense, and was a reproof to the boy.

"Before sunrise," Verlis said, "when there is enough light, we must go into the desert and plant the seeds I have brought. We must use our spears for plows and our very fingers for spades. We must make purposeful love to the earth in order that we may be spared oblivion."

"But we hunt before the heat of the day," objected a man called Pelsu.

"Today we must plant," Verlis told him.

"In this place?" Pelsu went on incredulously. "A day's walk from Adiro? If we plant here, we tie ourselves to the desert."

"So we do. But it seems you've had a good hunt already. The meat on hand and that procurable while we tend our crop will ease our stay in the gorge. In any case, not everyone need remain here."

"What are we growing?" Pelsu asked.

"Our fellows. Our descendants."

Hrul made an impertinent noise in the back of his throat, and no one reprimanded him. Evmauna, however, stood up and wiped her hands down her coarse thighs, after which the grain in her skin glistened like the veined flooring in Verlis's workroom. A tall woman, Evmauna captured the others' eyes with her bearing and her commanding voice.

"It's almost dawn," she said. "We'd best go planting."

When Verlis and Theleh led the others out of the shadows of the cliffs, the flat of the gorge was liver-colored with predawn light. Looking behind her, the girl saw Atmega and Hrul in the vanguard of the trailing hunters. Hrul put a finger in each broad nostril and nodded his head toward Verlis to suggest that the old man's brain was fly-ridden. Solemnly, in both exasperation and pity, Theleh shook her head no and quickly faced forward again—the boy was incorrigible, he reveled in his cynicism.

"We must break up the earth," Verlis told everyone when the hunters stood before him in a semicircle. "We must prepare the ground lovingly.".

"We haven't yet slept," protested a woman called Onveb.

"Afterward. Use your weapons, or your hands, or pieces of rock. Chop the soil fine. Strain the lumps with your fingers." Kneeling, the old man demonstrated. He jabbed at the hard ground with a rock from the cliff face. "If you go deep enough, you'll find a niggardly moisture."

Everyone imitated Verlis. The sky grew lighter and lighter, crowding the stars out of existence.

"Now," he commanded, his voice like worn leit-cloth, "you must shape mounds as high as your forearms with the soil you've made. Help each other. We need forty of these."

The mounds were made, and the sun at last cleared the edge of one of the cliffs. The bodies of the people in the gorge had already begun to simmer inside their skins.

"Good," Verlis declared. "Now we must plant." He gathered the hunters around him again and opened the bag he had brought down from Adiro. "Each of you must take a seed and plant it. The remaining ones Theleh and I will sow ourselves, giving them gently to the desert."

Twenty-three people planted the seeds Verlis had distributed. Then they watched as the old man and the girl moved from mound to mound poking finger-long shafts in the crumbling soil and depositing the queer rune-embossed kernels with a persnickety tenderness.

Even Hrul watched, and Theleh was conscious of him—terribly conscious of him—a grave-faced skeptic hovering about the borders of their garden like some sort of beastie with mischief on its mind. Soon the sun was high and hot, and Hrul went back to the shelter of the cliffs with the others. Theleh, when she and Verlis had finished, was glad enough to get there too. But she stood for a long time in the cliff shade looking at their landscape of new-made miniature pyramids and temples.

"A fine city," Verlis said, and he draped her shoulders with a moist piece of cloth.

During the days that they waited for their crop to spring up, the old man kept to himself. Late and early, he took solitary walks. Theleh missed his company, but she didn't begrudge him his solitude—this was a trying time for one who had spent his last several turnings as a misunderstood recluse with but a single goal. And in the mornings before dawn Verlis did supervise the sprinkling and the mixing-in of the nutrients and water crystals Theleh had carried down from Adiro. Her mentor, the girl knew, was too afraid of failure to be gone all the time.

One morning a man named Denlot—who had developed an intense loyalty to Verlis's project—stayed out among the seeded pyramids almost until midday. On the one occasion that Evmauna called to him, he smiled at her and waved off her warning. He was busy working bead capsules into the soil and reshaping the more wind-eroded mounds. He was happy in these tasks, happy in his admiration of the garden.

Then, with stunning suddenness, the flesh on Denlot's face split from pate to chin, and the man fell unconscious in the row he had been working. Evmauna saw him fall and raised a cry of alarm.

Theleh was one of the first to reach Denlot. She lifted him from the ground with the aid of Thami and Sardogra, and back in the cliff shade she helped the others remove his belt and mantle. Denlot was an old man—not so old as Verlis, but eighteen or nineteen turnings at least. His age, Theleh felt sure, was one of the reasons he was so in sympathy with Verlis's efforts to save the Dying People. Now the man looked maimed and blistered.

"It's the false death," Sardogra said. "We must take him from his skin before the false becomes real."

Evmauna appeared. With a strigil she split the skin beneath Denlot's throat and drew a line to just above the fork of his legs; then she drew lines from the insides of his thighs to his ankles. Her cuts were expert. A moment later Denlot's sixth skin came away from his body almost of itself, and Thami carried it away to prepare it for the rites of resurrection. But Theleh didn't go with the bearer of the skin; she stood staring at Denlot's near corpse and at the vivid, oddly glistening hide of a new triple-turning.

"See there," Sardogra said. "If we could each of us do that forever, we would not have to toil in Verlis's garden. Denlot is new again."

"So new that he will not be able to work for days," said Evmauna sourly, her voice heavy with an anxiety as thoroughgoing as Verlis's—an anxiety grounded in the same hopeful impatience. She touched the unconscious man's forehead.

Theleh, despite these avowals of Denlot's newness, could not help noticing on his face and lower belly the shadows of old creases on the vivid, fresh skin. Ahead of him, at best, he had only two more sheddings. He would not live so long as Verlis, for life had used him harshly. Nor did the man have any children. His "newness" was a mockery.

Pensively Theleh turned and sought out the lean-to where Atmega was playing a thin, evocative melody on a wood flute.

Nine days later, when Denlot had fully recovered from his false death, Atmega swept into the camp after a night of hunting and roused everyone with her shouts of excited joy. Whooping, she ran from shelter to shelter, then back out onto the plain of the gorge itself. She made such an unseemly din that it was impossible not to get up and stumble out into the desert after her. There Theleh saw Atmega dancing nimbly about their garden, a wraithlike figure in the first weak glow of dawn.

"He has succeeded!" Atmega cried. "Verlis has redeemed us! He has done what we believed impossible!"

If she squinted and cocked her head, Theleh could see a great many lopsided ocher tips protruding from the mounds they had made. These tips wobbled in the morning breeze. Along with many others Theleh approached the garden, and

walking among its rows they saw the leaf-wrapped, featureless heads of the "weed-wheat people" Verlis had made
in their image. Her companions, Theleh could tell, felt the
same magnificent awe that now held her speechless, and for
a long time the silence on Hond was as loud and fearsome
as the persistent rolling of summer thunder.

Then Theleh gripped Hrul's hand, and Hrul took Ebeth's,
and Ebeth took Sardogra's, and so on and so on—until all
the hunters who had not returned to Adiro were hallooing
together like children in their first skins. Verlis had succeeded! The Dying People were not irremissibly doomed!
Atmega led the others, and everyone danced. Old chants
were chanted, and speculation about their embryonic siblings in the soil was on every hunter's lips. The rising sun
had no power to confound their joy.

Theleh, dancing, saw Evmauna coming toward them
from the shelters. The woman halted at the garden's verge
with her legs spread and her arms akimbo. By her very
presence Evmauna brought the others' celebration to a
standstill. Her look was a troubled one.

"My thoughts at this moment are a little different from
yours," she told her people. "We are a long way from
harvest. Everyone understands this, but no one wishes to
confront the fact."

"This is a *hopeful* moment!" Atmega cried. "Don't ruin
it for us!"

"Theleh," Evmauna said, ignoring the other girl, "find
Verlis and bring him here. He may wish to see what he has
wrought."

Theleh departed and found Verlis sleeping amid a jumble of broken rock halfway up the cliff and told him what
had happened and brought him back down to the hunters'
encampment and the garden beside it. He admired the leaf
tips from the shade of the cliff and said nothing. That
evening, however, he took Theleh among the rows with him
and squatted in front of one of the rounded spikes nodding
above the soil. He probed its sheath with his thumbs.

"Our brother," he whispered, canting his face up to
Theleh's. "And I think that he will live. Yes."

Verlis's garden grew. In twelve more risings and fallings
of the sun his forty earthbound protégés had lifted their
heads to the height of Theleh's shoulders. They split be-

neath their middles into matching leg stalks and began to shed the dull ocher sheaths protecting their faces.

"Their first false death has come early," Evmauna said. "Their first shedding is only thirteen days."

"They will have several more," Verlis replied.

But in another two days it became clear that the "people" he had made all resembled—in a grotesque and deformed way—a younger version of himself. Indeed, Theleh could go into the field and feel herself to be surrounded by callow, crippled Verlises. This feeling bred a quiet discontent and sense of betrayal in the girl—but others who experienced it, particularly Hrul and the woman called Onveb, could not keep their unhappiness or their suspicions to themselves. They thought Verlis a monster of deception and self-love, and they publicly said so. Since the old man continued to absent himself from the encampment except in the mornings, they could speak against him without having to face him. Not only did Hrul and Onveb indict Verlis for his great and overweening vanity, they charged that his "genius" was nothing more than senile self-indulgence. All one need do to confirm this judgment was stroll through the nodding miscreations in his garden.

Theleh was torn. She did not know whose side to be on —or if, in fact, she must commit herself to a side at all.

"I can no longer look at the real Verlis," Hrul said one evening as the hunters ate, "without seeing in his face an image of one of his malformed effigies. Let's plow his forty 'babies' under and return to Adiro."

"I urge the same," Onveb added. "Verlis has committed sacrilege."

"In what way?" Evmauna asked. "By seeking to redeem us?"

"By seeking to deify himself through this stupid replication. We are barren. His energies would have been better spent attempting to rescue us from our barrenness."

Theleh secretly felt that the old man's detractors, Hrul chief among them, were jealous and short-sighted—but the hideous evidence of Verlis's crop made it impossible for her to speak her opinion. Each day the eerie weed-wheat people declined from a crooked hardiness into unmistakable disease. Their limbs were half-formed and mismatched, their unblinking eyes stared out on the gorge from behind a rheumy film reminiscent of the fluid in the old man's wounds. Verlis, the girl thought, your project has gone wrong, all wrong.

"Tomorrow night," Evmauna said, "we will speak to the genius himself. Theleh, will you see to it that he comes to our assembly?"

Her throat too tight for words, Theleh nodded.

On the following evening Denlot was the first to speak. Surprisingly, he argued against Verlis. Still uncomfortable in his new skin, he told the old man, "I championed you once—but now we must admit that our labor has gone for nothing, that this attempt at redemption is a botch."

Sitting with her chin on her knees, Theleh gave only part of her mind to Denlot's argument. Hrul was beside her to her right, and Verlis sat across the fire from her beside Evmauna. But because Atmega was altogether missing from the circle, Theleh could not help turning her head toward the darkened emptiness of the gorge for some indication of her sister's return. Why had she chosen this night of all nights to be away from their encampment?

"We might as well admit it," Denlot was saying. "Those 'people' out there"—he gestured at the night—"will never pull up their legs and walk as we do. And if they did, their heads are utterly empty—they know nothing. Can we expect them to mate as real people do, or must we prepare to see them seed one another through the aid of pocsit flies? And what will they produce, Verlis? Only more monsters, I'm afraid."

Verlis sighed disgustedly and spat at the fire.

"Like Hrul and Onveb," Denlot concluded, "I ask that our crop be plowed under."

"Of course you do," Verlis replied. "You are as shortsighted as they."

"It seems to me," Evmauna interjected, "that to reach his conclusion Denlot has taken the long view."

"Think again. To plow under what all of us about this fire have so devotedly tended would be both suicide and murder, Evmauna. Suicide and murder!"

Theleh looked at her mentor. Debate had halted against the terrible dead end of his last two words, and no one could find the necessary resolve to speak again.

Could it be murder, Theleh asked herself, to cover the weed-wheat people with the earth from which they had sprung? And if Verlis's offspring were so interred, would the Dying People really be committing suicide? The girl could not find it in herself to answer these questions affirmatively. She began to believe that Verlis, a good and well-meaning man, was now the victim of his own delusions. Even though all the most telling signs pointed to his work's futility and failure, he sought to save it only out of pride. Was he even aware of his motives in resisting the others' arguments?

When Verlis broke a stick against the ground and declared, "No one plows under our crop," Theleh was filled with a heartbreaking pity. She turned her face toward the darkness.

And saw Atmega striding out of it into the circle of light at the camp's center. "I have news that bears on this," she announced. "And for that reason I must cast my lot with Denlot and Hrul."

"What news?" Evmauna asked her.

"Even though it isn't time for them to leave, the iguabi have deserted the gorge. It's impossible to find one, impossible even to stumble upon their spoor."

"How do you know? We haven't hunted since Verlis's arrival."

"I have. I have hunted every night. And I have speared not a single iguabi. They're gone, Evmauna. They've been driven out, I believe, by the presence of Verlis's weed-wheat people. And since this crop is not the sort to yield meal for our bread, I ask that it be destroyed before the Dying People find their true deaths in starvation rather than sterility."

A pretty speech. Theleh realized now that Atmega had rehearsed it before stepping out of the darkness—but its premeditation in no way invalidated the girl's argument, and Theleh both feared and hoped that it would end their debate. Surely the old man would give in now. The iguabi were too precious to frighten from the gorge, too precious to risk on an uncertainty like his Hond-grown people. . . .

"No one," Verlis the Maker told the hunters quietly, intractably, "no one plows under our fellows and heirs." That spoken, he rose and left the encampment.

No one plowed them under. But despite the stewardship of Theleh and one or two others, the weed-wheat people went figuratively and literally to seed. Their fibrous bodies cracked, and hairlike scarlet silks grew from their chests and fell beneath their shoulders weighted by seeds exactly like the ones Verlis had created in the fortress at Adiro. When the wind blew with especial fierceness these seeds detached themselves and tumbled away as if propelled from within by tiny demons. And the iguabi, which had become harder and harder to find, even when the hunters scoured the far ends of the gorge, seemed now to have abandoned the planet altogether.

Hunger crept upon the ten or twelve people tending the old man's shabby garden; and, forty times over, the mummies growing there ridiculed the hunters with their distorted visages of Verlis. Theleh knew that those who had returned to Adiro were also beginning to feel the pinch of famine, and she did her daily work with a numb diligence.

One morning she awoke to find Atmega leaning over her in the grainy light. Hrul was absent from her side.

"Come, Theleh. Out to the fields with us."

Theleh bolted up from her slab. The hunters, she reflected groggily, were about to destroy the old man's garden. They wanted her participation, and she was not at all averse. Her stomach, after all, felt like a rock with ice expanding destructively in its secret seams.

"What about Verlis? Where is he?"

"He drowses on," Atmega told her. "Come silently. Most of the others have already gathered."

They stalked past the rock awning beneath which Verlis had elected to spend the night and joined their comrades among the weed-wheat people. Hrul—hook-footed Hrul—grinned at Theleh as if to say, I knew you'd see things our way; and she realized that in a moment they would all be at their little atrocity together, throttling the old man's plants with their bare hands, gutting them with knives, and stripping them down to their meaty innards for both themselves and the people at Adiro. Her heart pounded like the midday sun in dread and anticipation.

In their desire to finish before the old man awoke, the hunters murdered Verlis again and again. As they uprooted their victims the weed-wheat people's eyes clouded and closed—but none cried out, or otherwise protested, and it was hard for Theleh to view their stealthy harvest as a massacre. How, finally, were the Dying People related to these deformed reflections of the oldest man among them? In no way at all, it seemed.

"Eat," Hrul urged Theleh from a row away. "Eat, girl. We've earned the right with our work and with our over-

long tolerance of Verlis's madness." He folded back the dry
leaves enveloping an organ very like a heart and bit into it
with no apparent qualms.

Others about Theleh were doing the same—Denlot,
Thami, Sardogra, Onveb, Atmega, and even Evmauna,
who had strangled weed-wheat people with an astonishing
skill and rapacity. Eagerly, then, Theleh tore a dessicated
organ-fruit from one of the uprooted corpses and sank her
teeth into it. A flavor as of ashes and dry soil filled her
mouth, but she ate in spite of the taste. So did everyone
else. Who am I, one of the youngest here, to demur? the
girl asked herself; and before the sun had fully risen, they
had devoured an eighth part of their crop.

At last Hrul stood up and said, "We'll never be able to
survive on such a diet. The taste is far too brackish and
earthy."

"No," said Verlis the Maker, and the hunters swung
about to see the old man gazing down upon them from a
rock beside the garden. "You'll not be satisfied, Hrul, until
you've actually begun eating one another."

Theleh saw Verlis's face as a wrathful black disc, toward
which she must lift her hands imploringly.

But Verlis turned aside from her, climbed lamely down
from his rock, and began walking in the general direction
of Adiro. It would be full sun in a little while, and he risked
death if he continued homeward through the middle of the
gorge. Theleh dropped her hands and ran after him.

"Verlis, take shelter. You'll kill yourself this way."

His previous shedding, which he wore as a cloak, rippled
and snapped in the wind. He caught it at his throat. He
looked at Theleh out of a pair of familiar, Hond-weary
eyes.

"Verlis, forgive me."

"For what, your hunger?" He halted and touched her
face. "I have work to do, Theleh. Let me go back to it."

"But the heat—"

"How many skins have I worn?" He waved a hand, dismissing her concern. "Go back to your hook-footed infant."

She watched him proceed up the gorge. After a time he
angled off to the left and disappeared among the shadows
of various outcroppings below the cliff face. Verlis would
reach home safely, Theleh knew, and she returned to the
people with whom she had murdered his children. The ashy

taste in her mouth was an accusation she could neither ignore nor rationalize.

The following day Evmauna led the others back to the Adiro Cliffs. Their return marked the beginning of a severe quarter-turning. The Dying People had a difficult time finding vegetation fit to eat and edible varieties of game to replace the cunningly fled iguabi.

Occasionally they would see from their vantage high above the gorge a stunted weed-wheat person thrusting up through the feverish soil, and Hrul, despite his crippled foot, took great pains to proceed to these places and uproot the random stalks. They had to be destroyed, of course, so that the iguabi might the sooner return—but it seemed to Theleh that Hrul cut them down with a cruel viciousness and delight. He had not forgotten that Verlis's sole word of reprimand to the hunters had been addressed directly to him. In this season of near famine, then, the boy's cynicism had taken on a repulsively sullen and vindictive cast. Theleh, despite Evmauna's decree, refused to lie with him.

"It's a sin to refuse redemption with him," Atmega told her.

"Did you take your turn with him this morning?"

"Of course."

Theleh spat. "If by sun-high that has become a diamond, you will live to bear his child."

Atmega bridled visibly, then softened her look to one of dim puzzlement. "You are more like Hrul than you know," she said. From across the plateau Onveb beckoned, and, after lifting a hand to touch Theleh's shoulder, Atmega hurried off to join the woman in her foraging.

This was a time when the Dying People dug sanli gourds out of the ground, crisped the husks of insects for flour, and set traps for the small winged reptiles that sometimes nested among the steepest of Adiro's cliffs. There was dried iguabi from past quarter-turnings, but not much, and no one really wanted to begin plundering it. It was a hope held in reserve.

Verlis kept to himself. No one took him food, and no one saw him forage. Hrul began to argue that the tunnels and towers in which the old man spent his time must contain a remarkable quantity of foodstuffs. How else could he survive? And, Hrul went on, if Verlis did have such supplies on hand, he ought by rights to share them.

"Unless his mind has so completely failed him that he has begun to eat his old sheddings."

"His mind is occupied with something besides our hunger," Theleh said.

"And what is that?"

"Our survival."

"Very good, Theleh. How quick you are. Will you answer me one question, then?"

"What is it?"

"Just this: If we starve to death, has Verlis secured our survival?"

"Our hunger isn't yet that great."

"Maybe *yours* isn't, Theleh—but, then, your hungers have not been very demanding of late. A sign of surrender."

"Go to him, Hrul, and ask him for food. He won't refuse."

Atmega, who had come upon her spouses in the course of this argument, put in, "No one wishes to enter the labyrinths, Theleh. I've heard that Verlis is growing further copies of himself in metal troughs. Pelsu says that he has heard these beings speaking and laughing—the echoes of their voices haunt him at night. Soon they will rise from their troughs and walk as we do. An army of Verlises, over which the old man will have a sterner command than Evmauna has over us."

"I saw nothing like this when I entered the metal inside the rock, Atmega. The only images of himself he had were his old skins on the wall."

"That was a long time ago. How many rooms did you enter?"

"Only one. A very large one."

"Then what do you know of what is happening now, Theleh?"

Hrul remained silent during this exchange, curiously silent, and the following morning Pelsu—who claimed to have heard voices echoing outward from the labyrinth—found a ripped and battered effigy of the old man hanging in the tunnel entrance through which Verlis had once led Theleh to his workroom. The dummy, a crude thing made of leit-cloth and weed-wheat ticking, had ashes smeared across its face. Pelsu hurried to tell the others, and in a little while everyone at Adiro but Verlis had gathered to watch his effigy revolve limply in the morning breeze—an impotent, shoddy replica of the one person among them

who understood the dimensions of the Dying People's predicament. Theleh was outraged.

"Help me," she said. "Help me cut it down."

No one moved.

"Evmauna," Theleh said pleadingly.

At last Evmauna came forward, lifted Theleh to her
shoulders, and held the girl still beneath the dummy so that
she could cut it free with her knife. When it was down,
Theleh methodically dismembered it, ripped open its torso,
and strewed its ticking out over the gorge in defiant hand-
fuls. She wanted the perpetrator of this petty wickedness to
know her anger, and she hoped that Hrul had some insight
into the depth and certainty of her knowledge.

In small numbers the iguabi returned to the gorge. Hunting parties went out, and slew them, and came back to
Adiro with hides on their belts and meat in their long-
empty booty sacks. The days of near famine were over for
a time, and the smell of roasting flesh ascended from the
many fires on the cliffs. The people feasted, and one evening
a small party of Dying People who lived to the south came
into their midst and asked their hospitality. This—now
that Theleh's people had plenty—was ungrudgingly given.
Everyone ate and talked.

After a time Verlis appeared. "As the oldest here at
Adiro," he told Evmauna, "I should have been summoned
to receive our guests."

"We didn't know how to summon you," Evmauna said,
clearly temporizing. She hadn't even thought of calling the
old man to their feast, Theleh knew, but she could not admit this to him.

"You might have sent Theleh."

"Please, Verlis, you are here now," Evmauna said in an
excess of courtesy. "Sit with us and eat."

"How is it that he should eat with us when he did nothing to contribute to our feast?" Hrul asked loudly from
Theleh's right. "It's fortunate that we have meat at all,
considering Verlis's ability to frighten off game."

Everyone looked at the boy. The faces of their guests,
Theleh noted, were full of surprise and tentative censure.

"He eats with us by age-right," Evmauna said.

"I think he would have forfeited any claim on our
stores," Hrul insisted, "by denying us his when we were in

want. Does age-right abrogate one's obligations to his
people?"

One of the guests stood up, a woman who had apparently known Verlis during a past triple-turning. "How can you
speak against this man?"

"What do you know of the concerns of Adiro?" Hrul re-
torted. "Sit down. Eat of our charity."

Theleh realized that the boy had overreached himself. He
had compelled Evmauna to show her authority, and even
now the older woman was rising to exercise it. Verlis, understanding the delicacy of Evmauna's position, held his
tongue and waited.

"Relinquish your place to Verlis," Evmauna said. "And
leave us."

Hrul stood up and crossed to the old man. He put a
piece of roasted iguabi in Verlis's hands. "I relinquish not
only my place," he said, "but a portion of my kill. Do not
choke on it, old one."

He limped away into the darkness, and Theleh, watching
him go, was bewildered by how precisely his lameness
seemed a reflection of Verlis's age-ridden walk. Was this
conscious mockery, or did the boy always favor his bad
foot in this way? Theleh, quite unhappy, could like neither
Hrul nor Verlis very much now. Why hadn't the old man
stayed in his tunnels, as he had for so long seemed content
to do?

Theleh excused herself early. Hrul was not in the place
that she and Atmega nightly shared with the boy. . . .

Several days passed. Their guests had long since gone
back to their own encampments, and Verlis didn't come out
of his residence in the rock at all. Pelsu spoke again of
ghostly laughter in the tunnels, and even Atmega had fallen
completely to the rumors of a weed-wheat army with Verlis's face. More than likely, she said, he would use this
army to avenge himself on Hrul and any others who had
affronted him. He had even got to the point of making
female Verlises so that his creations could mate sexually
and reproduce endless copies of himself. The man's vanity
was more dangerous than the Dying People's barrenness.

"Once he allows them to come into the light," Atmega
told Theleh, "it won't even be possible to slay the old man.
We will not know which of the many Verlises we see is the
true one."

"He will be the oldest," Theleh said. "You needn't worry."

She herself, however, worried and continued to worry. No one had spoken before, even hypothetically, of slaying Verlis, and that Atmega should do so seemed an ominous alteration in her friend. Had Pelsu's rumors so poisoned her spirit that she could now think seriously of the most heinous of all crimes on Hond as a redemptive one? Had Hrul been talking to her of the old man's "dangerousness"? The Dying People, Theleh feared, were dying before their time.

Several more days passed, and Verlis went on playing the hermit. He did not even come out of his fortress to take a little of the morning sun, and this neglect of a somewhat habitual action began to unnerve Theleh. So, too, did the fact that the rumors of imminent attack by an army of Verlis's caricatures were a thing of the past—no one spoke against Verlis at all anymore, for no one so much as mentioned his name. It was as if the old man had never existed.

One night Theleh grabbed Hrul by the arm and turned the boy toward her with a rude yank. "Where is Verlis?"

He smiled and removed her hand. "In his metal labyrinth."

"You're lying, Hrul!"

"I jest sometimes," Hrul informed her, "but I never lie." He stretched himself out languorously and showed the girl his naked back. The boy was not lying, Theleh realized; and she understood, too, that if Verlis was indeed in his metal labyrinth, he was probably dead.

While the others slept, Theleh crossed the wind-swept summit of the cliff and found herself standing before the tunnel where someone—Hrul, perhaps—had strung up the effigy of the old man. She had gone through it once before. Why should she quail at navigating it a second time? The answer to her question was self-evident: she didn't wish to find what she knew she must. But putting aside both her fear and her people's prohibition against entering the sheath inside the rock, Theleh stepped into the silver-black corridor and followed it to its first turning.

She heard no laughter, no conversation, no hint at all of an unnatural army in sinister bivouac. All she heard were the terrible rhythms of her own breathing and the flute sounds the wind made across the tunnel mouth.

As if activated by her presence, a cylinder of light sur-

rounded Theleh. She walked through it to the room where
Verlis had showed her his rune-embossed seeds. His old
skins were still on the wall, as were the diamond-shaped
shields with their engraven hieroglyphics. But the glassware
that had once graced the room's counters now lay scattered
across the floor in jagged, glittering fragments—like tiny
galaxies of glass. Looking at this debris, Theleh felt that the
entire night sky had just fallen in upon her and broken at
her feet.

"Verlis!"

No one answered.

Then the girl saw that one of the double-plated doors
beyond the last counter was open. Gingerly, being careful
of her feet, she crossed the room and went through this
door into a chamber lined with metal troughs.

Verlis lay on the floor with his throat slit, his ninth skin
still clinging tenaciously to his frail bones. The smell of
decomposition was harsh and overpowering. Somehow
Theleh did not fall back from it. As if in a trance, she went
about the chamber and saw for herself the butchery in the
nutrient-filled beds lining the walls. What she saw recalled
the harvest of Verlis's garden in which she had once, long
ago, taken part. Nausea beset the girl like a wind, but she
fought the attack and triumphed over it.

Kneeling beside Verlis, horrified by what the old man
had become in his death, Theleh freed him from his mortality—as Evmauna had once freed Denlot from an intimation of his. The last skin Verlis would ever wear. Theleh
put it about her shoulders and retreated purposefully from
the slaughterhouse.

"Hrul," she said.

The boy woke up and turned toward her on his slab.
When it seemed to her that he was alert enough to plumb
her motives, Theleh lifted her knife from its scabbard and
showed it to him. His face clouded. Before he could summon the intelligence to thwart her, she used the knife to
slit his throat.

Flailing an arm, Hrul lurched upward and staggered out
into the night. Then fell to the ground and lay upon it,
spurting blood.

Atmega screamed, "What have you done? Your brother,
your husband!"

"He murdered Verlis. Therefore, this."

"Pelsu and Evmauna murdered Verlis," Atmega cried. "The rest of us merely destroyed the old man's bastard children. Hrul could never have taken one of the true people's lives, Theleh—not even Verlis's. Evmauna and Pelsu did so only to preserve the rest of us."

A crowd had gathered. All of the Dying People of Adiro were there to see her with blood on her hands.

"But I—" Theleh began.

"You were not told," Evmauna said, pushing her way to the fore, "because of your affection for the old man. We didn't wish to implicate you."

Theleh stared at the woman. No one spoke. At last the girl threw down her knife and wept openly, tearlessly.

"We have all turned murderer," she managed. "We are dying, and we have all turned murderer to speed the process." She took Atmega's hand from her arm. "Let go of me. From this day forward, I have no people."

She moved her belongings several hundred strides from the main encampment at Adiro, and no one tried to stop her. She made herself a home in the rocks, wearing the old man's ninth skin as a cloak against the cold. That this was against custom had no significance for her or any of the others.

The effigy of Verlis in her path nods blankly, rattles in the wind. The law, to which she has refused to subscribe for nearly three sheddings, says that she must uproot the thing and crush it underfoot. But how long has it been since she or anyone else has seen one? Theleh cannot adjust to her discovery that here on the gorge bottom another of the old man's weed-wheat persons has lifted its crippled head from the dust.

There is wonder in the fact. Wonder and hope.

But if anyone else sees this thing, Theleh knows that they will interpret it as an evil omen. They will view it as Verlis's last insult from the aftertime, a fleer at the inevitability of their extinction.

These considerations in mind, Theleh pulls the plant from the ground and crushes it underfoot. For a moment she believes that Verlis's effigy has gasped her name, has tried to dissuade her from its murder—but the heat has more than likely influenced her imagination in this. She gazes down at the plant's travesty of a face and holds at bay her gathering remorse.

Verlis, forgive me. I have killed another of your off-spring. How is it that something so imperfect can be so haunting? How is it that its death should so deeply wound me?

In the wind sweeping across the gorge there is nothing at all of Verlis's soothing voice. Theleh listens, and there is only the equivocal promise of the wind.

THE HOUSE OF
COMPASSIONATE SHARERS

*And he was there, and it was not far enough, not yet, for
the Earth hung overhead like a rotten fruit, blue with
mold, crawling, wrinkling, purulent and alive.*

—DAMON KNIGHT,
"Masks"

IN THE Port Iranani Galenshall I awoke in the room
Diderits liked to call the "Black Pavilion." I was an engine,
a system, a series of myoelectric and neuromechanical
components, and The Accident responsible for this clean
and enamel-hard enfleshing lay two full D-years in the past.
This morning was an anniversary of sorts. I ought by now
to have adjusted. And I had. I had reached an absolute
accommodation with myself. Narcissistic, one could say.
And that was the trouble.

"Dorian? Dorian Lorca?"

The voice belonged to KommGalen Diderits, wet and
breathy even though it came from a small metal speaker to
which the sable curtains of the dome were attached. I
stared up into the ring of curtains.

"Dorian, it's Target Day. Will you answer me, please?"

"I'm here, my galen. Where else would I be?" I stood up,
listening to the almost musical ratcheting that I make when
I move, a sound like the concatenation of tiny bells or the
purring of a stope-car. The sound is conveyed through the
tempered porcelain plates, metal vertebrae, and osteoid
polymers holding me together, and no one else can hear it.

"Rumer's here, Dorian. Are you ready for her to come
in?"

"If I agreed, I suppose I'm ready."

"Damn it, Dorian, don't feel you're bound by *honor* to see her! We've spent the last several brace-weeks preparing you for a resumption of normal human contact." Diderits began to enumerate: "Chameleodrene treatments . . . holo-gramic substitution . . . stimulus-response therapy . . . You ought to want Rumer to come in to you, Dorian."

Ought. My brain was—is—my own, but the body Diderits and the other kommgalens had given me had "instincts" and "tropisms" peculiar to itself, ones whose templates had a mechanical rather than a biological origin. What I ought to feel, in human terms, and what I in fact felt, as the in-habitant of a total prosthesis, were as dissimilar as blood and oil.

"Do you *want* her to come in, Dorian?"

"All right. I do." And I did. After all the biochemical and psychiatric preparation, I wanted to see what my reac-tion would be. Still sluggish from some drug, I had no exact idea how Rumer's presence would affect me.

At a parting of the pavilion's draperies, only two or three meters from my couch, appeared Rumer Montieth, my wife. Her garment of overlapping latex scales, glossy black in color, was a hauberk designed to reveal only her hands, face, and hair. The way Rumer was dressed was one of Diderits's deceits, or "preparations": I was supposed to see my wife as little different from myself, a creature as in-tricately assembled and synapsed as the engine I had be-come. But the hands, the face, the hair—nothing could disguise their unaugmented humanity, and revulsion swept over me like a tide.

"Dorian?" And her voice—wet, breath-driven, expelled between parted lips . . .

I turned away from her. "No," I told the speaker over-head. "It hasn't worked, my galen. Every part of me cries out against this."

Diderits said nothing. Was he still out there? Or was he trying to give Rumer and me a privacy I didn't want?

"Disassemble me," I urged him. "Link me to the control systems of a delta-state vessel and let me go out from Diroste for good. You don't want a zombot among you, Diderits—an unhappy anproz. Damn you all, you're tortur-ing me!"

"And you, us," Rumer said quietly. I faced her. "As

you're very aware, Dorian, as you're very aware . . . Take my hand."

"No." I didn't shrink away; I merely refused.

"Here. Take it."

Fighting my own disgust, I seized her hand, twisted it over, showed her its back. "Look."

"I *see* it, Dor." I was hurting her.

"Surfaces, that's all you see. Look at this growth, this wen." I pinched the growth. "Do you see that, Rumer? That's sebum, fatty matter. And the smell, if only you could—"

She drew back, and I tried to quell a mental nausea almost as profound as my regret. . . . To go out from Diroste seemed to be the only answer. Around me I wanted machinery—thrumming, inorganic machinery—and the sterile, actinic emptiness of outer space. I wanted to be the probeship *Dorian Lorca*. It hardly seemed a step down from my position as "prince consort" to the Governor of Diroste.

"Let me out," Rumer commanded the head of the Port Iranani Galenshall, and Diderits released her from the "Black Pavilion."

Then I was alone again in one of the few private chambers of a surgical complex given over to adapting Civi Korps personnel to our leprotic little planet's fume-filled mine shafts. The Galenshall was also devoted to patching up these civkis after their implanted respirators had atrophied, almost beyond saving, the muscles of their chests and lungs.

Including administrative personnel, Kommfleet officials, and the Civi Korps laborers in the mines, in the year I'm writing of there were over a half-million people on Diroste. Diderits was responsible for the health of all of them not assigned to the outlying territories. Had I not been the husband of Diroste's first governor, he might well have let me die along with the seventeen "expendables" on tour with me in the Fetneh District when the roof of the Haft Paykar diggings fell in on us. Rumer, however, made Diderits's duty clear to him, and I am as I am because the resources were at hand in Port Iranani and Diderits saw fit to obey his governor.

Alone in my pavilion, I lifted a hand to my face and heard a caroling of minute copper bells. . . .

*   *   *

Nearly a month later I observed Rumer, Diderits, and a stranger by closed-circuit television as they sat in one of the Galenshall's wide conference rooms. The stranger was a woman, bald but for a scalplock, who wore gold silk pantaloons that gave her the appearance of a clown, and a corrugated green jacket that somehow reversed this impression. Even on my monitor I could see the thick sunlight pouring into their room.

"This is Wardress Kefa," Rumer informed me.

I greeted her through a microphone and tested the cosmetic work of Diderits's associates by trying to smile for her.

"She's from Earth, Dor, and she's here because Komm-Galen Diderits and I asked her to come."

"Forty-six lights," I murmured, probably inaudibly. I was touched and angry at the same time. To be constantly the focus of your friends' attentions, especially when they have more urgent matters to see to, can lead to either a corrosive cynicism or a humility just as crippling.

"We want you to go back with her on *Nizami*," Diderits said, "when it leaves Port Iranani tomorrow night."

"Why?"

"Wardress Kefa came all this way," Rumer responded, "because we wanted to talk to her. As a final stage in your therapy she's convinced us that you ought to visit her . . . her establishment there. And if this fails, Dorian, I give you up; if that's what you want, I relinquish you." Today Rumer was wearing a yellow sarong, a tasseled gold shawl, and a nun's hood of yellow and orange stripes. When she spoke she averted her eyes from the conference room's monitor and looked out its high windows instead. At a distance, I could appreciate the spare aesthetics of her profile.

"Establishment? What sort of establishment?" I studied the tiny Wardress, but her appearance volunteered nothing.

"The House of Compassionate Sharers," Diderits began. "It's located in Earth's western hemisphere, on the North American continent, nearly two hundred kilometers southwest of the gutted Urban Nucleus of Denver. It can be reached from Manitou Port by 'rail."

"Good. I shouldn't have any trouble finding it. But what is it, this mysterious house?"

Wardress Kefa spoke for the first time: "I would prefer

that you learn its nature and its purposes from me, Mr. Lorca, when we have arrived safely under its several roofs."

"Is it a brothel?" This question fell among my three interlocutors like a heavy stone.

"No," Rumer said after a careful five-count. "It's a unique sort of clinic for treatment of unique emotional disorders." She glanced at the Wardress, concerned that she had revealed too much.

"Some would call it a brothel," Wardress Kefa admitted huskily. "Earth has become a haven of misfits and opportunists, a crossroads of Glaktik Komm influence and trade. The House, I must confess, wouldn't prosper if it catered only to those who suffer from rare dissociations of feeling. Therefore a few—a very few—of those who come to us are kommthors rich in power and exacting in their tastes. But these people are exceptions, Governor Montieth, KommGalen Diderits; they represent an uneasy compromise we must make in order to carry out the work for which the House was originally envisioned and built."

A moment later Rumer announced, "You're going, Dor. You're going tomorrow night. Diderits and I, well, we'll see you in three E-months." That said, she gathered in her cloak with both hands and rearranged it on her shoulders. Then she left the room.

"Goodbye, Dorian," Diderits said, standing.

Wardress Kefa fixed upon the camera conveying her picture to me a keen glance made more disconcerting by her small naked face. "Tomorrow, then."

"Tomorrow," I agreed. I watched my monitor as the galen and the curious-looking Wardress exited the conference room together. In the room's high windows Diroste's sun sang a Capella in the lemon sky.

They gave me a private berth on *Nizami*. I used my "nights," since sleep no longer meant anything to me, to prowl through those nacelles of shipboard machinery not forbidden to passengers. Although I wasn't permitted in the forward command module, I did have access to the computer-ringed observation turret and two or three corridors of auxiliary equipment necessary to the maintenance of a continuous probefield. In these places I secreted myself and thought seriously about the likelihood of an encephalic/neural linkage with one of Kommfleet's interstellar frigates.

My body was a trial. Diderits had long ago informed me

that it—that *I*—was still "sexually viable," but this was something I hadn't yet put to the test, nor did I wish to. Tyrannized by morbidly vivid images of human viscera, human excreta, human decay, I had been rebuilt of metal, porcelain, and plastic *as if* from the very substances—skin, bone, hair, cartilage—that these inorganic materials derided. I was a contradiction, a quasi-immortal masquerading as one of the ephemera who had saved me from their own short-lived lot. Still another paradox was the fact that my aversion to the organic was itself a human (i.e., an organic) emotion. That was why I so fervently wanted out. For over a year and a half on Diroste I had hoped that Rumer and the others would see their mistake and exile me not only from themselves, but from the body that was a deadly daily reminder of my total estrangement.

But Rumer was adamant in her love, and I had been a prisoner in the Port Iranani Galenshall—with but one chilling respite—ever since the Haft Paykar explosion and cave-in. Now I was being given into the hands of a new wardress, and as I sat amid the enamel-encased engines of *Nizami* I couldn't help wondering what sort of prison the House of Compassionate Sharers must be. . . .

Among the passengers of a monorail car bound outward from Manitou Port, Wardress Kefa in the window seat beside me, I sat tense and stiff. Anthrophobia. Lorca, I told myself repeatedly, you must exercise self-control. Amazingly, I did. From Manitou Port we rode the sleek underslung bullet of our car through rugged, sparsely populated terrain toward Wolf Run Summit, and I controlled myself.

"You've never been 'home' before?" Wardress Kefa asked me.

"No. Earth isn't home. I was born on GK-world Dai-Han, Wardress. And as a young man I was sent as an administrative colonist to Diroste, where—"

"Where you were born again," Wardress Kefa interrupted. "Nevertheless, this is where we began."

The shadows of the mountains slid across the wraparound glass of our car, and the imposing white pylons of the monorail system flashed past us like the legs of giants. Yes. Like huge, naked cyborgs hiding among the mountains' aspens and pines.

"Where I met Rumer Montieth, I was going to say; where I eventually got married and settled down to the life of a

bureaucrat who happens to be married to power. You anticipate me, Wardress." I didn't add that now Earth and
Diroste were equally alien to me, that the probeship *Nizami*
had bid fair to assume first place among my loyalties.

A 'rail from Wolf Run came sweeping past us toward
Manitou Port. The sight pleased me; the vibratory hum of
the passing 'rail lingered sympathetically in my hearing,
and I refused to talk, even though the Wardress clearly
wanted to draw me out about my former life. I was surrounded and beset. Surely this woman had all she needed
to know of my past from Diderits and my wife. My annoyance grew.

"You're very silent, Mr. Lorca."

"I have no innate hatred of silences."

"Nor do I, Mr. Lorca—unless they're empty ones."

Hands in lap, humming bioelectrically, inaudibly, I
looked at my tiny guardian with disdain. "There are some,"
I told her, "who are unable to engage in a silence without
stripping it of its unspoken cargo of significance."

To my surprise the woman laughed heartily. "That certainly isn't true of you, is it?" Then, a wry expression playing on her lips, she shifted her gaze to the hurtling countryside and said nothing else until it came time to disembark
at Wolf Run Summit.

Wolf Run was a resort frequented principally by Kommfleet officers and members of the administrative hierarchy
stationed in Port Manitou. Civi Korps personnel had built
quaint gingerbread châteaus among the trees and engineered two of the slopes above the hamlet for year-round
skiing. "Many of these people," Wardress Kefa explained,
indicating a crowd of men and women beneath the deck of
Wolf Run's main lodge, "work inside Shays Mountain, near
the light-probe port, in facilities built originally for satellite-
tracking and missile-launch detection. Now they monitor
the display boards for Kommfleet orbiters and shuttles;
they program the cruising and descent lanes of these vehicles. Others are demographic and wildlife managers, bent
on resettling Earth as efficiently as it may be done. Tedious
work, Mr. Lorca. They come here to play." We passed below the lodge on a path of unglazed vitrofoam. Two or
three of Wolf Run's bundled visitors stared at me, pre-
sumably because I was in my tunic sleeves and conspicuously undaunted by the spring cold. Or maybe their stares
were for my guardian. . . .

"How many of these people are customers of yours, Wardress?"

"That isn't something I can divulge." But she glanced back over her shoulder as if she had recognized someone.

"What do they find at your establishment they can't find in Manitou Port?"

"I don't know, Mr. Lorca; I'm not a mind reader."

To reach the House of Compassionate Sharers from Wolf Run, we had to go on foot down a narrow path worked reverently into the flank of the mountain. It was very nearly a two-hour hike. I couldn't believe the distance or Wardress Kefa's stamina. Swinging her arms, jolting herself on stiff legs, she went down the mountain with a will. And in all the way we walked we met no other hikers.

At last we reached a clearing giving us an open view of a steep pine-peopled glen: a grotto that fell away beneath us and led our eyes to an expanse of smooth white sky. But the Wardress pointed directly down into the foliage.

"There," she said. "The House of Compassionate Sharers."

I saw nothing but afternoon sunlight on the aspens, boulders huddled in the mulch cover, and swaying tunnels among the trees. Squinting, I finally made out a geodesic structure built from the very materials of the woods. Like an upland sleight, a wavering mirage, the House slipped in and out of my vision, blending, emerging, melting again. It was a series of irregular domes as hard to hold as water vapor—but after several redwinged blackbirds flew noisily across the plane of its highest turret, the House remained for me in stark relief; it had shed its invisibility.

"It's more noticeable," Wardress Kefa said, "when its external shutters have been cranked aside. Then the House sparkles like a dragon's eye. The windows are stained glass."

"I'd like to see that. Now it appears camouflaged."

"That's deliberate, Mr. Lorca. Come."

When we were all the way down, I could see of what colossal size the House really was: it reared up through the pine needles and displayed its interlocking polygons to the sky. Strange to think that no one in a passing helicraft was ever likely to catch sight of it. . . .

Wardress Kefa led me up a series of plank stairs, spoke once at the door, and introduced me into an antechamber so clean and military that I thought "barracks" rather than "bawdyhouse." The ceiling and walls were honeycombed, and the natural flooring was redolent of the outdoors. My guardian disappeared, returned without her coat, and escorted me into a much smaller room shaped like a tapered well. By means of a wooden hand-crank she opened the shutters, and varicolored light filtered in upon us through the room's slant-set windows. On elevated cushions that snapped and rustled each time we moved, we sat facing each other.

"What now?" I asked the Wardress.

"Just listen: The Sharers have come to the House of their own volition, Mr. Lorca; most lived and worked on extrakomm worlds toward Glaktik Center before being approached for duty here. The ones who are here accepted the invitation. They came to offer their presences to people very like yourself."

"Me? Are they misconceived machines?"

"I'm not going to answer that. Let me just say that the variety of services the Sharers offer is surprisingly wide. As I've told you, for some visitants the Sharers are simply a convenient means of satisfying exotically aberrant tastes. For others they're a way back to the larger community. We take whoever comes to us for help, Mr. Lorca, in order that the Sharers not remain idle nor the House vacant."

"So long as whoever comes is wealthy and influential?"

She paused before speaking. "That's true enough. But the matter's out of my hands, Mr. Lorca. I'm an employee of Glaktik Komm, chosen for my empathetic abilities. I don't make policy. I don't own title to the House."

"But you *are* its madam. Its 'wardress,' rather."

"True. For the last twenty-two years. I'm the first and only wardress to have served here, Mr. Lorca, and I love the Sharers. I love their devotion to the fragile mentalities who visit them. Even so, despite the time I've lived among them, I still don't pretend to understand the source of their transcendent concern. That's what I wanted to tell you."

"You think me a 'fragile mentality'?"

"I'm sorry—but you're here, Mr. Lorca, and you certainly aren't fragile of *limb,* are you?" The Wardress laughed. "I also wanted to ask you to . . . well, to restrain your crueler impulses when the treatment itself begins."

I stood up and moved away from the little woman. How had I borne her presence for as long as I had?

"Please don't take my request amiss. It isn't *specifically* personal, Mr. Lorca. I make it of everyone who comes to

the House of Compassionate Sharers. Restraint is an unwritten corollary of the only three rules we have here. Will
you hear them?"

I made a noise of compliance.

"First, that you do not leave the session chamber once
you've entered it. Second, that you come forth immediately
upon my summoning you . . ."

"And third?"

"That you do not kill the Sharer."

All the myriad disgusts I had been suppressing for seven
or eight hours were now perched atop the ladder of my
patience, and, rung by painful rung, I had to step them
back down. Must a rule be made to prevent a visitant from
murdering the partner he had bought? Incredible. The
Wardress herself was just perceptibly sweating, and I noticed too how grotesquely distended her earlobes were.

"Is there a room in this establishment for a wealthy and
influential patron? A private room?"

"Of course," she said. "I'll show you."

It had a full-length mirror. I undressed and stood in front
of it. Only during my first "period of adjustment" on
Diroste had I spent much time looking at what I had become. Later, back in the Port Iranani Galenshall, Diderits
had denied me any sort of reflective surface at all—looking
glasses, darkened windows, even metal spoons. The waxen
perfection of my features ridiculed the ones another Dorian
Lorca had possessed before the Haft Paykar Incident. Cosmetic mockery. Faintly corpselike, speciously paradigmatic,
I was both more than I was supposed to be and less.

In Wardress Kefa's House the less seemed preeminent. I
ran a finger down the inside of my right arm, scrutinizing
the track of one of the intubated veins through which cir-
culated a serum that Diderits called hematocybin: an efficient "low-maintenance" blood substitute, combative of
both fatigue and infection, which requires changing only
once every six D-months. With a proper supply of hematocybin and a plastic recirculator I can do the job myself,
standing up. That night, however, the ridge of my vein,
mirrored only an arm's length away, was more horror than
miracle. I stepped away from the looking glass and closed
my eyes.

*   *   *

Later that evening Wardress Kefa came to me with a candle and a brocaded dressing gown. She made me put on the gown in front of her, and I complied. Then, the robe's rich and symbolic embroidery on my back, I followed her out of my first-floor chamber to a rustic stairwell seemingly connective to all the rooms in the House.

The dome contained countless smaller domes and five or six primitive staircases, at least. Not a single other person was about. Lit flickeringly by Wardress Kefa's taper as we climbed one of these sets of stairs, the House's mid-interior put me in mind of an Escheresque drawing in which verticals and horizontals become hopelessly confused and a figure who from one perspective seems to be going up a series of steps, from another seems to be coming down them. Presently the Wardress and I stood on a landing above this topsy-turvy well of stairs (though there were still more stairs above us), and, looking down, I experienced an unsettling reversal of perspectives. Vertigo. Why hadn't Diderits, against so human a susceptibility, implanted tiny gyrostabilizers in my head? I clutched a railing and held on.

"You can't fall," Wardress Kefa told me. "It's an illusion. A whim of the architects."

"Is it an illusion behind this door?"

"Oh, the Sharer's real enough, Mr. Lorca. Please. Go on in." She touched my face and left me, taking her candle with her.

After hesitating a moment I went through the door to my assignation, and the door locked of itself. I stood with my hand on the butterfly shape of the knob and felt the night working in me and the room. The only light came from the stove-bed on the opposite wall, for the fitted polygons overhead were still blanked out by their shutters and no candles shone here. Instead, reddish embers glowed behind an isinglass window beneath the stove-bed, strewn wth quilts, on which my Sharer awaited me.

Outside, the wind played harp music in the trees.

I was trembling rhythmically, as when Rumer had come to me in the "Black Pavilion." Even though my eyes adjusted rapidly, automatically, to the dark, it was still difficult to see. Temporizing, I surveyed the dome. In its high central vault hung a cage in which, disturbed by my entrance, a bird hopped skittishly about. The cage swayed on its tether.

Go on, I told myself.

I advanced toward the dais and leaned over the unmoving Sharer who lay there. With a hand on either side of the creature's head, I braced myself. The figure beneath me moved, moved weakly, and I drew back. But because the Sharer didn't stir again, I reassumed my previous stance: the posture of either a lover or a man called upon to identify a disfigured corpse. But identification was impossible; the embers under the bed gave too feeble a sheen. In the chamber's darkness even a lover's kiss would have fallen clumsily. . . .

"I'm going to touch you," I said. "Will you let me do that?"

The Sharer lay still.

Then, willing all of my senses into the cushion of synthetic flesh at my forefinger's tip, I touched the Sharer's face.

Hard, and smooth, and cool.

I moved my finger from side to side; and the hardness, smoothness, coolness, continued to flow into my pressuring fingertip. It was like touching the pate of a death's-head, the cranial cap of a human being: bone rather than metal. My finger distinguished between these two possibilities, deciding on bone; and, half-panicked, I concluded that I had traced an arc on the skull of an intelligent being who bore his every bone on the outside, like an armor of calcium. Could that be? If so, how could this organism—this entity, this *thing*—express compassion?

I lifted my finger away from the Sharer. Its tip hummed with a pressure now relieved and emanated a faint warmth.

A death's-head come to life . . .

Maybe I laughed. In any case, I pulled myself onto the platform and straddled the Sharer. I kept my eyes closed, though not tightly. It didn't seem that I was straddling a skeleton.

"Sharer," I whispered. "Sharer, I don't know you yet."

Gently, I let my thumbs find the creature's eyes, the sockets in the smooth exoskeleton, and both thumbs returned to me a hardness and a coldness that were unquestionably metallic in origin. Moreover, the Sharer didn't flinch—even though I'd anticipated that probing his eyes, no matter how gently, would provoke at least an involuntary pulling away. Instead, the Sharer lay still and tractable under my hands.

And why not? I thought. *Your eyes are nothing but two pieces of sophisticated optical machinery. . . .*

It was true. Two artificial light-sensing image-integrating units gazed up at me from the sockets near which my thumbs probed, and I realized that even in this darkness my Sharer, its vision mechanically augmented beyond my own, could *see* my blind face staring down in a futile attempt to create an image out of the information my hands had supplied me. I opened my eyes and held them open. I could see only shadows, but my thumbs could *feel* the cold metal rings that held the Sharer's photosensitive units so firmly in its skull.

"An animatronic construct," I said, rocking back on my heels. "A soulless robot. Move your head if I'm right."

The Sharer continued motionless.

"All right. You're a sentient creature whose eyes have been replaced with an artificial system. What about that? Lord, are we brothers then?"

I had a sudden hunch that the Sharer was very old, a senescent being owing its life to prosthetics, transplants, and imitative organs of laminated silicone. Its life, I was certain, had been *extended* by these contrivances, not saved. I asked the Sharer about my feeling, and very, very slowly it moved the helmetlike skull housing its artificial eyes and its aged, compassionate mind. Uncharitably I then believed myself the victim of a deception, whether the Sharer's or Wardress Kefa's I couldn't say. Here, after all, was a creature who had chosen to prolong its organic condition rather than to escape it, and it had willingly made use of the same materials and methods Diderits had brought into play to save me.

"You might have died," I told it. "Go too far, Sharer— go too far with these contrivances and you may forfeit suicide as an option."

Then, leaning forward again, saying, "I'm still not through, I still don't know you," I let my hands come down the Sharer's bony face to its throat. Here a shield of cartilage graded upward into its jaw and downward into the plastically silken skin covering the remainder of its body, internalizing all but the defiantly naked skull of the Sharer's skeletal structure. A death's-head with the body of a man . . .

That was all I could take. I rose from the stove-bed and, cinching my dressing gown tightly about my waist, crossed to the other side of the chamber. There was no furniture in the room but the stove-bed (if that qualified), and I had to content myself with sitting in a lotus position on the floor. I sat that way all night, staving off dreams.

Diderits had said that I needed to dream. If I didn't dream, he warned, I'd be risking hallucinations and eventual madness; in the Port Iranani Galenshall he'd seen to it that drugs were administered to me every two days and my sleep period monitored by an ARC machine and a team of electroencephalographers. But my dreams were almost always nightmares, descents into klieg-lit charnel houses, and I infinitely preferred the risk of going psychotic. There was always the chance someone would take pity and disassemble me, piece by loving piece. Besides, I had lasted two E-weeks now on nothing but grudging catnaps, and so far I still had gray matter upstairs instead of scrambled eggs. . . .

I crossed my fingers.

A long time after I'd sat down, Wardress Kefa threw open the door. It was morning. I could tell because the newly canted shutters outside our room admitted a singular roaring of light. The entire chamber was illumined, and I saw crimson wall-hangings, a mosaic of red and purple stones on the section of the floor, and a tumble of scarlet quilts. The bird in the suspended cage was a redwinged blackbird.

"Where is it from?"

"You could use a more appropriate pronoun."

"He? She? Which is the more appropriate, Wardress Kefa?"

"Assume the Sharer maculine, Mr. Lorca."

"My sexual proclivities have never run that way, I'm afraid."

"Your sexual proclivities," the Wardress told me stingingly, "enter into this only if you persist in thinking of the House as a brothel rather than a clinic and the Sharers as whores rather than therapists!"

"Last night I heard two or three people clomping up the stairs in their boots, that and a woman's raucous laughter."

"A visitant, Mr. Lorca, *not* a Sharer."

"I didn't think she was a Sharer. But it's difficult to believe I'm in a 'clinic' when that sort of noise disrupts my midnight meditations, Wardress."

"I've explained that. It can't be helped."

"All right, all right. Where is *he* from, this 'therapist' of mine?"

"An interior star. But where he's from is of no consequence in your treatment. I matched him to your needs, as I see them, and soon you'll be going back to him."

"Why? To spend another night sitting on the floor?"

"You won't do that again, Mr. Lorca. And you needn't worry. Your reaction wasn't an uncommon one for a newcomer to the House."

"Revulsion?" I cried. "Revulsion's therapeutic?"

"I don't think you were as put off as you believe."

"Oh? Why not?"

"Because you talked to the Sharer. You addressed him directly, not once but several times. Many visitants never get that far during their first session, Mr. Lorca."

"Talked to him?" I said dubiously. "Maybe. Before I found out what he was."

"Ah. Before you found out what he was." In her heavy green jacket and swishy pantaloons the tiny woman turned about and departed the well of the sitting room.

I stared bemusedly after her for a long time.

Three nights after my first "session," the night of my conversation with Wardress Kefa, I entered the Sharer's chamber again. Everything was as it had been, except that the dome's shutters were open and moonlight coated the mosaic work on the floor. The Sharer awaited me in the same recumbent, unmoving posture, and inside its cage the redwinged blackbird set one of its perches to rocking back and forth.

Perversely, I had decided not to talk to the Sharer this time—but I did approach the stove-bed and lean over him. *Hello*, I thought, and the word very nearly came out. I straddled the Sharer and studied him in the stained moonlight. He looked just as my sense of touch had led me to conclude previously . . . like a skull, oddly flattened and beveled, with the body of a man. But despite the chemical embers glowing beneath his dais the Sharer's body had no warmth, and to know him more fully I resumed tracing a finger over his alien parts.

I discovered that at every conceivable pressure point a tiny scar existed, or the tip of an implanted electrode, and that miniature canals into which wires had been sunk veined his inner arms and legs. Just beneath his sternum a concave disc about eight centimeters across, containing neither instruments nor any other surface features, had been set into the Sharer's chest like a stainless-steel brooch. It seemed to hum under the pressure of my finger as I drew my nail silently around the disc's circumference. What was it for? What did it mean? Again, I almost spoke.

I rolled toward the wall and lay stretched out beside the unmoving Sharer. Maybe he *couldn't* move. On my last visit he had moved his dimly phosphorescent head for me, of course, but that only feebly, and maybe his immobility was the result of some cybergamic dysfunction. I had to find out. My resolve not to speak deserted me, and I propped myself up on my elbow.

"Sharer . . . Sharer, can you move?"

The head turned toward me slightly, signaling . . . well, what?

"Can you get off this platform? Try. Get off this dais under your own power."

To my surprise the Sharer nudged a quilt to the floor and in a moment stood facing me. Moonlight glinted from the photosensitive units serving the creature as eyes and gave his bent, elongated body the appearance of a piece of In-hodlef Era statuary, primitive work from the extrakomm world of Glaparcus.

"Good," I praised the Sharer; "very good. Can you tell me what you're supposed to share with me? I'm not sure we have as much in common as our Wardress seems to think."

The Sharer extended both arms toward me and opened his tightly closed fists. In the cups of his palms he held two items I hadn't discovered during my tactile examination of him. I accepted these from the Sharer. One was a small metal disc, the other a thin metal cylinder. Looking them over, I found that the disc reminded me of the larger mirrorlike bowl set in the alien's chest, while the cylinder seemed to be a kind of penlight.

Absently, I pulled my thumb over the head of the penlight; a ridged metal sheath followed the motion of my thumb, uncovering a point of ghostly red light stretching away into the cylinder seemingly deeper than the penlight itself. I pointed this instrument at the wall, at our bedding, at the Sharer himself—but it emitted no beam. When I turned the penlight on my wrist, the results were predictably similar: not even a faint red shadow appeared along the edge of my arm. Nothing. The cylinder's light existed internally, a beam continuously transmitted and retransmitted between the penlight's two poles. Pulling back the sheath on the instrument's head had in no way interrupted the operation of its self-regenerating circuit.

I stared wonderingly into the hollow of redness, then looked up. "Sharer, what's this thing for?"

The Sharer reached out and took from my other hand the disc I had so far ignored. Then he placed this small circle of metal in the smooth declivity of the larger disc in his chest, where it apparently adhered—for I could no longer see it. That done, the Sharer stood distressingly immobile, even more like a statue than he had seemed a moment before, one arm frozen across his body and his hand stilled at the edge of the sunken plate in which the smaller disc had just adhered. He looked dead and self-commemorating.

"Lord!" I exclaimed. "What've you done, Sharer? Turned yourself off? That's right, isn't it?"

The Sharer neither answered nor moved.

Suddenly I felt sickeningly weary, opiate-weary, and I knew that I wouldn't be able to stay on the dais with this puzzle-piece being from an anonymous sun standing over me like a dark angel from my racial subconscious. I thought briefly of manhandling the Sharer across the room, but didn't have the will to touch this catatonically rigid being, this sculpture of metal and bone, and so dismissed the idea. Nor was it likely that Wardress Kefa would help me, even if I tried to summon her with murderous poundings and cries—a bitterly amusing prospect. Wellaway, another night propped against the chamber's far wall, keeping sleep at bay . . .

Is this what you wanted me to experience, Rumer? The frustration of trying to piece together my own "therapy"? I looked up through one of the dome's unstained polygons in lethargic search of the constellation Auriga. Then I realized that I wouldn't recognize it even if it happened to lie within my line of sight. Ah, Rumer, Rumer . . .

"You're certainly a pretty one," I told the Sharer. Then I pointed the penlight at his chest, drew back the sheath on its head, and spoke a single onomatopoeic word: *"Bang."*

Instantly a beam of light sang between the instrument in my hand and the plate in the Sharer's chest. The beam died at once (I had registered only its shattering brightness, not its color), but the disc continued to glow with a residual illumination.

The Sharer dropped his frozen arm and assumed a posture more limber, more suggestive of life. He looked . . . expectant.

I could only stare. Then I turned the penlight over in my hands, pointed it again at the Sharer, and waited for another coursing of light. To no purpose. The instrument still burned internally, but it wouldn't relume the alien's inset disc, which, in any case, continued to glow dimly. Things were all at once interesting again. I gestured with the penlight.

"You've rejoined the living, haven't you?"

The Sharer acknowledged this with a slight turn of the head.

"Forgive me, Sharer, but I don't want to spend another night sitting on the floor. If you can move again, how about over there?" I pointed at the opposite wall. "I don't want you hovering over me."

Oddly, he obeyed. But he did so oddly, without turning around. He cruised backward as if on invisible coasters—his legs moving a little, yes, but not enough to propel him so smoothly, so quickly, across the chamber. Once against the far wall, the Sharer settled into the motionless but expectant posture he had asumed after his "activation" by the penlight. I could see that he still had some degree of control over his own movements, for his long fingers curled and uncurled and his skull nodded eerily in the halo of moonlight pocketing him. Even so, I realized that he had truly moved only at my voice command and my simultaneous gesturing with the penlight. And what did *that* mean?

Well, that the Sharer had relinquished control of his body to the man-machine Dorian Lorca, retaining for himself just those meaningless reflexes and stirrings that convince the manipulated of their own autonomy. It was an awesome prostitution, even if Wardress Kefa would have frowned to hear me say so. Momentarily I rejoiced in it, for it seemed to free me from the demands of an artificial eroticism, from the need to figure through what was expected of me. The Sharer would obey my simplest wrist-turning, my briefest word; all I had to do was *use* the control he had literally handed to me.

This virtually unlimited power, I thought then, was a therapy whose value Rumer would understand only too well. This was a harsh assessment, but penlight in hand, I felt that I too was a kind of marionette. . . .

Insofar as I could, I tried to come to grips with the physics of the Sharer's operation. First, the disc-within-a-disc on his chest apparently broke the connections ordinarily allowing him to exercise the senile powers that were still his. And, second, the penlight's beam restored and amplified these powers but delivered them into the hands of the speaker of imperatives who wielded the penlight. I recalled that in Earth's lunar probeship yards were crews of animatronic laborers programmed for fitting and welding. A single trained supervisor could direct from fifteen to twenty receiver-equipped laborers with one penlight and a microphone.

"Sharer," I commanded, blanking out his reverie, pointing the penlight, "go there. . . . No, no, not like that. Lift your feet. March for me. . . . That's right, a *goosestep*."

While Wardress Kefa's third rule rattled in the back of my mind like a challenge, for the next several hours I toyed with the Sharer. After the marching I set him to calisthenics and interpretative dance, and he obeyed, moving more gracefully than I would have imagined possible. Here—then there—then back again. All he lacked was Beethoven's piano sonatas for an accompaniment.

At intervals I rested, but always the fascination of the penlight drew me back, almost against my will, and I once again played puppetmaster.

"Enough, Sharer, enough." The sky had a curdled quality suggestive of dawn. Catching sight of the cage overhead, I was taken by an irresistible impulse. I pointed the penlight at the cage and commanded, "Up, Sharer. Up, up, up."

The Sharer floated up from the floor and glided effortlessly toward the vault of the dome: a beautiful aerial walk. Without benefit of hawsers or scaffolds or wings the Sharer levitated. Hovering over the stove-bed he had been made to surrender, hovering over everything in the room, he reached the cage and swung before it with his hands touching the scrolled iron work on its little door. I dropped my own hands and watched him. So tightly was I gripping the penlight, however, that my knuckles must have resembled the caps of four tiny bleached skulls.

A great deal of time went by, the Sharer poised in the gelid air awaiting some word from me.

Morning began coming in the room's polygonal windows.

"Take the bird out," I ordered the Sharer, moving my penlight. "Take the bird out of the cage and kill it." This command, sadistically heartfelt, seemed to me a foolproof, indirect way of striking back at Rumer, Diderits, the Wardress, and the Third Rule of the House of Compassionate Sharers. More than anything, against all reason, I wanted the redwinged blackbird dead. And I wanted the Sharer to kill it.

Dawn made clear the cancerous encroachment of age in the Sharer's legs and hands, as well as the full horror of his cybergamically rigged death's-head. He looked like he had been unjustly hanged. And when his hands went up to the cage, instead of opening its door the Sharer lifted the entire contraption off the hook, fastening it to its tether, and then accidentally lost his grip on the cage.

I watched the cage fall—land on its side—bounce—bounce again. The Sharer stared down with his bulging silver-ringed eyes, his hands still spread wide to accommodate the fallen cage.

"Mr. Lorca," Wardress Kefa was knocking at the door. "Mr. Lorca, what's going on, please?"

I arose from the stove-bed, tossed my quilt aside, straightened my heavy robes. The Wardress knocked again. I looked at the Sharer swaying in the half-light like a sword or a pendulum, an instrument of severance. The night had gone faster than I liked.

Again, the purposeful knocking.

"Coming," I barked.

In the dented cage there was a flutter of crimson, a stillness, and then another bit of melancholy flapping. I hurled my penlight across the room. When it struck the wall, the Sharer rocked back and forth for a moment without descending so much as a centimeter. The knocking continued.

"You have the key, Wardress. Open the door."

She did, and stood on its threshold taking stock of the games we had played. Her eyes were bright but devoid of censure, and I swept past her wordlessly, burning with shame and bravado.

*   *   *

I slept that day—all that day—for the first time since leaving my own world. And I dreamed. I dreamed that I was connected to a mechanism pistoning away on the edge of the Haft Paykar diggings, siphoning deadly gases out of the shafts and perversely recirculating them through the pump with which I shared a symbiomechanic linkage. Amid a series of surreal turquoise sunsets and intermittent gusts of sand, this pistoning went on, and on, and on. When I awoke I lifted my hands to my face, intending to scar it with my nails. But a moment later, as I had known it would, the mirror in my chamber returned me a perfect, unperturbed Dorian Lorca. . . .

"May I come in?"

"I'm the guest here, Wardress. So I suppose you may."

She entered and, quickly intuiting my mood, walked to the other side of the chamber. "You slept, didn't you? And you dreamed?"

I said nothing.

"You dreamed, didn't you?"

"A nightmare, Wardress. A long and repetitious nightmare, notable only for being different from the ones I had on Diroste."

"A start, though. You weren't monitored during your sleep, after all, and even if your dream *was* a nightmare, Mr. Lorca, I believe you've managed to survive it. Good. All to the good."

I went to the only window in the room, a hexagonal pane of dark blue through which it was impossible to see anything. "Did you get him down?"

"Yes. And restored the birdcage to its place." Her tiny feet made pacing sounds on the hardwood. "The bird was unharmed."

"Wardress, what's all this about? Why have you paired me with . . . with this particular Sharer?" I turned around. "What's the point?"

"You're not estranged from your wife only, Mr. Lorca. You're—"

"I know that. I've *known* that."

"And I know that you know it. Give me a degree of credit. . . . You also know," she resumed, "that you're estranged from yourself, body and soul at variance—"

"Of course, damn it! And the argument between them's been stamped into every pseudo-organ and circuit I can lay claim to!"

"Please, Mr. Lorca, I'm trying to explain. This interior 'argument' you're so aware of . . . it's really a metaphor for an attitude you involuntarily adopted after Diderits performed his operations. And a metaphor can be taken apart and explained."

"Like a machine."

"If you like." She began pacing again. "To take inventory you have to surmount that which is to be inventoried. You go outside, Mr. Lorca, in order to come back in." She halted and fixed me with a colorless, lopsided smile.

"All of that," I began cautiously, "is clear to me. 'Know thyself,' saith Diderits and the ancient Greeks. . . . Well, if anything, my knowledge has *increased* my uneasiness about not only myself, but others—and not only others, but the very phenomena permitting us to spawn." I had an image of crimson-gilled fish firing upcurrent in a roiling, untidy barrage. "What I know hasn't cured anything, Wardress."

"No. That's why we've had you come here. To extend the limits of your knowledge and to involve you in relationships demanding a recognition of others as well as self."

"As with the Sharer I left hanging up in the air?"

"Yes. Distance is advisable at first, perhaps inevitable. You needn't feel guilty. In a night or two you'll be going back to him, and then we'll just have to see."

"Is this the only Sharer I'm going to be . . . working with?"

"I don't know. It depends on the sort of progress you make."

But for the Wardress Kefa, the Sharer in the crimson dome, and the noisy midnight visitants I had never seen, there were times when I believed myself the only occupant of the House. The thought of such isolation, although not unwelcome, was an anchoritic fantasy: I knew that breathing in the chambers next to mine, going about the arcane business of the lives they had bartered away, were humanoid creatures difficult to imagine; harder still, once lodged in the mind, to put out of it. To what number and variety of beings had Wardress Kefa indentured her love . . . ?

I had no chance to ask this question. We heard an insistent clomping on the steps outside the House and then muffled voices in the antechamber.

"Who's that?"

The Wardress put up her hand to silence me and opened

the door to my room. "A moment," she called. "I'll be with you in a moment." But her husky voice didn't carry very well, and whoever had entered the House set about methodically knocking on doors and clomping from apartment to apartment, all the while bellowing the Wardress's name. "I'd better go talk with them," she told me apologetically.

"But who is it?"

"Someone voice-coded for entrance, Mr. Lorca. Nothing to worry about." And she went into the corridor, giving me a scent of spruce needles and a vision of solidly hewn rafters before the door swung to.

But I got up and followed the Wardress. Outside I found her face to face with two imposing persons who looked exactly alike in spite of their being one a man and the other a woman. Their faces had the same lantern-jawed mournfulness, their eyes a hooded look under prominent brows. They wore filigreed pea jackets, ski leggings, and fur-lined caps bearing the interpenetrating-galaxies insignia of Glaktik Komm. I judged them to be in their late thirties, E-standard, but they both had the domineering, glad-handing air of high-ranking veterans in the bureaucratic establishment, people who appreciate their positions just to the extent that their positions can be exploited. I knew. I had once been an official of the same stamp.

The man, having been caught in midbellow, was now trying to laugh. "Ah, Wardress, Wardress."

"I didn't expect you this evening," she told the two of them.

"We were granted a proficiency leave for completing the Salous blueprint in advance of schedule," the woman explained, "and so caught a late 'rail from Manitou Port to take advantage of the leave. We hiked down in the dark." Along with her eyebrows she lifted a hand lantern for our inspection.

"We *took* a proficiency leave," the man said, "even if we *were* here last week. And we deserved it too." He went on to tell us that "Salous" dealt with reclaiming the remnants of aboriginal populations and pooling them for something called integrative therapy. "The Great Plains will soon be our bordello, Wardress. There, you see: you and the Orhas are in the same business . . . at least until we're assigned to stage-manage something more prosaic."

He clapped his gloved hands together and looked at me. "You're new, aren't you? Who are you going to?"

"Pardon me," the Wardress interjected wearily. "Who do *you* want tonight?"

The man looked at his partner with a mixture of curiosity and concern. "Cleva?"

"The mouthless one," Cleva responded at once. "Drugged, preferably."

"Come with me, Orhas," the Wardress directed. She led them first to her own apartment and then into the House's midinterior, where the three of them disappeared from my sight. I could hear them climbing one of the sets of stairs.

Shortly thereafter the Wardress returned to my room.

"They're twins?"

"In a manner of speaking, Mr. Lorca. Actually they're clonemates: Cleva and Cleirach Orha, specialists in Holosyncretic Management. They do abstract computer planning involving indigenous and alien populations, which is why they know of the House at all and have an authorization to come here."

"Do they always appear here together? Go upstairs together?"

The Wardress's silence clearly meant yes.

"That's a bit kinky, isn't it?"

She gave me an angry look whose implications immediately silenced me. I started to apologize, but she said: "The Orhas are the only visitants to the House who arrive together, Mr. Lorca. Since they share a common upbringing, the same genetic material, and identical biochemistries, it isn't surprising that their sexual preferences should coincide. In Manitou Port, I'm told, is a third clonemate who was permitted to marry, and her I've never seen either here or in Wolf Run Summit. It seems there's a *degree* of variety even among clonal siblings."

"Do these two come often?"

"You heard them in the House several days ago."

"They have frequent leaves, then?"

"Last time was an overnighter. They returned to Manitou Port in the morning, Mr. Lorca. Just now they were trying to tell me that they intend to be here for a few days."

"For treatment," I said.

"You know better. You're baiting me, Mr. Lorca." She had taken her graying scalplock into her fingers and was holding its fan of hair against her right cheek. In this posture, despite her preoccupation with the arrival of the Orhas, she looked very old and very innocent.

"Who is the 'mouthless one,' Wardress?"

"Good night, Mr. Lorca. I only returned to tell you good night." And with no other word she left.

It was the longest I had permitted myself to talk with her since our first afternoon in the House, the longest I had been in her presence since our claustrophobic 'rail ride from Manitou Port. Even the Orhas, bundled to the gills, as vulgar as sleek bullfrogs, hadn't struck me as altogether insufferable.

Wearing neither coat nor cap, I took a walk through the glens below the House, touching each wind-shaken tree as I came to it and trying to conjure out of the darkness a viable memory of Rumer's smile. . . .

"Sex as weapon," I told my Sharer, who sat propped on the stove-bed amid ten or twelve quilts of scarlet and off-scarlet. "As prince consort to the Governor of Diroste, that was the only weapon I had access to. . . . Rumer employed me as an emissary, Sharer, an espionage agent, a protocol officer, whatever state business required. I received visiting representatives of Glaktik Komm, mediated disputes in the Port Iranani business community, and went on biannual inspection tours of the Fetneh and Furak District mines. I did a little of everything, Sharer."

As I paced, the Sharer observed me with a macabre, but somehow not unsettling, penetration. The hollow of his chest was exposed, and, as I passed him, an occasional metallic wink caught the corner of my eye.

I told him the story of my involvement with a minor official in Port Iranani's department of immigration, a young woman whom I had never called by anything but her maternal surname, Humay. There had been others besides this woman, but Humay's story was the one I chose to tell. Why? Because alone among my ostensible "lovers," Humay I had never lain with. I had never chosen to.

Instead, to her intense bewilderment, I gave Humay ceremonial pendants, bracelets, earpieces, brooches, necklaces, and die-cut cameos of gold on silver, all from the collection of Rumer Montieth, Governor of Diroste—anything, in short, distinctive enough to be recognizable to my wife at a glance. Then, at those state functions requiring

Rumer's attendance upon a visiting dignitary, I arranged for Humay to be present; sometimes I accompanied her myself, sometimes I found her an escort among the unbonded young men assigned to me as aides. Always I ensured that Rumer should see Humay, if not in a reception line then in the promenade of the formal recessional. Afterward I asked Humay, who never seemed to have even a naive insight into the purposes of my game, to hand back whatever piece of jewelry I had given her for ornament, and she did so. Then I returned the jewelry to Rumer's sandalwood box before my wife could verify what her eyes had earlier that evening tried to tell her. Everything I did was designed to create a false impression of my relationship with Humay, and I wanted my dishonesty in the matter to be conspicuous.

Finally, dismissing Humay for good, I gave her a cameo of Rumer's that had been crafted in the Furak District. I learned later that she had flung this cameo at an aide of mine who entered the offices of her department on a matter having nothing to do with her. She created a disturbance, several times raising my name. Ultimately (in two days' time), she was disciplined by a transfer to the frontier outpost of Yagme, the administrative center of the Furak District, and I never saw her again.

"Later, Sharer, when I dreamed of Humay, I saw her as a woman with mother-of-pearl flesh and ruby eyes. In my dreams she *became* the pieces of jewelry with which I'd tried to incite my wife's sexual jealousy—blunting it even as I incited it."

The Sharer regarded me with hard but sympathetic eyes.

Why? I asked him. Why had I dreamed of Humay as if she were an expensive clockwork mechanism, gilded, beset with gemstones, invulnerably enameled? And why had I so fiercely desired Rumer's jealousy?

The Sharer's silence invited confession.

After the Haft Paykar Incident (I went on, pacing), after Diderits had fitted me with a total prosthesis, my nightmares often centered on the young woman who'd been exiled to Yagme. Although in Port Iranani I hadn't once touched Humay in an erotic way, in my monitored nightmares I regularly descended into either a charnel catacomb or a half-fallen quarry—it was impossible to know which—and there forced myself, without success, on the bejeweled automaton she had become. In every instance Humay waited for me underground; in every instance she turned me back with coruscating laughter. Its echoes always drove me upward to the light, and in the midst of nightmare I realized that I wanted Humay far less than I did residency in the secret subterranean places she had made her own. The klieg lights that invariably directed my descent always followed me back out, too, so that Humay was always left kilometers below exulting in the dark. . . .

My Sharer got up and took a turn around the room, a single quilt draped over his shoulders and clutched loosely together at his chest. This was the first time since I had been coming to him that he had moved so far of his own volition, and I sat down to watch. Did he understand me at all? I had spoken to him as if his understanding were presupposed, a certainty—but beyond a hopeful *feeling* that my words meant something to him I'd had no evidence at all, not even a testimonial from Wardress Kefa. All of the Sharer's "reactions" were really nothing but projections of my own ambiguous hopes.

When he at last returned to me, he extended both hideously canaled arms and opened his fists. In them, the disc and the penlight. It was an offering, a compassionate, selfless offering, and for a moment I stared at his open hands in perplexity. What did they want of me, this Sharer, Wardress Kefa, the people who had sent me here? How was I supposed to buy either their forbearance or my freedom? By choosing power over impotency? By manipulation? . . . But these were altogether different questions, and I hesitated.

The Sharer then placed the small disc in the larger one beneath his sternum. Then, as before, a thousand esoteric connections severed, he froze. In the hand still extended toward me, the penlight glittered faintly and threatened to slip from his insensible grasp. I took it carefully from the Sharer's fingers, pulled back the sheath on its head, and gazed into its red-lit hollow. I released the sheath and pointed the penlight at the disc in his chest.

If I pulled the sheath back again, he would become little more than a fully integrated, *external* prosthesis—as much at my disposal as the hands holding the penlight.

"No," I said. "Not this time." And I flipped the penlight across the chamber, out of the way of temptation. Then, using my fingernails, I pried the small disc out of its electromagnetic moorings above the Sharer's heart.

He was restored to himself.

As was I to myself. As was I.

A day later, early in the afternoon, I ran into the Orhas in the House's midinterior. They were coming unaccompanied out of a lofty, seemingly sideways-canted door as I stood peering upward from the access corridor. Man and woman together, mirror images ratcheting down a Moebius strip of stairs, the Orhas held my attention until it was too late for me to slip away unseen.

"The new visitant," Cleirach Orha informed his sister when he reached the bottom step. "We've seen you before."

"Briefly," I agreed. "The night you arrived from Manitou Port for your proficiency leave."

"What a good memory you have," Cleva Orha said. "We also saw you the day *you* arrived from Manitou Port. You and the Wardress were just setting out from Wolf Run Summit together. Cleirach and I were beneath the ski lodge, watching."

"You wore no coat," her clonemate said in explanation of their interest.

They both stared at me curiously. Neither was I wearing a coat in the well of the House of Compassionate Sharers— even though the temperature inside hovered only a few degrees above freezing and we could see our breaths before us like the ghosts of ghosts. . . . I was a queer one, wasn't I? My silence made them nervous and brazen.

"No coat," Cleva Orha repeated, "and the day cold enough to fur your spittle. 'Look at that one,' Cleirach told me; 'thinks he's a polar bear.' We laughed about that, studling. We laughed heartily."

I nodded, nothing more. A coppery taste of bile, such as I hadn't experienced for several days, flooded my mouth, and I wanted to escape the Orhas' warty good humor. They were intelligent people, otherwise they would never have been cloned, but face to face with their flawed skins and their loud, insinuative sexuality I began to feel my new-found stores of tolerance overbalancing like a tower of blocks. It was a bitter test, this meeting below the stairs, and one I was on the edge of failing.

"We seem to be the only ones in the House this month,"

the woman volunteered. "Last month the Wardress was gone, the Sharers had a holiday, and Cleirach and I had to content ourselves with incestuous buggery in Manitou Port."

"Cleva!" the man protested, laughing.

"It's true." She turned to me. "It's true, studling. And that little she-goat—Kefa, I mean—won't even tell us why the Closed sign was out for so long. Delights in mystery, that one."

"That's right," Cleirach went on. "She's an exasperating woman. She begrudges you your privileges. You have to tread lightly on her patience. Sometimes you'd like to take *her* into a chamber and find out what makes her tick. A bit of exploratory surgery, heyla!" Saying this, he showed me his trilling tongue.

"She's a maso-ascetic, brother."

"I don't know. There are many mansions in this House, Cleva, several of which she's refused to let us enter. Why?" He raised his eyebrows suggestively, as Cleva had done the night she lifted her hand lantern for our notice. The expressions were the same.

Cleva Orha appealed to me as a disinterested third party: "What do you think, studling? Is Wardress Scalplock at bed and at bone with one of her Sharers? Or does she lie by herself, maso-ascetically, under a hide of untanned elk hair? What do you think?"

"I haven't really thought about it." Containing my anger, I tried to leave. "Excuse me, Orha-clones."

"Wait, wait, wait," the woman said mincingly, half-humorously. "You know our names and a telling bit of our background. That puts you up, studling. We won't have that. You can't go without giving us a name."

Resenting the necessity, I told them my name.

"From where?" Cleirach Orha asked.

"Colony World GK-11. We call it Diroste."

Brother and sister exchanged a glance of sudden enlightenment, after which Cleva raised her thin eyebrows and spoke in a mocking rhythm: "Ah ha, the mystery solved. Out and back our Wardress went and therefore closed her House."

"Welcome, Mr. Lorca. Welcome."

"We're going up to Wolf Run for an afterbout of toddies and P-nol. What about you? Would you like to go? The climb wouldn't be anything to a warm-blooded studling

like you. Look, Cleirach. Biceps unbundled and his sinuses
still clear."

In spite of the compliment I declined.

"Who have *you* been with?" Cleirach Orha wanted to
know. He bent forward conspiratorially. "We've been with
a native of an extrakomm world called Trope. That's the
local name. Anyhow, there's not another such being inside
of a hundred light-years, Mr. Lorca."

"It's the face that intrigues us," Cleva Orha explained,
saving me from an immediate reply to her brother's question. And then she reached out, touched my arm, and ran
a finger down my arm to my hand. "Look. Not even a
goose bump. Cleirach, you and I are suffering the shems
and trivs, and our earnest Mr. Lorca's standing here bare-
boned."

Brother was annoyed by this analysis. There was something he wanted to know, and Cleva's non sequiturs weren't
advancing his case. Seeing that he was going to ask me
again, I rummaged about for an answer that was neither
informative nor tactless.

Cleva Orha, meanwhile, was peering intently at her
fingertips. Then she looked at my arm, again at her fingers,
and a second time at my arm. Finally she locked eyes
with me and studied my face as if for some clue to the
source of my reticence.

Ah, I thought numbly, she's recognized me for what
I am. . . .

"Mr. Lorca can't tell you who he's been with, Cleirach,"
Cleva Orha told her clonemate, "because he's not a visitant
to the House at all and he doesn't choose to violate the con-
fidences of those who are."

Dumbfounded, I said nothing.

Cleva put her hand on her brother's back and guided
him past me into the House's antechamber. Over her shoulder she bid me good afternoon in a toneless voice. Then
the Orha-clones very deliberately let themselves out the
front door and began the long climb to Wolf Run Summit.

What had happened? It took me a moment to figure it
out. Cleva Orha had recognized me as a human-machine
and from this recognition drawn a logical but mistaken
inference: she believed me, like the "mouthless one" from
Trope, a slave of the House. . . .

*   *   *

During my next tryst with my Sharer I spoke for an hour, two hours, maybe more, of Rumer's infuriating patience, her dignity, her serene ardor. I had moved her—maneuvered her—to the expression of these qualities by my own hollow commitment to Humay and the others before Humay who had engaged me only physically. Under my wife's attentions, however, I preened sullenly, demanding more than Rumer—than any woman in Rumer's position—had it in her power to give. My needs, I wanted her to know, my needs were as urgent and as real as Diroste's.

And at the end of one of these vague encounters Rumer seemed both to concede the legitimacy of my demands and to decry their intemperance by removing a warm pendant from her throat and placing it like an accusation in my palm.

"A week later," I told the Sharer, "was the inspection tour of the diggings at Haft Paykar."

These things spoken, I did something I had never done before in the Wardress's House: I went to sleep under the hand of my Sharer. My dreams were dreams rather than nightmares, and clarified ones at that, shot through with light and accompanied from afar by a peaceful funneling of sand. The images that came to me were haloed arms and legs orchestrated within a series of shifting yellow, yellow-orange, and subtly red discs. The purr of running sand behind these movements conferred upon them the benediction of mortality, and that, I felt, was good.

I awoke in a blast of icy air and found myself alone. The door to the Sharer's apartment was standing open on the shaft of the stairwell, and I heard faint, angry voices coming across the emptiness between. Disoriented, I lay on my stove-bed staring toward the door, a square of shadow feeding its chill into the room.

"*Dorian!*" a husky voice called. "*Dorian!*"

Wardress Kefa's voice, diluted by distance and fear. A door opened, and her voice hailed me again, this time with more clarity. Then the door slammed shut, and every sound in the House took on a smothered quality, as if mumbled through cold semiporous wood.

I got up, dragging my bedding with me, and reached the narrow porch on the stairwell with a clear head. Thin starlight filtered through the unshuttered windows in the ceiling. Nevertheless, looking from stairway to stairway to stairway inside the House, I had no idea behind which door the Wardress now must be.

Because there existed no connecting stairs among the staggered landings of the House, my only option was to go down. I took the steps two at a time, very nearly plunging.

At the bottom I found my Sharer with both hands clenched about the outer stair rail. He was trembling. In fact, his chest and arms were quivering so violently that he seemed about to shake himself apart. I put my hands on his shoulders and tightened my grip until the tremors racking him threatened to rack my systems, too. Who would come apart first?

"Go upstairs," I told the Sharer. "Get the hell upstairs."

I heard the Wardress call my name again. Although by now she had squeezed some of the fear out of her voice, her summons was still distance-muffled and impossible to pinpoint.

The Sharer either couldn't or wouldn't obey me. I coaxed him, cursed him, goaded him, tried to turn him around so that he was heading back up the steps. Nothing availed. The Wardress, summoning me, had inadvertently called the Sharer out as my proxy, and he now had no intention of giving back to me the role he'd just usurped. The beautifully faired planes of his skull turned toward me, bringing with them the stainless-steel rings of his eyes. These were the only parts of his body that didn't tremble, but they were helpless to countermand the agues shaking him. As inhuman and unmoving as they were, the Sharer's features still managed to convey stark, unpitiable entreaty. . . .

I sank to my knees, felt about the insides of the Sharer's legs, and took the penlight and the disc from the two pocketlike incisions tailored to these instruments. Then I stood and used them.

"Find Wardress Kefa for me, Sharer," I commanded, gesturing with the penlight at the windows overhead. "Find her."

And the Sharer floated up from the steps through the midinterior of the House. In the crepuscular starlight, rocking a bit, he seemed to pass through a knot of curving stairs into an open space where he was all at once brightly visible.

"Point to the door," I said, jabbing the penlight uncertainly at several different landings around the well. "Show me the one."

My words echoed, and the Sharer, legs dangling, inscribed a slow half-circle in the air. Then he pointed toward one of the nearly hidden doorways.

I stalked across the well, found a likely seeming set of stairs, and climbed them with no notion at all of what was expected of me.

Wardress Kefa didn't call out again, but I heard the same faint, somewhat slurred voices that I'd heard upon waking and knew that they belonged to the Orhas. A burst of muted female laughter, twice repeated, convinced me of this, and I hesitated on the landing.

"All right," I told my Sharer quietly, turning him around with a turn of the wrist, "go on home."

Dropping through the torus of a lower set of stairs, he found the porch in front of our chamber and settled upon it like a clumsily handled puppet. And why not? I was a clumsy puppetmaster. Because there seemed to be nothing else I could do, I slid the penlight into a pocket of my dressing gown and knocked on the Orhas' door.

"Come in," Cleva Orha said. "By all means, Sharer Lorca, come in."

I entered and found myself in a room whose surfaces were all burnished as if with beeswax. The timbers shone. Whereas in the other chambers I had seen nearly all the joists and rafters were rough-hewn, here they were smooth and splinterless. The scent of sandalwood pervaded the air, and opposite the door was a carven screen blocking my view of the chamber's stove-bed. A tall wooden lamp illuminated the furnishings and the three people arrayed around the lamp's border of light like iconic statues.

"Welcome," Cleirach Orha said. "Your invitation was from the Wardress, however, not us." He wore only a pair of silk pantaloons drawn together at the waist with a cord, and his right forearm was under Wardress Kefa's chin, restraining her movement without quite cutting off her wind.

His disheveled clonemate, in a dressing gown very much like mine, sat cross-legged on a cushion and toyed with a wooden stiletto waxed as the beams of the chamber were waxed. Her eyes were too wide, too lustrous, as were her brother's, and I knew this was the result of too much placenol in combination with too much Wolf Run smallmalt in combination with the Orhas' innate meanness. The woman was drugged, and drunk, and, in consequence of these things, malicious to a turn. Cleirach didn't appear quite so far gone as his sister, but all he had to do to strangle the Wardress, I understood, was raise the edge of his forearm into her trachea. I felt again the familiar sensation of being out of my element, gill-less in a sluice of stinging salt water. . . .

"Wardress Kefa—" I began.

"She's all right," Cleva Orha assured me. "Perfectly all right." She tilted her head so that she was gazing at me out of her right eye alone, and then barked a hoarse, derangedsounding laugh.

"Let the Wardress go," I told her clonemate.

Amazingly, Cleirach Orha looked intimidated. "Mr. Lorca's an anproz," he reminded Cleva. "That little letter opener you're cleaning your nails with, it's not going to mean anything to him."

"Then let her go, Cleirach. Let her go."

Cleirach released the Wardress, who, massaging her throat with both hands, ran to the stove-bed. She halted beside the carven screen and beckoned me with a doll-like hand. "Mr. Lorca . . . Mr. Lorca, please . . . will you see to him first? I beg you."

"I'm going back to Wolf Run Summit," Cleirach informed his sister, and he slipped on a night jacket, gathered up his clothes, and left the room. Cleva Orha remained seated on her cushion, her head tilted back as if she were tasting a bitter potion from a heavy metal goblet.

Glancing doubtfully at her, I went to the Wardress. Then I stepped around the wooden divider to see her Sharer.

The Tropeman lying there was a slender creature, almost slight. There was a ridge of flesh where his mouth ought to be, and his eyes were an organic variety of crystal, uncanny and depthful stones. One of these brandy-colored stones had been dislodged in its socket by Cleva's "letter opener"; and although the Orhas had failed to pry the eye completely loose, the Tropeman's face was streaked with blood from their efforts. The streaks ran down into the bedding under his narrow, fragile head and gave him the look of an aborigine in war paint. Lacking external genitalia, his sexless body was spread-eagled atop the quilts so that the burn marks on his legs and lower abdomen cried out for notice as plangently as did his face.

"Sweet light, sweet light," the Wardress chanted softly, over and over again, and I found her locked in my arms, hugging me tightly above her beloved, butchered ward, this Sharer from another star.

"He's not dead," Cleva Orha said from her cushion. "The rules . . . the rules say not to kill 'em, and we go by the rules, brother and I."

"What can I do, Wardress Kefa?" I whispered, holding her. "What do you want me to do?"

Slumped against me, the Wardress repeated her consoling chant and held me about the waist. So, fearful that this being with eyes like precious gems would bleed to death as we delayed, each of us undoubtedly ashamed of our delay, we delayed—and I held the Wardress, pressed her head to my chest, gave her a warmth I hadn't before believed in me. And she returned this warmth in undiluted measure.

Wardress Kefa, I realized, was herself a Compassionate Sharer; she was as much a Sharer as the bleeding Tropeman on the stove-bed or that obedient creature whose electrode-studded body and luminous death's-head had seemed to mock the efficient mechanical deadness in myself—a deadness that, in turning away from Rumer, I had made a god of. In the face of this realization my disgust with the Orhas was transfigured into something very unlike disgust: a mode of perception, maybe; a means of adapting. An answer had been revealed to me, and, without its being either easy or uncomplicated, it was still, somehow, very simple: I, too, was a Compassionate Sharer. Monster, machine, anproz, the designation didn't matter any longer. Wherever I might go, I was forevermore a ward of this tiny woman's House—my fate, inescapable and sure.

The Wardress broke free of my embrace and knelt beside the Tropeman. She tore a piece of cloth from the bottom of her tunic. Wiping the blood from the Sharer's face, she said, "I heard him calling me while I was downstairs, Mr. Lorca. Encephalogoi. 'Brain words,' you know. And I came up here as quickly as I could. Cleirach took me aside. All I could do was shout for you. Then, not even that."

Her hands touched the Sharer's burns, hovered over the wounded eye, moved about with a knowledge the Wardress herself seemed unaware of.

"We couldn't get it all the way out," Cleva Orha laughed. "Wouldn't come. Cleirach tried and tried."

I found the cloned woman's pea jacket, leggings, and tunic. Then I took her by the elbow and led her down the stairs to her brother. She reviled me tenderly as we descended, but otherwise didn't protest.

"You . . ." she predicted once we were down, "you we'll never get."

She was right. It was a long time before I returned to the House of Compassionate Sharers, and, in any case, upon learning of their sadistic abuse of one of the wards of the House, the authorities in Manitou Port denied the Orhas any future access to it. A Sharer, after all, was an expensive commodity.

But I did return. After going back to Diroste and living with Rumer the remaining forty-two years of her life, I applied to the House as a novitiate. I am here now. In fact as well as in metaphor, I am today one of the Sharers.

My brain cells die, of course, and there's nothing anyone can do to stop utterly the depredations of time—but my body seems to be that of a middle-aged man and I still move inside it with ease. Visitants seek comfort from me, as once, against my will, I sought comfort here; and I try to give it to them . . . even to the ones who have only a muddled understanding of what a Sharer really is. My battles aren't really with these unhappy people; they're with the advance columns of my senility (I don't like to admit this) and the shock troops of my memory, which is still excessively good. . . .

Wardress Kefa has been dead seventeen years, Diderits twenty-three, and Rumer two. That's how I keep score now. Death has also carried off the gem-eyed Tropeman and the Sharer who drew the essential Dorian Lorca out of the prosthetic rind he had mistaken for himself.

I intend to be here a while longer yet. I have recently been given a chamber into which the light sifts with a painful white brilliance reminiscent of the sands of Diroste or the snows of Wolf Run Summit. This is all to the good. Either way, you see, I die at home. . . .

IN CHINISTREX FORTRONZA
THE PEOPLE ARE MACHINES

or, Hoom and the Homunculus

IN THE empery of Chinistrex Fortronza on the planet Blaispagal, Inc., the people were machines. For as long as anyone could remember the people had been machines, as had the animals in the whirring forests, and the fish in the lubricating seas, and the birds that hummed and chittered in Blaispagal, Inc.'s electric air: all were perpetually wound, spontaneously self-repairing automata.

Maybe once there had been organic creatures on this world of cybernetic ascendancy, but archaeology was not a science of any repute among her mechanical citizens; and if beings of blood, bone, and mortal flesh had ever existed here, they lay fossilized and forgotten in the faulted, striated strata of beautiful Blaispagal, Inc.'s ferriferous red earth: time-torn architectures of Death, a condition of which the Blaispagalians knew almost nothing since for them the ultimate entropic disaster was merely a repairable malfunction. Tap into the circuitry of the emperor (who in Chinistrex Fortronza was called the Parmalee), and *voilà! mon frère*, you are well again.

By religion, then, the people were deists, for God of course was the transcendent Watch Maker who had wound them all up and then benignly left them to their own devices. Organizationally (you and I would say "politically"), in each and every one of the planet's several autonomous corporate bodies, the people were mechanostatists believing in the divine right of 'chines and therefore practicing a pert, ta-pocketa-pocketa obeisance to whichever august

113

automation had evolved to a probity of operation and control so *dependable* that it never, no, never, broke down.

In Chinistrex Fortronza this esteemed entity was the two-meter-tall, artificial bird of paradise Pajetric Stat, Parmalee to More Than Half a World and Cybernetic Wonder Universally Unparalleled.

Of hammered gold and gold enameling was the Parmalee Stat mainly made, and for a mild eternity he had sat on the highest bough of the golden throne-tree at the bottom of a glass-and-aluminum shaft in the minareted Command Center of Chinistrex Fortronza, alertly attuning himself to the pulses and pistonings of his empery, showily cantilevering his silver-wimpled wings and issuing melodious decrees in every variety of computerese and mechanical patois known to his people. Now and again, in his function as priest as well as parmalee, Pajetric Stat would lift a series of formulae to the erstwhile Watch Maker who had wound them all up. It was a happy and well-regulated existence that the Parmalee both monitored and embodied, this monarchial bird of paradise.

From the many other corporate emperies of Blaispagal, Inc., came an influx of automata—efficiency units, robo-aestheticians, optical scanners—to tour the facilities of Chinistrex Fortronza, and to time-share audiences with Pajetric Stat. From the corporations of Datcoa, Selestron, Randland, Ampide, Bzz, and Divroid Phic came these representatives, and once home again each one of them unreeled printout upon printout extolling the virtues of Chinistrex Fortronza: from the climate control, to the exquisite synchronization of the populace, to the opulent dependability and near-omniscience of Pajetric Stat. Indeed, their praises hummed. Upon occasion, so mightily had these visits worked upon the cluck-a-clucking emissaries, their eulogies ratcheted out in rhymed dactylic hexameters. . . .

Oddly enough, however, the visitors reserved their lengthiest comment and most puzzled praise for the only denizen of Chinistrex Fortronza that the Parmalee, even as Most High Regulator and Monitor of his people, had never felt pulse from or fed energy to: the Homunculus.

The Homunculus?

In some reports this machine was called, in Blaispagalian equivalencies, the Mennikin, the Dwarveter, or the Orangouman. But most often, the Homunculus.

Said the messages sped from synapse to synapse through the microminiaturized neuristors of Pajetric Stat, "But of all the marvels of Chinistrex Fortronza the most remarkable is the Homunculus." Over and over again among the visitors' relayed printouts this sentiment occurred, provoking something vaguely like a glitch in the Parmalee's heretofore glitch-free systems. Indeed, his cryotrons overheated. But the only outward sign of annoyance or possible (minuscule) malfunction he made was an overly showy cantilevering of his silver wings and sapphire-eyed tail, which, the hall being empty, no one witnessed.

What was the Homunculus? The accounts indicated that this machine, who dwelt secretly in the private forest, or paradise, of the Parmalee, mimicked to perfection the attributes of a strange consciousness that was neither digital nor analogical.

Although an automaton like the other inhabitants of Blaispagal, Inc., the Homunculus had the behavioral capacity to suggest *emotion:* it could *laugh,* piteously *keen,* yea, even shed *tears.* Much was made of the affective nature of this last operation, of how the visual perception of the Homunculus's tears—lachrymal gemstones produced at will in polymer-coated ducts behind its "eyes"—could throw off your rheostats or make your flywheels falter.

Even so, the servitors in Pajetric Stat's wooded and crystal-hung paradise often paused in their labors to register the wail of the Homunculus, or, distance seldom being a let to the high-powered robo-rangers, to record the magnitude of brilliance of one of its glinting tears. Swinging through the dark, dark park the Homunculus would flash on the sensor units of the rangers and disappear. Sometimes its ululating keen lingered in undulant lambency on their stomach oscilloscopes. Its presence, though, lingered even longer than that, a haunting quasi-glitch. . . .

The Homunculus, you see (and this is information not even the emissaries of Datcoa, Selestron, Randland, Ampide, Bzz, and Divroid Phic gleaned during their visits), was the immortal representative of a single generation of machines programmed in secrecy before the decline and fall of organic consciousness on Blaispagal, Inc., when in fact the planet had been unincorporated and called by such names as Azúl, Organdy Dancer, Sweetflame, and other equally mawkish, nonmechanical tags. This may account for some of the Homunculus's strange accouterments. Tiny copper bristles overlay the *head, shoulders,* and bandy *arms* of the Homunculus, giving it what no other machine or electronic unit in Chinistrex Fortronza, or anywhere else, possessed: a shaggy copper-colored *fur.* Moreover, it had a totally plastic (in several senses) *face,* which it could contort, wrinkle, or stretch when an esoteric internal mechanism triggered the proper stimuli for these responses. In addition, it suffered a built-in *grief* for its extinct and dimly remembered creators, a grief that occasioned its poignant keening and compelled it to avoid the congregating places of later species of machine.

The origin of the Homunculus millennia in the past, then, and its deliberate solitariness explain in part the Parmalee's ignorance of its existence; the awe of the Chinistrex Fortronzans before so odd and illogical, albeit wonderful, a phenomenon must explain the Parmalee's remaining so long in the dark. But now Pajetric Stat had been enlightened—cruelly enough, by foreigners.

"What is this Homunculus, this Mennikin, this Dwarveter, this Orangouman?" he wondered for the 10^{29}th time. "What is this marvel that is the 'most remarkable' in Chinistrex Fortronza? Am I to learn about my own corporate empery from the printouts of traveling robo-aestheticians?"

Pajetric Stat tapped into the bowels of his right-hand wing-rider, the computer on wheels RunAbout Most High. It was RunAbout Most High's function to compile and store lists of all the empery's employees, complete with duty descriptions, vital statistics, and maintenance records. He also performed for the Parmalee whatever command responsibilities required mobility.

Barrel-shaped and tentacled, RunAbout delighted in busy-bodying from place to place piping out pitch-coded instructions and tweaking the exposed console bulbs of the Command Center chamber-aides. If anyone but the Parmalee ventured to tap into him RunAbout ostentatiously lit up a buzzer-accompanied message-panel spelling out *"Tilt!"*: a response designed to minimize impertinent feedback.

Tapped the Parmalee, "What can you tell me, RunAbout, about a machine called the Homunculus? Courtesy tapes from recent visitors inform me that it can laugh, lament, and let fall tears; that, indeed, it is the 'most remarkable' marvel in all Chinistrex Fortronza."

RunAbout Most High scanned his integrated innards. "No info bit regarding a mechanism and/or solid-state unit registered as the Homunculus, Your Parmalee. . . . Zizizi, click, rescan. . . . No, Your Paradisiacal Birdship, no bits, no info, no news."

"But it exists, RunAbout, it nevertheless exists."

"Zizizi, click, rescan: I don't see how you can be so certain, Your Parmalee. All my components tell me otherwise." Sententiously RunAbout appended, "Digesting as empirical truth the printouts of ill-constructed foreigners is seldom an energizing pastime."

"However, RunAbout, I have one such printout with the imprimatur of the Mechanarch of Divroid Phic, and *his* structural integrity I do not doubt. The story must be true. Therefore, I wish that the Homunculus, whatever it may be, appear before me this evening at 2100 hours in the well of the throne-tree to laugh, lament, and let fall tears, that Pajetric Stat escape an ignorance unbecoming to your Parmalee. Go, RunAbout, and find this 'marvel.'"

For a short period RunAbout Most High ran about, mostly out of mild mechanical trauma: he realized that should he fail to fetch back the Homunculus by 2100 hours Pajetric Stat would cut the juice to every one of the automata and servitors in the Command Center. Indeed, the Parmalee might even induce a punitive infestation of ferric oxide in their capacitors and diodes! "Zizizi, click, rescan," murmured RunAbout Most High, inefficaciously. He then began to roll back and forth through the air-conditioned tunnels of the Command Center in search of the Homunculus; to levitate up and down the glass-walled, hologramic storage-shafts.

By happy and not altogether random chance RunAbout encountered in the vestibule of the Center a robo-ranger from the Parmalee's paradise: this simple servitor, ycleped Smoky, was there seeking a replacement for a burnt-out cathode-ray tube. One too many times had Smoky's stomach oscilloscope reverberated to the keening of the bandy-armed, rubber-faced Homunculus. "But I no mind," it said in husky, pidgin FORTRAN. "The Homunculus scream just so, you know, it drop-drop the diamond tears, I warble-hum inside. Is really a Homunculus, O RunAbout Most High; is really, you know."

"Robo-ranger," RunAbout said, "lead me to the Homunculus. Do you so, and I will give you a stationary installation beneath the throne-tree of Pajetric Stat, from whence you may witness the majestic wimpling of the underside of his many-eyed tail."

"Gracious thanks," said Smoky.

Into the forest of the Parmalee's paradise they ventured together, along with a retinue consisting of an omnivorous vacuum cleaner called Univac, a musical synthesizer answering to Morp, and a pair of nameless mobile generators. The woods burped, burbled, and roared with static.

At 1940 hours RunAbout Most High registered a distant wailing and Smoky picked up the Homunculus's telltale spoor: a trail of tears. This they followed, Univac sucking up same, and at 1952 hours were rewarded by a glimpse of their elusive prey. Morp the Synthesizer, programmed to emulate the dwarveter's every lamentation, keened and keened, burbling a bit more electronically than did the Homunculus itself. Even so, the Homunculus paused to record this untoward and imperfect aping of its audible grief, and at 2009 hours the party from the Command Center drew up beneath the living conifer, draped with pastel filaments of quartz, in which their prey now resided, curious mechanism that it was.

It stared down, they stared up, and a chunk of moon evermore in synchronous orbit with Blaispagal, Inc., littered the paradise's shaggy trees with starlike sparklings.

"O Homunculus," RunAbout Most High began, the sensor screens of his retinue all lifted to the thing above them, "Parmalee Pajetric Stat wishes you to laugh, lament, and let fall tears for him." Even as he made this request, RunAbout flooded his own information centers with questions: How could so ungainly, so loosely bisymmetrical a machine fulfill any purpose whatever? Of what utility were laughing, making high moan, and shedding gemstonelike tears? In the lineaments of the Homunculus, in fact, slept something repellent, something invidious to good organization and efficient command. At least on first impression.

But then, contorting its lugubrious plastic face, the Homunculus chortled sadly, shaped with its crazy speaker unit a howl much purer than Morp's, and littered the ground with a rain of worthless, utterly worthless, diamonds. The spectacle, all inutile as it was, sent the logic circuits of RunAbout Most High pleasantly awry: "Zizizi, click, rescan." Smoky's oscilloscope burned out another tube, but somehow the loss was a psychomechanical reward. Univac hiccuped, happily hiccuped, and Morp fell awestrickenly silent.

RunAbout implored the Homunculus to return with them to the Command Center; he set Morp the Synthesizer off as a sort of guide-piper to their crew.

And, unpredictably enough, the Homunculus followed: a squat, heavy shadow swinging through the sparkles cast down by Blaispagal, Inc.'s seemingly stationary moon.

By 2100 hours, just as the Parmalee had directed, the orangouman was standing under the throne-tree in the control shaft of the Command Center: body hunched, arms hanging, head thrown unkemptly back to scan the artificial bird of paradise who had summoned it. Once, the Homunculus recalled (an archetypal hum coursing from switch to switch in its belly), creatures more like itself—aye, *creatures*—had commanded its time, punched in its duties, applauded its creaturely responses. A familiar grief then began coursing in its innards, a counterpoint to the hum of memory. How good, though, to be commanded again, even if by a digital intelligence rather than an organic one.

"If you would, Homunculus," the Parmalee said from aloft, cantilevering wings and tail, "do for me as you did for RunAbout and the others: laugh, make moan, and show me these things called tears."

And so, spreading its copper-haired arms as if to embrace the old grief that powered it, the Homunculus did. With this exception: its laugh was a sob, it could not this night bypass the ancient templates of its programmed sorrow.

As for Pajetric Stat, in a detonation of wonder he realized the correctness of the printouts of the emissaries of Blaispagal, Inc.'s other corporate emperies, and for the first time in the presence of another machine he released through the speaker in his golden beak that complicated, mathematically intense, baroque concerto he had long ago composed to help him cope with moments of electronic overload. The glass-and-aluminum control shaft echoed with this melody, and the Homunculus, humbled, felt itself well repaid for its own brief performance. It had heard the Parmalee sing!

The next day Pajetric Stat permitted the other calculators, servitors, and chamber-aides in the Command Center to audit through telemetry and time-sharing the relayed talents of the Homunculus. Closed-circuit holovision let them optically apprehend the dwarveter's tears.

And from that day forward the Homunculus was as famous in Chinistrex Fortronza as Pajetric Stat himself. Ordinarily staid machines began purposely simulating "emotion": they laughed (so to speak), wept, and burbled in premeditated, ratchety runs up and down the chromatic scale, some even lapsing into dodecaphonic feedback squeals that blew fuses, shorted out sockets, and larruped up work schedules. The Parmalee tolerated this—indeed, he never once threatened to cut off their juice—because when his machines *weren't* homunculing around, they performed with a pizzazz and verve unprecedented in the history of the Command Center. Besides, none of them had yet managed to manufacture tears, which were, after all, potentially computer-room-cluttering.

The robo-rangers in the Parmalee's paradise elected the Homunculus their official mascot: The Machine Who Weeps Starlight, they dubbed him. (As cathode-ray tube repairs continued to rise, a minor efficiency unit in the Command Center determined that the forest servitors didn't need oscilloscopes anyway.)

RunAbout Most High installed in himself an entire bank of circuitry devoted to digesting and responding to queries about the new Corporate Resource of Chinistrex Fortronza: the Homunculus. Less and less often did his message-panel buzz out *"Tilt!"* when an auxiliary unit of some sort tapped into him for advice or general amplification.

Morp the Synthesizer composed, in an accessible binary code, a temper-balancing ditty entitled "Homunculi, Homuncula." Two days later the whole empery was humming it compulsively on ordinarily unused channels of private communication.

Then, one day, there arrived at the Command Center a large aluminum box with a number of holes bored into each one of its six faces. So unusual was this box that the machines that brought it into the vestibule didn't even notice the emissary—who looked like an abbreviated lightning rod surmounted by a frosted glass globe—who had come along with it. RunAbout Most High was summoned, and when he appeared he demanded of the offloaders, "What is this obstruction? Why are you mucking about?"

"I am the Mechanarch of Divroid Phic's messenger," the

globe-surmounted lightning rod averred. "And I have brought a gift for your illustrious Parmalee. Please usher me in to him."

"Here is a terminal," said RunAbout, gesturing to a wall console, "from which you may call in your request or message."

"No," the emissary said firmly. "I must see the Parmalee, as it were, in the very metal. So the Mechanarch, Pajetric Stat's counterpart, has commanded me."

Since it could not be got around, RunAbout Most High ordered the box trucked into the control well and accompanied the visitor from Divroid Phic to the base of the throne-tree. There the gift was uncrated. "What a strange machine," said the Parmalee, cocking his golden head and gazing down.

"It is not a machine at all, Your Parmalee," said the emissary, and at once both Pajetric Stat and RunAbout Most High realized that the *thing* they were looking at resembled—in almost every way but its utter want of copper-bristle fur—the Homunculus who, for the past twenty-odd fiscal periods, had captured the neuristors and vacuum tubes of the empery. Oh, yes, another difference: the gift was conspicuously *more* misshapen than the Homunculus. And there it stood at the bottom of the well, all unadorned and shivering.

"Not a machine?" Pajetric Stat said.

"Then what?" RunAbout Most High inquired.

With their gift blubbering to itself like a small vat viscously boiling mud, the emissary from Divroid Phic explained that upon first hearing of the Homunculus in Chinistrex Fortronza, his Mechanarch had decreed a crash program to develop a machine with similar capabilities. Computer research, however, had suggested that this might best be done not through exclusively cybernetic methods but instead by the application of the principles of a new science which D.Ph.'s Chief Engineer ADMA 7 had cryptically tagged "bionics." "What is this *bio?*" the Mechanarch had asked; and ADMA 7, unable to communicate this concept adequately, had tapped out, "Trust me, Your Dependableness," and proceeded to discard from his team's researches even the familiar and comprehensible group of studies signaled by the suffix *-onics*. To create a homunculus on a par with the wonderful one of Chinistrex For-

tronza, ADMA 7 said, would require not something more
but something other. . . .

"Although no one but he fully understands it," the
frosted globe continued, pulsing—at least to Pajetric Stat's
divination—a bit maniacally, "ADMA 7, who is a genius
by virtue of a serendipitous foul-up in the initial stamping
of his circuitry, discovered a whole new complex of systems and sets: *biology!*"

The Parmalee and RunAbout exchanged tiny surges of
uncoded current: the morpheme *bio,* carrying no more
semantic freight for them than it had for the Mechanarch
of Divroid Phic, struck them as somehow improper.

Then the frosted globe began telling them, in a monologue that was no doubt prerecorded, how ADMA 7 had
enlisted the aid of *nucleic acids* in his researches; how he
had plumbed the *prebiotic formation of carbohydrates and
fats;* how he had effected the *polymerization of amino
acids into proteins;* how he had isolated the specific functions of the acid *glycine;* and how, finally, he and his team
had *animated* all this alien material into systems that were
entirely independent of mechanical or electronic impetus.

The end result was the thing that now hunkered and
shook, rubber-necked and whimpered, at the base of Pajetric Stat's throne-tree: "Organic intelligence," the emissary
said.

Emanations from the gift gave the Parmalee's olfactory
sensors pause, but since they were so seldom exercised his
Paradisiacal Birdship was not offended.

"This is as far as ADMA 7 and his team could take
their experiments," the visitor continued, his dogmatism at
last mediating into a nice mechanical humility. "In com-
parison to the Homunculus of Chinistrex Fortronza it is a
sorry specimen, a clumsy and insulting mock-up—but the
Mechanarch, out of respect for you, apologizes for its short-
comings and hopes that you will find it diverting in moments of programmed off-time.

"Its name is Hoom, and it runs, disgustingly enough, on
chlorophyl patties, H_2O, and internally produced fuels
that ADMA 7 has labeled its *neuroses.* We have given you
a supply of each." With that, the emissary took his leave.

What now? the Parmalee wondered, and RunAbout
Most High hurried after the globe-surmounted lightning
rod to give him a seemly and machinely send-off: "Zizizi,
click, rescan."

Hoom, its organic intelligence alert to the departure of its guardian, commenced to lament and let fall tears. Although an involuntary scan revealed that the tears were salt water rather than gemstones, Pajetric Stat found this a refreshing change. Hoom's tears would evaporate; the Homunculus's had to be swept up. Then the Mechanarch's gift began to crack his crimson knuckles, pound its breast-plates (which were neither metal nor plastic, the Parmalee divined), and batter its hairless head against the lowest branches of the throne-tree. Here was a grief at least three exponents more violent and demonstrative than that the Homunculus usually manifested. The effect on the Parma-lee, then, was by just that degree intensified. No complex concerto escaped his speaker unit, but instead a shrill, high whistle as strange as the creature that had provoked it. It surprised Pajetric Stat.

Also surprised, Hoom left off its heartfelt histrionics. Hoom fell silent. Then Hoom laughed; ca-ca-cackled like a battery of breaking console lights.

Not often or for very long did the real Homunculus laugh: its programmed grief always overcame it. Metering his reaction, Pajetric Stat discovered that the novelty of Hoom's laughter pleased him, registered well on those calibrating mechanisms arrayed like clockwork inside his golden breast. Quite a while, after all, had gone by since the Homunculus's first appearance in the control well, and the edge had gone off everyone's appreciation of the original dwarveter's still inexplicably affecting talents. Morp's "Homunculi, Homuncula" had long since given way, on the private channels of Chinistrex Fortronzans, to a Muzak melody entitled "Do Not Staple, Spindle, or Fold." A population cyberlutionarily evolved to cope with tedium and routine had developed a taste for variety; likewise, the Parmalee.

The day after Hoom was delivered, Pajetric Stat called the Homunculus into the control well, confronted him with the organic consciousness incarnate in the misshapen crea-ture from Divroid Phic (whose resemblance to itself the Homunculus did not fail to detect), and asked that the two laugh, lament, and let fall tears *together*.

This was not a success. Both attempted what was asked, but the Homunculus could not sustain its own laughter nor synchronize its keening with that of the obstreperous

Hoom. And when the mechanical dwarveter began producing tears, Hoom, face streaked with wetness, began picking them up, rattling them together, and thrusting them up at the fluorescents overhead to make them sparkle.

The sparkling made Hoom laugh, and the performance, come full circle (assuming the circle somewhat oblate), therefore broke down: *"Tilt!"* RunAbout Most High wasn't even around to signal the breakdown with a buzz. Hoom, though, kept laughing at random intervals and the Parmalee emitting his shrill, appreciative whistle, so that the Homunculus, grief for its millennia-dead creators switching into personal channels, left the Command Center, swung back into the depths of Pajetric Stat's paradise, and disappeared.

No one noticed, although in the crystal-hung woods the robo-ranger Smoky (RunAbout Most High, you see, had failed to come through with a Center-based sinecure) again picked up the familiar ululations of the Homunculus and felt, down where its oscilloscope had used to be, a pleasant heat.

When it was discovered back in the Command Center that the real orangouman had left them, an epidemic of indifference broke out.

And why not? The Parmalee—recording, amplifying, and broadcasting the capabilities of Hoom to every unit in the complex—had given his machines a multitude of new concepts to store and toy with. Prime among these was the phenomenon of organic excretion, since Hoom *sweated, eliminated,* and, in occasional fits of wall-banging passion, *bled.* It was true that the people of Blaispagal, Inc., gave off heat and light, but about Hoom's (perhaps) analogous processes there flitted an aura of the elemental and earthy, as if before the elements had been numbered and the earth refined. The Homunculus was forgotten. Now the computer consoles, the servitors, the chamber-aides—all the corporate automata—spent their leisure simulating Hoom-like *waste matter* and *smells.* Too, they engaged in cross-circuited powwows the purpose of which was to derive a formula for credible electronic laughter.

In praise of the organic homunculus, Morp composed a song adroitly punning on computerese grammar: "Who Is Subjective, Hoom is Objectionable" (in rough translation). The lyrics made a point of contradicting the title:

> *Who is subjective,*
> *Hoom is objectionable.*
> *But whoever's selective*
> *Finds Hoom delectable.*

This ditty quickly replaced "Do Not Staple, Spindle, or Fold" on the hit parade tapes of the empery. In gratitude and joy RunAbout Most High presented Morp the Synthesizer with its own independently operable powerpak.

And for the next five revolutions of Blaispagal, Inc., Hoom, its novelty undiminished, its affective capabilities intact, chittered impudently in Pajetric Stat's throne-tree, chortled freely in the echoing command shafts, chased wantonly among the tunnels of the complex. Its fame was assured, its position secured.

Meanwhile, beyond the Center, the Homunculus of old—the *real* Homunculus—made high moan for whichever servitors in the Parmalee's paradise might be listening and littered the ground with gemstones. It was half in love with easeful malfunction, but nevertheless continued to self-repair.

Then one day, right there in the control well, Hoom collapsed and did not get up. The Parmalee had seen Hoom turn itself off before, often for hours on end while its various internal and psychomechanical units, he supposed, revitalized themselves. But this was different. This was the result not of a revitalization but of a bankload of breakdowns.

Two X-ray–equipped scanning machines found alien, apparently inimical particles of a microscopic nature in Hoom's *bloodstream* (this being its curious analog of a machine's electronic circuitry), and the larger of the robodiagnosticians said to Pajetric Stat, "Hoom continues to function at automatic, nonconscious levels, Your Paradisiacal Birdship, but is still very close to terminal shutdown."

For the duration of an entire fiscal period, thirty slow rotations of the planet, Hoom lay inert and incommunicative beside a monitoring console in a subsidiary tunnel of the Command Center. It dwelt, said the monitor, in a hinterland between *on* and *off.* Intravenously, Level-1 mechanics conscripted for "bio duty" plied the malfunctioning creature with liquefied chlorophyl patties and lactase-spiked lubricants. Who knew precisely what would work, what fail?

During Hoom's maddening dormancy a failure of another sort captured the attention of Pajetric Stat: the gross corporate product of Chinistrex Fortronza, for the most recently concluded fiscal period, had fallen below that of Divroid Phic for the first time since . . . who could remember? Yea, the C. Fortronzan g.c.p. was being challenged even by such lightweight emperies as Selestron and Bzz! Efficiency had fallen off, the pizzazz and verve of times past had degenerated into a mopy, glitch-ridden languor. Why? Easy to say: Hoom was terminating, and the citizens of Chinistrex Fortronza had registered the fact in all its computer-counted ramifications.

What or who, with Hoom gone, would touch them in those enigmatic recesses—recesses neither digital nor analogical—that they'd not been previously conscious of? Who or what would restore them to peak temper and dependability?

The answer came at once to Pajetric Stat (as it must surely have already come to you): only the Homunculus, only the Homunculus.

But could the Homunculus be enticed from its self-imposed banishment in the eerily neat depths of the Parmalee's paradise? Had it perhaps been *hurt*—the Parmalee struggled with the abstruseness of this notion—by their attentions to Hoom? Yes; most certainly. As a consequence, had it manufactured a quantity of *pique?* Again, most certainly. Logic confirmed the undeniable likelihood of both possibilities. And sending out RunAbout Most High, Smoky, Univac, and Morp the Synthesizer to retrieve the Homunculus would hardly work a second time.

Once bidden, once sly.

Hoom continued operable a second fiscal period, and a printout from Divroid Phic's ADMA 7, in response to pleas for cooperative research on the problem, said that the organic homunculus would most likely . . . *die:* the same thing had happened, in time, with all their other decanted intelligences.

The term *die* was then explained in a sheaflet of printouts designed as a footnote to ADMA 7's initial reply; the footnote included analogies, graphs, experimental examples. Pajetric Stat, scanning them, could not help applying these statistics and prophecies to the g.c.p. of Chinistrex Fortronza: down, down, and *dead*. Soon even tiny Bzz, ruled, as a rumor had it, by an abacus, would be capable of becoming a majority shareholder in their empery.

The Parmalee's wings ratcheted up, ratcheted down, in overwarm unison, light playing upon them with unhealthy incandescence.

At the end of the second fiscal period there occurred a drop in the g.c.p. commensurate with Hoom's monitored decline. About this time RunAbout Most High disappeared from the Center: he had defected, it was later learned, to Ampide. . . .

"Dear, dear, Homunculus," Pajetric Stat murmured to himself, "when will this irrationality and glitchiness end?"

Would Hoom recover?

Would the Homunculus return?

As the Watch Maker of all Blaispagalians would have it, Hoom *died*. The last pulsebeat went out of the creature, tiers of telemetering equipment went fuzzily blank.

When the Parmalee informed his people of the organic homunculus's *death*, work stopped altogether. Morp the Synthesizer broadcast over the entire empery a single reverberating grief-filled chime. Servitors and sedentaries stopped humming long enough to record the protracted *bong* from Morp's woofers and to say to each other, "Yes, it's true: the bell tolls for Hoom."

The organizational structure of Chinistrex Fortronza was disintegrating; and contemplating this from the isolation of the control well, from the topmost branches of his thronetree, Pajetric Stat, fighting overload, warbled the whole of his complex concerto to an empty room. Or so he thought.

When he looked down again, he saw the Homunculus beneath him, diamonds poised on its cheeks like glass commas. Quietly, the dwarveter began to weep—wept because it had forgotten how to laugh, wept because it had again heard the Parmalee sing. Almost at once Pajetric Stat overcame his surprise and switched on the mechanisms that would relay the sights and sounds of the joyously lamenting Homunculus to all the citizens of his empery: no time to lose, no time to lose. That done, the Parmalee addressed the Machine Who Weeps Starlight in terms of genuine gratefulness and affection.

"Long, long ago, Homunculus, I should have turned Hoom out, I should have sent it back to the Mechanarch of Divroid Phic."

"Not so, Your Paradisiacal Birdship, for Hoom served you well and would still be doing so if it had not been who and what it was: an organic entity. Its misfortune was greater than our own, the misfortune of mortality. Do not revile it either for temporarily replacing me or for so inconsiderately terminating. I am back now, and coming and going as I please, I will continue to influence—by my bitter laughter, my lamentations, and my lachrymal displays—the hidden sensibilities of our people. I will touch the mortal in them that lies unsuspected and impetuous under their immortal skins. And under yours, too, my Parmalee."

"So be it," said Pajetric Stat.

And so the Homunculus did, its grief for its dead creators an incentive and an inspiration for its fellow citizens. In the very next fiscal period Chinistrex Fortronza recovered its cybernetic leadership of the corporate emperies of Blaispagal, Inc., and a press printout from Ampide reported that a pack of indigenous robots, unprogrammed primitives, had cannibalized RunAbout Most High for parts and bartered these for sturdier varieties of scrap metal. Upon receiving this news, the machines in the Command Center unanimously elected the Homunculus to the late RunAbout's position, and the Homunculus, a bit against expectations, accepted.

And everyone functioned happily ever after: literally.

On the other hand, poor dead Hoom was the only citizen of Chinistrex Fortronza who ever went to a paradise other than the Parmalee's coniferous and crystal one. Or who, to be fair, needed to go there.

Zizizi, click, rescan.

LEAPS OF FAITH

AT NINE o'clock on Tuesday morning, Ridpest Ltd. dispatched Heinz Jurgens to Kudzu Valley, a small town nearly an hour away, and Heinz drove there in a blue Volkswagen with the blue and white company emblem on its doors.

The Mayers of Kudzu Valley, his dispatch notice said, had fleas—fleas slipping through the piles of their carpets, fleas doing Calaveras antics on the kitchen linoleum, fleas pirouetting in the shrubbery around the Mayers' foundation and porch stoops. Heinz's mission was to commit genocide upon the Mayers' fleas. An additional recommendation was that he impress upon this family the desirability of year-round control. As a newly trained Ridpestman knowledgeable in the ways of ants, book lice, carpet beetles, centipedes, house crickets, roaches (four varieties), silverfish, *and* fleas, Heinz would himself perform this monthly service for the Mayers, once they were under contract. He would cheerfully and professionally execute his duties.

Yes: execute.

As he turned into the Mayers' grass-grown driveway, Heinz felt a familiar headache coming back. Immediately his mind poised to leap away from the pain, but he actively resisted this movement and tried to concentrate on the business at hand.

The Mayers' house was two stories tall, a gingerbread monument to the turn of the century. Its gables suggested an enormous attic wherein all sorts of rascally vermin

129

could foregather and breed. Heinz imagined them knocking and rustling in the night, vying for hegemony. If you saw the house as a living organism, that nightly warfare would be tantamount to a headache, the whole house beneath the attic (a vast two-story basement) standing aghast at the disorder upstairs. Just like my body now, thought Heinz. He recalled that you could divide the body of a flea into three parts too: head, thorax, and abdomen. But it wasn't likely that fleas had invaded the attic unless squirrels or bats had preceded them. You had to have a host, after all; that was essential for ectoparasites.

A man in blue jeans and sandals was inching his way around the perimeter of the house carrying an unwieldy bag. White powder sprinkled down from the mouth of the bag like sifted Bisquick. It was probably lime. Nimble but balding, the man going around the house was trying to lay down a chemical Maginot Line against the fleas *that were already inside*. As if a prophylactic measure could also be curative! Too little, too late. A melody began playing inside Heinz's migraine, and he wished that he were somewhere else, singing lustily. With difficulty he resiled to the moment and walked toward the house.

He was met at the kitchen door. The man with the lime sack wiped his palms on his thighs, and they shook hands. " 'Shot' Mayer," the owner of the house announced. "Nice to meetcha."

"Heinz Jurgens. Eventually I've come from Columbus, to answer your call." He held up his company clipboard.

"What's that first name again?"

"Heinz. As in Heinz 57. Jurgens, as in the lotion." The timeworn explanation.

"Right. Right. And mine's 'Shot.' As in *shoot, shot, shot*. The past tense, you know—since I'm retired."

"You look very young to be retired." Introductory small talk. Through it all Heinz could feel his brain loading energy into a tight little ball: an elastomer whose thermodynamic release would spring him miles away and persons apart unless he kept its catches engaged. To relax the spectral muscles controlling these catches would be to do violence to reality.

"Well, I didn't really retire. I quit. This was during the bombings of Cambodia. I was a captain, flew B-52s. When it came time to reenlist, well, I just didn't." Mayer picked a flea off his bare ankle and smushed it between the nails of his thumb and forefinger. Heinz heard the faint click of its exoskeleton's collapse.

"If it isn't seeming too personal," he began, looking at the torn screen door, fidgeting to get on with his work, "what line is it you're in now?" That enables you to be home on a Tuesday? he wanted to add.

"I'm a househusband," said Shot Mayer. "I take care of the kids and tend to the house."

The ball in Heinz's brain got smaller and smaller; the catches restraining its release wobblier and wobblier. It was November, cold. Somewhere there must be a statute requiring "househusbands" to wear sandals in November. The grass around the Mayers' kitchen stoop was leaping with life in spite of the cold, and Heinz could see black specks, like flakes of pepper, just below the knees of his Ridpest coveralls. Fleas . . .

"I've decided to do the work myself," Shot Mayer was explaining. "Bought this lime from Wilson & Cathet's. Have an aerosol bomb of flea and tick killer too. That ought to take care of the carpets. I've already sprayed."

"Mr. Mayer—"

"Shot. Just call me Shot."

"Sir, you telephoned long-distance our company. It's an hour's drive from Columbus. All this way I came."

"I know, Heinz. I phoned again as soon as I knew I was going to do it myself, but you'd already left, see, and I guess your cars"—he nodded at the VW in the driveway—"don't have radios."

"No. Radios they don't have. And I drove forty-five miles to watch you dump such . . . such junk around your foundation. It isn't going to work, Mr. Mayer. Not when you have fleas *inside*. I'm . . . I'm . . ."

"Hey, settle down—"

"This little headache I have . . . it's something only I can know about. Up and down to Kudzu Valley not to do anything. All right, all right." Heinz waved a hand, compressed his lips. "A pretty ride, a pretty ride."

"Calm down, fella. Just slow down a bit." Shot Mayer was loading energy too, mostly in his biceps. His upper body was cocked, but it seemed that a kind of tentative sympathy had engaged a catch against his anger. Heinz could tell that Mayer wasn't going to lose control, not this good-humored man. "Like I said, I'm sorry. But we don't really need a Ridpestman now. This is the third day of our siege, and we're startin' to win. . . . Hey, it *is* a pretty ride, you take it slow."

"Ach," Heinz said, turning around disgustedly.

His catches disengage, and he catapults all the way from November to February, his saltatorial reflexes conveying him backward a distance of 272 days at an acceleration of 140 g's. This is accomplished in little more than a millisecond. He lands at a right angle to the point of his departure and reorients himself by squinting against the light and shuffling around so that he can see himself. On the old Gramophone his father has given him, the Airmen of Note, a service dance band, are playing "At the Hop," a moldy oldie first popularized by Danny and the Juniors. In his mirror Heinz sees the members of this group wearing Ridpest Ltd. coveralls and the formal mess jackets of air force enlisted men. Thus attired, Danny and the Juniors are singing to him. It isn't the sort of music he cares for, but as he lifts a razor blade toward the throat of the sandy-haired young man confronting him in the glass, he mouths the rusty lyrics: "Let's go to the hop, O baby, let's go to the hop," etc., etc. He scrapes the blade against his soapy cheek and then lets it fall stubble-gummed into the wash basin. This place in February, he realizes, is a substratum that must be escaped if he is going to survive either then or here, now or there. His migraine begins, automatically, to reload. . . .

"You're not being a very good host, Shot. Forty-five miles for nothing, and you don't even offer him a Coke."

"You want a Coke?"

"Please."

"Well, please forgive our fleas." Shot Mayer opened the screen door, and Heinz passed through it and the inner wooden one into the kitchen. Mayer's wife was there in a laboratory coat such as those worn by Ridpest Ltd.'s R & D people; she looked like a dark-haired Lee Remick instead of Wernher von Braun, however, and she was holding two beaded glasses out to Heinz and her husband.

"Miriam, Heinz. Heinz, Miriam."

"Very pleased." Heinz took his drink and shook the woman's hand.

A furry green puppet was popping in and out of a trash

can on the TV set in a farther room; and two preschoolers
sat rapt, unsmiling, watching the puppet. At least Heinz
supposed their faces were serious. Since they both wore triangular dust masks, to be certain of their expressions was
impossible. Something had been sprayed in the room, something caustically sweet. Flea and tick killer? It drifted into
the kitchen like a heavily cologned guest unaware of the
offense he gives.

"They won't budge from there when that's on," Mayer
apologized. "So I made them put on the masks we wore to
sand down the bookshelves in the library."

"Roust them out, Shot. It's not so cold they can't stand
to go out. This isn't good for them."

"OK, OK." The television set went off with a familiar
click, suddenly extinguished. It then took Mayer five minutes to get the kids out of the viewing room. Bundled into
parkas, they whimpered about missing their program and
not being able to move. Once outdoors they stood like two
fireplugs, one blue, one maroon, beside a sunken sandbox
beyond the kitchen's pilot-house window. Mayer went back
to slinging lime around the foundation.

"You don't have any animals?" asked Heinz, finishing his
Coke. "No dog? Not a cat? Do you know how all the fleas
came in?"

"With me, I'm afraid. They escaped."

"Yes? From where?"

"I'm working with them upstairs," Miriam Mayer said.
"Several different species. It's a shame Shot has to kill the
ones that got out."

"Let me—let Ridpest, I ought to say—kill them."

"No, Shot's made up his mind. But you've come all this
way, can you give us a general inspection? I'm not promis-
ing that we'll accept monthly service, understand, but maybe you could tell us how the house looks—if we're under
any sort of potentially lethal attack, I mean. Then later—"

"Ach, I hear that all the time. 'Then later' never comes,
Mrs. Mayer. If I leave your house without a contract,
eventually I'll never hear from you again. Give me a break.
I'm here. Let me do something."

"I'm trying to let you do something. But I can't commit
my family to year-round service. Our finances won't permit
it. Really. Would you like to see our bankbook?"

"No, no. It's not for me to seem personal, Mrs. Mayer."
He waved his hand. His headache had very nearly loaded

to capacity again, and Heinz's body sought to orient itself in unfamiliar surroundings before being dragged away after his leaping mind. A crucial leap of faith, he knew, lay ahead or behind, awaiting whatever tensive trigger would squeeze it into focus. Not yet, not yet . . . "What line are you in, if I may ask?"

"I'm a free-lance researcher."

"Oh," Heinz responded. "Very good." Put upon or not, he decided to give this house a free inspection. And going upstairs behind Miriam Mayer, he leapt to a conclusion unpredicated on any previous experience.

Heinz is climbing a windless face of Mont Blanc. Below, Shelley's Ravine of Arve is mistily visible. Behind him comes Miriam Mayer in fur-lined galoshes and a thermally padded laboratory smock. She carries a thermometer in one hand and with the other sweeps over the snow a box containing a microphone and a miniature amplifier. "It's six degrees Celsius," she shouts at him excitedly, "and the microphone's picking up activity from the substratum." "Our footsteps?" Heinz ventures, turning to face her. "No, no, definitely not. I designed this instrument to register sounds in a low range of audibility; it *screens out* crunches." "Ah. From where do these noises come, then?" "Up ahead, Heinz. Keep going." Farther up the slope they see mobile specks on the snow, like little periods and commas leaping about on a huge sheet of foolscap. "Bird fleas!" Miriam exclaims. "A whole community of bird fleas! Even at this temperature they're leaping. Heinz, it's living confirmation of resilin's ability to release energy independently of temperature. Mere muscle isn't capable of that." *"Resilin?"* he wonders. "They're waiting for eagles, I suppose," Miriam goes on, oblivious. "The only hosts Mont Blanc can offer them are eagles." Gleams of a remoter world dance enigmatically in the eyes of Shot Mayer's wife, and with a crowd of homeless bird fleas leaping all about them in the Alpine cold, Miriam's amplifier crackling like a Geiger counter, Heinz takes this vibrant, sympathetic woman in his arms and kisses her deeply. . . .

"Where do you want to start?"

Heinz tried to collect himself. He began gathering his thoughts and compressing them into the inevitable little ball he helplessly believed to be the source of all his headaches:

physical, psychic, social. Unless he did this, however, he
wouldn't be able to function in the real world without in-
viting accusations of madness. Migraines were the price he
paid to be considered sane. But more and more often the
catches disengaged and flung him out of himself like a pro-
jectile. Why? Well, sometimes he simply let them go. . . .

"It doesn't matter. I can begin wherever you want, I
think." They were in a child's room. The wallpaper repeated six or seven different forest animals against a muted
yellow ground. (Two of the animals were designated in the
company brochure as "pests.") Not terribly long ago the
room had been sprayed with the same commercial product,
intended for dogs, that Shot had used downstairs.

"Do you usually go into attics?"

"Sometimes. If possible."

Mrs. Mayer pointed to a passageway overhead. It was
nothing fancy, a square of wood you pushed upward and
set aside as you pulled yourself through. But the opening
was a good twelve feet up, and no ladder or footstool in
sight. "We don't go up there very often," Mrs. Mayer apologized.

Heinz decided he wouldn't even try. "If you'd heard
something guh-nawg-ing up there," he said, "eventually you
would have called somebody by now. Right?"

"If I'd heard something what?"

"Guh-nawg-ing," Heinz repeated. "Chewing." He held
his knuckles to his mouth and gnawed at them in demon-
stration.

"The first *g* is silent, Heinz, and there isn't any *g* in the
middle. It's *gnawing*."

"OK. However you pronounce it." He thrust his hands
into the pockets of his coveralls and peered about the room.

"Well, I have heard *something* up there, a squirrel more
than likely. But a few mothballs thrown about ought to
take care of that, don't you think?"

"You sure you want an inspection, Mrs. Mayer?"

"No. It was Shot who called you. Then he changed his
mind. Really, Heinz, I'm just trying to let you do something while you're here. And I'm *not* trying to put you off
by saying we can't afford anything until after Christmas.
That's true. It's also true we'd like to have your company's
initial service, *when we can afford it*. Do you see?"

"OK. I believe you." Heinz smiled and shook some of

the tightness out of his shoulders. "Praise the Lord, I'm not a doubter like a few months ago is what I say."

"You're from Germany originally?"

"Naturalized American citizen. My father retired Fort Benning five or six years ago. Complicated deal."

"Well, if you want to, Heinz, you can start by looking around in here. Leave the attic be. As things stand now, it's probably dangerous to go up there." Her lab coat crisping about her legs, Mrs. Mayer moved toward the door.

"In a little town like Kudzu Valley," Heinz asked suddenly, taking a squeeze bottle of roach powder from his belt, "what do you do for amusements? If I'm not being too personal."

Mrs. Mayer halted and turned around. "There's not much, that's for sure. Shot and I go into Columbus sometimes, for a movie or a play. Here there's reading, or television, or bicycle rides when it isn't too cold. And my work itself is often an amusement, I'm afraid. Why?"

"I like reading, too," Heinz responded, rehooking the squeeze bottle to his belt and fumbling for his wallet. "Winter quarter I'm eventually going back to school, Columbus College."

"Oh, good. In what?"

"Abnormal psychology." He extracted a business card from his wallet and approached Mrs. Mayer. "But gospel singing is my thing. Hymns, too. Also my thing." He was self-conscious about his use of American slang, even after several years in the States, and the card somehow slipped from his fingers to the carpet.

Mrs. Mayer retrieved it. "The Witness of Glory Interdenominational Singers," she read. "Owen Bob Anderson, Director."

"Yes. It's been on television, Mr. Anderson's singers. From Atlanta. But not me, you see; I'm still just a new one."

She lifted her eyebrows slightly. "Does sound familiar, Anderson's name." Heinz knew that she was trying, with the very best intentions, to be polite.

"Well, if you're not busy on the last Saturday of this month"—he took a pen and wrote on the card—"I'd like to invite you and Mr. Mayer to come to our singing. Here. At this fellowship hall." He wrote the address.

"OK. I'll keep your card. It's just very hard for me to say what we'll be doing that far ahead. We've got a child in

school who dictates some of these things, especially around
this time of year."

"I understand. You put the card someplace where you
can see it. On your mirror is good, I think."

"I'll do that. . . . The fleas are pretty much under control
here, Heinz, but you go ahead and inspect for other things.
Roaches and whatnot. I'll be in my workroom at the end of
the hall. That OK?"

"Very good."

Heinz knelt and examined the crevices under the baseboards. He shone his flashlight into the cracks around the
fireplace, in front of which sat a propane-burning space
heater. He squirted roach powder into those cracks. An
inch or two into one of them he saw the corpse of an
American roach. . . . Not too bad. This was an old house.

Heinz began humming "Amazing Grace," almost as if the
energy-loading ball in his head didn't exist. The Mayers
were very good hosts. They knew how to make you comfortable even if they didn't particularly want you around.
Maybe that wasn't the way to put it, exactly. . . . He walked
on his knees to a desk across the room and shone his flashlight about beneath it. One or two fleas jumped feebly for
his trousers, but they were survivors, desperate passengers
already done for. Seventy-two hours unfed and a good
dousing from Shot's aerosol bomb were just about as effec-
tive as anything Ridpest Ltd. could do. Cheaper too. He had
to admit it.

". . . *That saved a wretch like me,*" Heinz vocalized
softly, standing up. "*I once was lost, but now——*"

What he saw on the desk surprised him, brushed him
back like an unexpected blow. He put his hand out to touch
it. A children's book, upon whose yellow cover a little boy
in a bright red tunic was frozen in the midst of a prodigious
leap. Below him stood a crenelated castle on a hillside.
Heinz's mind sprang helplessly after the boy, catapulted by
a taut recollection inside his migraine.

"*The Big Jump,* by Benjamin Elkin," Heinz reads. Trudi,
aged four, snuggles on his lap and turns the pages for him.
The story is about a king who promises a dog to a little boy
if the boy can do the "Big Jump" to the top of his castle.
The boy eventually wins the dog by jumping *one step at a
time* to the castle's summit; the illustrations imply, however, that the king can do so in a single bound, like Super-

man. Although Heinz understands that the story's point lies in the boy's cleverness rather than in the king's super-human abilities, Trudi insists on asking about the king: "How does he do that, go jumping so high?" "I don't know," Heinz answers with some peevishness (this is the third night he's been interrogated this way); "he's a king, *mein Liebchen.*" "Kings can't do that," Trudi pipes, each word a different note; "they're only people." "And this is only a book, Trudi. In books people can do all sorts of things, I think." This—the random license of books in assigning or denying powers—is an argument he hasn't used before. Will it still his daughter? No. As clever as the boy in Elkin's tale, Trudi goes at once to the heart of the argument: "Then why can't the boy go jumping so high, like the king?" Silence. Then Heinz bursts out laughing and hugs his daughter to him. When she begins bouncing about on her bed in celebration of his laughter, he takes off his shoes and joins her. The boxsprings under the mattress go *schproing, schproing,* and to escape Trudi's mother, who is hurrying through the house toward them, cursing audibly under her breath, Heinz on one bound from the bed knocks a trapdoor in the ceiling aside and on the next lifts Trudi with him into the attic. The attic is like heaven, another world. Up here a Salvation Army band in Ridpest Ltd. coveralls is singing "Amazing Grace," and for a time he and Trudi are safe among these smiling, winged musicians. . . .

Heinz found himself at the end of the hall. Light came through the transom above Mrs. Mayer's workroom. He knocked.

"Come on in, Heinz. You can look around in here, too, if you like."

The room was the largest one upstairs. Opposite him were three tall dormer windows, with window seats; light spilled in through their uncurtained panes like eggnog, thick and fragrant. The walls were light brown, the floor covering a linoleum in a brown-and-gold cobblestone pattern—not the soft, nappy carpeting that connected the other upstairs bedrooms and provided a petlike hiding place for the Mayers' escaped fleas. Mrs. Mayer herself was standing at a long table cluttered with glass jars, retorts, tongs, and a jumble of equipment unfamiliar to Heinz. Another long table flanked this one. Despite the dormer windows, a chemical-stained wing-backed chair, and the cozy window seats, the room had the appearance of a kitchen-cum-laboratory, homey and businesslike at the same time.

"So," Heinz exhaled, glancing about. "This is where you invent, I suppose?"

"Research, yes. It's probably a crazy thing to try. Big companies and government agencies do this sort of thing so much better, but this . . . well, this is where we've chosen to live, and Kudzu Valley's only industry is a poultry-processing plant."

"Can you make money doing this, working alone? I mean . . ." He could feel his face reddening.

"Don't worry, Heinz; you're not overstepping the bounds of propriety. . . . I've had small retainers from Du Pont and the Phillips Petroleum Company in the past, and now I have a small government grant. Very oddball setup, I know. Sometimes I go to the state university to work, when I need someone else's opinion or access to a fuller range of equipment. Not often. I don't like to leave, really."

Heinz busied himself inspecting baseboards and squirting roach powder. Over his shoulder he asked, "Fleas? Is this your research?"

"Indirectly." She carried a bell jar from one table to the other. "They provided the jumping-off place, both literally and figuratively. Do you know anything of their anatomy?"

"Oh, yes." He straightened. "Every Tuesday night—tonight is one, by the bye—we must go to additional training classes, to stay up on all latest chemical methods and new regulations of the Environmental Protection Agency. Also pest facts. Sometimes we're tested on the pest facts—habits, anatomy, suchlike."

"Sounds like good policy. You know what the pleural arch is, then?"

"Never heard of it." Heinz laughed at himself and Ridpest Ltd.'s mandatory Tuesday nights. "We're stronger on habits than anatomy, I suppose."

"Why not? I can't see where knowing what a pleural arch is would be of much benefit to someone whose job is extermination."

"No," Heinz agreed. "What is it, this pleural arch?"

"An area above the flea's hind leg on its thorax. Poor species of jumpers have either reduced or altogether absent pleural arches, you see."

"Ah. You discovered this and the government gives you money? . . . May I look in this closet?"

"Go ahead. . . . No, I didn't discover that; others did, long, long before me. The important thing is that the arch corresponds to the wing-hinge ligament in flying insects like dragonflies and locusts, and it contains—in the form of a ligament—a protein called resilin. That's what I'm researching now, a way to synthesize resilin in large quantities. I had four or five species of flea up here so that I could observe, firsthand, just what resilin is capable of doing for our little friends and, eventually, for us. That's what my grant's for, Heinz."

"Resilin?" Heinz came out of the closet as if into a vale of stinging light. He found himself staring into a jar containing several fleas. The fleas leapt while a microphone and an amplifier kept count.

"It's very nearly the perfect rubber, resilin is. Torkel Weis-Fogh of Cambridge calculated that it yields nearly ninety-seven percent of its stored energy when it's stretched and released." Mrs. Mayer went on to explain that this figure represented only a three percent dissipation of energy as heat, whereas with commercial rubbers the average loss stood at about fifteen percent. Resilin's thermodynamic efficiency accounted for the flea's ability to jump over a hundred times its own body length, even in low temperatures at which mechanogenic muscles fail to relax and contract rapidly enough to power such leaps.

About this classically precise explanation, Heinz felt, there was something familiar and disturbing. It fascinated him, but it made him uneasy. Extinguishing the life of a flea meant nothing (except, possibly, the restoration of order in a household overrun with them), and yet . . . and yet their tiny bodies were crafted with such watchmaker exactitude and love that surely they—the fleas themselves—must mean *something*. Pinching one between your fingers was like breaking a valuable timepiece with a ball-peen hammer. Spraying for them was as great an affront to God's Daedalian genius and artistry as . . . well, as what? Auschwitz? Dachau? Heinz shook his head and stepped back from the bell jar on Mrs. Mayer's lab table.

You have a flea in your brain, he told himself. Didn't Susanna like to call you flea-brained when she was trying to teach you English? That was when, even before Trudi was born, she had you read from children's books. . . .

Mrs. Mayer was staring at him. Heinz roused himself.

"What uses will this resilin have, Mrs. Mayer, if it's possible to . . . to . . ."

"Synthesize it?"

"Yes. Synthesize."

"Well, there's been some talk of incorporating it into the hip assemblies of either space suits or cybernetic organisms intended for use on the moon—as a means of exploratory locomotion, you see. The moon's low gravity would partially offset the additional, unf!ealike weight of a human being or a cyborg, and the ungodly cold wouldn't have any effect at all on the resilin in the hip assemblies."

"Ah. Human fleas on the moon." He could see them skipping from crater to crater, searching. . . . What were they looking for?

"That's one way to put it, I guess. I hope they won't be merely ectoparasites out to deface the moon and suck its blood. Resilin's supposed to have many stay-at-home commercial uses too, if that makes you feel any better."

"I don't know, Mrs. Mayer. These are things I can't envision."

"No, I can't envision many of them myself, and that's part of my job, really. It's hard to predict the exact uses to which one's work will be put. Research is a dicey field, Heinz. In several ways."

Somehow a test tube was dislodged from its metal rack. Heinz didn't know if he or Mrs. Mayer had upset it, but he watched from a great distance as it spiraled down from the table and fragmented on the linoleum, splintering like an icicle. Maybe he had taken it absentmindedly in his hands. He stepped back. Then he leapt.

Susanna's bottle—his bottle, too—has shattered on the table edge. The scent of Jim Beam hangs medicinally between them, like an anesthetic. Trudi, thank God, is asleep. "Slow down, Susanna. You must get quiet, I think, before we can talk." "You made a big deal of it, Heinz; you made a big deal of it in front of Trudi." She's talking about dinner. She served frankfurters and sauerkraut, and when he attempted to cut into one of the plump sausages nestling in the cabbage, he discovered that it was enclosed in a nearly invisible membrane of plastic. Susanna had boiled the frankfurters without unwrapping them! "I just laughed," Heinz soft pedals; "I just laughed is all. That's not making a big deal." "It's what the laughter implies, Heinz, it's what

it says about me and my worth and everything else! I can't
take this kind of open ridicule from my own husband. Isn't
it bad enough . . . bad enough . . . ?" She stops. (For several weeks she's been looking for a job.) As in an old
gangster or waterfront movie, Susanna is holding the neck
of the Jim Beam bottle in her fist, pointing its jagged ring
at his belly. Weeping, wiping her eyes, she begins to stalk
him. Heinz turns, dashes toward the living room's plate-
glass window, and plunges through it like Errol Flynn or
Douglas Fairbanks. Unscathed, he lands amid a circle of
Christmas carolers dressed as angels. They're singing
"Silent Night" in the original German, but the words are as
alien as the costumed children mouthing them, and he
bounds away across the lawn in search of a translator.
Columbus College, he tells himself, has a good language
department. . . .

"That's all right. There wasn't anything in it."
"There could've been. Mrs. Mayer, I'm sorry. I'm clum-
sier than usual; it's this headache, off and on, off and on."
"Can I get you something?"
"No. I'd better finish, I think. Then maybe I could make
a call—collect, of course—to tell them I'm eventually on
my way back."
Mrs. Mayer followed Heinz downstairs. He went under
the house and looked at the water pipes; two or three of
them were dripping slightly, providing the moisture that
roaches require and giving him an additional reason to urge
monthly service on the Mayers. (You didn't suggest a
plumber. That was "counterproductive.") In the kitchen he
made his telephone call to the company's dispatcher's
office.
"I'll be back in an hour. . . . No, not a great deal to do
here. . . . Let me give you my report when I'm back, OK?
. . . OK."
Shot came in. "That's two bags around the house,
Miriam. I think we've pretty much got 'em." He turned
to Heinz. "Taking off, hey?"
"Yes, sir."
"I'm sorry we—*I*, I mean—did this to you. The long trip
and all."
"That's all right," Heinz responded, picking up his clipboard from the kitchen table. "I'm deciding, I think, to quit
my job, anyway."

"Why?" Mrs. Mayer asked. She sounded genuinely startled.

"I don't like it, I guess. Maybe I must test my faith. Lilies of the field." He stepped outside and looked toward the children perched on the edge of their sandbox. The Mayers exited behind him. "Do you go to church regularly, Mr. Mayer?" he asked abstractedly when they were all outside.

"I'm Jewish, Heinz. Miriam's a lapsed Episcopalian."

"You don't believe in God?" Heinz asked Mrs. Mayer, turning on her the same startled look she had just given him.

"That's not it really, Heinz. I'm just not exclusively a Christian any longer, I'm afraid."

"Why? Everything I have, Mrs. Mayer, is from God, I think. Everything." He had forgotten his call to the dispatcher's office. The Mayers needed him. Him, Heinz Jurgens; not the Ridpest exterminator in whose coveralls he had necessarily appeared. . . .

Mrs. Mayer was at his elbow, maneuvering him gently across the yard to his Volkswagen. Beside the automobile she picked a flea off her ankle and cracked it between her fingernails, as Shot had done earlier. Then she examined the nail on which the tiny corpse lay broken.

"Aren't they amazing jumpers? They evolved from ancestors that flew, it seems. Natural selection modified the flight mechanism so that it could be used for these ridiculous death-defying leaps. And they *are* death-defying, you know. If a flea doesn't make it from the substratum to a host, that's it, Heinz: 'The End.' No more flea. And resilin's the agency linking the two mechanisms." Mrs. Mayer was elsewhere for the moment, on a secret Alp of her own.

"Faith is a kind of resilin," Heinz blurted, finding the woman's wrists and clutching them with a frightened urgency. Then, standing in the cold, he explained how he had lost his marriage, custody of his daughter, and his own self-esteem in a series of alcohol bouts and senseless recriminations with his former wife. "In February, Mrs. Mayer, I was thinking of taking . . . the easy way out. I was down at the bottom. Then came people helping me to see for myself what I really am. Now I go to church where we sing our praises, where we talk in tongues, and every day I give my life to God, you know, and pray that whatever headaches I have He'll take from me. Once, like angels, we could all fly—but now we have to jump. Mrs. Mayer,

I've jumped. Eventually it's better than being on the bottom, down and out. Eventually it's much better."

"I know, Heinz. I'm glad for you. I truly am. And I hope you're not making a mistake in quitting your job."

"No, no, surely not," he dismissed this concern impatiently. "Won't you and Mr. Mayer come hear us, Mr. Anderson's singers? You have the card I gave you?"

Back from her spirit's Alpine outpost, Mrs. Mayer promised him nothing. She told him that for two years while her husband was in the air force she had taught Sunday school, out of a sense of duty. She had finally resigned because she could not reconcile her knowledge of the world with what she was teaching the fourth-graders entrusted to _her_ each Sunday. "And now I'm happier than I've ever been, Heinz. I wouldn't wish everyone to follow me, that's true, but not because I'm somehow unfulfilled. Even with the compromises and deal-making life demands of you, I'm almost wholly fulfilled. Or _feel_ as if I am. And I hope you don't wish that feeling away from me because I don't believe as you do."

"No, Mrs. Mayer, I don't." Heinz released the woman's wrists. "Surely I don't." He brushed a sandy lock off his forehead and stared at the high, wispy contrails blowing across the sky. His migraine was coming back. "I like you. I like your personality, which is honest. . . . Will you let me say a prayer? I feel like saying a prayer."

"All right. If you like."

While Shot Mayer rummaged in the garage for a tool of some sort, rattling pickaxes, shovels, hoes, and wooden and metal-pronged rakes, Heinz folded his hands at his belt buckle and leapt upward to the God who had saved him from disaster in February of his adopted country's bicentennial year. What a cranky, unpredictable month February was. It would soon be coming around again, and he was thankful that in the interval he had found a point of focus for his wandering aspirations and loves. A host. Words came to his lips of their own accord, and he asked that the same joy and serenity slowly becoming his take a tenacious hold in the hearts of Miriam Mayer's family.

When he had finished praying, he found Mrs. Mayer's eyes on his; in them was a scintillation of light signaling a world of things she was powerless to explain, at least on a cold Tuesday in November when the sole issue uniting them was the slaughter of a menagerie of on-the-lam fleas. How, as human beings, could they close with each other . . . ?

"Goodbye," Heinz told her. "I've enjoyed it, my inspection."

"Us too. Goodbye, Heinz."

He backed his VW out of the driveway and waved at the children in the blue and the maroon parkas. Surprisingly, they returned his wave, as did the adults who had joined each other in front of the garage. In three minutes Heinz was beyond the Kudzu Valley city limits, on his way back to Columbus.

"A strange one," Shot ventured.

"Yes. Almost as strange as you."

She took her husband's hand. He took hers. Just who initiated the touching neither of them could have said.

Twelve miles outside of Kudzu Valley he could feel the intricate little catches preparing to disengage. The sky was suddenly full of snow clouds. He took his VW to the shoulder, put his arms across the steering wheel, and lowered his head to his arms.

Three hours later a Ridpestman dispatched to find Heinz and hurry him back to work stopped his own vehicle on the road to Kudzu Valley and stared across the highway at the parked Volkswagen. Heinz didn't appear to be injured, nor was the VW damaged. A light snow was falling. The Ridpestman got out of his car and approached his fellow employee.

"Engine trouble? Come on. I'll drive you back."

A youthful man in company coveralls turned to look at him briefly, then revolved his eyes to the sky. After a small struggle the Ridpestman got him out of the Volkswagen and across the road to the other car—but Heinz Jurgens was somewhere else entirely, far, far away, and fetching him back wasn't going to be easy. . . .

ON THE STREET
OF THE SERPENTS

**or, The Assassination of Chairman Mao
as Effected by the Author in Seville, Spain
in the Spring of 1992
a Year of No Certain Historicity**

I

THIS narrative takes place in one of those strange eddies
of time that are fed, downstream, so to speak, by the fierce
maniacal tributaries of the mind. Though such a notion may
frighten or discourage you, don't leave. I cannot leave,
frightened of this idea as I am, and for you to do so would
be to abandon me utterly to the pull and suck of these
psychological whirlpools. I have a story to tell. Therefore,
heed me awhile. As a concession to your reluctance, I will
lead you into the water slowly—by beginning in the past,
progressing to this purely hypothetical moment (this one,
this very one) that finds me hunched over a pale blue typewriter, and proceeding, without apology, to a 1992 that may
never fulfill itself as this narrative directs.

But one has the right to rape the Muse of History if he
adheres to the Aristotelian precepts of structure. Or so I
have convinced myself.

The setting is Seville. I know something of Seville because, in 1962, as a callow and shock-haired adolescent, I
lived there with my father and his second wife in a high-
ceilinged apartment that simmered above the cobblestones
of one of the city's back-street plazas. Beneath us was a

foyer with a wrought-iron grate and, next to this, a cramped *bodega* smelling of sawdust and olives. My father, a forty-three-year-old enlisted man in the United States Air Force, frequented this establishment religiously and often stood me to a glass of beer or a *vino rojo* costing three pesetas. Rather than lean over the damp counter in the bar's cramped breathing space, we sat at the collapsible green tables on the sidewalk outside the door.

From the sidewalk I could look at the balcony railing that fortified the half-casement of my own bedroom. At seventeen I believed myself a sophisticated amalgam of the late James Dean and the even later Ernest Hemingway: during the day I drank with my father, and, late at night, I brooded in the sheltered place between the casement sashes, imbibing the sounds and stinks of Seville through my very pores.

It was a good time, a time that actually happened.

But there were strange occurrences, too, and some of these have made the sort of indelible striations on the psyche that, years later, call one out of a sound sleep with their raw thrummings.

Upstairs from us there lived the family of a Japanese-American airman whose name was Pete Taniguchi. Taniguchi's wife, a tall blonde German girl with heavy features, put me in mind of a folk-legend milkmaid translated against her will to a land of querulous swarming gnomes, so out of place did she seem. The two of them—Taniguchi and the milkmaid—had a daughter, certainly little more than three years old, who could speak pidgin varieties of Spanish, German, and English. *Elfin* is the word that most accurately describes her, for she had inherited the small bones and nut-brown coloring of her father. I sometimes played intricate little games with her on the rooftop aerie of our tenement, enticing her to put together phrases in odd combinations of her three "native" languages.

The most successful of these may have been *"The gato es schlepping,"* which she piped whenever she encountered my stepmother's cat Toro basking in the dapples under the clotheslines. Pigeons swooped above us, like ghosts cruising between the rooftop crucifixes. The little girl's name was Nisei; I often said this name aloud, testing it on my lips.

Although she was not usually reticent with me, on one spectacular occasion I frightened Nisei into an apoplexy of speechlessness:

It was early afternoon. My father had sent me downstairs to the bar, and I was returning with a bottle of seltzer water in one hand and a bottle of wine in the other. I had left the gate in the foyer open. I squeezed through the gate on my way back, pushed it to with my hip, and began to climb the tile steps to the second landing. Outside, the sun burned. The stairwell, however, might have existed in a totally different universe. I climbed through its mosaic coolness wearing khaki shorts, a cotton undershirt, and a pair of bathroom thongs.

Suddenly, Nisei appeared in the semidarkness above me, her small body as naked as a thumb. She flashed against the inlaid tiles of the stairwell, tiles blue and brown; flashed upon some peripheral part of my awareness. The apparition startled me, and, looking up, I fell forward as one perfidious thong slid from my foot and tripped me.

Under pressure, the bottle of seltzer water struck the edge of a step and exploded. Only the fact that the barman had placed the bottle in a wire-mesh hood prevented this explosion from filling me with crystalline shrapnel. The wine bottle also broke. I lay pitched headlong in glittering glass and a sticky veneer of wine.

The wine was red, it smelled sour, and the tall enamel stairwell in which I finally regained my feet seemed a shaft dropping me into another dimension. Sopping wet, I looked up again and saw the Taniguchis' little girl staring at me with unabashed horror. I called her name, and she began to scream, an eerie wail that echoed icily up and down the well. For, after all, I stood there in broken glass, my elbow and chin actually bleeding and my cotton T-shirt drenched with the merciless incarnadine of my father's sour wine. No wonder that she fled inarticulate, sobbing, up the cold steps. Perhaps she paused at the top to look back down at me—I don't know, for only a moment later I heard the foyer's grating unlatch and felt a hand on my elbow, my uncut elbow.

At my shoulder stood a tall man in uniform. The man was oblivious to the ruin that my stained hands could work on his martial spotlessness; he supported me. This, I realized vaguely, was a member of the Guardia Civil, the Generalissimo's unique national police force. The man smelled of new leather, gun metal, and gabardine; and when I at last brought my eyes into focus, I saw that he had lived only four or five years longer than I—and that

his smooth brown face bore upon its cheek the spidery
magenta of a birthmark. Beneath the guard's tricornered
patent-leather hat, his eyes regarded me with a limpid
concern. Slung over his shoulder he wore a sleek gleaming
weapon that I could not identify, so alien did it seem.

"You are hurt," he said.

This observation required no comment. I wondered how
he had got past the iron latticework because, having
bumped the gate with my rear end, clumsily balancing two
bottles, I knew that it had shut behind me. From high in
the stairwell Nisei's frail voice thinned and died. The young
guardsman tilted his head to catch its final dying note.

"Qué va," he said to himself, not even a question. Then:
"The explosion of the bottle sounded like a gunshot. And
the screaming, of course. Who is screaming, man?" For
man he said *hombre,* a peculiarity of address which, considering my age, I might have taken for a compliment. In
fact, I so took it. Despite the glaring birthmark, the guardsman inspired in me a grateful acquiescence. "Nisei," I said
in answer to his question. "Nisei is screaming." But I spoke
in English. Then I leaned my full weight against the front
of his immaculate olive-drab uniform. Nevertheless, he
accepted me and nodded as if he understood. Without staring, without protesting, he guided me through the glass and
up the sucking steps, gummy with wine, toward my apartment.

Before we had got very far, I thought, *Members of the
Guardia always travel in pairs,* and I looked over my shoulder at the hard pink light that came through the scrollwork
of the grating. Looking down, I saw nothing but a square
of sidewalk and the shadow of the guardsman's bicycle.
Apparently my escort was alone. "Attention to where you
place your feet," he said and led me to my door, where my
stepmother, who had heard none of Nisei's screaming because of a huge electric fan in the dining room, put two
knuckles in her mouth at the sight of me.

The guardsman saluted and took his leave.

I do not remember the exact moment of his leaving, nor
do I pretend to know how he once again got through the
outside door unassisted. Our landlady, whose name was
Consuela, frowned on all trespassers (their legitimacy as
civil agents notwithstanding) and kept her building as in-
violately secure as the Generalissimo must have kept his
private bedchambers. But the soldier with the birthmark

had come and gone as easily as if he had possessed Consuela's keys from the pockets of her housecoat.

My father had been napping. We woke him, and he drove me in our red and white 1955 Buick to San Pablo, an auxiliary air force installation that lay several miles outside Seville. There in the military infirmary, an anonymous doctor sewed the lips of my wounds together and sent me back home with an admonition to be more careful with volatile seltzer bottles.

Riding back in the dark, I could not believe that we were in Spain, a foreign country, the underslung belly of Old Europe. As the anesthetic wore off, the banality of my pain assailed me. I might as well have been in Kansas or Oklahoma, and imagined that I was. Only the faint neon luminance of the *Cruz del Campo* sign, far away on our left, convinced me that we were indeed in Andalusia, that the emptiness I felt had an Old World antecedent. The factory beneath the neon sign manufactured beer. If suddenly it, and the countryside, and the distant city lights, had all dissolved in mist, I would have accepted the phenomenon as a judgment akin to a beer hangover, mustard-yellow and foggy. The Buick hummed.

Later that evening I went up to the Taniguchis' apartment to demonstrate to Nisei that I was no longer the ensanguined monster from which she had so precipitously fled. She accepted this revelation readily enough that evening, but in the following weeks she avoided me as if I were the most heinous of ghosts—the implacable spirit of the *Enola Gay* given flesh. At any rate, I detected something esoteric and cultish in her attitude. Moreover, her mother seemed to me an accomplice in these evasions, and I spent a great deal of time alone on the roof, looking toward the cathedral and spire that the Spanish call La Giralda. Once I thought I saw Nisei watching me from the doorway to the stairwell. If I did see her, she stuck her tongue out at me, a flickering of crimson, and hastily retreated.

In those lonely weeks I learned how to negotiate all the city's twisting back streets and alleyways. My facility at getting from one place to another began to amaze me. About the time that Nisei resolved to accept me back into her fickle graces, I had forgotten the accident that had expelled me from them. But an incident on the Calle de

Sierpes, or Street of the Serpents, brought that wellhead of our falling out forcibly to mind once more.

Again, it was a hot afternoon. I had come into the kaleidoscopic human traffic on the Calle de Sierpes from a dirty side street. Vehicles are not permitted, but so insistent are the feet and shoulders on this pedestrian thoroughfare that if one stumbled he would have no more chance than a stray dog on the streaming raceway at Indianapolis. I headed up the Way of the Serpents in the direction of the Hotel Cristina. The heads of the oncoming crowd formed an irregularly budded surface that unrolled continuously, like the tongue of history. The tongue buckled. It glistened. And the faces of a thousand bustling foreigners rode its broad carpet as if they, too, had been swallowed. But there burned a little Spanish in my head that summer, and I tried, knowing my own inadequacy, to comprehend both the strange voices—the babel of sweltering words—and the strange visages.

"*Lotería para hoy*," a blind man standing in a doorway shouted. "*Lotería para hoy*."

Then a businessman in wraparound sunglasses and a brown Continental suit apologized when my abrupt stop carried him into my back. He moved on, and traffic flowed around me as if I were a stone, an insentient breakwater. It seemed that I had not quite enough Spanish to comprehend what I saw: a plate-glass window rippled darkly on the façade of a billiard parlor and bar. I saw, through that window, two figures sitting at a white metal table. Even though the awning that shaded this section of the street made it difficult to identify the two figures, I knew jealousy. My mind thudded; my mind blanked out the ubiquitous din of the street. I fought the crowd and drew closer to the window. Gazing in, I felt betrayed.

Nisei sat in one chair. She wore a high-collared navy-blue dress with white trim around the cuffs. Her hands gripped an outsized glass that contained an orange drink of some kind, probably a Fanta. She scarcely reached the edge of the table. She did not see me because she was too busy with her drink and because she was listening politely to the adult who sat opposite her. At her back, like a menagerie of ugly mythological animals, hunkered the dim shapes of the billiard tables and the green silhouettes of the game-sters. The adult with Nisei was neither a parent nor one of the family's favorite babysitters. In fact, I might not have recognized him at all had I not seen the filamentous blotch of color that stained his right cheek.

It was the young guardsman. But rather than his dread uniform he wore a pair of gray slacks and a white shirt open at the collar. With one sandaled foot crossed over his knee, he appeared both worldly and ingenuous. The way Nisei ignored her orange drink to listen to him was disquieting; it indicated that I had a rival of no small consequence. How had he ingratiated himself with her? What circumstances had brought him into her life as more than an impersonal emissary of state?

I went away from the window before they could see me, up the street and into the crowd. But I stopped in a doorway, turned about, and pressed myself against a wall. My head ached.

Perhaps the young guardsman lived in the neighborhood of our apartment building, perhaps on the little avenue of Leoncillos itself. If he had grown up there, he might indeed have a key to Consuela's foyer gate as Consuela's acknowledgment of his social worth. She mistrusted the barmen and laborers in the *barrio,* and it would have been like her to attempt to capture her very own Guardia Civil as a sort of status-imparting footman. On the other hand, perhaps Consuela had a real affection for the boy and wished to demonstrate it through the gift of the key. And since the landlady kept company with the Taniguchis more frequently than with the Bishops, it followed that she might have introduced the guardsman to Nisei's parents, all unbeknownst to me.

But on the teeming Way of the Serpents I had no idea how legitimate these speculations were; they came and went like feet over unyielding flagstone.

Temples pulsing, I watched the doorway of the billiard parlor. At last, Nisei and the young man with the birthmark emerged and melted into the general confluence. Because I, too, stepped into the arcade and followed with my eyes the stiff formal jouncing of Nisei's dress, they did not immediately disappear. But they did disappear, and with a cold suddenness. Passersby bumped me, shoved me, pushed past like hungry fish in an aquarium.

Standing there gazing wistfully after the guardsman and the girl, I had a vision of the Calle de Sierpes filled with all the unknowable peoples of the globe: Latins, blacks, Scandinavians, other whites of every ilk, bushmen, Eskimos, aborigines, Pygmies, Arabs, Polynesians, Mongoloids;

primitives and technathropes alike. And even as this vision worked inside me, my terrible separation from these people swept over me like a salt-estranging comber from the planet's last tidal convulsion. My mouth choked on the brackishness of it all, and I realized that not one, not one, in those thronging numbers shared my language. Nevertheless, turning to face the genuine pedestrians who gave me bruisingly genuine bumps, I tried to put words together, struggled to be understood. But my vision began to evaporate; and when it was altogether gone, I desisted and let myself go, floating on the back of the serpent's tongue. No other alternative remained.

It was a long way home.

I believed that no one could be so lonely and that the summer would never end.

II

December 6, 1971

But of course the summer did end, and my loneliness perished with the coming of the white Andalusian autumn and the beginning of school. Time passed. Now I am twenty-six years old, and my attitudes have changed so alarmingly that the picture of that other self—staring across the rooftops toward the great fifteenth-century cathedral, moving like a somnambulist on the tongue of the serpent, standing drenched in the blood-red wine of what may have been a prophecy—that picture, I say, no longer has significance for me. I am changed. Spain has become a bundle of stored impulses that only infrequently prick me into recollection; it has become a news item.

In today's Denver *Post,* for instance, I ran across an article that had this headline: RUSS-SPANISH TRADE FIRMING. From habit, I scanned the columns. "Despite occasional outbursts from the Spanish right," one sentence reads, "there seems little doubt that Spain and the Soviet Union are moving toward establishing diplomatic relations."

Last week, in this same newspaper, I read an article about how a number of Spanish women have begun to protest the traditional masculine-oriented law of that nation. Change, you see, is the only constant. Even the staid Generalissimo, grown grayer and more benign with the years, has allowed the serpent's tongue to touch inside him a responsive chord of metamorphosis. Change occurs in Spain. Still, it is difficult for me to believe that in the eight years since my departure the Generalissimo has managed to resist the ultimate personal change, the act of dying. Why, the man has outlived Churchill, de Gaulle, Khrushchev! He rules the knotted underbelly of Europe like a mildly shifting, comfortably ancient tumor. One forgets that he is there at all. I have forgotten him innumerable times.

But in these last few weeks the news of the world has been constantly in our minds. The President is going to China. The announcement of that visit, so smugly made and so promiscuously startling in its implications, may well have been the first half-turn of the key that admitted Chairman Mao's grinning retinue into the councils of the U.N. We fought very hard, but that organization did not choose to recognize two Chinas. In fact, a goodly number of our allies, bridling beneath the weight of a ten percent surcharge on imports, took singular delight in chasing the tattered Paper Tiger all the way back to Taiwan, *miaow, miaow, miaow*. Perhaps, after all, we were unrealistic. The Tiger would not have stood still to be decorated with Communist decals (tiny red stars, I suppose), and Mao, rotund as a benevolent cherub, would in no case have permitted the papier-mâché beast to hang ignominiously from his neck.

Perhaps it is best.

I have very little understanding of international relations; the same hatreds, allegiances, and gut fears that move the multitudes move me. So deep do these things run that they exert an archetypal influence. Sometimes I envision a rabid Confucius and a splenetic Christ locked in combat in my bowels, and the suspicion always arises that our erstwhile savior is either lacking in experience or tragically outnumbered. Then the gut fear overtakes me. Nor is it a pretty captivity: it smells of the glands, the bowels, the lily flesh itself. I come back to the world only by imagining the President strolling the parapet of the Great Wall in the company of several genial Chinese. What visceral changes will his visit accomplish? As ignorant of diplomacy as I am, I am certain that our lives will indeed be subtly changed. For isn't the Great Wall, too, as tortuous as the shape of history? Doesn't it have a mystic affinity with my well-remembered Way of the Serpents? I pray that it does.

My prayers, however, are not so altruistically universal

in scope as they might seem. I hone them; I refine them. In consequence, they reflect a shining domestic happiness. You see, it will be four weeks tomorrow since I became a father, since I stood by my wife in the delivery room and shared with her, as much as a man is given to share it, the long pain and the exultant fatigue of birth.

And then, a son.

He emerged with a misshapen head, wearing the purple-and-yellow motley of new nakedness; emerged like a small clown from Cathay; emerged into the gloved hands of the waiting Dr. Schindler. Healthy, perfectly healthy, despite these passing evidences of the birth struggle. Miracle it has been called myriad times, and I (even I who once doubted) have contributed a thread to the tapestry that creates itself by endlessly unraveling. Afterward, my wife's face was that of a madonna, and they rolled her on a hospital cart to a room where she could sleep away her weariness under a blanket that had been warmed under hot yellow bulbs.

Our son's name is Christopher James. Tonight, as I write, he lies uncharacteristically serene in his bassinet, sleeping beneath the bright glimmer of the television. Jeri has left the set on while she works nearby in the kitchen; it functions as a sort of inanimate but garrulous nurse. In fifteen minutes Jeri will take him up to feed him. Awake, he will roll unfocused eyes and make hungry mewlings in his throat as Jeri spoons in the rice cereal, talks nonsense to him, and catches the pasty overage that he tongues back out. In his tilted infant-seat he resembles nothing quite so much as a pale-blue Buddha, swaddled in terrycloth.

I am writing this story for him, even though he will no doubt put off reading it for a time. When he does come to read it, he will not recognize the purely hypothetical entity (the baby Christopher James) whom I have just described. How, therefore, may he recognize himself?

The question fills, brims, overflows.

It may be that he will define himself through a series of metaphysical comparisons with his father, the father who orders this narrative so traditionally. Because, despite the confessional tone of this section of my story, I have not forgotten the reader. Bear with me a moment. The past we have looked at. My infant son is the present. Some, I suppose, would argue that he embodies also the future, for children, like rocket stages, carry us one step nearer our common destiny. However, I don't choose to usurp Jamie's future here. Nor anywhere else. To do so would be to negate the unthinking primordial gift that this gift cannot approximate.

As Jamie eats, I will halt for the night. Tomorrow it may snow, and the month of December looms ahead of us now like a gigantic white package that we will open only to discover newer months, colder months. Still, one must finish what one has begun.

December 8, 1971

We have our snow, and I have been away from this narrative for an entire day. The reader, of course, must view this passage of time as largely an illusory thing (unless the break between sections signaled for the reader, too, a logical stopping place); but for Jamie, who little realizes what he loses, the passage of time has been a reality. Certainly he has not counted the clock ticks, but, by paternal proxy, I have done so for him, aware that the day we have lost, the fourth-week anniversary of his birth, cannot be recalled. It pains me to think that he has *lived* this lost time more fully than I, albeit with less consciousness. I merely fretted about the minutes that sifted down around me like snowflakes.

The white space above *December 8, 1971* is even whiter than it appears.

Yesterday evening I found myself grading themes. A prosaic business, this task occupied me for two hours. Outside the snow continued to fall, not wet and heavy, not feathery, but dry and silver like scales of mica from the back of an iridescent reptile. Jeri talked consolingly to the baby, whom she had placed full length on her lap; and I impatiently flipped through papers with titles like "Population and Subsistence," "The Question of the Universe," and "Man, the Immortal," this last being an extrapolative account of how man may attain virtual immortality within the next 150 years, provided he learns a thing or two in the interval. The Air Force Academy (yea, even its preparatory school) attracts students with strong aptitudes for the sciences; the titles of my themes are testimonials to this fact. Forward-looking young men, my students seldom quail at the thought of leaping light-years or of confronting the next century on its own ineluctable terms. I cannot restrain them, even with a red felt-tipped marker and a hand that brooks no comma splices.

In spite of this, I marked—marked and commented, marked and despaired—hoping by a vivid enough display of red to wipe out their ingenuous prophecies. The winter night urged me to obliterate the futures they predicted, just as the fall of snow had obliterated our lawn under a blanket of slate. I marked and marked. At the end of those two hours I almost believed that all the red on their papers had been tapped from my veins. I put the felt marker aside, empty. Absolutely empty.

It was ten o'clock, again Jamie's feeding time.

Since I could not abide the thought of disciplining myself to a false rapport with my typewriter, I avoided my study altogether. I put a record on. In a well-worn red leather chair in our living room, I listened to Bach's *Brandenburg* Concertos. Eighteenth-century baroque. I know very little about music, but I like these pieces; and Jeri's mother, who was here briefly after Jamie's birth, gave these recordings to me as a belated birthday gift. A pair of introspective Scorpios only three days apart, Jamie and I share November.

Pablo Casals conducts. He, like Franco, is Spanish, but an expatriated Spaniard of even greater age. Sitting in my chair, I listened to the strands of melody that he coaxed from his small orchestra, but listened with a dreaming attention, for Bach, depending on the state of receptivity that the listener chooses to assume, has the ability not only to stimulate but to lull. Exhausted, I chose to be lulled and permitted the music to inundate me with its richness.

After a time I took Jamie from my wife and, still sitting in my tottering red chair, began to give him his last bottle of the day. Cradled in my arms, he rooted for the warm nipple, fists clenched under his chin, eyes fixed uncertainly on the lamp at my shoulder. His small round face, as he suckled seemingly in time to the music, conveyed the impression of a bland astonishment. Again and again the world surprised him. What was he doing in my arms? What forces had compelled him to this attitude of unthinking dependence? Because his astonishment seemed so genuine, I asked these questions for him.

Of course, I had no answers. Not satisfying ones, at any rate. For the world continued to surprise me, too, surprise me with the perpetual dullness of its cruelties, with the familiar clash of its alarms and seizures. Israel wants our jets; we play coy. Pakistan slaughters its own; India prepares for war. Belfast smolders. Meanwhile, having gutted ourselves of all rectitude on the *bluddlefilths* of Southeast Asia, we throw up a sanctimonious façade and persevere in making our moral commitments on the basis of a coin toss, or worse. In fact, in this matter of the Asian subcontinent we are incongruously aligned with the Red Chinese.

No, I had no answers yesterday evening; I have none now. As I held Jamie and concentrated on his rhythmical ingestion of formula, world politics could not have been more removed from my thoughts. His bottle was a world in its own right, his bottle and my arms. Let the snow come down. Let the global burden be borne by those who have sought to assume it, even if they lead us into moral hinterlands.

Aloof to such considerations, I watched my son drink.

The final concerto advanced solemnly into its second movement. The day was nearly gone, and I had written nothing.

But as Jamie drank, I ran a finger over his silkenly wrinkled forehead. I remarked an oddity. Beneath the weaving of downy hair that covered his scalp farther back, an angry redness gleamed. I let my fingers push the delicate hairs aside to reveal this phenomenon more clearly. The redness, however, was merely a birthmark, nothing more. Although shaped uncannily like our common birth sign, this nevus did not threaten to brand Jamie a freak. Once his hair had completely grown out, it would not show at all. There was no reason for me to feel uneasy.

But I did. I did indeed.

And last night my dreams were surfeited with a single image: that of an armored arachnid with its stinger upraised, dripping poison. The morning came early, and I went to my seven-thirty class weighted down with a briefcase full of themes about the promise of the future. My uneasiness has persisted all day, even to this purely hypothetical moment.

III

In 1992 I returned to Spain for the first time in thirty years. The world and I had both changed, and in the spring of that year I followed my tired memory to Leoncillos

Street and the old apartment building where the Bishops and the Taniguchis had taken their secluded residence, surrounded by an alien city.

I was forty-six years old: gray, disillusioned, a trifle paunchy. But I had come back to Seville with a sense of mission, and when I first looked at the city, it seemed that no time had passed at all. Pigeons still left their feathers on rooftop laundries. Hunched over curbstones, urchins still played at catching dragonflies with reeds. And the bars, of course, remained open long hours into the night, just as before.

In the bright sunlight, I stood looking at the old apartment building. For some time I did not dare to cross the cobbled street and sound the buzzer inside the shadowy foyer.

I was afraid that no one would answer that buzzing.

The building had a collapsed look, as if it had been empty the entire thirty years since the Bishops' departure. Two huge timbers propped up the face of the building. My old brooding place, the narrow balcony above the sidewalk, was barricaded with cardboard and scrap wood. Red tiles from the roof had fallen into the street. Like Poe's meticulous narrator, I suppose I ought to add that a fissure ran down the face of the building from the cornice to the stone molding at its base. That would not be strictly true. Nevertheless, the emptiness and corruption of that tottering structure would no doubt have delighted Edgar Allan, even if he had had to experience them, as I did, in the Mediterranean coolness of a spring morning. It was *Semana Santa,* Holy Week.

Surprisingly, nothing else on the street seemed to have changed. The pigeons, the children, the bars—all unaltered. Somewhat reassured, I crossed the cobbles, took up a chair at one of those old sidewalk tables, and sat in the midst of the neighborhood noises sipping a *vino rojo.* Of course, I did not recognize the barman, but that was the sort of alteration that time must necessarily work; I appreciated the absence of any need to explain my return to a doddering tavernkeeper who, from some quirk in my behavior, might have deduced my identity. The reason for my return concerned no Old Worlder, least of all an ignorant barman.

Why, in fact, had I come back to Spain?

Because somewhere after my twenty-sixth year either

history or I had become so incomprehensible that action
had to be taken. The center of things had shifted; the focus
of human events had revolved away from the old arenas.
Consequently, I had returned to Spain to ensure that my
life did not conclude on the distorted periphery of this
new lens.

I had come to Spain to murder Mao Tse-tung, Chairman
of the New Chinese Communality.

He, in turn, had come to Spain to celebrate with Generalissimo Franco the fifth anniversary of the signing of a
Sino-Iberian friendship pact. The original event had coin-
cided, by design, with the festivities of *Semana Santa,* and
now the Chairman had chosen this week, this week, to rein-
force that pledge with a personal visit. It was said to be
his first excursion outside of Peking in eleven years, at
which time he had traveled secretly to Moscow to aid in
the drafting of the Ecumenical Charter of New Socialism.
The most astounding provision in that document had been
the abolition of all arbitrary frontiers between the Soviet
Union and the People's Republic of China. The precedent
established by the Ecumenical Charter had had far-reach-
ing effects in both Asia and Europe; the American press
made it directly accountable for the breakdown in national
distinctions that took place in the succeeding decade. Now,
however, our press avoids publicizing these almost daily
occurring treaties and conscientiously suppresses any men-
tion of the Chairman himself. In fact, in that year I learned
of his visit to Spain from a Chilean-based radio broadcast
that our government used to make a halfhearted nightly
effort to jam. Although I understood that such broadcasts
deserved jamming, I felt fortunate to have obtained this
clue to Mao's plans. The broadcast gave me valuable direction; it steeled my resolve to attempt a restoration of the
old balance.

It also hinted ambiguously that only a month before his
scheduled trip to Madrid and the Spanish provinces he had
undergone a major operation, one of considerable scientific
import. At the time, this morsel of innuendo had gone undigested; it meant nothing to me. Since both Franco and
Mao were nearly a hundred, an operation probably signi-
fied that the Chinese had found a way to reeducate senile
digestive tracts, possibly through a variation on acupunc-
ture or some such esoteric Oriental procedure. I had no
idea. On the following day, however, the entire bizarre

story of Mao's operation was revealed to me in a conversation as improbable as the operation itself. But since artful storytelling involves a respect for chronology (as well as a symmetrical spacing of climaxes), I'll delay transcribing this conversation until it meshes more exactly with my narrative.

On that spring morning I drank my wine and studied the condemned building that loomed up from the sidewalk so imposingly.

I had no place to stay.

My trip to Spain had cost me the last meager residuums of a savings account and the respect of my family, whom, of course, I had told nothing of my purposes in leaving them. Besides, over the years we had come to have less to say to one another, so that my physical desertion of them—Jeri, Christopher, and Stephanie—must have seemed a rather anticlimactic *fait accompli.* Why, they must have wondered, had I taken so long to sever the final frayed thread of kinship?

Still, Jeri and I had done better than most of our acquaintances. During the last ten years nearly three-quarters of the couples we had known in the early seventies had either unamicably separated or gone through bitter divorce proceedings. By ironic contrast, our marriage had been a model union. Statistics indicated that disenchantment between man and wife had become a nationwide phenomenon, one paralleled by the increase in racial conflicts in most of the country's major cities.

Perhaps, I mused, feeling the wine uniting with my blood, Yeats's rough beast was slouching toward a Bethlehem of a peculiarly American impress. And I was afraid.

Would Jeri think that I had come to Spain, to Europe, to partake of their spirit of mellow community? I had not, I had not. For no one had seemed to deduce that we suffered in direct proportion to the Old World's steadily accumulating prosperity. The center had shifted. But one right-thinking man might manipulate the circumference of events so as to compensate for the shift. My family would benefit, my wife and my children. Therefore, I had come to Spain, where I had no place to stay, no place to shelter.

But on a subliminal level of consciousness, even while musing about the Sino-Iberian pact and my estrangement from my family, I had been formulating a solution. The solution was right before my eyes. The condemned apartment building. Yes, the condemned apartment building would house me; it would serve, it would serve me very well.

I finished my wine and left a coin that I could scarcely afford to sacrifice on the moist, grainy surface of the table. It would not be possible to enter the old building until after dark, and I had the whole afternoon ahead of me. Astonishingly, my memory of Seville's back alleys had not become pock-ridden with the long disease of time, nor had the alleys themselves much altered. I navigated them with all the skill of my seventeen-year-old self—but for one thing, that is. Now I was encumbered with a piece of luggage, a stout leather valise. It contained a change of clothes, some shaving equipment, several paperback books, and the sinister but uncomplicated paraphernalia with which I would effect Mao's assassination. The weight of the valise, its aching pull on my arm, forced me to shift it from hand to hand as I walked or to stop now and again on the fatiguingly uneven cobbles. Children stared at me. Outside a hole-in-the-wall *pescaría,* from which the smell of frying fish floated on hot gusts, a swarthy little girl briefly looked me over and then showed me the mottled pink tip of her tongue: a tiny contemptuous snake. Immediately she was gone. With the fragrance of fried octopus (*calamares,* the Spanish had called them) haunting my leave-taking, I followed the shadow of her shadow down the long canyon of the *barrio.*

Almost at once I was on the Way of the Serpents.

The feeling of déjà vu that I experienced then probably had its foundation in the simple fact that the street had been frequently in my dreams during these last thirty years. Yes, I had been on the street before; but never had I been on it when it teemed with so heterogeneous a population of human beings, even though—strangely—I felt that I had. The people who streamed about me might have constituted one shambling amorphous company of fashion models, each model flaunting, or casually presenting, or merely moving in, the costume of a different nationality, so that the shadows in the street rippled with so many undercurrents of color and foliage that I believed myself a hunter in a tropical jungle rather than a pedestrian on the Calle de Sierpes. Granted, working Spaniards comprised the largest number of these people, but the abnormal incidence of other foreigners could hardly be attributed to *Semana Santa* alone. However, at the moment, that was my conclusion. I could reach no other. Dizzied by the reeling procession, I shifted my sight from sarongs to muu-muus, from kilts to kimonos, from pyjamas to jodhpurs, from fezes and berets and bowlers . . . to slickly gleaming tricornered hats.

These last belonged to members of the Guardia Civil.

A pair of state soldiers strolled toward me against the lesser flow of traffic, both young of face and vigorous; both, to my surprise, neither gripping nor wearing any sort of weapon. Although unarmed, these men made me nervous. With moist hands I caught up my valise and held it in front of me, a conspicuous shield, until, not seeing me at all, they had passed and fused with the costumed throng.

I had forgotten about the guardsmen. They were perhaps the most telling obstacle to the sure completion of my plans. But my near meeting with two of the Guard's members snapped my mind to attention. I had come to the Way of the Serpents for a reason, a reason connected with the Guard. Consequently, I ignored the thoroughfare's distractions of color and movement in order to find the sightless, stationary man who would enable me to thwart La Guardia.

I found the man I was looking for: the blind man who sold lottery tickets from the doorway of one of the street's many shops.

He was a lean man of middle age, with a square forehead and tall graying temples. He wore his hair in a backward-combed flattop which, in combination with the exaggeratedly erect posture that his blindness apparently demanded, gave him the look of either a stern military man or a genial Frankenstein monster. His head scarcely moved. When I touched his arm, his yellow-tinted sunglasses cut not a fracture of an inch toward the pressure. The white tip of his cane, rigid as the staff of a caduceus, remained fixed on the same damp spot of sidewalk. Nothing in the man flinched.

In English I said: "I want to talk to you."

"Quién es?" he said behind his motionless lenses.

In English I said: "Someone who wants to talk to you."

He tilted his head back a very, very little and pursed his lips as if savoring a taste he had almost forgotten. But something in his unmoving attitude indicated that his tongue might at any moment come awake to that old experience. I waited. The hum and scuffle of the street made me put my face a breath away from his in order to hear.

"An Englishman?"

"No," I said. "An American."

The hard yellow glasses turned toward me, coruscating like mirrors. I felt that the eyes behind the lenses had momentarily regained their sight. Then the blind man's face revolved back to its original set.

"Do you wish to purchase a lottery ticket?"

"I want to talk to you."

"You are the first American who has spoken to me since the bases were removed." His brow contracted; the yellow glasses rose in response. *"Más que doce años."*

"What?"

"More than twelve years it has been. How goes the world in *los Estados?* Has your government finished the walls?"

That set me back. Then I remembered. He referred to the nearly three-hundred-mile-long barricade that had stretched from the northeasternmost extremity of New Hampshire across Vermont to the Saint Lawrence Seaway in upper New York: the Canadian Wall. In the mid-1970s the residents of these three New England states had begun to agitate for a closed-door policy when a heavy influx of French-Canadian youths flooded their cities and hamlets preaching the gospel of Continental Reunionism. (Almost self-mockingly laconic, the citizens of Maine had accepted this unique foreign incursion as if it were no more unusual than a clambake.) Erected by a strange hysteria, the "walls" began to go up—at first, nothing but intermittent sections of chicken wire and old lumber possessing not even the continuity of a tune played on a jew's harp. But eventually the sections began to connect, and the three state governments replaced the chicken wire with stone.

When the two Germanies reunified in 1983, the Canadian Prime Minister suggested that it was time for American contractors to place bids on the fallen Berlin barricade; after all, these bricks, these pieces of rubble, would make a neatly symbolic contribution to our own structure. For most Americans, the Prime Minister's angry radio speech marked their first knowledge of the collapse of the wall in Berlin. The knowledge shamed us. The hysteria subsided. We let the Canadian Wall crumble of its own accord—although this news had apparently not reached the ears of Europeans like my blind friend.

"There's no longer a need for the walls," I said. "The countries that border us respect our territorial integrity."

Reminiscently, the blind man nodded.

"I want to talk to you," I said again. "Not here."

"Buy me a drink, *Americano*. Anisette would be very good."

"I don't have enough money," I said, embarrassed. Then I tried to explain: "It's true. I spent most of my money getting here."

The yellow lenses glinted. "Oh, I believe it's true," he said. "That is not a difficult thing to believe now." He touched my coat sleeve. "I will buy *you* a drink. *Venga!*"

He stepped into the crowd. I also entered the torrent of voices and feet. We walked up the Way of the Serpents until the white tip of his cane, like a divining rod, led him to the entrance of a nameless establishment. We went inside. The darkness of the place required some visual adjustment, but the blind man sought out a table without even pausing to determine if it might be occupied. His tapping cane guided me to the same table.

Seated before a smoky plate-glass window, I looked around and saw that we were in a combination billiard-parlor-and-bar. My pulse quickened.

The blind man ordered two anisettes. When they came, he took a careful sip and raised his yellow sunglasses so that they rested on his forehead. His irises had no color whatsoever, and his pupils looked like exploded drops of ink.

"What do you wish to talk?"

Now that the man sat across from me, intimate and cooperative, I did not know how to broach my purpose. In fact, I could not talk about my purpose at all. What I wanted to know would have to be pulled from the blind man by indirection and finesse, like a magician deftly removing a victim's shirt and disencumbering him of it through the sleeve of his sports coat. Maybe not quite that difficult, for the blind man appeared talkative enough, but I would have to be careful. As the anisette coated my throat with a licorice warmth, the blind man waited.

"I want to know if you always sell your tickets from the doorway where I found you today." *Very little indirection there; almost no finesse.*

"Why?"

His question gave the liqueur I was sipping an unexpected sting. I put my glass down. "So that I can find you again if I need to."

"*Sí*," the blind man said. "What for?"

"To buy lottery tickets. When I have the money."

"No," he said. "A sickly reason. You wanted to talk to me, you did not want tickets."

I sipped my drink, the ancient smell of the felt billiard tables hovering over us. "Listen," I said, leaning forward. "I came to Spain to see the Chinese leader and your own Generalissimo in company together. America plays me false; nothing happens there anymore. If I can see these men—these two distinctly different statesmen—on the Calle de Sierpes, I intend to applaud them publicly and denounce my government for its isolationism. On my flight from Lisbon I heard that the street will be cordoned when the Generalissimo initiates the tour. The rumor I heard suggests that only the businessmen on the Way of the Serpents will be permitted to remain between the cordons. I believe you are one of these?"

"Yes," he said. "A merchant without a shop."

"I want to stand beside you on the day they come through. I want to stand at your elbow as would a helpful relative."

"I need no help. Nor are you a relative."

"But if you had been ill, it would be reasonable that you should wish someone at your side in case you began to feel faint. The authorities would not question a relative at your side under such circumstances."

"Why ought I to pretend that I have been ill?"

"So that I can make my declaration to Chairman Mao and the Generalissimo, to prove to them that the New World is not made up entirely of idiots. If you care at all about International Reunionism, you must abet me."

I took no delight in these fabrications; they were clumsy and nonsensical, but the necessity of gaining an ally outweighed my disgust at deceiving the blind ticket-seller. Worse would follow. The alliance (as I had no way of knowing while we talked) would become a sordid usurpation of his identity.

"I could do what you ask," he said. "It would not be difficult."

"Will you do it? You hold the key."

The blind man pushed his sunglasses back into place, a courtesy for which I was grateful. Slowly, he said: "For the reasons you give me, I will do it. The reasons are mad ones, but we have always been a people susceptible to the charm of madmen. The great Don Quixote is my personal patron saint, *Americano*."

"Good," I said. "Good." I relaxed a little and began to enjoy my drink. "What day will the dignitaries tour your street?"

"*Viernes*," he said. "The day that follows tomorrow. Friday."

"That gives you very little time to feign illness."

"For you I will miss working tomorrow. One day will be sufficient. Because I have no family in Seville, no one will be surprised that my *relative* has an unfamiliar face." He laughed. "Do you resemble me at all, friend?" His laughter was deep, coarse.

"I don't think so. Not very much."

"Not important," he said. "At this time of year everyone is every other one's brother. There is great reconciliation."

"Of course," I said. "*Semana Santa* and the *Feria*."

"And the election this year, *señor*. The election that will be held at the completion of these festivities."

I had heard absolutely nothing about an election. As I have said, news did not flow freely between the European continent and the United States. I put my glass, empty, on the table. "What election?" I asked. "What sort of election in Spain?"

"To determine if the Generalissimo should remain in power or step down in favor of a successor voted upon by the people. The ballot is open to anyone who registers his name before the end of the *Feria*. Already there are a hundred names on the ballot, and the Generalissimo promises to give way to any candidate who achieves a plurality. He promises to give way for the purpose of a runoff in the event he does not earn fifty percent of the people's support. It is a democratic celebration in the honor of the Generalissimo's one hundredth birthday. Why, even Juan Carlos must run if he hopes to succeed to rulership! Spain has never experienced such a thing."

"No," I said. "I realize that." In 1962, I remembered, I had talked to a man, a simple laborer, who had come into the bar beneath our apartment; with him was his three-year-old son. The man had made a prediction. *"This boy,"* he said, touching his son's tousled hair, *"will be the president of Spain one day—if we have a president."*

"There is great reconciliation," the blind man went on. "The renowned Picasso has made public his intention to return to Spain for this election, and the Generalissimo has extended the artist his personal assurance that he may return in safety. The people rejoice."

"I thought Picasso had died."

"Not so. He has nearly one hundred eleven years, certainly—but it may be that in his new incarnation he will never die. *La muerte no es tan poderosa.*"

"What 'incarnation'? What are you talking about?"

"Another drink!" the blind man called. The waiter came and poured two more thick dollops of anisette into our glasses. When he had gone, the ticket-seller told me the story of Picasso's new incarnation, the first of two bizarre tales that I was to hear in a thirty-hour period. Somehow the smoky warmth of the liqueur made the account palatable, and I did not question very much of what the blind man said.

On the verge of death, the artist had lain semiconscious in his home in France. Europe had prepared to mourn. ("This all took place," the blind man said, "about seven years ago, perhaps eight.") When all hope appeared gone, an emissary from Peking—where, so far as I knew, they had always thought abstractionism decadent—arrived and gained a bedside audience with the dying Picasso. That same evening a number of indefatigable hangers-on and tourists saw a flag-draped bier emerge from the artist's home, accompanied by the Chinese emissary and his silent henchmen. Rumors flew. The Master had perished; had asked for burial in the People's Republic; had been borne away by efficient representatives of something called the Resurrection Guard. Nearly all the rumors were without foundation. For the Chinese government had made a highly confidential arrangement with a surgeon of cybernetics at a large hospital in the southwestern portion of the United States; their officials, in fact, had obtained grudging permission to fly the artist to these facilities, and at a bleak cold hour before dawn their hulking jet had arrived in this great southwestern city.

"What *southwestern* city?" I asked, irritated. He had

used the word twice, both times with a kind of mocking emphasis.

"Dallas. Where your young president was killed."

In Dallas, the surgeon in whom the Chinese had placed an inordinate trust began to earn it. Working without rest or food for thirteen consecutive hours, he directed his five-man team through the ticklishly minute details of the transfer procedure. At the end of that time Picasso existed—nay, *lived*—in the platinum turret of a wonderfully animate computer system. He saw, heard, smelled, tasted, felt. Moreover, he had the ability to move of his own volition and to attend to his own needs more capably than most athletic young men. Inside the platinum turret, his brain, like an embryo in the womb, floated in an electrotonic gelatin under the conditions of near-vacuum. The wine of oxygen rose to his brain from the supply of circulating plasma maintained in the computer system's plastic torso. Beautiful, this contrivance, beautiful. The only thing denied the Master, the blind man told me, was the questionable blessing of speech.

"Speech!" he said contemptuously. "Who would miss it? Certainly not he! Other means of expression Picasso has." The blind man laughed. "Why, he is more fortunate than I!"

"But his art? How did he resolve to give it up in this way? Wouldn't he have preferred death?"

"He gave up nothing, for the surgeon gave him the most fantastic—how do you say it?—*prosthetic* hands, hands such as artists are not born with: strong, delicate, nimble. Fantastic hands!"

"Then he's still capable of working?"

"Prodigies come from his easel, miracles blossom at the tips of his fingers! Three years ago he did a mural larger than his famous *Guernica,* but this time in primary colors—a mural which is meant to be the antithesis of that earlier one. *Americano,* it is as if Brueghel had returned as a neocubist and painted the new millennium with his drunken life's blood. Our papers ran full-color reproductions of this masterpiece, and now Picasso himself is coming back to us."

"Seeing? Hearing? Experiencing all his senses, even though he no longer has the necessary organs?"

"He has the brain, which is the seat of sensation. And his doctor made him rich in experience through the clever interlinking of the many, many nerve cells."

"Meanwhile," I said, "the surgeon made himself rich in money. And no one in America ever knew that anything had happened."

Laughing, the blind man said: "Yes, yes. The Chinese paid your doctor much money, no doubt, and then returned Picasso to his home in France. We suppose that their motive was goodwill, perhaps the payment of a kind of debt." Again, the coarse laugh.

I shoved my chair away from the table, but did not get up. Dust motes swam in the cognaclike dimness of the billiard parlor; and I had the upside-down notion that the room, in its dark sentience, desired *to get out from around me*—not for me to leave, understand, but for the room to displace itself somewhere that I was not. Nonsense, I freely confess; but I was both angry and a little drunk. Across the table, turning his yellow sunglasses on me like tracking discs, the ticket-seller somehow read my mind. I gave him no opportunity to question.

"Thanks for the drinks. I'm going on a tour of my own. When your working day is over, I'll be back for you. You can spend this evening and tomorrow at my apartment on Leoncillos."

"I have a place to stay," he protested.

"I'll be back for you," I said. "At six o'clock."

With that, I left the bar and reentered the blinding shadows on the Way of the Serpents. All afternoon I walked the city. Lugging my valise from one plaza to another, I killed the hottest hours of the day. With the anisette as a propellent I climbed the switchbacking ramps inside the tower of Seville's lofty cathedral. My legs ached. I came down and strolled beside the Guadalquivir River. I walked by the bullring. Early in the evening I found a low-ceilinged bar in the vicinity of the Hotel Cristina and sat down on a bench out of view of the barman. The marbled, pink carcasses of hams hung from the low rafters, as did cheeses and garlic strings. It was like resting in a pungent crypt. At six o'clock I returned to the Calle de Sierpes and the blind seller of lottery tickets.

"Come with me," I said.

"It's too early to leave, *Americano,* too soon to retreat."

"You're not feeling well," I said. "Come on."

"First, something to eat," he said. "Then I'll go with you gladly enough. I buy, of course."

We ate fish and salad and drank beer at a sidewalk table as the streets grew gradually darker and the sky filled up with needlepoints of light. Then, gripping his elbow, I led the blind man through the alleyways to Leoncillos.

In the evening chill we found the foyer of my old apartment building and entered it like two thieves, for no one had gone to bed yet and people milled about restlessly in the cul-de-sac of the square. Transistor radios reverberated with a music that sounded like an endless succession of polkas; no one seemed to mind either the music's tastelessness or its overweening volume. Inside the foyer, our voices echoed. I tore several boards away from the iron gate and saw that it would not be too difficult to get past it to the pitchy stairwell. The gate's latch was broken, rusted inside its iron sheath.

"Qué va?" the blind man said. "What sort of building do you live in?"

"A very old one." I took his arm and led him through the heavy gate, now groaning inward on its hinges. The blind man moved reluctantly and tensed against the sound and smell of the building. "There are some steps here," I said. "We're going up three flights to the top."

His face tightened. Enough light fell through the stairwell for me to see the pale green prominence of his cheekbones and the moist hollow under his bottom lip. His feet shuffled through the debris of some fallen tiles; the toes of his shoes stopped at the base of the first step. I stood poised over him on that first step; the arm I held was raised toward me somewhat defensively, like the arm behind a shield.

"Who are you?" he asked suddenly. "Who are you?"

"We're going to the roof. There are beds in the laundry shack up there. Beds and blankets. It'll be cold in one of the apartments. The heat's off and the floors are like stone."

The acrid odor of animal waste came down the stairwell on a chill gust of wind. The building stank; it moaned disconcertingly. The blind man turned his head toward the street, toward the concert of surrealistic polkas that oompah-pahed from countless transistors. The color of thin milk, his face flowed into the set of its controlling emotion: fear. He feared me, he feared me beyond anything else in the entire liberated hemisphere. I had not sought that reaction.

Hysterically, he began to shout in Spanish. *"Ayúdame!"* he called. *"Ayúdame!"*

I swung my valise awkwardly, striking him under the chin. He fell backward into the wall and slipped into a clattering heap of tiles. His glasses twirled away. Struggling to rise, he continued to call out in Spanish. He held his exploded eyes fixedly on my face and called out like an infantry sergeant. I struck him several more times with the valise until he had ceased calling and the street's incessant beer-hall music threatened to spill into my heart.

Then I leaned over the blind man's body and put my ear to his chest. Certain that he was dead, I wept. I had planned to lock him in the laundry shack until Friday, not to kill him. The sordidness of the deed made me physically ill, and I squatted beside the blind man's body trying to hold back the raw congestion in my throat. Squatting there, I wept.

Several minutes went by. I got up and rummaged through the debris on the floor until I had found the yellow sunglasses. The lenses had not been broken. I put the glasses in my inside jacket pocket.

Then, realizing that my position in the foyer was hardly an intelligent one, I managed to lift the body from the floor and balance it clumsily against my back. The arms hung over my shoulders like two ropes. Holding them, I climbed the stairs all the way to the roof. At each landing I rested, but the hard knot in my throat and the exertion of the afternoon had begun to empty me of strength. When I reached the roof, I dumped the body on the stones and coughed up a thin stream of bile. I couldn't vomit; the food I had eaten would not dislodge itself.

A number of cats were miaowing on an adjacent roof, their silhouettes prowling back and forth along the cornice.

The door on the laundry shack refused to open. I kicked it aside, then carried the dead man into the mildewed stink of the laundry cubicle. A piece of moon grinned down through the doorframe, and I saw that the bed (there had never been more than one up there) had been removed and that the concrete sink in the corner stood pooled up with a sheen of water. It would be impossible to spend the night in such a place. If I left the body there, however, no one would be likely to discover it for a while. And one of the apartments downstairs would accept me as an occupant as willingly as it accepted the rats that skittered between its cold, vacant rooms. After removing his wallet and papers, therefore, I left the blind man in the laundry shack and pulled the broken door to.

But I did not go downstairs at once. I went to the building's parapet and looked across the city toward the cathedral. Ancient, dark, remote, its tower seemed nearly as indifferent as God. I thought of my wife and of Stephanie and of Christopher James, too, who was then studying medicine at the first totally integrated university in South Africa. The fear that they would not understand my motives, not forgive my blunders, not accept the legitimacy of my gift, stilled me on that high rampart and took away my conviction. But I gripped the stone ledge until these doubts had grown as pale as my knuckles. How far away the spire was, how far away my family.

Faint music came up to me from the streets, this time the spirited flamenco of the Spanish gypsies. They were one people, at least, who had maintained their sense of identity.

A little revived by the night air, I descended the three flights of steps to the foyer and retrieved my valise. Then I climbed to the second landing, tried the door to my old apartment, and stood back as it collapsed off its hinges in a choking billow of dust. A cat, surprised in the act of hunting down vermin, streaked through the living room. Seeing the open door, it turned and sped by me up the steps.

In the settling dust the apartment was as dead as a bombed-out museum. I almost expected to meet myself— my adolescent self—emerging from the bedroom doors behind which, thirty years ago, I had kept the pitiful artifacts of my growing up: books, photographs, notebooks full of unfinished poems, a distorted self-portrait in oils, and the typewriter on which I am recording this narrative. Because no one emerged from those french doors, I went through them and frightened away two or three more four-legged shadows. Otherwise this room, too, was empty.

That night I slept in a corner of my old room. Wrapped in a torn bedsheet smelling of turpentine and resting my head on a nest of crumpled toilet paper, I slept without dreaming.

On Thursday morning I awoke with a headache and a frightening absence of memory about the previous day. Sunlight, streaming down through the unevenly spaced slats on the front window, fell on me with the weight and consistency of mucilage; it glued me to the floor. My body ached. When at last I recollected the situation, I sat up painfully and pulled my valise over the tiles toward my improvised bedclothes.

My hands wavered like a pair of ugly medusoid sea creatures. Consequently, it took me a moment or two to undo the latches. The valise opened. I saw the dried blood on the bottom lip of the case. Brown like Spanish earth, that encrustation reminded me of what I had done. Never before in my life had I killed another human being. That remorse for the man's brutal execution might negate my sense of purpose became a real possibility. Because the horror of the act had reasserted itself, I turned quickly to business.

"Let's enumerate," I said aloud.

I took items one by one out of my valise and laid them on the floor: three paperback novels, a dry-shave kit, a clean shirt, and a small package containing the last of my Spanish money, perhaps three hundred pesetas. But these were the mundane items. Under the shirt, the socks, the underwear, lay the essentials with which I would rectify three decades of misdirection and embarrassment.

These things, too, I took from my valise, and arranged on the filthy apron of the bedsheet. For the task before me it was not a particularly profound assemblage of instruments: three hollow cylinders that slipped one into another to form a convincing replica of the blind man's white-tipped cane.

A single difference existed.

Into the bottom segment of the "cane" I wedged an intricately shaped firing mechanism. If one jammed this concealed mechanism violently against another's body, the system exploded a cartridge that shattered bone and tore flesh. Of course, one could not afford to fail on the first attempt. For that reason I had selected a cartridge of savagely high caliber, a bullet for the diaspora of mankind back into its proper camps. I assembled the segments and jabbed the weapon listlessly at the tall front window where the morning sunlight tumbled in.

"Ludicrous."

Someone else, after all, ought rightly to have been doing what I—a dilettante, an academician, a failed writer—proposed to carry out the following morning on the Way of

he Serpents. Yesterday's exertions had already come to
aunt me in the flesh of my middle age; I didn't belong in
he role I had scripted for myself. Someone, however, *must*
>e the protagonist; otherwise, events go aimlessly in search
>f a power to bring them about. That the task had de-
cended to me by default disappointed and bewildered; it
>ordered on farce.

To complete the emptying of the valise, I took one final
hing out and held it contemplatively between my fingers.
A cyanide capsule. It, too, was ludicrous and seemed to
>rove how quickly farce could turn into melodrama. But
after murdering the Chairman, there would be no escape.

fully intended to use the capsule, even though the act of
>iting through its thin outer shell had a certain artistic
>aucity about it——for I would not be questioned. I would
aot be made to justify!

Slowly I disassembled the cane and put it back into my
valise.

For the rest of the morning I read one of the paperback
aovels and thought vaguely about getting something to eat.
Neither polkas nor flamencos disturbed my reading.

Now I come to one of the more improbable episodes of
his story: the conversation that I mentioned several pages
ago, and the entirely fortuitous encounter that occasioned
t. Here you must go on with me, suspending your doubly
>ffended disbelief, or else you must altogether cease to
rust this account. I refuse to apologize for a parallel time's
murderous assault on credulity, especially an assault by a
>arallel future time. At that moment in my high-ceilinged
>ld bedroom, shut off from the currents of time, I sought
apologies only from the world I knew. Momentarily iso-
ated, I had no way of preparing for my random encounter
vith Mrs. Euralinia Weik.

It happened because my conscience prodded me out of
he torn bedsheet, out of my bloodstained shirt, out of the
>laster silt of my old bedroom. Newly dressed and shaven,
climbed to the building's roof and emerged into a sky as
>ellucid as quinine water; its thin blueness hurt my eyes,
and the air stung with the chill of early spring.

I went to the laundry shack.

The broken door hung there like an upraised palm, halt-
ng me. I didn't want to flout its unequivocal DO NOT OPEN;
I didn't wish to have proof that last evening's nightmare

had come true in the light of day. But I overcame these
negative scruples and pushed the weather-ruined door inward. The beginnings of a very basic smell had begun to
taint the laundry shack's wonted atmosphere of concrete
and dirty water.

On the floor, the blind man lay just as I had left him.
But the sink had overflowed, dripping, dripping, dripping,
and a damp grayness outlined his corpse. The slow dripping
went on monotonously in the shack's far corner. I thought,
This room is a limestone grotto. And the word *grotto*
sounded in my head like a small bell, triggering a strange
association; I thought of the Spanish word for cat: *gato*.
This thought, in turn, summoned up the object itself, for
when I looked closely at the blind man's corpse, I saw that
perched on his back, as if attempting to homestead an
island, there was a black kitten with murky gold eyes. It
stared at me. It made no move to dart past me onto the
roof. Whether indolence or ignorance made it docile, I
don't know; but I picked the creature up and carried it out
of the shack thinking how hideously, how pathetically
gothic was its presence in that place. A blind man and a
cat, locked up together. The cat did not protest my cradling
it out of the darkness.

Absentmindedly, I stroked the animal and listened to its
acquiescent purr. I went to the parapet and faced the
cathedral; the cat went to sleep, purring a nearly inaudible
counterpoint to the wind. Again, I stood there transfixed by
the distant tower and all the hazy rooftops in between.

A voice said, *"Hola. Qué haces aquí, hombre?"*

I turned. "What?" A noise more than a word.

"English," the woman said, coming onto the roof. "Very
well. I merely asked what you were doing up here. Looking
at this building from the street, I didn't expect to find a
soul anywhere in it—much less on the roof appearing
affluent and pensive at once."

I looked away from the woman's face, blurring her
features—looked toward the door of the laundry shack.
The door stood partially open. My pulse began to work in
both temples. Would the smell give me away? Would I
have to protect my interests in Spain by still another act of
violence?

I let my eyes go back to the woman's face, a brown face
framed by dark hair, but still did not really see her. I said:
"Affluent, no. Not that."

Suddenly she was approaching me. Her small body moved in a knee-length leather skirt, flat shoes, and an unattractive jacket that buttoned at the collar; the skirt, the shoes, and the jacket were all gray. With a conscious effort I tried to measure and weigh the emotions in the face above these clothes. But it approached me so quickly, looking not at me but at the cat in my arms, that I could determine only that the woman had a small mouth and eyes with delicate epicanthic folds. Her hair shone like a helmet of polymer, bravely.

I stepped back.

"Oh," she said, reaching out. *"The gato es schlepping."* She stroked the animal.

"Nisei?" I said.

She turned her face up. I am not a tall man, but she had inherited the diminutive stature of Pete Taniguchi rather than the Amazonian proportions of her mother; consequently, I dwarfed her. But the upturned face now belonged to a woman well into her thirties, and its Oriental openness had suffered a closing in of small crow's-feet, of probably much larger disappointments. A brave but imperceptibly bruised face. Even then, confronted with the crisis of her being there, I took time to decide that she was not as attractive an adult as she had been a child. Her clothes didn't suit her; her face, though brave, looked altered away from the familiar.

"No one calls me that anymore," she said. "Except my parents. And they live in Germany."

"That was all I ever knew to call you."

"Who are you?"

Since she had continued to stroke the cat, I carefully shifted the animal into her arms, where, awake, it eyed me with golden indifference, and then let its lids slide shut.

I told her my name. I put my hands in my pockets and sauntered along the parapet, talking. "We lived in the apartment just below yours when your father was in the air force. My father, too. One of your favorite expressions was *'The gato es schlepping.'* I scared you nearly to death one afternoon when a seltzer bottle broke and wine went all over my clothes." At the laundry shack I turned and faced her. "Do you remember that?" Casually, I pulled the door to and remained there for a moment letting my heart run casually down.

"No," she said, 'I don't remember that. But I think I

remember you. I remember you riding me on your back on this same roof."

"Yes, that was me. A different me, but the same one."

She laughed. She nodded her head, humoring the dead adolescent. "Very profound. 'A different me, but the same one.'"

"Please don't ask me to make consistent sense, Nisei." I came back toward her. "The world confuses me nowadays, and occurrences such as this one put gray in my hair."

She tilted her head and studied me, strained to see my temples. "You've experienced this sort of thing many times, then." A pause. "Aren't you older than your father was when our families lived in this building?"

"Yes." I gave a startled laugh. "Yes, Nisei, I am."

"My name isn't Nisei anymore."

"No, I suppose not."

"And I don't want you to call me that if you can help it. As soon as I was old enough to know what it meant, I began to hate the name."

"Why?"

"Because it's not a girl's name. It's not even a boy's name—its a generic term for a child born in America of immigrant Japanese parents. It doesn't have anything to do with me, and I can't understand how my father could have given me such a name."

"Somehow it fit you when you were little. What's your name now? I'll call you by it if I can remember."

"Euralinia," she said.

"Taniguchi?"

"No, *Weik*. Euralinia Weik."

I didn't say anything.

Stroking the cat, she asked: "You're not surprised that I married, are you? Am I so unattractive?"

"No," I said. "I was thinking about your name."

"And?"

"The name is unattractive."

This comment stilled her hand on the cat's electric lamp-black fur. It put an angry but evanescent charge in her eyes. Looking into those eyes, I regretted the remark but understood, too, the rightness of my evaluation. The name was grotesque. The syllables of the first name sounded well enough, but the word they created had something wrong with it; something dissonant despite the fluid vowels. And her last name suggested the hard iron thwack of the con-

queror's sword, implacable and mocking. I felt cut down
by her eyes.

"I don't like that," she said. "It's unkind. Rude. It's the
sort of comment that doesn't have to be said aloud."

"I apologize."

"You mouth an apology, like an eel caught out of the
water."

Still holding the cat, she turned. She walked along the
parapet. She put the animal, half-asleep, on its own feet.
Then looked back at me.

"Why don't you go downstairs now—*Mike*, is it? You've
had your turn. I came up here because I hadn't seen this
old building since our families moved out. My parents
gave me the address, and when I found the gate downstairs
open, I had to come up. I didn't expect to interrupt a
reverie—but since I have, it's my turn to start one of my
own. I don't see any reason why we should both be up
here at the same time."

The cat, overcoming its sleepy surprise at being abandoned, lay down in a wide patch of sunlight and began in-
delicately to preen itself. I couldn't leave Nisei—*Euralinia
Weik*—on the roof, not while the corpse of the blind man
decomposed fleshmeal in the damp heat of the laundry
shack, an insult to justice, yes, but a mephitic menace to
my assassination plans. The woman's indignation had to be
dealt with, soothed, siphoned off.

"I agree with you," I said. "I don't see any reason why
either of us should be up here. Let me buy you something
to eat."

Turning her back on me, she gripped the handrail and
stared toward the cathedral, La Giralda. Three pigeons
dipped coolly down from the sky over an adjacent rooftop, fell between the clotheslines, and strutted in the sun
with iridescent breasts. Nisei stared at the cathedral,
watched the pigeons, totally ignored me.

"A real apology," I said. "Not an eel's involuntary
mouthings."

"I'm not hungry."

"A drink, then. Downstairs at Antonio's bar, or *whom*-
ever it belongs to now." The inflection was for levity's
sake. "Please, Mrs. Weik. Forgive me my lack of tact. The
quality seems to disappear in me whenever I have proofs
of my age."

In a moment or two she had accepted my apology, and

together we went down to what had once been Antonio's *bodega,* where we found a sidewalk table and sat down opposite each other. The small black cat stayed on the roof; Nisei—surprisingly, I thought—voiced not a single protest about our leaving it there. She obviously liked cats, but she behaved as if this one ought by rights to be exactly where it was, alone and undisturbed on the roof of a collapsing apartment building.

On the sidewalk beside that building, we drank wine and talked about our lives since our departures from Spain in 1963—although, by no design of my own, she did most of the talking, beginning almost from the summer of our departure. As she talked, I looked into my wine glass and saw the image of two golden eyes hovering in the liquid redness there. But Nisei held stage-center, and the illusion disappeared with the dregs of my wine.

"We left Spain because Papa had been reassigned to the States," Nisei said. "We were sent to Eglin Air Force Base in Florida, and I can remember that for a long time I did not truly realize that we had left Spain. We spent many days on the hot white beaches between Fort Walton and Panama City, and to my simple mind those beaches—so glittering and sea-warmed—were merely extensions of the sands that formed bright aprons around the cities of Cádiz and Torremolinos. The Mediterranean and the Gulf of Mexico were one and the same for me.

"Five years later Papa was reassigned again, this time to Lincoln, Nebraska, and things began to fall apart for us as a family. I remember seeing snow for the first time and walking home from school through the dirty slush by the curbings. Mama argued with Papa about all sorts of things from the weather, to her homesickness, to the foolishness of his job; and he argued back. Sometimes I left the house and went out into the snow to be away from their shouting. Then one day Mama told me that she and Papa had had a divorce and that just the two of us would have to love each other. That seemed to me even stranger than the fact that the beaches near Cádiz and Panama City were not on the same continent. I did not see Papa again for nearly seven years, until I had become a grown woman of nineteen and a serious university student."

"You and your mother came back to Europe?"

"Yes. We returned to Mama's home in Munich and lived with her parents until Mama could find a job of her own. In some ways, of course, Munich reminded me of Lincoln"—here Nisei giggled and whirled the wine in her glass—"but really only in that both cities slumbered in the wintertime under fat quilts of snow. I missed my father very much, and I had to work hard at recovering the German I had lost. But somehow, Mike, the snow in Munich seemed friendlier, even when seething across the streets and hissing angrily between the houses. It always seemed to sweep down over me like an unraveling sheet of gauze, white and calming."

"I get the same feeling after too many brandies," I said. A falsely jocular remark. Nisei nodded distractedly. Then I asked: "Is your father still alive? You said that you saw him again."

"Oh, yes. He and Mama remarried when I was twenty. They're living together in Munich now—although when I was little Papa used to swear that Germany was a land of barbarians and warriors and that he wouldn't dignify it by settling there. Mama told him Japan was the same way, and the United States, too. This made Papa swear; not comically, but like a person raised in the gutters on onions and sour bread. It was frightening. And he had never been to Japan in his entire life."

"But now your parents are remarried and living in Munich?"

"Yes."

"How did this miracle in human relations come about?"

"Mama's parents urged her to write 'Mr. Taniguchi' in the States and tell him the news about his daughter. Mama argued that 'Mr. Taniguchi' had not written her and that he probably hoped his daughter had gone into the streets for want of paternal guidance. But my grandparents prevailed. Mama wrote. First, she had to write the big air force base in Texas where they keep the addresses of all their American servicemen, and through these people she found out that Papa had been sent to a duty station in California. Then she wrote Papa. The two of them exchanged letters for three years, and finally he came to Munich.

"We welcomed him home—yes, *home*—on a gauze-gray day filled with streamers of snow, like the ticker tape they toss out of windows for the parades in New York. I missed my university classes, and Papa told us that he had left the air force for good, only two years away from his pension.

Less than two years away from his pension, in fact. We laughed. Then we wept. We wept together like a family."

"Probably because he had forfeited his pension."

"Oh, no," Nisei said, but she acknowledged this second forced witticism by raising her glass and clinking it against my own. "We wept because we were so happy together, together again. The marriage came so much later only because Papa would not establish a home until he had a secure position. He became the executive foreman of one of the biggest automobile service-centers in Munich. Mama and I taught him the language."

"A garage mechanic," I said. "Glorified, of course."

"Yes, a garage mechanic." She blinked. "Then a foreman."

This aspect of her narrative irritated me; it shared a covert but very real common denominator with the turnabout in European history, a turnabout that dated from the early seventies. I tried to make my voice the instrument of a new seriousness: "Your father left the service with less than two years remaining, Nisei. That was irresponsible. He might have been drawing a comfortable allotment right up to the present day had he simply thought for a moment. He wouldn't've had to worry about becoming an 'executive foreman.' Don't you see, Nisei?"

"A man can die in two years' time."

"I realize that," I said. "I realize that."

"And my name isn't Nisei anymore."

"No. You're a grown-up girl and you're married. I'm sorry. I'm sorry, *Mrs. Euralinia Weik.*"

On the dusty sidewalk, no longer able to maintain any sort of composed veneer (either haughty or schoolgirlish), sitting there in full view of a hundred pedestrians, Nisei broke down and cried. At the moment I believed my inadvertent boorishness to be the cause of her tears, and I tried to calm her by leaning forward and apologizing again and again. But she shook her head, indicating that the fault wasn't mine. She shook her head and wept as if to stop would be to still her heart.

I sat back stiffly in my chair. The barman came from behind his counter to the open doorway and looked at us. So did the table-sitters around us. When Nisei at last managed to control her convulsing shoulders, the barman returned to his den of warm sawdust and soap-filmed glassware.

"I'm sorry, too," Nisei said, wiping her eyes.

"You did get married, didn't you? You're not still a Taniguchi."

"Yes," she told me. "But my husband is dead. My husband's dead, and I can't . . . I can't make myself accept . . ." She broke off, but her voice dovetailed into a feeble sob, avoiding the inarticulate shrillness of her former weeping. The barman stayed behind his counter.

"Oh, Nisei."

She looked me straight in the eyes, her eyes filled with a defiant lambency, her jaw set. "But what makes it worse— what makes it a thousand times worse—is that he *isn't* dead. He's dead, Mike, but he isn't. His walking about is the terrible thing, the thing I can't accept, knowing that he's dead. Knowing that he's . . ."

Again, the slow rhythmic sobbing that forced her face into her hands.

I had to wait. I waited five minutes. Ten. Occasionally I spoke to her under my breath, mouthing the ritualistic hurt-softeners that have no meaning outside of their audible proof that someone is near. We drank no more wine, but I bought a bottle and had it brought to the table as an excuse to remain where we were.

The story of Nisei's marriage and its wholly fantastic aftermath came out haltingly over the period of the next two hours. Nisei spoke in a voiced whisper, and I ignored the high passing of the sun, even though the sidewalk had no shade and the early afternoon had lost its coolness.

In the university at Munich (her story went), she had majored in languages. By the age of twenty-three she could speak fluent German, Spanish, English, French, Italian, and Russian. She was conversant with the classical languages and had enough of several Slavic tongues to be able to read them with good understanding. As easily as leaves come to a tree, words came to her lips and budded in patterns of beautiful coherence. No one, it seemed, stood outside her ability to communicate. In the snows of Munich she planted the tender green shoots of language and watched them grow out of that whiteness into myriad interlocking vines.

As something of a prodigy, she moved into the arena of communicating her skills, and her perhaps incommunicable deftness, to others. She was not a teacher, but others

sought her out. The experience frightened Nisei, and she
backed away from many of these people—particularly the
young Oriental men who expected her to speak with them
in Japanese, or Amoy, or Korean, and who invariably concluded by berating her, always in the mildest and most
humorous of terms, for neglecting the linguistic heritage
of her father (who himself, as they had no way of knowing,
had long since forgotten the tongue of *his* fathers). These
young men, bright as scrubbed copper, represented the
vanguard of a continuing influx of Eastern exchange students; sometimes it seemed that their earnest faces had
usurped every study nook, classroom, and seminar discussion in the university. An uneasiness took possession of
Nisei. Although these copper faces crowded upon her with
the message of something left incomplete, she refused to
acknowledge the incompleteness. In hallways and empty
lecture rooms she declined supper dates from these young
men and clotured, unilaterally, their attempts to drill her
in the rudiments of Mandarin. She would not learn from
them. And it did not take them long to give her the distance she seemed to want, leaving her to all the fawning
and incestuous scions of the Indo-European persuasion.
She would not cultivate the exotic shoots of the East, and
Munich's snow during this winter began to dinge—so that
it reminded her of another time, another place.

Then she met Theodor Weik.

At thirty, Theodor Weik came into the university system
with a startlingly consummate command of the Sino-Tibetan languages. He resembled, Nisei told me, the tall
ascetic-looking actor, blond and gaunt, who had worked
in so many of Ingmar Bergman's films. But Theodor Weik
had spent the major portion of his life not in the cold
northern reaches of Scandinavia, but rather in the teeming
British colony of Hong Kong, where his father had worked
as an international correspondent. (Of course, the British
had long since departed—those British in administrative
positions, that is; but many remained in the city, in sharply
diminished roles, for sheer love of their obstreperous port.)
As a boy little more than twelve, Weik had learned all the
major dialects of China and more than a scantling of
Vietnamese. This last he had learned, surprisingly enough,
from the American soldiers who had been sent to Southeast
Asia by their government, but who came on leave to Hong
Kong by personal choice. His father knew many of these

men, and young Theo digested the crudely imparted fragments of vocabulary and grammar they had to offer and
combined these into a mosaic of intuitive symmetry.

His talent with the Sino-Tibetan languages was commensurate with Nisei's understanding of the European
tongues. When they met at the university in Munich, it
was as if each one had found his tally, the opposite but
complementary half of one's being that Plato permits
Aristophanes to speak of in the *Symposium:* the pursuit of
the whole which he, Aristophanes, termed Love.

"After we had married," Nisei said, "we spoke in just
this way about our coming together and laughed at the
seeming absurdity of it. But, on a subsurface level, I don't
believe we thought it so ridiculous an analogy. For, although we were completely different, we found each other
and married—just as the Greek playwright explains the
comical process in Plato's dialogue."

For three more years the Weiks remained in Munich; for
Theo had become one of the young lions of the language
faculty, a lion with velvet manners and the intense, recon-
ciliatory instincts of a woman. Many of the Oriental young
men whom Nisei had rebuffed, he invited to their home. In
a small upstairs apartment furnished more after his tastes
than hers, they sat on the floor, the Weiks and their guests,
and talked long into the night; they talked, in fact, in the
dialects she had once fled from. Out of necessity, Nisei
heeded the strange cadences, the emphatic vowels, the
changes in pitch. Laughter punctuated their discussions of
politics and literature and the new science, and she moved
easily through her own laughter toward the languages that
were the vehicles of their gentle hilarity.

Things fell into place; the center of her life expanded,
from a point to a circle, from a circle to a solid sphere.

Then Theo talked with her about his goals and decided
that the time had come to change directions. With strong
recommendations from the senior members of his department and from a Chinese diplomat whose son had been
under his tutelage, Theodor Weik went to the ambassa-
dorial secretariat of Reunified Germany. He asked for a
position in the Far East. The staff of the secretariat inter-
viewed, tested, cross-examined him. In less than a month's
time they had approved his application and had assigned
him as a "diplomat apprentice" to the German consulate

in Peking. Nisei and he left Munich in the summer of 1986, of one ambitious mind to confront and encompass the ongoing revolution of their time.

"He achieved everything he wished," Nisei said. "Always."

Mesmerized by her own story, she held her hands folded on the table. A slanting of shade cut across her head and hands. Despite the fact that I was sweating in the one remaining triangle of sunlight on the walk, I did not interrupt her.

"Always," Nisei continued. "In a year's time he had met and conversed with all the leaders of the Communality, including the Chairman himself. The Chairman developed a mentorlike fondness for Theo. Toward me he behaved like a father who had once deserted his children but who now hoped to rectify things by all sorts of silly attentions. I could not imagine him working as a librarian, as he had once done, or organizing a peasant army, or penning the sententious little sayings that sound as if they were written by a middle-class Machiavelli. He joked with us. He teased. He was very nice. Almost twice a month we ate with him privately, with him and his third wife. Theo challenged him with an an Occidental mind that had transcended its origins, and it also pleased Mao to tease me about marrying a blond neocapitalist. Sometimes our conversations wearied him and forced him to retire before he would have liked, but he continued to invite us. Soon he would talk to no one in the German diplomatic corps but Theo.

"Like a Shansi version of the Cheshire cat, he grinned at other emissaries but faded into silence when they approached him. It was amazing, the access to his person that he granted us. No one could believe it, and just before our third full year was over, one of the German 'elder statesmen' returned to Berlin for good and Theo was immediately appointed to succeed him.

" 'Nisei,' he told me, 'now I can pull down the walls.' "

I laughed. "He called you Nisei, too, then?"

"Oh, yes." She echoed my laugh and unfolded her hands. "I never minded the way it sounded when Theo said it."

But we were getting near the end of her story, and Nisei abruptly stopped smiling. With her forefinger she drew interlocking circles in the dampness on the tabletop. I waited—waited a minute—waited two minutes—waited until her finger spiraled to a standstill and her head came back up.

"Last year," she said, swallowing, "last year a disease—a growth—a viral cancer struck Theo and grew through his brain like a weed sending roots into a clump of moss. It gave no indication of its presence except a slight recurring headache that Theo ignored; in fact, he didn't even tell me about the headaches until they had been going on for three or four weeks, and then we put off determining their cause for still another three or four weeks. Theo was too busy . . . pulling the walls down.

"Even though the diseased cells had not spread through his bloodstream to other parts of his body, the localized cancer was enough. He would die. All they could do was irradiate the surface tissues of his brain, slow the malignancy a little, prolong his life a small nasty bit, and ultimately . . . inevitably . . . let the cancer grow into the unaffected tissues outside the brain." She stopped for a moment. "He was going to . . . going to die. All very clinical, all very final—despite what they claim they can do now."

What they could do was quite a lot; not, by any means, what Nisei would have desired, but quite a lot.

The Chairman, though himself in a weakened and febrile state, took a personal interest. He installed Theodor Weik in a red-draped hospital room and visited the stricken man in a prim avuncular way that excluded, for long stretches, even Nisei herself. The two men conferred. Ill but spirited, they shared the community of their diseases and of their dreams. At last Nisei heard of their jointly formulated plan, the product of these colloquies; and her husband, adamant in his decision, argued with her the better part of a night until two white-frocked attendants came barging through the door in response to her hysteria and denied Nisei her supposedly unrestricted visiting privileges. The voluted draperies moved eerily, she noted, as they forced her from her husband's bedside. Her eyes were full of acid.

The plan itself she felt was inhumane, unnatural. Granted, the plan involved trust and sacrifice—but the sacrifice would be Theo's, while the trust, if he could muster it, would belong to the apprehensive but undaunted Chairman. Nisei stood alone on the periphery, forgotten.

On the night after her expulsion from her husband's

room, a great gleaming aircraft, lights coldly atwinkle, landed on the longest runway at the airfield outside Peking. A convoy escorted the deplaning passengers into the city. These passengers were a surgeon of cybernetics, of undeservedly small renown and five highly trained specialists with whom he had long since established an uncanny rapport. They arrived at the hospital at a bleak, cold hour just after midnight. In a circular amphitheater located two floors below ground level, they discovered a facility to rival the one they had left: an operating room lit as if by klieg lights, and instruments of poignant stainless steel.

"They had decided to effect the transfer," Nisei said slowly, "before Theo's cancer invaded some other part of his body . . . before it made his . . . his *corpse* . . . uninhabitable. Since he was doomed to die no matter what he chose, that would have been a shameful waste, a sin against the people. And Theo—Theo, God forgive him—agreed."

Her voice was no longer hers; it rose huskily on an undercurrent of remembrance.

"I don't know how long they took, how long they cut and probed and stitched and played witch-doctor gods, but Theo didn't let me see him again as himself, didn't give me a moment to lie next to him before the knife came down.

"When he awoke, he didn't awake. His eyes opened with somebody else behind them; and his brain, all cancer-ridden and horribly aware, they killed with electricity and incinerated in a stainless-steel cylinder. Theo had become a nearly one-hundred-year-old man. His eyes didn't belong to him anymore, and he had forsaken me—forsaken me by leaving in his stead a brutal doppelgänger who will never, no matter how pitifully I beg him, never forsake me.

"Oh, God," she said. "My dear God."

"Are you telling me that your husband walks about only because his mind has been usurped by the Chairman's intelligence?"

To herself she said, "My dear God," and fell silent, the noise of her grief and incredulity no more audible than the purring of a kitten. Again, I gave her a minute or two.

"Has he attempted to take your husband's place?"

The question made a slow assault on her understanding. She lifted her head. "No," she said. "No, he hasn't."

"But the Chinese must see such an operation as a traitorous perversion of their identity. Do they know of it? Do they accept it?"

"Expedient. The Chairman admits that it was an expediency—also the supreme gesture of goodwill toward the West. Deliberately assuming the body of a Nordic." With some bitterness she said: "He doesn't touch me, I couldn't stand . . . couldn't tolerate . . . so he never touches me. But he is solicitous, always solicitous, and it's so damnably eerie, so frighteningly cruel."

"Won't he let you go home to Munich?"

"I've been home briefly. I came to Seville because I wanted to. I had to see where it had all started."

"Just to see this old building? Is that what you mean?"

"No. Not just to see this old building."

"What else, then?"

Abruptly she pushed her chair back and stood up, a gray Oriental woman with whom I shared nothing in common. Heads at other tables turned toward us. She lifted the blue-black curtain of hair against her left cheek with a quick hand and let it drop behind her shoulder. Exposed fully in the noonday glare, her face in no way resembled that of the little girl who had screamed in the stairwell. She said, "I have to go."

"Where? Are you staying with your husband?"

"My husband's dead!" she shouted, and began to move away.

"With the Chairman, I meant." Trying to get up, I knocked the wine bottle over. "Nisei, I'm sorry. I meant, with the Chairman." In front of so many unabashed onlookers, I felt naked. The beginnings of a migraine unbalanced me; I swayed. I set the wine bottle back on the table, still half-full.

"The *Chairman* is in Madrid today," she said. "When he arrives here tomorrow, I'll meet him. Just meet him. That's all." She was now in the thoroughfare, facing me across the cobbles. I had turned 180 degrees to follow her angry retreat. "That's all!" she shouted.

"Nisei!"

"Don't call me that!" She waved her arm. "That old building," she waved her arm again, "isn't my building. Goodbye, Mike. Go back to where you belong. Go back."

A small automobile went by her. Two men in the bar across the street exchanged what sounded like either threats or obscenities. But Nisei simply turned her back on me and walked until the battered side of a bus advertising a Spanish cognac interposed itself and caused me to lose sight of her among the faded blue shirts of several pedestrians. Then, undoubtedly, she was gone from the dirty plaza—and I could do nothing but stare at the façade of a rundown drugstore and look at the movie posters pasted on the bricks.

I sat back down, the center of some unasked-for attention, and poured from the bottle of wine. Everything but the wine and the task before me, I ignored. First, the blind man's story of Picasso's new incarnation; now, this account of the Chairman's relocation of intelligence in the body of a Caucasian. Both stories were troubling—intensely so now that the blind man lay dead in the laundry shack and Nisei had disappeared like a wintry apparition back into her own place in time. I could question neither the blind man nor the woman any further; they had been taken from me, driven from me. Nevertheless, all I really wanted was a more detailed description of what the Chairman now looked like. He looked like Nisei's dead husband; yes, like an actor who had once worked in the pearl-bright films of Bergman.

I wished I had asked Nisei if she had a photograph.

For in the morning, I would strike down the venerable Chairman of the Communality, no matter in whose borrowed flesh he continued to walk about. I had come too far —we had all come too far—to be denied retribution by this grotesque duplicity of skins, this hideous doffing and dooming of another's bones. It didn't matter. I would kill Nisei's husband again, if that was what was required.

I went back into the building.

In my old room I settled down for the heat of the day. For a time I slept; for an hour or so I read. When the room began to grow dim and murky with evening dust motes, I dared to tear down three or four of the rotten slats that covered my casement window. This made an inevitable cracking noise—alarmingly acute to me—but the transistor radios had begun playing again and the people on the sidewalk at Antonio's *bodega* were engaged in animated debate. No one looked up.

By the thin light from the window, I assembled the parts of my cane and inserted the concealed firing mechanism that would end the Chairman's second go-round at youth and power.

I rumpled my suit. I put on the blind man's yellow sunglasses. I walked around the rubble-strewn floor practicing the smooth halt-and-hitch of the blind man's walk. When the light had almost gone (attenuated nearly to extinction behind the yellow lenses), I stopped and checked my pockets. Inside my jacket I found the blind man's identification papers. These I unfolded, squinted at, folded again, and replaced in the pocket next to my heart.

The last thing I found was the capsule of cyanide. In the dark, shining with a hairline plastic scar, it seemed even more ludicrous than it had that morning. My heart did timpani rolls, muffled beatings. My hands began to sweat.

As near to midnight as I could gauge, I left the apartment, descended the stairs, and struck out haltingly toward the Street of Serpents. I wore my glasses. Even when night falls, a blind man's sight does not return, and so I emulated the reality. Few people were about, the alleys were ill-lit, and at every uncertain step I fought the urge to abandon my role and heed Nisei's advice to go back where I belonged. But my other senses asserted themselves as if I were indeed blind, and reaffirmed in me my commitment to go through to the end: the cold bricks under my fingers, the smells of baking bread and stale laundry, the cries from the courtyard tenements, the taste of my own saliva. By these signs I knew where I belonged, where I was going.

At the foot of the Calle de Sierpes, preparations for the morning's tour had already begun. Men in uniform, members of La Guardia, moved about like olive-drab specters; they directed the workmen who were setting up sawhorses and tying off every entrance to the street with ropes of plush red velvet. The street itself, except for the presence of an occasional guardsman, lay before me as inviolate as new snow, a broad, vacant swath stretching toward the distant avenues where motorized traffic was permitted.

The moon hung in the sky like a candled egg, lopsided and warm.

Voices echoed in the empty street; and, hollow of will, I approached the first barricade, tapping my cane, regretting my poor command of the language. No one questioned me until I had gone past a pair of ropeless sawhorses into one of the pools of light that shimmered on the street.

"Alto!" A man's face bloomed in front of me like a giant rose with sagging petals.

Through my glasses I could tell only that the man was angry, that his jowls labored flaccidly under the weight of the admonition he was giving me. His hands gripped my shoulders. Another man came up beside him. This second man I had time to scrutinize, and I could see that he was a young officer with considerably more poise than his comrade. I tried to keep my head still, my eyes steady, my posture expectant. The young officer engaged the rose-faced man in a brief discussion, and then turned to me.

"*Señor. Cómo se llama?*"

A challenge. But in some ways my confrontation with the guardsmen was the finest self-acquittal I managed in that seventy-two-hour period. I gave them the blind man's name and rummaged inside my jacket for his papers. The angry man checked my name against a list of the shopkeepers on the Calle de Sierpes, while the young officer, singing a popular song under his breath, summarily looked over my identification. He was untroubled, and I searched my memory and constructed a phrase or two in Spanish to keep him so. It was remarkably easy. When he asked me why I had not been on the street that day, I answered, "*He estado enfermo—muy enfermo,*" speaking the vowels like a true Andalusian. Neither man so much as looked up to examine my face.

The officer returned my papers and dismissed his heavy-jowled comrade—who went sullenly back to directing the placement of sawhorses and the stringing of red velvet.

The officer asked me why I had come to the street at so awkward an hour of the night.

"*Quiero esperar el Generalissimo y su huésped distinguido,*" I said. "*Si possible, quiero conocerlos y hablar.*" The words came full blown into my head; and if they had a certain foreign awkwardness, my confidence in speaking them deceived the young officer—who laughed and said, "*Bueno, bueno, bueno.*"

Still laughing, he indicated that I could proceed to my accustomed place on the street and cautioned me that it would be a long night, one lacking in any real amusements. I nodded, said, "*Sí, comprendo,*" and began tapping my lethal cane toward the doorway where I could await the Chairman's coming.

All night I stood in that doorway, intermittently dozing. When the morning came, it spread a pink watercolor wash under the low clouds, over the brick gray buildings, through the netting of canopies that hung furled like sails above the Street of the Serpents.

Traffic noises, far away and joyous, set the pavement

humming under my feet. I saw the Guardia at both ends of the thoroughfare checking papers and admitting shop-keepers. Grinning nervously and rubbing their palms to-gether, these men hurried to their shops, lifted the grates over their doorways, and opened for the Generalissimo's pleasure. A few hailed me cursorily, and I lifted the top of my cane a little in reply.

Everyone was too busy to stop and talk, but somehow I believed I could handle any conceivable difficulty, should any businessman decide to greet me at closer range and, failing to recognize me, challenge my right to be there. I had the language in my mouth, the cunning in my head: *"The ticket-seller of your acquaintance is ill, señor, but the Guardia wish the street to appear as it always does. Con-sequently, I am here in his stead."* When fate ordains that one complete his mission in life, no power may arise to thwart him.

So it was with me on that spring morning as merchants babbled, policemen strolled, and the sounds of opening shops made metallic moan. At one point, a busboy from the nearest bar brought me a glass of anisette with the com-pliments of his employer, and I accepted it with trembling fingers and a nod. The boy stared at me for a moment, but went away when I began to sip the cloudy liquid, my tongue caressing the rim of the glass.

The two hours that I waited after the arrival of the shop-keepers seemed even longer than the seven or eight hours that I had waited that night.

But presently a commotion at the head of the street told me that I would need to wait only a little longer. In one of the street's shadowy S-coils a party of dignitaries emerged into my direct vision. A great many people swelled the bottleneck where they strolled abreast, unconcernedly jab-bering. There was laughter.

Once past this narrow place the party came on with mad-dening slowness, for the stoop-shouldered man about whom the other dignitaries revolved took very small steps and paused at frequent intervals to gesture with his hands or point out things of interest. He wore a uniform with shoul-der boards and ribbons and a brilliant loop of braid. His face was birdlike. I knew him immediately for the General-issimo. But the men around him had no distinction for me, blurring one into another like eidolons. I saw other uni-forms, vaguely Oriental faces, business suits, pale exposed

wrists, perhaps even the hem of a woman's skirt. Flashbulbs
scoured these people's clothes with brief bursts of light, but
still I could not tell if the Chairman walked with them.

I sought two different faces, one Mongoloid, one Nordic.

But neither one appeared among the faces that descended
upon me at such an enragingly leisurely rate. Had the blind
man lied to me about the Chairman's visit? Had Nisei, to
punish my boorishness, concocted the bizarre tale of Theodor Weik's death and resurrection? Standing there, I realized that all the information I possessed had come to me
secondhand. Doubt took hold, and I cursed my trust in
the dead and the deceitful.

Tapping with my cane, I stepped out of the doorway.

Almost at once I saw a tall figure with graying blond
hair, a man with sunken blue eyes and a long jaw. He
moved from behind a knot of smaller men and took up his
place beside the Generalissimo. Incongruously, he wore the
high-necked jacket and the loose trousers of a member of
the Chinese Communality. It was Nisei's former husband,
now merely the living husk in which there resided the locust
mind, the insatiable maw, of an unparalleled villain.

"Lotería," I cried. "Lotería para hoy."

They saw me and smiled. Shapeless, slow, hungry for
novelty, the group of dignitaries and reporters came rolling
toward me. The sensation of their spreading approach was
claustrophobic. I would have precious little room to strike
Theodor/Mao, not an inch in which to retreat. Their bodies
would be upon me in an instant. But like a basketball player
among school children, the Chairman towered over his
Spanish hosts, his Chinese comrades, and strode toward me
with impetuous boldness.

"Lotería," I cried again.

The Chairman halted, spoke something over his shoulder,
laughed, and came on relentlessly. The others crowded behind him, and suddenly their infuriating slowness had become one great tidal rush. Men and flashbulbs surrounded
me. I stepped back. Looking up through the opening between my face and the lenses of my glasses, I saw a pigeon
floating in the slit of blue sky. I longed to fly into that
vacancy with it, free of the self-imposed onus of assassinat-
ing a man who no longer resembled himself. The actor
drew near.

He looked over his shoulder again. "Generalissimo," he
said in Spanish, addressing the aged homunculus in the

majestic uniform, "this man need not remain blind. No one must. We have the means to restore his sight."

Blond as northern wheat, supple as a lean cat, the Chairman extended toward me his beautiful hands and smiled an other-worldly benediction. I could see no one but him. All the others might have been cardboard figures meant to dress a prosaic backdrop. And all the time—past, present, future—condensed into that moment and ran in my veins like a fiery serum.

In English I shouted, "Die, you monster!" and sprang forward so violently that the sun dimmed, the air burned, and the earth heaved under the pavement in volcanic shudders; all creation aghast at the magnitude of my deed.

Up came the tip of my cane as I swung the weapon first sideways and then unerringly forward. It split the space between the Chairman's outstretched hands, homing on his heart.

Several flashbulbs exploded.

The Chairman's body turned; his head went back. A sound like steam escaping a kettle filled the causeway as the accompanying dignitaries let their astonishment slip past their lips. I twisted the cane and banged it against the Chairman's breastbone, a trifle off-target because of the twisting he had involuntarily done. But the cartridge tore into his chest, ripped away the facing of his gray garment, burrowed into the hollow that his lungs bordered. Shouts overrode the hissing sounds of the crowd.

The recoil of the weapon shoved me down; the weapon fell from my hands. Falling, I saw the plush red stain on the Chairman's torso and then stared for a moment into his water-blue unbelieving eyes. Two men supported his tottering body. But the intelligent blue eyes watched me fall and then rolled into their own milky whites before closing. The body sagged. Still, I had a fraction of a second in which to note that the effect had been all wrong, the expression not at all what I had desired. It came to me instantly that perhaps I had made a mistake. *A mistake!*

This thought died at once, for a man's knee came up under my chin and cracked my head against a storefront.

My yellow sunglasses skittered away—but somehow I got my hands under me and crabwalked frantically along the concrete molding of the shops, retreating from my pursuers. A pair of heavy knees—in olive-drab gabardine, above

shiny lubricated boots—bore down on me. The gleaming
boots were almost in my face. I kicked out at one of them
and took advantage of their stumbling to lever myself up to
a standing position.

Desperately, I tried to extract the cyanide capsule from
one of my trouser pockets.

"No!" a woman's voice screamed. "You mustn't let him
do that!"

The man who had momentarily stumbled was upon me.
He wore a tricornered hat and appeared to be an extremely
important officer in the Guardia. With one brusque sweep
of his forearm he broke my jaw and sent the flimsy pod of
plastic sailing into infinity, irrecoverable. The man was
older than I, I saw, but demonstrably stronger. He gripped
my lapels and pushed me along the façade of storefronts
until my back was to a wide tinted window. I knew what
was coming, read the direction of his rage.

He spat in my face. *"Hijo de noche."*

Then his forearms stiffened against my chest, powerfully,
like coiled springs, and thrust me into the collapsing wall
of glass so that shards dropped around me, sprigs of crystal
caught in my hair, excruciating powders abraded my back.

I lay sprawled, legs up, in the darkened serving area of
the billiard parlor where the blind man and I had discussed
the Chairman's impending visit. Now the Chairman was
dead, and the jagged opening above me filled with curious
faces, all somehow secondary to the stolid angry face of the
guardsman.

With the back of his hand he knocked several more
pieces of glass out of the window frame and climbed in
toward me. I was conscious. My jaw throbbed like the rail
over which a huge engine had just passed; my body was
riddled as if with bee stings and laser holes. In thrall to his
anger, the guardsman would kill me and end my suffering.

The prospect did not frighten me; I welcomed it.

But I was conscious, too, of the barman and busboys
inside the parlor and their pleas that my assailant desist so
that the wreckage not become more general. Jerked to my
feet, I listened to these cries as the guardsman slapped my
head from side to side and whispered a hissing torrent of
obscenities with every blow. It seemed that I was being
struck by an anonymous retributive power, for the man,
so far as I knew, had no face—only terrible extremities, the

boots I had fled from and the bruised hands that battered
me.

Like a plucked harp string, a woman's voice sounded in
the shattered opening: "No, Vicente, no. The Chairman is
dead. This man's death won't alter that."

Vicente, the guardsman, chopped at me with the edge of
his hand. He held me erect. He prepared to strike me again.

"For the sake of love," the woman cried, "stop yourself!"

At these words, Vicente backed away from me and gave
me an unobstructed view of the people crowded in the
window. The woman, of course, was Nisei. She had both
her hands to her face, several fingers twisted through the silk
curtain of her hair. Her eyes strained at the relative darkness we inhabited. Clearly, she did not recognize me—
though I could not tell why. When my knees began to
crumple and my eyes to glaze, the heavyset guardsman
grabbed my sleeve and shook me into another moment of
awareness. Held erect once more, I saw that my jacket was
gone, my shirtfront bloodied, my chest outlined beneath
the sucking wetness. Pain riveted me upright for a horrify-
ing second. "Nisei," I said. Then I slumped again. This
time Vicente let go of me.

Having penetrated my identity, Nisei began to scream.

I toppled into the carpet of dull glass and heard the
larger pieces go *crack* under my back, indifferently cutting.
Again, Vicente's head came down. His hands reached for
my absent lapels and tore my shirt. My consciousness was
going. I fought to fix my tormentor's face in my mind; I
struggled for a last remnant of lucidity. The man's breath
touched my lips and nose. Straining to focus, I turned my
head toward him and looked up at his swollen jowls.

Although thirty years had passed, one thing made this
man readily and forever familiar: the spidery magenta
birthmark on his left cheek. It was with this image in my
mind that the guardsman and all the spectators in the window faded into inconsequence. My pain faded, too. For the
certain knowledge that what I had accomplished was no
mistake spun a web of silver for me and trembled in the
gathering dark.

And as the darkness fell, a pigeon hovering in the blue
space between the canopies over the Street of the Serpents
disappeared; disappeared without moving. The serenity of
old cathedrals was finally mine.

Epilogue

As this document proves, they did not kill me. Do not ask
me why. Instead they committed me to this great prison.
When I first came here, there were other men behind the
walls. Now, however, I am the only one, for year by year
the number of prisoners has decreased with pardons,
natural deaths, and finally, at the turn of the new century,
a general amnesty. Only I am not released—though I may
go walking through any corridor I choose and even spend a
morning digging in the prison gardens.

From the window of my cell I can look down on olive
trees, gnarled little hardwoods that cast crooked shadows.
I write and think.

In the election of 1992 the Generalissimo won a resound-
ing victory over his many opponents. This year he won his
ninth consecutive springtime election. The guards keep me
apprised. It is by his decree, I am certain, that I remain
here—deferred to, humored, well cared for, but always
aware of my status as a prisoner. The guards, you see, do
not tell me everything, only the news that pertains directly
to Spain. For instance, after the Generalissimo's last election they informed me that Picasso had painted a com-
memorative mural entitled *The Dream and the Truth of
Franco* and that this mural now hangs in the Museo del
Prado. Sometimes I believe that the guards are liars, that
the blind man was a liar, that even Nisei must have deceived me.

I know nothing of what happened in China after I killed
Theodor/Mao. Of the momentous reactions of the world at
large I am completely ignorant. They keep me this way. The
guards conspire to see that I continue to go about in the
dark. Beyond daily pleasantries and a little gossip about
Franco, they will not venture.

They leave me to write and think. Consequently, I have
only one more brief episode to relate.

After my incarceration eight years ago, the authorities
permitted me a visitor. The elder of my two children,
Christopher James, flew up from Johannesburg and came
with a strange reticence into my cell. He was not yet
twenty-one, and it had been so long since I had last seen

him that I was surprised to note how tall he was. He did not sit down, but stared at me with his hands folded in front of him. So young, so young! His face had a healthy adolescent thinness, and his hair, worn at a moderate length, fairly shone. Even the palpable gloom of my cell could not quench that sheen—the vigor and sheen of his youth!

He would not talk to me about himself, although I asked him questions about his studies and even joked with him about the possibility of his becoming my personal physician. (At that time, my wounds still had not completely healed, and my jaw occasionally ached with a cruel fierceness.) None of my banter moved him. He stood looking down on me, passing judgment. When I asked him news of the world, he said, "They told me not to discuss that with you. And I won't, Father, because it isn't important."

"What do you consider important, then?"

"Your reasons for taking a man's life, for killing another human being. I'd like to know those things."

As briefly as I could, I explained. With some eloquence I laid all the pieces of the jigsaw puzzle before him and then proceeded to fit the edges together into a coherent pattern. When I was through, he shook his head and began to pace the flagstones beside my cot.

"Your family still loves you," he said at last. "But you aren't Moses. Your people aren't the Chosen People."

I laughed a little at that and then went on to say that just as I did not resemble Moses, he did not resemble Minos, one of the Greek judges of the dead. I would permit my children to sit in judgment of me, however, if they would agree to having their allowances curtailed. This nitwitticism—they had had no allowance from me for several years—unexpectedly broke the ice, and we fell into some pleasant, if slightly self-conscious, conversation.

An hour passed.

Jamie, summoned by a guard, told me goodbye and left me sitting disconsolately on my cot. The cell filled up with darkness. The sound of my son's footfalls faded. And in the intervening years I have not been permitted another visitor.

Still, I regret nothing. Though the years have wrinkled me as they will wrinkle even the youngest, I regret nothing. I killed a monster for my wife and children, and there is nothing in that to regret.

PIÑON FALL

THREE scrawny brown boys found him. It happened in the early part of October when the afternoon sun burned on the backs of the Sangre de Cristo mountains with a kind of transcendent bloodiness. The boys found him on the prairie among the scrub pines.

Whatever he was, he lay crumpled in a sculpted drift of snow without a single vesture of clothing on his body. The snow only partially covered him, and by the man's naked flanks the oldest boy could see a delicate orange powder. All three boys halted to stare at the man and to watch their breaths vaporize like skinless balloons.

The boys were brothers. The oldest brother was Jamie, and all three lived in the coal mining town that no longer mined coal. Tucked in an abandoned hollow fifteen miles from the Spanish Peaks, the town was called Huerfano. The word means *orphan,* but Jamie spoke the word with little concern for either symbolism or semantics. When they found the angular blue-jowled creature, Jamie was thinking only of the likelihood of bringing home several pounds of piñon nuts, the hard brown kernels that they had to husk from the sticky cones of the piñon trees. Although the first snowfall had come early, the season for piñon nuts was nearly over.

Jamie raised his quarter-filled fruit jar as a signal to stop, and then the brothers stared back and forth from the blue corpselike body to one another's uncomprehending faces.

"Who is it?" the youngest boy asked.

"Nobody we know," said Jamie. "Put down your jars and watch me—I'm going to see if he's dead."

Tonio, the second brother, pointed and said: "Look at the snow. It's a funny orange color next to his arms."

Jamie approached and knelt, his knee sinking gently into the stiffening white drift. He reached across the man's broad forehead and touched his oddly parted blue lips. The two younger boys stepped back.

"He doesn't look like he's breathing," Jamie said, "but his mouth is warm."

"Then he ain't dead, is he?" Tonio asked.

"No. I don't think he is."

The wind blew a bit of the orange powder across the snow, and Packie, the youngest boy, scraped at the smears of piñon resin that coated his fingers. Leaning over the man's elongated hairless skull, Jamie very carefully opened his shrouded eyes with a thumb and forefinger.

The huge eyes were black—and faceted.

On the edge of town, a Polish woman lived in the white-washed wooden house directly across the arroyo from their hovel. Mrs. Zowodny was fat, manlike in appearance, and crotchety. She wore coveralls under her monstrously ample dresses and lived among a menagerie of stuffed elks' heads and a brigade of porcelain figurines.

She hovered every day between the kitchen and the murky parlor, as if she could not make up her mind in which direction her appetites would most likely find fulfillment. She called the brothers "blackheads."

She called them blackheads, identified them in her mind with scar tissue and cancerous sores. It was as if the boys were physical blemishes on the sooty complexion of the town, on the old battered face of Huerfano. Jamie frequently pelted her house with clumps of mud or snow, depending on the season, so that she would come to the window, flushed and bulging-eyed, to shout at them.

"You little blackheads! You think you are 'Mericans; you are foreign trash cluttering the streets!"

Then Jamie would bulge out his eyes derisively and shout back the single word: "Slav!" He spat it.

At that he would turn, beckon to his brothers, and lead them in a scrambling retreat down the banks of the arroyo that separated their houses. Their arms and legs would flail the air like the blurring plastic spokes of a pinwheel. Fuming, Mrs. Zowodny would watch them go.

Soon neither the old woman nor the boys knew which of

the two occurrences had first established their enmity: the coining of the epithet "blackhead" or the ritualistic pelting of Mrs. Zowodny's house. The pelting or the epithet, the epithet or the pelting.

Now it did not matter at all.

Jamie slapped the man's face. Looking upside down into the opaque faceted eyes, he could see the image of himself and of his brothers. All three were milky slivers of light in the small flat planes, and with each slap the angular blue skull moved back and forth in the snow, flattening the snow, communicating a warmth to Jamie's hand.

"Hey, ain't he coming awake now, no?" Tonio asked.

"I don't know, but he's warm; warm as can be."

"He's wearing sompen on his eyes, no?"

"Maybe. They are certainly strange eyes if he isn't," Jamie said. "They are certainly strange."

Packie was standing a little way off in the snow; he put his hands on his knees and leaned forward, cocking his head from side to side.

"Grasshoppers have eyes like that," he said. "And flies, too."

"Yes," Jamie said. "It's hard to tell if he's alive, but he is very, very warm."

With a shudder of gray sinews and an indigo deepening of color the long body took on the sapphire luminosity of a dragonfly turning in the sun. The man's lips parted and he moved one leg, crossing it over his body to cover his exposed knotted groin. All three boys fell back at the movement, scrambling away, struggling in the icy powder. The sun balanced precariously between the Spanish Peaks.

"Please," the man said huskily. "Please cover me."

The boys crept back, but Jamie was aware that it would be virtually impossible to establish a rapport with the man, mostly because of the eyes, the terrible eyes. How could one make human contact with eyes that returned one's image in a thousand distorted permutations? How would it be possible to read the character of the entity—human or otherwise—who resided behind those eyes? Jamie stood to his full height, one foot hidden by the broken snow, and looked down into the creature's face. Tonio and Packie stood awed and poker-spined at a small distance.

The eyes, the black faceted eyes, glinted.

"Please cover me," said the odd mouth, grotesquely

orming the sounds. "The snow weighs down my own overings. I can't move."

"I'm going to help you up," Jamie said.

The boy knelt behind the stricken creature and grasped im beneath his spindly arms. The man's flesh was a uniorm grayish blue, crisp to the touch and incredibly warm. Iis musculature was strangely reticulated: his abdomen eemed almost to consist of hinged segments, the corrugaons of the flesh a darker color than the flesh that they pparently hinged. Jamie found it easy to lift the man to a artial sitting position, his body was so light. But then the an cried out in pain, huskily, inarticulately.

Jamie saw that growing from the man's narrow shoulder lades were the beginnings of two sets of wings. The wings nemselves lay outspread and icily laden beneath the culpted snow. In bringing the creature to a sitting position, amie had inadvertently twisted the sensitive membranes f those wings.

"Lay me down again," the creature said. "Lay me down nd cover me. Cover me against the cold."

"Hey, brother," Tonio said, "let's get out of here, no? Ie ain't a real person. He may be sompen else, but he ain't o real person."

Jamie took off his coat after easing the naked man back to the snow. Then he wrapped his threadbare woolen uffler around the man's neck, winding it once around his ard constricted chest, and finished by draping the corduoy coat over the man's chest and hips. But the coat was itifully small and did not begin to cover the man.

"Why don' we move the snow off his wings?" Packie uggested. The boys exchanged bewildered looks, and the an lay back in the orange-tinctured snow with nothing hatever alive in his faceted eyes, nothing at all.

Mrs. Zowodny had been alone all the first day the snow ell. Because her eyesight was failing and because she reused to turn on the electricity, she moved about among her usty statuary and mildewed elks' heads with a singular lumsiness. Her swollen feet navigated the dark areas beween ottomans and overstuffed chairs but only with diffiulty. At last she came to the small shuttered window in er kitchen, and paused.

There were colored bottles on the interior sill, above the

sink, and ugly glass ashtrays she had no need for; and these items had to be taken down before she could open the peeling shutters. She took them down and ranged them along the edge of the sink.

Outside, the drifts filled her yard, swan-necked peaks that curled like stiffened meringue. Her breath steamed the glass, but by squinting she was able to make out the alien thing that was lodged in the snow almost directly under the window, a soft cylindrical shell. She squinted and smacked her lips in consternation.

"Them blackheads," she muttered. "Them blackheads."

The shell was very much like an outsized cocoon. It lay in the snow somewhat lopsidedly, for it was attached by filaments of ice and strands of a glistening silken substance to a long plank; the plank itself was embedded in the snow. Mrs. Zowodny looked at the clutter in her yard, smacked her lips again, and muttered into a corner of her shawl. With a palsied hand she pushed the shutters to.

Jamie and Tonio were kneeling on opposite sides of the outstretched man, scooping up jars of snow and depositing the snow out of the way, behind the man's outstretched arms. Packie sat cross-legged under the piñion tree and continued to worry over the gooey white resin that adhered to his fingers. Beside him was his own widemouthed fruit jar, now brimful of piñon nuts: the two older boys had emptied their jars into his that they might remove the snow from the creature's wings. The creature admonished them.

"Dig very gently," he told them. "Keep your knees back and dig as gently as you can."

In twenty minutes Jamie and Tonio were through. Revealed to them were the soft paperlike membranes of the man's wings. He looked very much like a sallow, whey-faced saint from an El Greco painting, a saint miraculously invested with four diaphanous capes with which to shield his tortured body. The boys gaped, and the Sangre de Cristo mountains rose up on the west like a chiseled, living wall of white granite.

"Let me help you up," Jamie said.

He lifted the man to a sitting position for a second time, then awkwardly got him to his narrow trembling legs. Lifting him, Jamie remarked on the strange creature's astonishing lack of weight; the man seemed to consist only of air and the ethereal burden of his papery flesh. It was then, too,

hat Jamie noticed that the orange powder on the snow was
scaly dust from the man's multicolored wings, the dust that
had outlined his flanks.

But the wings were wet, wet from the snow and wet as
if they had only recently molted.

"The name that you may call me," the man said, "is
Papilio. That is not my given name, nor even an approxima-
tion; but it is what you may call me."

"Papilio," Jamie said.

"Yes."

In the failing sunlight the creature Papilio began very
slowly to manipulate his wings, moving them back and
forth, back and forth, covering and uncovering his naked
manlike body. As he moved them, the wings shimmered
beneath the emblazoned weight of red and orange peacock
eyes. Royal blue hieroglyphics also shimmered with the
movement of his wings, and the movement was rhythmic.
Jamie decided that those hieroglyphics easily could have
been the characters of an alien tongue, but he watched the
man and said nothing.

"I'm afraid that the sun is dying," Papilio said. "My wings
are still damp and I'm hungry, very hungry."

So the boys fed him piñon nuts. They cracked the tiny
nuts with their teeth and clumsily shelled them, picking at
the hard rinds like jewelers working over the mechanisms
in a watch. Having shelled the nuts, they gave the sweet
white kernels to Papilio and watched him eat.

As he ate, his emblazoned wings moved very slowly back
and forth, as thin and translucent as Japanese silk screens.
Jamie watched the sun and felt the wind.

Clouds were forming above the Spanish Peaks, presaging
another snowfall.

Mrs. Zowodny looked out through the frosted kitchen
window. Except to putter through the rubble in her own
fenced-in yard, she very rarely ventured outside. She had
a son who worked construction machinery on the new
passes that were being built through the Sangre de Cristo
range, and this young man brought groceries to the house
every Thursday afternoon. Although she bullied him about
his personal life, he remained dutiful; and she depended
on his visits for the opportunity to rail about the "blackheads" who vandalized the property of such industrious

Americans as herself. Soon the young man came only on Thursdays and only to deliver his mother's groceries.

More and more, Mrs. Zowodny was left to the creaking solitude of her house, left to stare at the lacy rime on the windowpanes.

But now she had made up her mind to go out. The thing beneath the kitchen window demanded that she approach someone with authority over the boys who pelted her house and who, apparently, had violated the sanctity of her yard. She put a scarf over her head and with considerable effort squeezed her swollen feet into rubber galoshes. Upon breathing the outside air that rushed coldly into her nostrils, she smacked her lips together in surprise. The front door banged shut on the dusty bric-a-brac within.

In coveralls and a frayed sweater, which she clutched tightly to her middle, Mrs. Zowodny trundled down the snow-blanketed side of the arroyo. Her scarf flapped, and her fat upholstered legs sank into the drifts. A solitary magpie watched her from the top of her own picket fence.

Struggling, she came up the gully's opposite bank and negotiated the wire gate and the stepping-stone walkway in the boys' front yard. For her it was a typical Chicano home, the kind inevitably constructed of mud and plaster, the kind with linoleum strips over the broken-out windows. Breathing through numb lips, she knocked on the door.

The woman who answered the knocking was thin and pale, though her paleness was plainly more the result of a washed-out weariness than of any actual whiteness of flesh. Mrs. Zowodny squinted at her, and the woman in the door made a helpless gesture with her left hand. Mrs. Zowodny leaned forward:

"You are the mother? You are the Mrs. Aguilera?"

"Yes."

"And the boys, where are they running at now?"

The helpless gesture with the left hand, made not in response but from weariness.

"You should be keeping track of where they go and what they did. I raised up a young man of mine own, I did; and you must watch their antics. Yes, you must!"

"They are out for the piñon nuts, Mrs. Zowodny. At two o'clock they left for the piñon nuts."

"They have been dropping their trash at my yard!"

"No," the Chicano woman said wearily. "No, Mrs. Zowodny."

For several minutes the two women stood in the fragile warmth of the open doorway and exchanged arguments tinged wth wholly disparate kinds of provincialism. Mrs. Zowodny argued heatedly, her lips giving rise to cold balloons, little captions of breath. Mrs. Aguilera lethargically resisted, guarding her doorway. Then the Polish woman's face drew into a contorted parody of itself, and she made a hissing sound.

"You think you are a mother. You are a Chicano slut!"

"No, Mrs. Zowodny." The woman stepped from the security of her doorway and closed the door behind her. She was wearing only a thin cotton garment, and her face, in profile, was a hard papier-mâché mask. Mrs. Zowodny moved instinctively out of her way. The Chicano woman strode on the stepping-stones to the wire gate and stopped there to look at the Spanish Peaks, two black granite shadows blocking the sun. "No, Mrs. Zowodny," she said.

Both hands reassuringly clutching her frayed sweater, Mrs. Zowodny followed the boys' mother to the gate. But she followed slowly.

Mrs. Aguilera turned.

"It is cold. Last night I had a dream about the snow, a very strange dream. Snow was falling over the whole world. It fell in Colorado and in Mexico. It was falling even on the deserts of Africa. The camels were standing in the snow."

"Camels in the snow?"

"Yes, Mrs. Zowodny. Shaggy, shaggy beasts looking up at the sky and watching the snow fall out of the sun."

Mrs. Zowodny stood three wet stones away from the Chicano woman; she ran her raw tongue over the fissures in her lips and blinked, angrily bewildered.

"Do you know what else?" Mrs. Aguilera asked. "There were *mariposas*. All over the world, huge butterflies swam in the white storms. And moths, too, shaggy moths that danced among the snowflakes. Moths and butterflies of every color that there is." She stopped and tightened her lips before speaking again. *"Yes, Mrs. Zowodny."*

"Oof!" the other said, registering disgust.

"And tonight the snow will come again. And if I dream, there will be camels in the snow, and butterflies."

"You should stop this dreaming and watch them boys."

"We will need wood for a fire," Mrs. Aguilera said to herself. "We will need wood."

Mrs. Zowodny remembered her rare mission beyond her own yard and drew her face into its doughy self-parody. She let Mrs. Aguilera's last words turn over in her mind. She made up the three stones between them and grasped Mrs. Aguilera's loose cotton sleeve. Her face twitched.

"You've got an axe? An axe for chopping wood?"

"Yes."

"I will borrow, then, your axe."

Mrs. Aguilera did not argue with the old woman. She found the axe in the empty woodbox beside the door and handed it to Mrs. Zowodny by its rusted head. The old woman took the axe in both hands, both visibly shaking hands.

"Thank you," she said. "Send the oldest boy to bring it back—if he don' stay out all night."

Then she left Mrs. Aguilera and crossed the arroyo to her own house, at first hefting the axe across her body and then dragging it by the long worn handle. A magpie flew up when she entered her gate. She could almost feel the sweat on her upper lip crystallizing.

In the backyard she went to the thing under the kitchen window and stared indecisively at its glistening bulk. It glistened with a peculiar whiteness.

Dusk enveloped the house and trees.

At last she brought the axe to her shoulder and let it drop listlessly into the soft integument of the thing. The cocoonlike shell ruptured. Suddenly Mrs. Zowodny's eyes blazed up. Again and again she chopped at the thing, the rusted axehead making clumsy arcs in the failing light. Membranous colors gushed out of the shell and spilled onto the snow, diaphanous capes of orange and scarlet and blue. The plank to which the thing had been attached lay broken in countless splinters.

Mrs. Zowodny was panting. Her armpits ached, and the axe fell from her trembling hands into the snow. She looked at her handiwork without comprehension, then went into the house and turned on a single electric light. Still sweating, she sat down in an overstuffed chair and let the shadows move across her doughy face.

It was nearly two hours before she got up and went into the backyard to see what she had done.

When the boys came into their own yard it was very late. A few frosted pinpoints of light were visible in the

eastern sky, but from the other direction came the burgeoning front of snowclouds that massed over the Sangre
de Cristo range and spread like a cancer into the regions
of clean night sky. Jamie led the boys into the yard. They
had returned with only two fruit jars, both of them empty.

Papilio had refused to venture as far as the house with
them, and they intuitively understood his reluctance. He
had remained in a mine opening several hundred yards beyond their adobe hovel, wrapped in the silken covering of
his wings, hiding his nakedness behind those beautiful
tapestried membranes. Jamie could still see him placing a
piñon nut on his strange indigo tongue, sucking the kernel
out of the shell and spitting out the shattered rind—all with
merely the efficient workings of his long papery mandibles.
So they had come home with the two empty fruit jars.

The younger boys went immediately to bed.

Mrs. Aguilera asked Jamie about the piñon nuts, and he
told her that he had left the jars in the woodbox outside
the door. He neither denied nor affirmed their emptiness.

"*Bueno*," the boy's mother said. "Then you know that
the woodbox is empty. And tonight it will be cold again,
with more snow."

"Yes."

"Mrs. Zowodny has borrowed the axe. Go over to her
house and bring the axe home. Tomorrow you will go out
for the wood."

"Let me go in the morning for the axe, too."

"No. Tomorrow you will have other excuses."

"Why did she borrow the axe? She has a coal furnace."

"I didn't put my nose in her business. Now, go."

Jamie found the stepping-stones in the dark, hobbled
through the gate, and plunged into the piles of drifted snow
in the arroyo. He pretended that the snow was a vast
hinterland of grassy meadow and clambered through it as
if its wetness were a wholly nonexistent quality. He pretended that zebras and wildebeest lay in wait for him in
the grasses of that hinterland. He saw the broken-crusted
footprints of a creature that had preceded him, and his
heart thumped hard against his chest.

His visions dissolved. The wind chilled him, blowing
powdery dust into the air; and he came upon the old
woman's dimly lit house with a sense of detached contempt
for his fantasies. The house was stolid, compact, and real.

It seemed to heave in the new darkness just as the snow shifted under his feet.

At the whitewashed gate he paused and listened. He heard an odd skittering inside Mrs. Zowodny's house, like the toenails of a tiny dog pattering over linoleum. Jamie turned and peered into the density of blackness from which he had come; what he saw was merely the blurred patina of light that emanated diffusely from the grouping of hovels on the other side of the arroyo. But he had heard something distinct from that direction, too.

A scraping on the snow; then a hollow fluttering that was barely audible over the sequent hush and wheezing of the wind. The nap of his corduroy jacket stiffened; he could feel bumplets of chicken flesh puckering in the small of his back. Then a clatter came from the house, a metallic din that diminished into a pattering and died.

Jamie turned rapidly again.

An odor hung in the air. It came into his nostrils with a kind of shocking subtlety, an odor that he knew would assert itself even if the smells of skunk and napthalene were also in the air. He coughed, put his hands over his mouth, and walked through the gate toward the noise that he had heard issue from Mrs. Zowodny's house. The porch light was on. The front door stood completely open.

As Jamie entered the house, snow began to fall: the stars fell as snowflakes.

In the oppressively warm foyer he waited for his eyes to adjust and wondered about his sudden nervousness. Why had Mrs. Zowodny borrowed an axe when her house possessed a coal-burning furnace? What was the smell that flooded him like the scent of a musty, organic cologne? Why had the old woman's door been open and her porch lamp on? Jamie focused on the outlines of weight and substance that were emerging from the darkness in the parlor.

What finally took shape for him was the hump-shouldered figure of Mrs. Zowodny herself. Her legs were braced in an awkward attempt to spraddle something on the floor; her head was down. The door behind the old woman was open, and Jamie saw past her doubled body into the backyard. Then he looked down. The thing that Mrs. Zowodny was doubled over was very like a sleeping bag from which the lining has been gutted and torn free. Remnants of that lining lay in scaly iridescence on the hardwood floor of both the hallway and parlor. The smell of the glandular perfume was stifling.

Snow whirled into the kitchen, and the door behind Jamie slammed shut in the draft. Mrs. Zowodny looked up in the half-light and stared at the boy from her huge pouchy eyes. He had arrested her in an action of some importance, and she was panting grotesquely from the physical effort involved. His own heart pounded uncontrollably. Mrs. Zowodny's blood-choked eyes blazed as she snarled the familiar epithet.

"You little blackhead! Why do you not knock?"

"The axe," he said, nearly stifling. "The axe."

Mrs. Zowodny's terrible bloody eyes grew larger. Even through his fear Jamie understod that she was no longer looking at him but instead at the gloom that deepened at his back. A rippling movement of air made him simultaneously whirl about and step backward from the door.

As he focused on Papilio's lean blue body and the peacock-eyed draperies of his wings, Jamie heard the rattle of the old woman's stunned voice. This time Papilio's faceted eyes gave back no images.

"She has killed the female of this region," he said.

"Papilio," Jamie said.

"That is not my name," Papilio said.

He strode past the boy, carrying his wings lifted and outspread, an entomological presence who made the walls of the house, the floor and ceiling, contract upon one another like the parts of a shrinking garment. Jamie followed in the cluttered wake of Papilio's wings and watched as the creature placed his segmented hands around Mrs. Zowodny's neck. Her eyes bulged in terror. Her fat speckled hands came up feebly, feebly to ward off the grip that was unremittingly carrying her to her knees.

"Stop it!" Jamie screamed.

He found a ceramic figurine on a small end table and brought it down on Papilio's elongated skull, striking him from behind. The odor in the house was now unbearable, and he could feel sickness coming on as the supple creature slumped away from the old woman and collapsed into the broken folds of his wings. Mrs. Zowodny opened and closed her mouth like a dying fish. Looking down at her with the base of the shattered figurine in his hand, Jamie saw a cold glint of acknowledgment in the old woman's eyes, just before they closed irrevocably.

"Many others will come," Papilio said. He lay crumpled between an overstuffed chair and the thing that the old woman had dragged in from the backyard. "They are coming now."

The glandular odor was overwhelming. As Jamie looked into the kitchen and into the backyard, he became aware of angular shadows dropping from the sky, threading their way through the gauzy snowflakes, dropping on outspread capes of blue and scarlet. The snow was full of wings, and the muted whirring that Jamie heard was a universal music.

Somewhere, miles and miles beyond the Sangre de Cristo mountains, camels were standing in the snow.

ROGUE TOMATO

The Metamorphosis of Philip K.

WHEN Philip K. awoke, he found that overnight he had grown from a reasonably well shaped, bilaterally symmetrical human being into . . . a rotund and limbless planetary body circling a gigantic gauzy-red star. In fact, by the simple feel, by the total aura projected into the seeds of his consciousness, Philip K. concluded that he was a tomato. A tomato of approximately the same dimensions and mass as the planet Mars. That was it, certainly: a tomato of the hothouse variety. Turning leisurely on a vertical axis tilted seven or eight degrees out of the perpendicular, Philip K. basked in the angry light of the distant red giant. While basking, he had to admit that he was baffled. This had never happened to him before. He was a sober individual not given to tippling or other forms of riotous behavior, and that he should have been summarily turned into a Mars-sized tomato struck him as a brusque and unfair conversion. Why him? And how? "At least," he reflected, "I still know who I am." Even if in the guise of an immense tomato he now whirled around an unfamiliar sun, his consciousness was that of a human being, and still his own. "I am Philip K. and somehow I'm still breathing and there must be a scientific explanation for this" is a fairly accurate summary of the next several hours (an hour being measured, of course, in terms of one twenty-fourth of Philip K.'s own period of rotation) of his thought processes.

As I Live and Breathe

Several Philip K.–days passed. The sufferer of metamorphosis discovered that he had an amenable atmosphere, a topological integument (or *crust,* although for the skin of a void-dwelling variety of *Lycopersicon esculentum* the word crust didn't seem altogether appropriate) at least a mile thick, and weather. Inhaling carbon dioxide and exhaling oxygen, Philip K. photosynthesized. Morning dew ran down his tenderest curvatures, and afternoon dew, too. Some of these drops were ocean-sized. Clouds formed over Philip K.'s equatorial girth and unloaded tons and tons of refreshing rains. Winds generated by these meteorological phenomena and his own axial waltzing blew backward and forward, up and down, over his taut ripening skin. It was good to be alive, even in this disturbing morphology. Moreover, unlike that of Plato's oysters, his pleasure was not mindless. Philip K. experienced the wind, the rain, the monumental turning of himself, the internal burgeoning of his juices, the sweetness of breathing, and he *meditated* on all these things. It was too bad that he was uninhabited (this was one of his frequent meditations), so much rich oxygen did he give off. Nor was there much hope of immediate colonization. Human beings would not very soon venture to the stars. Only two years before his metamorphosis Philip K. had been an aerospace worker in Houston, Texas, who had been laid off and then unable to find other employment. In fact, during the last four or five weeks Philip K. had kept himself alive on soup made out of hot water and dollops of ketchup. It was—upon reflection—a positive relief to be a tomato. Philip K. inhaling, exhaling, photosynthesizing, had the pleasurable existential notion that he had cut out the middleman.

The Plot Thickens

Several Philip K.–months went by. As he perturbated about the fiery red giant, he began to fear that his orbit was decaying and that he was falling inevitably, inexorably, into the furnace of his primary, there to be untimely stewed. How large his sun had become. At last, toward the end of his first year as a planetary tomato, Philip K. realized that his orbit wasn't decaying. No. Instead, *he* was growing, plumping out, generating the illimitable juiciness of life. However, since his orange-red epidermis contained an utterly continuous layer of optical cells, his "eyes," or The Eye That He Was (depending on how you desire to consider the matter), had deceived him into believing the worst. What bliss to know that he had merely grown to the size of Uranus, thus putting his visual apparatus closer to the sun. Holoscopic vision, despite the manifold advantages it offered (such as the simultaneous apprehension of daylight and dark, 360-degree vigilance, and the comforting illusion of being at the center of the cosmos), could sometimes be a distinct handicap. But though his orbit was not decaying, a danger still existed. How much larger would he grow? Philip K. had no desire to suffer total eclipse in a solar oven.

Interpersonal Relationships

Occasionally Philip K. thought about things other than plunging into his primary or, when this preoccupation faded, the excellence of vegetable life. He thought about The Girl He Had Left Behind (who was approaching menopause and not the sort men appreciatively call a tomato). Actually, The Girl He Had Left Behind had left *him* behind long before he had undergone his own surreal Change of Life. "Ah, Lydia P.," he nevertheless murmured from the innermost fruity core of himself, and then again: "Ah, Lydia P." He forgave The Girl He Had Left Behind her desertion of him, a desertion that had come hard on the heels of the loss of his job. He forgave . . . and indulged in shameless fantasies in which either Lydia P.—in the company of the first interstellar colonists from Earth—landed upon him, or, shrunk to normal size (for a tomato) and levitating above her sleeping face in her cramped Houston apartment, he offered himself to her. *Pomme d'amour*. Philip K. dredged up these words from his mental warehouses of trivia, and was comforted by them. So the French, believing it an aphrodisiac, had called the tomato when it was first imported from South America. *Pomme d'amour*. The apple of love. The fruit of the Tree of

Knowledge, perhaps. But what meaningful relationship could exist between a flesh-and-blood woman and a Uranus-sized tomato? More and more often Philip K. hallucinated an experience in which interstellar colonist Lydia P. fell to her knees somewhere south of his leafy stem, sank her tiny teeth into his ripe integument, and then cried out with tiny cries at the sheer magnificent taste of him. This vision so disconcerted and titillated Philip K. that for days and days he whirled with no other thought, no other hope, no other desire.

Ontological Considerations

When not hallucinating eucharistic fantasies in which his beloved ate and drank of him, Philip K. gave serious thought to the question of his being. "Wherefore a tomato?" was the way he phrased this concern. He could as easily have been a ball bearing, an eightball, a metal globe, a balloon, a Japanese lantern, a spherical piñata, a diving bell. But none of these things respired, none of them lived. Then why not a grape, a cherry, an orange, a cantaloupe, a coconut, a watermelon? These were all more or less round; all were sun-worshippers, all grew, all contained the vital juices and the succulent sweetmeats of life. But who-ever or whatever had caused this conversion—for Philip K. regarded his change as the result of intelligent interven-tion rather than of accident or some sort of spontaneous chemical readjustment—had made him none of those ad-mirable fruits. They had made him a tomato. "Wherefore a tomato?" *Pomme d'amour*. The apple of love. The fruit of the Tree of Knowledge. Ah ha! Philip K., in a suppura-tion of insight, understood that his erophagous fantasies involving Lydia P. had some cunning relevance to his present condition. A plan was being revealed to him, and his manipulators had gone to the trouble of making him believe that the operations of his own consciousness were little by little laying bare this plan. O edifying deception! The key was *pomme d'amour*. He was a tomato rather than something else because the tomato *was* the legendary fruit of the Tree of Knowledge. (Never mind that tomatoes do not grow on trees.) After all, while a human being, Philip K. had had discussions with members of a proliferating

North American sect that held that the biblical Eden had in fact been located in the New World. Well, the tomato was indigenous to South America (not too far from these sectarians' pinpointing of Eden, which they argued lay somewhere in the Ozarks), and he, Philip K., *was* a new world. Although the matter still remained fuzzy, remote, fragmented, he began to feel that he was closing in on the question of his personal ontology. "Wherefore a tomato?" Soon he would certainly know more, he would certainly have his answer. . . .

A Brief Intimation of Mortality

Well into his second year circling the aloof red giant, Philip K. deduced that his growth had ceased; he had achieved a full-bodied, invigorating ripeness that further rain and sunshine could in no way augment. A new worry beset him. What could he now hope for? Would he bruise and begin to rot away? Would he split, develop viscous scarlike lesions, and die on the invisible vine of his orbit? Surely he had not undergone his metamorphosis for the sake of so ignominious an end. And yet as he whirled on the black velour of outer space, taking in with one circumferential glimpse the entire sky and all it contained (suns, nebulae, galaxies, coal sacks, the inconsequential detritus of the void), Philip K. could think of no other alternative. He was going to rot, that was all there was to it; he was going to rot. Wherefore the fruit of the Tree of Knowledge if only to rot? He considered suicide. He could will the halting of his axial spin; one hemisphere would then blacken and boil, the other would acquire an embroidery of rime and turn to ice all the way to his core. Or he could hold his breath and cease to photosynthesize. Both of these prospects had immensely more appeal to Philip K. than did the prospect of becoming a festering, mephitic mushball. At the height of his natural ripeness, then, he juggled various methods of killing himself, as large and as luscious as he was. Thus does our own mortality hasten us to its absolute proof.

The Advent of the Myrmidopterans
(or, The Plot Thickens Again)

Amid these morbid speculations, one fine day-and-night, or night-and-day, the optical cells in Philip K.'s integument relayed to him ("the seeds of consciousness," you see, was something more than a metaphor) the information that now encroaching upon his solar system from every part of the universe was a multitude of metallic-seeming bodies. He saw these bodies. He saw them glinting in the attenuated light of Papa (this being the name Philip K. had given the red giant about which he revolved, since it was both handy and comforting to think in terms of anthropomorphic designations), but so far away were they that he had no real conception of their shape or size. Most of these foreign bodies had moved to well within the distance to Papa's nearest stellar neighbors, three stars forming an equilateral triangle with Papa roughly at the center. At first Philip K. assumed these invaders to be starships, and he burbled "Lydia P., Lydia P." over and over again—until stricken by the ludicrousness of this behavior. No expeditionary force from Earth would send out so many vessels. From the depths of ubiquitous night the metallic shapes floated toward him, closer and closer, and they flashed either silver or golden in the pale wash of Papa's radiation. When eight or nine Philip K.-days had passed, he could see the invaders well enough to tell something about them. Each body had a pair of curved wings that loomed over its underslung torso/fuselage like sails, sails as big as Earth's biggest skyscrapers. These wings were either silver or gold; they did not flap but instead canted subtly whenever necessary in order to catch and channel into propulsion the rays of the sun. Watching these bright creatures—for they were not artifacts but living entities—waft in on the thin winds of the cosmos was beautiful. Autumn had come to Philip K.'s solar system. Golden and silver, burnished maple and singing chrome. And from everywhere these great beings came, these god-metal monarchs, their wings filling the globe of the heavens like precious leaves or cascading, beaten coins. "Ah," Philip K. murmured. "Ah . . . Myrmidopterans." This name exploded inside him with the force of resurgent myth: Myrmidon and

Lepidoptera combined. And such an unlikely combination did his huge, serene visitors indeed seem to Philip K.

Onslaught

At last the Myrmidopterans, or the first wave of them, introduced themselves gently into Philip K.'s atmosphere. Now their great silver or gold wings either flapped or, to facilitate soaring, lay outstretched on the updrafts from his unevenly heated surface. Down the Myrmidopterans came. Philip K. felt that metal shavings and gold dust had been rudely flung into The Eye That Was Himself, for these invaders obscured the sky and blotted out even angry, fat Papa—so that it was visible only as a red glow, not as a monumental roundness. Everything was sharp light, reflected splendor, windfall confusion. What was the outcome of this invasion going to be? Philip K. looked up—all around himself—and studied the dropping Myrmidopterans. As the first part of the name he had given them implied, their torso/fuselages resembled the bodies of ants. Fire ants, to be precise. On Earth such ants were capable of inflicting venomous stings, and these alien creatures had mouthparts, vicious mandibles, of gold or silver (always in contrast to the color of their wings). Had they come to devour him? Would he feel pain if they began to eat of him? "No, go away!" he wanted to shout, but could only shudder and unleash a few feeble dermalquakes in his southern hemisphere. They did not heed these quakes. Down the Myrmidopterans came. Darkness covered Philip K. from pole to pole, for so did Myrmidopterans. And for the first time in his life, as either tomato or man, he was utterly blind.

The Tiresias Syndrome

Once physically sightless, Philip K. came to feel that his metaphysical and spiritual blinders had fallen away. (Actually, this was an illusion fostered by the subconscious image of the Blind Seer; Tiresias, Oedipus, Homer, and, less certainly, John Milton exemplify good analogs of this archetypal figure. But with Philip K. the *illusion* of new insight overwhelmed and sank his sense of perspective.)

In world-wide, self-wide dark he realized that it was his ethical duty to preserve his life, to resist being devoured. "After all," he said to himself, "in this new incarnation, or whatever one ought to term the state of being a tomato, I could prevent universal famine for my own species—that is, if I could somehow materialize in my own solar system within reasonable rocket range of Earth." He envisioned shuttle runs from Earth, mining operations on and below his surface, shipments of his nutritious self (in refrigerator modules) back to the homeworld, and, finally, the glorious distribution of his essence among Earth's malnourished and starving. He would die, of course, from these consistant depredations, but he would have the satisfaction of knowing himself the savior of all humanity. Moreover, like Osiris, Christ, the Green Knight, and other representatives of salvation and/or fertility, he *might* undergo resurrection, especially if someone had the foresight to take graftings home along with his flesh and juice. But these were vain speculations. Philip K. was no prophet, blind or otherwise, and the Myrmidopterans, inconsiderately, had begun to eat of him. "Ah, Lydia P.," he burbled at the first simultaneous, regimented bites. "Ah, humanity."

Not as an Addict (or, The Salivas of Ecstasy)

And so Philip K. was eaten. The Myrmidopterans, their wings overlapping all over his planet-sized body, feasted. Daintily they devoured him. And . . . painlessly. In fact, with growing wonder Philip K. realized that their bites, their gnawings, their mandibles' grim machinations, injected into him not venom but a saliva that fed volts and volts of current into his vestigial (from the period of his humanity) pleasure centers. God, it was not to be believed! The pleasure he derived from their steady chowing-down had nothing to do with any pleasure he had experienced on Earth. It partook of neither the animal nor the vegetable, of neither the rational nor the irrational. Take note: Philip K. could think about how good he felt without in any way diminishing the effect of the Myrmidopterans' ecstasy-inducing chomps. Then, too soon, they stopped— after trimming off only a few hundred meters of his orange-red skin (a process requiring an entire Philip K.- month, by the way, though because of his blindness he was

unable to determine how long it had taken). But as soon
as his eaters had flown back into the emptiness of space,
permitting him brief glimpses of Papa, a few stars, and the
ant-moths' heftier bodies, another wave of Myrmidopterans
moved in from the void, set down on his ravaged surface,
and began feeding with even greater relish, greater dispatch. This continued for years and years, the two waves
of Myrmidopterans alternating, until Philip K. was once
more a tomato little bigger than Mars, albeit a sloppy and
moth-eaten tomato. What cared he? Time no longer meant
anything to him, no more than did the fear of death. If he
were to die, it would be at the will of creatures whose
metal wings he worshipped, whose jaws he welcomed,
whose very spit he craved—not as an addict craves, but
instead as the devout communicant desires the wine and
the wafer. Therefore, though decades passed, Philip K. let
them go.

Somewhere over the Space/Time Bow

Where did the Myrmidopterans come from? Who were
they? These were questions that Philip K. pondered even in
the midst of his ineffable bliss. As he was eaten, his consciousness grew sharper, more aware, almost uncanny in its
extrapolations. And he found an answer . . . for the first
question, at least. The Myrmidopterans came from beyond
the figurative horizon of the universe, from *over* the ultimate curvature where space bent back on itself. Philip K.
understood that a paradox was involved here, perhaps even
an obfuscation which words, numbers, and ideograms could
never resolve into an explanation commensurate with the
lucid reality. Never mind. The Myrmidopterans had seemed
to approach Philip K. from every direction, from every
conceivable point in the plenum. This fact was significant.
It symbolized the creatures' customary *independence of* the
space/time continuum to which our physical universe belongs. "Yes," Philip K. admitted to himself, "they operate
in the physical universe, they even have physical demands
to meet—as demonstrated by their devouring of me. But
they belong to the . . . Outer Demesnes of Creation, a non-
place where they have an ethereal existence that this continuum (into which they must occasionally venture) always

debases." How did Philip K. know? He knew. The Myrmidopterans ate; therefore, he knew.

Moving Day

Then they stopped feeding altogether. One wave of the creatures lifted from his torn body, pulled themselves effortlessly out of his gravitational influence, and dispersed to the . . . well, the uttermost bounds of night. Golden and silver, silver and golden—until Philip K. could no longer see them. How quickly they vanished, more quickly than he would have believed possible. There, then gone. Of the second wave of Myrmidopterans, which he then expected to descend, only twelve remained, hovering at various points over him in outer space. He saw them clearly, for his optical cells, he understood, were now continuous with his whole being, not merely with his long-since-devoured original surface—a benefit owing to his guests' miraculous saliva and their concern for his slow initiation into The Mystery. These twelve archangels began canting their wings in such a way that they maneuvered him, Philip K., out of his orbit around the angrily expanding Papa. "Papa's going to collapse," he told himself, "he's going to go through a series of collapses, all of them so sudden as to be almost simultaneous." (Again, Philip K. knew; he simply knew.) As they moved him farther and farther out, by an arcane technology whose secret he had a dim intuition of, the Myrmidopterans used their great wings to reflect the giant's warming rays on every inch of his surface. They were not going to let him be exploded, neither were they going to let him freeze. In more than one sense of the word, Philip K. was moved. But what would these desperation tactics avail them? If Papa went nova, finally exploded, and threw out the slaglike elements manufactured in its one-hundred-billion-degree furnace, none of them would escape, neither he nor the twelve guardian spirits maneuvering him ever outward. Had he been preserved from rotting and his flesh restored like Osiris's (for Philip K. was whole again, though still approximately Mars-sized) only to be flash-vaporized or, surviving that, blown to purée by Papa's extruded shrapnel? No. The Myrmidopterans would not permit it, assuredly they would not.

The Nova Express

Papa blew. But just before Philip K.'s old and in many ways beloved primary bombarded him and his escorts with either deadly radiation or deadly debris, the Myrmidopterans glided free of him and positioned themselves in a halolike ring above his northern pole (the one with the stem). Then they canted their wings and with the refracted energy of both the raging solar wind and their own spirits *pushed* Philip K. into an invisible slot in space. Before disappearing into it completely, however, he looked back and saw the twelve archangels spread wide their blinding wings and . . . *wink out* of existence. In our physical universe, at least. Then Philip K. himself was in another continuum, another reality, and could feel himself falling through it like a great Newtonian *pomme d'amour*. Immediately after the winking out of the twelve Myrmidopterans, Papa blew; and Philip K., even in the new reality, was being propelled in part by the colossal concussion resulting from that event. He had hitched, with considerable assistance, a ride on the Nova Express. But where to, he wondered, and why?

Special Effects Are Do-It-Yourself Undertakings

In transit between the solar system of his defunct red giant and wherever he now happened to be going, Philip K. watched—among other things—the colors stream past. Colors, lights, elongated stars; fiery smells, burning gong-sounds, ripplings of water, sheets of sensuous time. This catalogue makes no sense, or very little sense, expressed in linguistic terms; therefore, imagine any nonverbal experience that involves those senses whereby sense may indeed be made of this catalogue. Light shows, Moog music, and cinematic special effects are good starting places. Do not ask me to be more specific, even though I could; allusion to other works, other media, is at best a risky business, and you will do well to exercise your own imaginative powers in conjuring up a mental picture of the transfinite reality through which Philip K. plunged. Call it the avenue beyond a stargate. Call it the interior of a chronosynclastic infundibulum. Call it the enigmatic subjective well that one may enter via a black hole. Call it sub-, para-, warp-, anti-, counter-, or even id-space. Many do. The nomenclature, however, will fail to do justice to the transfinite reality itself, the one in which Philip K. discovered that he comprehended The Mystery that the Myrmidopterans had intended him, as a tomato, to comprehend *in toto*. For as he fell, or was propelled, or simply remained stationary while the new continuum roared vehemently by, he bathed in the same ineffable pleasure he had felt during the many dining-ins of the gold and silver ant-moths. At the same time, he came to understand (1) the identity of these beings, (2) his destination, (3) the nature of his mission, and (4) the glorious and terrible meaning of his bizarre metamorphosis. All became truly clear to him, everything. And this time his enlightenment was not an illusion, not a metaphysical red herring like the Tiresias Syndrome. For, you see, Philip K. had evolved beyond self, beyond illusion, beyond the bonds of space/time—beyond everything, in fact, but his roguish giant-tomatohood.

How the Mandala Turned
(or, *What Philip K. Learned*)

Although one ought to keep in mind that his learning process began with the first feast of the ant-moths, this is what Philip K. discovered in transit between two realities: It was not by eating of the fruit of the Tree of Knowledge that one put on the omniscience and the subtle ecstasy of gods, but instead by *becoming* the fruit itself—in the form of a sentient, evolving world—and then by *being eaten* by the seraphically winged, beatifically silver, messianically golden Myrmidopterans. They, of course, were the incarnate (so to speak) messengers of the universe's supreme godhead. By being consumed, one was saved, apotheosized, and lifted to the omega point of man's evolutionary development. This was the fate of humankind, and he, Philip K., only a short time before—on an absolute, extrauniversal scale—an insignificant man of few talents and small means, had been chosen by the Myrmidopterans to reveal to the struggling masses of his own species their ineluctable destiny. Philip K. was again profoundly moved, the heavens sang about him with reverberant hosannas, all of creation seemed to open up for him like a blood-crimson bud. Filled with bright awe, then, and his own stingingly sweet ichor,

Philip K. popped back into our physical universe in the immediate vicinity of Earth (incidentally capturing the moon away from its rightful owner). Then he sat in the skies of an astonished North America just as if he had always been there. Millions died as a result of the tidal upheavals he unfortunately wrought, but this was all in the evolutionary Game Plan of the supreme godhead, and Philip K. felt exultation rather than remorse. (He did wonder briefly if Houston had been swamped and Lydia P. drowned.) He was a rogue tomato, yes, but no portent of doom. He was the messenger of the New Annunciation, and he had come to apprise his people of it. Floating three hundred fifty thousand miles from Earth, he had no idea how he would deliver this message, the news that the mandala of ignorance, knowledge, and ultimate perception was about to complete its first round. No idea at all. Not any. None.

Coda

But, as the saying goes, he would think of something.

SPACEMEN AND GYPSIES

BECAUSE my house is on the edge of a desert, I can look out through my patio doors and see the naked dunes standing as fluorescent as water under the moonlight. That particular night was a strange one, and my head ached with the arid murmurings of the sand. I had come into the desert to escape insomnia, to palliate the trauma of a recent loss. But my insomnia persisted; the loss continued to rankle in me, a gnawing sore.

I passed through the dark house and looked out the facing of glass, across the patio of inset marble tiles. Ordinarily my neatly structured gardens grade into the desert with a silent artfulness that makes one forget the distinctions between man's handiwork and nature's. But not on that night.

My view of the ineluctably rolling dunes was obstructed. The butterscotch moonlight fell not on the desert—but instead on the hodgepodge of garish wagons that had encamped, without my knowledge, between the marble mosaic of my patio and the sheer edge of the desert itself.

For, you see, there were gypsies in my backyard.

I could see the chrysalises of their slumbering bodies, the dark mounds of their bedrolls, shadows under the painted wooden carts of their caravan.

But one gypsy stood guard. His figure was crooked, grotesque in pantaloons and cap. He surveyed not the area around him, however, but the indigo skies, staring at the full orange moon that rocked and pitched, pitched and rocked, in the awesome night overhead. I determined to approach him and slid the patio doors aside. Although the

226

doors made no sound that I could detect, the gypsy turned his head and watched my robed figure emerge from the house, test the cold marble with my bare feet, and ascend toward him.

The gypsy's eyes reflected a moony sheen, like hard dark pieces of obsidian. In that long minute in which I approached him, his perspective became mine. I could tell that he was not at all disconcerted to see me coming.

Quietly, he greeted me, and we talked casually together, careful to let the others sleep.

The man's name was Lazarescu. Talking to him, I could see that he had lived more years than I had patio stones. The leathery flesh of his face had an ugly canaled quality, as if it had been tattooed from the inside of his mouth. His hands clasped and unclasped one another like amorous tarantulas. They held me fascinated, as Lazarescu told the following story; and I listened to him, neither impatient nor mystified, while all about us the desert and the wind conspired to cover my walkways and gardens with sand.

Lazarescu's voice was old, his English only faintly accented. In fact, he spoke like a learned scholar only recently estranged from his academy:

Yes, I am an old man. An old man with blear eyes and a memory that more and more frequently fails me. But I know what we are doing in this windy desert and why my people have chosen me to stand the watch. You, on the other hand, are a settled person; you require answers. Well, I have the voice to give them, the eyes to see through your astonishment, and the memory to relate this latest of our sufferings.

My name is Lazarescu.

In the days gone by, the people came to my summons, followed where I led, listened to my counsel. But latterly I have been the follower, an old man nodding on the wagon seat, going where the nomadic spirit of our newer gypsy blood has prompted. But tonight the new blood slumbers, the young men rest, and Lazarescu—blear-eyed but worthy —stands the watch. I have asserted myself again.

But you would know why we have encamped by your home.

This is the story. During the April that is past, our caravan crawled through the Balkans. We were coming down out of the upland mists that made us wish for heavier

mantles, coarser shawls, drier climes. It was the thaw, and
evil going. Wagons toppled. We set them right again. Two
children were born, and we sang in our coming down with
the force and joy of this new unbartered blood. In May
we reached the Adriatic. The sky burned so fiercely blue
that the air seemed alcohol on fire. Our wagons creaked
on their newly thirsty wheels, and mouths turned black
with the heat and water-lust. Still we exulted. We exulted
in the thirst we had chosen and in the pleasure of the road.
On the last wagon rode Zoga, the tamer of bears, and his
young wife Selena.

Zoga chose to bring up the rear of our ungainly convoy
because attached to his own wagon, an additional weight
for his finely curried horses, was the bear cart. The bear
cart contained only one animal, but this one so nervous
and excitable that it must ride last in our procession or
else lacerate itself unmercifully against the bars of its
cage—pawing and thrashing at the horses that pulled the
trailing wagon. Therefore, Zoga and his wife came last.

But horse-drawn wagons were never made for such
highways as the *gago* travel in their motorcars. People
shouted from their speeding windows and shook their fists.
When they drew up behind our clattering caravan and
could not pass, they shouted obscenities about kettle-
makers and pilferers. We kept to the road. We kept to
the highway beside the hot blue shining sea and ignored
the blaring horns. But the horns blew louder. Our horses
stopped, alarmed and whinnying, as all around the noise
billowed up: whinnying and swearing, horns and horses,
so many noises that I trembled on the wagon seat. Zoga's
bear growled ferociously.

Before the officials came, a brawny man got out of one
of the stalled motorcars behind us, skirted the bear cart,
and yanked Zoga down from his wagon. The brawny man
smashed Zoga's face with his hard red hands and tore
away his neckerchief and vest. I watched, leaning from my
seat. Zoga's bear made heavy complaint. A shaggy black
monster, it raged at the red-haired man and rocked its
flimsy wooden cage. I dismounted and ran lamely, belated-
ly, to Zoga's aid. I could see the bear's whiplashing saliva,
its matted black beard, and, on down the highway, the
doors opening on the little Fiats and motor vans as red-
faced people emerged to watch the fight. Some clearly
wished to join in.

It was fortunate that the police arrived, for I am no fighter. The government officials and the police came just before the brawny man could kill Zoga, and they made us pull our caravan off the roadway. I do not know what they did with the man.

They questioned us. They would not believe that we had come all the way from the Stara Planina, the high mountains, to this roadway on the Adriatic in so short a time. But it was true. We were fewer than four hundred kilometers from Trieste, following our blood north along the west-winding sea. Nor would they permit us to leave the unsheltered encampment where they had forced us off the government roadway.

In the late afternoon a huge truck growled into our midst. The driver wore a heavy revolver on his hip, and his two companions carried long, pointed sticks. We could do nothing against these uniformed men when, cursing all the Romany and prodding with their sticks, they transferred Zoga's bear from its flimsy cart to the cattle-sullied bed of their truck. It was rules, they said. So menacing a beast could not go about the civilized countryside in a mere cart. Growling, both the truck and Zoga's bear departed from us forever.

I was glad that the bruised tamer lay abed, unaware of this new duplicity.

Night came down on our wagons.

Zoga lay in his wagon on a pallet of straw; he moaned so that his voice had the plaintiveness of the Adriatic, the sorrow of a people infinitely old. Selena crouched over her husband, tending his wounds. All this I knew simply by moving stealthily, with an old man's stealth, through the camp. Zoga's moaning continued. When I could support it no longer, I took action.

With my neckerchief I throttled the government official who had been assigned to stay beside us. One government official. He was unarmed, sleeping in his motorcar, and I do not believe that he ever awoke. But his stupidity was only an extension of the government's, and it was impossible to feel remorse.

Just as it is tonight, the moon was full and bright. I wasted no time.

From the old days I remembered how the blood ran when a man assumed the leadership of his people. The blood ran that way in me. I roused Rudolfo in the first wagon and told him that we had a journey to embark upon. Together we woke the others. In only a few brief minutes we had tied down all the rattling spoons, kettles, pots, and basins that hung from our carts. Silently we left the place of our forced encampment and began traveling north, true north, by that sort of wagon rut only a gypsy can find. Behind us the Adriatic moaned like a bereaved woman.

We traveled for a long period of time. A period of time that had no dependency on the markers of day and night. The air grew incredibly thin, and we bundled in our mantles and shawls against the cold.

At last we came down out of the naked gray mountains into the Mare Crisium, the deepest of all the moon's waterless seas, where the cold was not so penetrating.

Our horses always respond well to the lowland regions of Mother Luna, for their hooves touch but lightly in that inviolate powdered soil. And for us, of course, the Earth hangs in the skys like a blue crystal ball, clouded with possible misfortune. It is always good to go back to the moon. You, who possess this fine glass house, know what returning home accomplishes for the wanderer. Well, man, our people have no home but Mother Luna, and to be sojourning in her seas is all we know of the settled man's homecoming.

We had resolved to span the Mare Crisium and pass leisurely from the moon's forward face to the dark. In that darkness of stars and crater shadows we would purge our bodies of the cloying Earth. Our crimson and yellow caravan would thread the passes of each of the three mountain ranges that encircle the Oriental Sea. That was the haven we sought. Darkness heals. We were in need of healing; and Zoga, who still carried the scars of his encounter with the brutish Yugoslav, had demanded that our destination be a dark-side sanctuary. Since he was yet in mourning for his bear, no one opposed him. Therefore, bathed in ambiguous Earthlight, we moved through the Sea of Crises.

But we had misgivings, and our misgivings bore fruit.

You see, when our ancestors plied the moon oceans, they feared nothing—not the cold, not the dark, not the void, not the perpetual hunger. A man had only to suffer these things, and Mother Luna granted him all her desolate privacy, the grandeur of her barrenness. In these days the gift has not been withdrawn. But it has been extended to others whose birthright includes nothing of either our hunger or our blood.

And a gypsy is a jealous creature.

We had traversed nearly half the sea's diameter when the crisis befell us. In the mare's surface we found a slump pit, a great cavity that would house us better than our wagons; and we encamped. On that lunar night no one stood watch. The necessity did not exist. But I am an old man who has difficulty sleeping; and when the thing that you would call a *module* came dropping from the pitchy sky, I saw nearly every moment of its descent. Enormous and squat. Spitting little tatters of fire. Dropping with no more grace than a clumsy silver octopus.

I climbed to the slump pit's rim and stood there in the numbing cold among the horses.

The module fell to its bed only a few kilometers from our camp. Three hours I stood on the parapet of our huddling place, staring through the black emptiness—until at last a speck of silver began rolling down the side of the sea bottom's bowl. What an unlovely speck it was. For the *gago* had invented a motorcar for the moon. It rolled like the ironclads that had growled up and down the Apennines many years ago. Such things have always frightened my people, and I awoke them that we might flee.

Our wagons struggled onto the sea bottom. The horses snorted indignantly at having to pull their burdens so soon again after our encampment. But the moon is a silent place (we talk to one another with signs, free of such voices as this ancient croaky one that now assails you), a place where the rolling of wood over stone cannot by itself betray. Nevertheless, my friend, we looked back to see the spacemen's motorcar pursuing us, like a wolf hoping it will be mistaken for a pariah dog and fed. *A morsel*, the wolf asks, *some fallen morsel*. Not receiving that, the wolf runs ahead to nip at the horses' fetlocks.

So it was with the moon car. Following and then overtaking us, it halted our caravan and trembled metallically in our path. Without their voices, the horses screamed.

I was in the lead wagon beside Rudolfo, and the dust from the horses' scuffling sifted down on my hands and thighs. The spacemen's motorcar was big. It sat in our path like a boulder, but a boulder about to split open and loose bodiless demons. Rudolfo's face looked ashen in the blue light that Earth gives, and I touched his knee.

Calm thyself, I said in signs.

For the demons that came out of the motorcar from its winglike doors had no appearance of danger about them. Both men wore bulky suits and helmets—so that I could not help thinking of tired government officials, in overcoats and fedoras, trudging through the snow in Warsaw or Budapest. But the suits they wore were clean and white, like pieces of new soap, and I was ashamed of my fear. Sometimes, however, it is difficult to accept the lessons of Mother Luna's generosity, the fact that she now receives gentiles and gypsies alike.

What a confrontation, my friend.

It was a philosophic thing, the spacemen in their phosphorescent white suits staring at Rudolfo and me. How can I explain the events that followed if not by emphasizing the enmity that flowed between us? How tell you what the four of us felt, naked on the naked lunar sea? Gradually, our horses calmed.

But the spacemen argued with each other.

It was clear that the argument proceeded apace inside their helmets, like a bee buzzing back and forth between two jars. An invisible bee, for Rudolfo and I could hear nothing. Then the spacemen ceased gesticulating with their great gloved paws, and one of them came up to our wagon and stood beneath us, looking up. I was greatly afraid.

Inside the heavy helmet the spaceman's face seemed blue, as if daubed with the indigo dye of a Moslem nomad. But when the man turned his head and I saw the sweat on his brow, this comforting blueness faded away.

The man touched Rudolfo on the ankle. Rudolfo did not move. The other white-suited man approached a few steps.

The bee flew between their helmets.

Although the spacemen then moved very slowly to bring their heavy square guns out of holster, neither Rudolfo nor I could do anything. Our horses began to skitter sideways in harness; I tightened the reins against them, an instinct. To have let the horses go skittering might have gained us an advantage, but I was bloodless, and cold, and too frightened to consider strategies.

Get down! Get down! the closer of the spacemen was signaling. Never before had a gypsy been ordered about on Mother Luna's surface. Consequently, it was only from earthly habit that Rudolfo and I got down from that high place and submitted to their orders. From earthly habit and from the always sublimated fear of a dying people. But, my friend, even a dying people may have faith in the resurrection of their genius; and when the nearer spaceman struck Rudolfo over the head with his weapon, I had just such a resurgence of implacable faith. I, Lazarescu, the goat-bearded old wanderer! Even though I did nothing myself.

Because it happened as in a ballet.

Suddenly—at the very moment Rudolfo slumped into the slate-gray dust—my people came whirling and pirouetting from the wagons behind. Men and women alike. Spinning their blossomed sleeves, twirling crimson scarves between their sinuously supple hands. No ballet company of any state, my friend, ever performed more gracefully before its audience than did the people of our caravan. They encircled the two spacemen and danced a flowing rope between them. Such leaps and glides it is not possible to behold on Earth!

Terrified and enraptured at once, those spacemen stood spellbound by our pantomime. Their weapons were useless against us because the minds that wielded them had popped, like fuses in the glass temples where all such *gago* dwell. Even you, my friend.

The more furious the dancing, the more subdued our horses. Here was gypsy revelry, and they grew docile, gently rippling their flanks. The silence was boisterous.

Then came Zoga and Selena into the crowd of dancers. Husband and wife, they celebrated our blood with a rustic *pas de deux* which they performed between the two spacemen. I was standing near, and I looked through the helmet glass of the man who had struck Rudolfo. That man's face was white, white as a grub, and his eyes paled before the dance as if he were witnessing spirits where there should have been only solid flesh. Half his manhood had drained away. The other half stood there inside the fat, corrugated suit, stiffly unbelieving. Then I saw Zoga's face; he was well again, but his look—even in the act of dancing—was bitter.

The silent music faded.

Selena knelt and kissed Rudolfo on the forehead, but Zoga strode disdainfully to each spaceman and removed the guns from their thick insulated hands. Then he put the guns in the bottom of our wagon seat and returned to his wife. She was still kneeling over Rudolfo. No one danced

any longer. Everyone stood beside our crimson wagon in
the moon's immense chill, and waited. Waited for Selena to
make some sign. At last she looked up.

On the indifferent ether she made the sign of the death's-
head. She held her cupped hands out before her as if in
supplication. My friend, you must try to imagine the manifold depths of Mother Luna's silence, for that tiny group
of people on the floor of the Mare Crisium knew a profound silence indeed. No bees droned inside our heads, but
still we listened.

This lasted briefly. Then Zoga flew into a rage, a fury
of grimaces and gestures. On the Adriatic a gypsy might
be beaten with impunity, but not on the primal Sea of
Crises. The less demonstrative of the two spacemen Zoga
killed outright, jerking tubes from his humpback and
slashing the spongy sleeves of his suit with a tanner's knife.
None of us intervened in this. Although it may be diaboli-
cal to admit such a thing, we experienced a calm satisfaction in watching the spaceman die. Zoga's impulsiveness
spoke for all, and the outcome of his anger was purifying.

The more aggressive of the two men he dealt with
differently. The bear cage at the end of our procession
remained empty, and Zoga thought to remedy so unhealthy
a circumstance by introducing the spaceman to a world
of straw, wooden slats, and awkward jouncings. How like
a bear the man already looked! A great white bear with a
glass head and a humpbacked body. Zoga prodded the man
with his knife, prodded him threateningly in his padded
ribs, and smiled like Satan. Yes, like Satan himself, for the
light-bearer also struck back when he had suffered humilia-
tion.

We laughed bitterly, all our laughter silence.

Then we fell back from the circle in which the two
dead men lay and watched Zoga prod that upright motorcar of a man into dance. It was not a thing that the spaceman took to readily, but we were not disappointed. Just
as Zoga's old bear, the one stolen from us on Earth, had
lumbered about our campfires with melancholy clumsiness,
so the *gago* lumbered. He waltzed inelegantly, lifting one
foot, then the other, letting his paws hang free like a
puppet's arms. All the while, Zoga played his wooden flute
and waved a neckerchief in front of the spaceman's great
television set of a head. But the man could not be provoked or distracted; for the first time in his life, my friend,

that dumbfounded creature—and this I swear to you—
understood true spontaneity in the discipline of a captive
bear. He lifted one big foot, put it down again. He bowed
and twirled. He dragged his encumbered body about to the
soundless melodies of Zoga's pipes.

Such a formal spontaneity.

At the end everyone applauded, even old Larzarescu
himself. And I had detected that the dancer's naturalness
was in part an artificial thing; hypnotized, any man is
sincere. When we had applauded the dance, Zoga took the
spaceman and put him in the bear's cage.

Only much later did we begin to fear that others might
miss the bees' voices humming from the moon and resolve
to cut short our journey. And by then we had very nearly
crossed the hairline shadow between light and dark.

We were merry. The wagons rolled well. Our horses
pulled in harness gladly, as the Earth's blue seas tumble
gladly in theirs. We left the moon car paralyzed, its doors
open, in the middle of a lifeless sea. And about that we
made hand signs to one another, silent mouthings, jocular
obscenities. A gypsy does not mourn for long because he
knows that the dead come back, always they come back.
Even the dead of the pruned and civilized.

Rudolfo, lifeless, sat beside me on the wagon seat.
Mother Luna does not require that the dead go several
meters underground for preservation's sake, and many
times Rudolfo had spoken of sitting out eternity atop a
dark-side peak, moon boulders propping him erect that
he might forever watch the coursing stars. It would be
granted him, this boon; and that knowledge gave our people even less cause to mourn his death.

But we were careless of the spaceman.

He died. The oxygen in his humpback spilled away into
his lungs, and was gone. It was many hours later before
we found him slumped against the bars in the bear's cage,
a white heap of canvas. We were passing through the
awesome Cordillera Mountains, resting in a deep sluiceway, and Zoga went back to the cage to scoff at his dancing
prisoner. That was when we discovered our carelessness,
my friend, and all but the bear tamer repented of it.

Nevertheless, the man was dead. Zoga came to me with
a scornful smile to report the accident but did not return
with me.

Under the merciless stars I went into the cage and eased

the man backward onto its straw-covered flooring. Then I removed his helmet, twisting it, unscrewing it like a bottle cap. When I saw the man's face, I felt a painful pity—for he was very young, freckled like a farm girl, shocked over with red hair brighter than fire. No one was with me in the cage, not even Zoga the keeper. I put the boy's helmet back on his head and went for help.

The others came. Together we carried the body to a depression in the sluiceway. In only a few moments we had installed him there, like an appliance. Zoga removed his helmet again, against my remonstrances, and became enraged at the sight of the boy's flaming hair. He insisted with many gestures that we cover the spaceman with rocks, gravel, dust—anything to deprive his corpse of a view of the heavens. In the end we accomplished Zoga's will, for he would tolerate no gainsaying, not even from his wife Selena, whom he struck viciously across the mouth at her suggestion that the boy's burial place be granted a small marker.

When we at last recommenced our journey toward the Mare Orientale, the bear cage was once more empty, and Zoga wore over his own stocking cap the dead man's alien helmet. It was a spoil, a prize of battle. My heart troubled me in this, for our people were long ago admonished of the Father never to war among nations.

Zoga behaved unnaturally. He wore the helmet every waking moment. His face warped into a sinister travesty of itself behind the glass, and Selena refused to share his wagon. Dancing and singing ceased altogether among us.

On the seventh Earth's day that we were in the Oriental Sea, we found Zoga dead. He lay in the bear cage, where he had gone more and more often of late to nurse his bitterness, his purpled fingers clutching at the base of the stolen helmet. No matter our combined exertions of will, we could not remove the helmet from Zoga's head. But a gypsy accepts such mysteries, my friend, and feels no need for questions.

It was fitting retribution.

Then we began to see lights crossing the sky above our sheltered encampment: pinpoints of fire. A good people come after their dead, seek to redress injustices. How were they to know that the injustices worked against their own foolish spacemen had already been atoned for? That Zoga the keeper lay dead? Even with their precious radios they did not know. Therefore, they had come with bright machines and fire-forged wills.

How cold my blood ran to witness this thing. I demanded that we leave, return to Earth to escape the camera eyes and weapons of these relentless adversaries. To my wonder, the people agreed; all showed a willingness to follow my directives. All but one, my friend, and that one was Selena. She refused to journey with us, claiming that a covenant bound her to the spirit of the very husband who had betrayed her. A covenant more binding in death than in life. She would walk the craters and rills of Mother Luna, she told us in signs, for as long as there were gypsies alive in a silent universe. She would make her complaint to the stars.

Therefore, we left her and embarked upon the void.

Yesterday we came into your desert, a people dying under the heel of change. This evening we encamped by your sprawling house. Now we ask only a little room in this vast new country, sterile as it may be. That is our only request.

That, my friend, is our story.

The moon was gone.

Lazarescu fell silent. I had stopped him once or twice during his narrative to ask a question, but for the most part he had engaged in a monologue. What you have just read was set down as nearly as possible in the flavor of his idiom, but Lazarescu's voice and my own have at many points melted into one another. That is not surprising.

For, you see, when Lazarescu stopped speaking, I bent down with great composure, picked up a rock that was braking one of the wheels on the old man's wagon, and struck him a terrible blow on the forehead. Then I caught the old man's body and lowered him to the sand so that he would not awaken the others. He looked at me with glazed but accepting eyes.

"Why?" he asked. The question did not accuse.

"Because those men were my friends," I said. "Because I am what you call a *spaceman:* an astronaut just like those others. It's impossible for me to forgive you the hideousness of their deaths. Tonight—for the first time in several weeks—I may be able to sleep. But only because I've done this."

Lazarescu said. "You have killed a part of yourself." Then he closed his eyes and died.

I stole through the sleeping caravan and entered my house. But I did not sleep. All that night I stared at the ceiling. Strange changes worked themselves in my body. In the morning I looked out my broad glass doors to see that the caravan had departed. Not a trace of the gypsies' night encampment remained. The wind had swept a layer of desert silt over the patio and gardens, and the dunes looked as if they were encroaching ever closer and closer on my house.

Three days have gone by. My phone lines are dead.

A moment ago I looked at the bathroom mirror and discovered that my face is no longer that of a young man. Brown and leathery, the skin presses against my skull with constricting force. This is not the most frightening thing, however. I keep remembering Lazarescu's words: "The dead come back, always they come back." For on the last two nights a monstrous white bear has come out of the sand dunes and stood on his hind legs against the glass of my patio doors. The animal is not clumsy. He is ragged, supple, insistent. And his eyes, which radiate small pinwheels of fire, are hard as obsidian, dark as smoked marble.

Meanwhile, my mind—my mind does not fit this ancient face.

I had just returned from a ten-month sojourn among the Parfects in Azteca Nueva, nearly two thousand miles across the Carib Sea, where these transcendental human beings permitted me to wander among them—just as we tolerate a pet dog to run underfoot at one of our sacramental bayside weddings. The Parfects, who enforce mankind's exile here on Guardian's Loop, the winged island, refuse to come among us; but occasionally they require detailed knowledge of our moods, our numbers, our intramural repressions. At these times they compel the Navarch to provide them with an envoy. On the past two such occasions, our Navarch, Fearing Serenos, selected me to represent the two million dying and doomed human beings of Windfall Last.

And gladly I performed the Navarch and the Parfects' will.

But on the Christmas of my second (and I hoped, my last) return, I was a man consummately weary and dispirited. No human being can live among the Parfects for ten months without coming to feel himself a wholly contemptible creature, wanting in reason, purpose, and ultimate grace. The experience enervates and destroys. Even the wisest comes back to Guardian's Loop with the stench of his own humanity suffocating him and tainting his reunion with the old friends who seek to celebrate his return. Time becomes a necessity as great as food or shelter. One must recover. One must shake off the malaise produced by nearly three hundred days among the tall naked mutants who rule, without punishments or statutes, their own golden earth. For I was as an envoy to another planet, conscious every moment of the racial superiority of my hosts. At forty-one, I needed time to grow back into myself and my people. Those close to me understood and attempted to aid me in my recuperation.

I left Windfall Last. Fresh winds blew across the waters of Pretty Coal Sack, and ruffles of white lace spilled over the coral barrier in the bay. The sky shimmered with the bluish white of noon.

I rode horseback along the beach, spurring my horse with incredible ferocity toward our destination. Soon—even had I reined in the horse and turned him about—I could not have seen the cancer shape of globes and turrets and aluminum minarets that is the skyline of Windfall Last. Palm fronds and the curve of the beach blotted

out that skyline with as much finality as if a fission bomb
had fallen on the administrative sanctuary of Fearing
Serenos himself. Galloping on horseback, the wind in my
mouth, I rode free of mankind and its madnesses.

The horse belonged to Dr. Yves Prendick. I spurred it
along the water's edge, now and again forcing the good
doctor's docile beast away from the stretches of sand and
broken shells and up into the moist varnished-green foliage
that lay inland. I rode to keep a rendezvous with Prendick's
twenty-six-year-old daughter. It was my fourth day back,
Christmas Eve Day, and Prendick had given me the horse
and suggested that I go find Marina at the gutted sailing
vessel that a hurricane had long ago swept up and depos-
ited several hundred meters from the edge of the sea. The
vessel was a unique landmark.

"Marina's camping there," he had told me, "studying the
vegetation, the migratory waterfowl."

"My God, Prendick, is she out there all alone?" Our
centuries-old Navarchy had decreed no one could leave
Windfall Last but the duly licensed and authorized (among
whom Prendick and I and other counselors to Fearing
Serenos counted ourselves), but enforcing such a decree
among two million imperfect subjects presents special
problems. I feared for Marina.

"She's all right, Mark. She has a pistol, and she knows
how to use it. Take Paris, go down the beach and find
her. Stay out there awhile if you like. You need quiet company, a woman's voice."

And so I urged Paris, Prendick's dappled gelding, to
aid me in seeking out Marina. In the glory of the white
afternoon Paris's mane undulated like silken grass.

I found Marina when the sun had begun to fall a little
toward the west. (Perhaps our first meeting after my return
was a metaphor, who can say?) The old ship, the *Galleon
of the Hesperides* as Marina and I had called it, lay
wracked and rotting on the side of a small rise; and the
sea had managed to cut a channel—a narrow channel—
through the sand and then through the clamoring vegetation so that water sloshed and echoed in the caved-in
opening beneath the galleon's forecastle. This same channel
was fed in part from a freshwater runoff from the interior.

The ship dated from the 5100s; it had been built by the
Parfects as an experiment in restoration, most likely, and
then abandoned with their characteristic whimsicality to

the elements. Somehow, its wood had not wholly decayed, in spite of the vegetation and the wet. The upper decks suffered under the liquorish weight of this vegetation; as a consequence, the *Galleon of the Hesperides* resembled a great basket of flowers: amazing varieties of cineraria grew there, as did acanthus, melilot, mallow, and fenugreek, plants one would not have anticipated growing in the West Indian tropics.

And it was on the upper deck that I saw Marina, dark, lithe, and inattentive to my approach, stooping over a bouquet of plush blue flowers. She was drawing in a sketchbook. She wore khaki shorts, a sort of sleeveless mesh-cloth hauberk, and, of course, a pistol. I halted Paris on the slope above the galleon and watched her with the eyes and heart of a man who knows himself too well. My eyes and heart ached. The wind was blowing from her to me, and it carried upon it the intimations of old perfumes.

Then Paris whinnied, drawing her attention. Paris danced sideways on the slope a little, and I had to pull him up with the reins.

Marina, below on the ship's deck, dropped her sketchbook, stood to her full height amid the blue flowers, and drew her pistol, all seemingly in a single motion. Her left arm came up to shield her eyes, and what I had forgotten during my ten months with the Parfects came back to me with heartbreaking cruelty.

Marina had been born with a left arm that terminated, just below the elbow, in a splayed paddle of flesh. It was a cruel and heartbreaking reminder of our ancestors' brinksmanship: the ash was always with us.

Whenever I remembered Marina, I remembered her without deformity. It was as if my mind unconsciously extrapolated from the tenderness of her nature and gave her the faultless physical beauty that she deserved. I *saw* the flat and slightly curved blade at the end of her arm, yes, but it had no genuine reality for me—only enough reality to make my eyes and heart ache in a way different from that provoked by simply beholding her face. Therefore, I suppose, that reality was enough.

Her father, a surgeon, might have softened the hard cruelty of her "hand" when she had come of age. But when she came of age, she would have none of his reshaping and plastisculpting. "I am as I am," she told her father. "I accept myself as I am. Besides, my seawing"—Fearing Serenos, our Navarch, had been the first to call her deformed hand and forearm a *seawing*—"serves to remind me of where we came from and what we've done to one another." Moreover, Serenos himself, whose face and hands bristled with a covering of atavistic fur, frowned on surgical remedies.

The result was that Prendick obeyed his daughter; he refrained from angering his hirsute and bestially ruthless lord.

And the further result was that Marina now shielded her eyes with the stump of her seawing and in her good hand held a pistol that was aimed at my heart. At her back, the sea sparkled under the white sun of noonday, laving the distant beach with foam. The pistol glinted blue.

"Don't shoot," I called. "If you miss me, you might kill your father's horse. You know how your father is about his horses."

"Markcrier!" She smiled and holstered the gun. "Markcrier, come down here. Leave Paris on the hill."

"To run away? A fine Christmas gift for your father."

"Paris won't run away. If you get off his back and unbridle him, he'll graze and be happy for the chance."

I did as Marina bade me and then descended to the galleon. Boarding the run-aground vessel, I felt like a pirate who has fought for doubloons but who discovers that his captives' sea chests all contain roses. But I am a bad pirate; I was not disappointed. Marina had more the odor of roses about her than the metallic tang of old coins, and I kissed her. She pressed her lips against mine with no little ardor. The sea laved the beach with foam.

I was a little surprised at the degree of Marina's ardor.

We had known each other for almost her entire life, for I had met Yves Prendick in 5278 when he was elevated to the council and made the Navarch's personal surgeon. Marina had been five years old and I a precocious twenty. Even then, Serenos had trusted me more deeply than he did the fawning old magi twice and three times my age. I paid no attention to the children of fellow council members, however, and it was not until I returned from my first diplomatic excursion to the Parfects, eleven years later, that I became aware of Marina.

She was a self-possessed young lady, and our relationship developed into something subtle and significant—although I refused to acknowledge that it might be the prelude to

marriage. The erotic aspect was not there, not even the first
hints of a shy amorousness. Marina had other interests; so
did I. When she turned twenty and I began to think about
her as a possible wife, a political incident removed me from
the council and the circle of my closest friends.

Fearing Serenos took umbrage at a semisardonic comment that I made in council session (a remark, I swear, that
I cannot even recall) and ordered me to leave his chambers.
I compounded this error by standing my ground and ques-
tioning the state of his mental health. How could so small
a thing, I asked, provoke such a disproportionate response?
Had the Navarch not loved me, I might have been killed.

Instead, I was exiled for almost fourteen months among
the fishermen who live in the licensed colony of Barbos on
Marigold Island, which lies to the south of Guardian's
Loop. These men had been made fishermen and sent to
Barbos because they were mutants, but, unlike most of us,
mutants who offended either by their appearance or their
nephitic odor, the last the result of unbalanced body chem-
istries. Many of them looked and smelled like rheumy-eyed
beasts, but they treated me well; and I became one of them,
working with boats and nets through the entirety of my
exile. Serenos relented only when I had promised him, by
messenger, to obey him in everything.

Upon my return I found that I had little time to think of
Marina or of marriage. My duties, strangely enough, had
multiplied. I handled countless administrative functions
for the Navarch at the Palace of the Navarchy and spent
many days at a time in the pressurized sacristies of the
Sunken Library. At the bottom of Pretty Coal Sack, I
worked with men who were carrying on the monastic tradition of preserving mankind's accumulated knowledge.
Technically, regardless of professed affiliations, everyone
on Guardian's Loop was either a monk or a nun under
the supreme authority of our abbot, the Navarch. But the
gradual—the miraculously gradual—crumbling of belief
had turned Windfall Last into a secular community, rigidly
stratified and stringently ruled. The monkish work in the
Sunken Library went on only because the Parfects had
built the library for us and demanded that we continue to
transcribe and catalogue the intellectual achievements of
man. Therefore, we did so. And Fearing Serenos kept me
totally occupied supervising these labors and innumerable
others in the city itself.

Marina and I saw each other very seldom.

Eventually I protested that I would collapse from fatigue if not given a respite, a chance to communicate with other people. The Navarch reminded me of my vow. I kept silence ever after, until one day Serenos dropped his heavy arm over my shoulder and told me that after my next sojourn to Azteca Nueva, under the dead volcano, he would permit me to retire on full pension from his service —provided that he might call upon me now and again for advice and comradeship.

I agreed.

But to the day of my departure, not one whit did my work abate. I seldom saw anyone but those engaged in the same projects and activities as myself. I had no time for horsemanship, no time for poetry.

On the evening before I was to leave for the Parfects' homeland, however, Marina came secretly to my apart-ment/office and talked with me about other times. We talked for several hours, sipping rum from crystal glasses. When she was ready to go, Marina told me to take care and give me a chaste girlish kiss on the nose: goodbye to her second father.

Now she was kissing me with the welcoming kiss of a woman for her lover, and I returned the compliment, hav-ing realized it for a compliment, more devoutly, tonguing the warmth between her lips. At last we stopped. She stepped back and looked at me.

"Hello," I said. The sun raged small and white.

"Hello, Markcrier."

"I'm not used to such welcomes. The Navarch merely shook my hand; then he turned me over to the council members for thirty hours of debriefing. And in three days not one of those bastards kissed me."

"Not even Father?"

"No. When we were done, he loaned me a horse and told me to get lost."

"And now you're lost?"

"Less so than I might have thought. Show me what you're doing, where you're camping. Does the old *Galleon of the Hesperides* still hold together well enough to provide a lady botanist shelter?" I pointed at the channel that the sea had cut beneath the ship. "That looks ominous."

"It's not," she said. "Come."

We crossed the deck. Our legs brushed past and an

mated the umbels, stalks, and gleaming leaves that grew from the accumulated soil on the deck's planking. The salt breeze reanimated this vegetation when we were by, and perfume was everywhere.

Down into the forecastle we went.

By the light that came through the planks overhead I could see that Marina had swept this area and made it her own. She had suspended a hammock across two corners of the room and stacked several books and sketch pads beside the hammock. But a section of the tilted floor near the vessel's bow had fallen in, and through the ragged opening one could look down and see the dark water that had undercut the galleon. The light was stronger here, and a million flowers grew in the clumped dirt on both sides of the encroaching rivulet. The water here was only minutely saline because rain had apparently flushed the sea back upon itself several times during the recent rainy season. As we stood looking into the flower pit, the hollow sound of water lapping at wood made primordial echoes in our ears. At last we turned back to the rustic boudoir.

"Very good," I said. "But where's your transportation?"

"Oh, Hector. I gave him his head yesterday. He's up the beach most likely, nibbling at the green shoots that grow in one of the coastland swales."

"Yes, Hector. Good old Hector. Will he come back on his own?"

"With wet fetlocks and a matted chest. Don't worry."

"I'm not worried. I'm hungry."

"Me too."

We sat cross-legged on the askew planking, and Marina fed me. We ate biscuits and dried fruit and sucked on the stems of a canelike plant that Marina assured me was not poisonous.

"Are you glad to be back?"

"Now I am."

"Markcrier?" She let my name hang above the sound of echoing water.

"Yes?"

"What's it like living among the Parfects for so long?"

"Like being five years old again. Like being continuously embarrassed for wetting the bed. Like being caught in the act of liberating the legs from an all-too-alive grasshopper. I don't know, Marina. The experience has no corollaries."

"How did they behave toward you? Were they contemptuous?"

"No, no, nothing like. They were kind but . . . *aloof*. *Aloof* is a perfect word to characterize them because even when they engaged me in conversation, some part of their intellect remained . . . disengaged, uncommitted. Simply because there was no need for them to commit this withheld part, I suppose. But they were always kind."

"Were they always"—her voice became humorously insinuative—"*naked?*"

"Always. I'm surprised you're interested."

"Why? Everyone has a prurient streak." Marina handed me another biscuit and spat out a piece of fiber from the plant stem she had been sucking on. "What I really want to know is, did they go naked all year? Even when it was cold?"

"Every day, rain or shine."

"How could they?"

"No morals," I said.

"No, I don't mean that. I mean, how could they tolerate the cold?"

"I don't know. It never seemed to bother them."

"And you? Did you—?" She stopped.

"Go naked?"

"Yes."

"You're asking that of me? A member of the Navarch's council?"

"Yes. Did you?"

"No," I said. "They never expected that of me. Besides, the disparity between my own physique and the Parfects' would have been painful to me. No prepubescent lad ever likes to shower with the big boys."

"Oh, I see. The matter was not simply physical, but sexual as well."

"No, no."

"Well, then, what are they like?"

"I don't know. Like us, but more elegant."

"*Elegant* is an equivocator's word. Markcrier, you're trying to put me off; you're trying to tease me."

"I'm not. Besides, your curiosity is too much for me. And the word *elegant* says it all; it encapsulates the essence of the Parfects. You're teetering on an abyss, young woman, when you correct a sometimes poet on his diction."

"Very sorry, I'm sure. But I want to know what they're like."

"They're prigs, if you want the truth. They make love openly, they refrain from sermonizing, they speak whatever they feel—but somehow, don't ask me to explain it, they're still prigs. For nine months and two weeks of the time that I spent in the shadow of Popocatepetl, I was bored. My bones ached with ennui."

"I don't believe you."

"After the first two weeks they scarcely paid me any heed. And when they did, their kindness ran over me like cane sap."

"Did you write poetry, then? In all that time you were alone?"

"No."

"Why not? You used to complain of a lack of time."

"Marina, poetry is a spiritual need. Many of us in Windfall Last turned to poetry when we lost faith in the mythologies of our still-lying church. But it's impossible to express the spirit when the spirit is submerged, and among the Parfects I had no more divinity in me than does a teredo, a wood-burrowing shipworm. I couldn't write a line."

"Then you really believe they're creatures without original sin?"

"Marina, I deny original sin—but I acknowledge that man is carnivorous and cannibalistic, spiritually so."

"But the Parfects are different; you've already said that."

"Different, yes. They lack the more obvious human vices, the ones that are ours by way of evolutionary bequest. Doubtless, they have vices of their own."

"Such as?"

"You ask painfully pointed questions, don't you?"

"Yes. What sort of vices?"

I had to pause. The ship seemed to creak with old tethers and old strains, the sea wrack of yesterday. At last I suggested, "How about the vice of being insupportably boring?"

Marina laughed, unconsciously rubbed her seawing with her good right hand, tapped her bare feet on the rough planking. I grinned at her. In a way, she had made me go through my second debriefing in four days, and I think she realized that I couldn't talk about the Parfects any longer without decorating the account with an uncontrolled and

perhaps subhysterical flippancy. She must have sensed m
precarious mental state. At any rate, she laughed at m
without malice and asked no more questions about my
mainland stay.

We finished our makeshift meal and went down to th
beach.

The whole of mankind on two islands in the Carib Sea
That thought kept bubbling in my head even as I hel
Marina's hand and walked with her along the water's edge
Incongruous. Wasn't every man a piece of the continent
a part of the main? It seemed not—not any more—in spit
of what the long-dead dean of St. Paul's had once written

Paris being content with his grazing, we were going u
the beach to find Hector; as we walked, Marina did no
permit me to dwell on the metaphysics of mankind's gen
eral exile.

She said, "You're done with the council now, aren't you
Now that you're back from the mainland, you'll be give
a pension and time to do what you want. Isn't that so
Markcrier?"

"So that accounts for my welcome. You're interested i
my money."

"It's true, then?"

"I don't know yet. Serenos hasn't mentioned the matte
since my return. How did you happen to know about it?'

"Can't you guess?"

"Your father?"

She nodded. "I ask only because I want it to be true. Fo
your sake, Markcrier—not because the matter might i
some way concern me."

I had nothing to say to that. The sea came up and cov
ered our feet, then slid back down the wetted shingles a
if unable to obtain purchase. I, too, was barefoot now, an
I wondered how many bare feet and how many beache
this one same wave throughout the world had laved, thi
one same wave since Troy.

"My father and I have seen Fearing Serenos many time
since your departure. We've been in his company ofte
Markcrier."

I looked at her. "Why?"

"Invitations. Always invitations."

"But just for you and your father. Never for Melantha
Never for your mother also?"

"Never."

I halted her and held her shoulders. "A transparent arrangement."

"Yes," she said. "But in the last two months I've been able to put him off. He's been busy, and I've spent a great deal of time sketching and collecting—with the *Galleon of the Hesperides* as my base."

"Has the Navarch mentioned marriage to you or your father?"

"No. That would be a loss of face, I suppose. He wants the first word to come from us, from either Father or me."

"Thank God for vainglorious scruple."

We looked at each other but said nothing. There was no need. We resumed walking, holding hands.

Finally we left the beach and clambered into the green underbrush. Marina ran ahead. I followed. We found Hector, a huge brown beast just as matted as Marina had said he would be, in a clearing beside a pond. His lips worked methodically on the greenness in his mouth, and his eyes unconcernedly blinked. Marina scratched him on the plane of his forehead and behind his ears. After drinking from the pond ourselves, we rode Hector back to the *Galleon of the Hesperides*. Although he wore no bridle, Hector responded to the pressure of Marina's knees and carried us surely home.

We arrived at four or five in the afternoon. The white blister of the sun had fallen farther toward the westward sea, and the light had thinned to a frightening paleness.

We released Hector at the foot of the rise upon which Paris still grazed, and the heavy mud-and-salt-encrusted creature plodded up the hillside to join his stablemate. Paris, glad for the company, tossed his mane, stomped, whinnied. Two convivial geldings at the top of the world, they murmured anecdotes to each other out of tirelessly working lips.

"Come on," I said to Marina.

"Where. We're home."

"Into the broken section of hull—where the flowers are."

She did not protest. She followed me. We waded into the long narrow channel that snaked up the beach from the sea; we splashed through this ankle-deep water toward the ship. At the hull's sea-ripped portal we had to duck our heads, but we passed through it without scraping flesh, without having to crawl. Inside, the smell of rotting wood, tempered by the smell of mallow and tropic rose, was not unpleasant. Though even paler here, the afternoon light ceased to frighten me; instead it cast a warm white haze over the groined interior walls, over the clover that sprang from the mud embankments on both sides of the rivulet. Marina and I faced each other. We might have been in a ballroom, so spacious and warm seemed that forward bilge of the *Galleon of the Hesperides*.

"We could have stayed outside," Marina said, not rebuking me. "I've seen no one on the beaches in all the time I've been camping and working here."

"I didn't want it that way. I wanted shelter and just you with me in the closeness of that shelter."

"Those things are yours, Markcrier."

I took her face in my hands and kissed her. We moved out of the rivulet, still kissing, and went down on our knees on one of the clovered embankments, went down together with infinite mansuetude and care. The sea exhorted us. Kneeling face to face, we unclothed each other. I removed the sleeveless hauberk from her shoulders and let the garment crumple to the ground behind her. She unlaced my tunic, she slipped it away from me, she pressed one perfect hand against my chest. Her eyes would not remove from mine.

"A child, Markcrier, are you afraid of a child?"

"No," I said. I had no time to say anything else.

"I'm not afraid of a child, even if we never married. But if it would displease you, the thought of my deformity being passed on; if you were to think me immoral for taking that chance——"

"There'll be no child," I said.

She looked at me expectantly, curiously, awaiting an explanation.

"There'll be no child because it isn't given to me to create one, Marina. We have both been visited by the ash, but my punishment is in some ways the crueler: sterility. Invisible but insidious."

After a moment she said, "Are you certain?"

"I'm forty-one years old." And I had some understanding of the medusa of man's heart. "Does it make a difference to you?"

She leaned forward. She kissed me briefly. "No. I would have borne your children gladly, but had they been . . . *wrong*, somehow like me . . . I would have hated myself for making them suffer."

I covered her mouth with my own. Then we broke apart and clumsily finished removing our clothes. Although we were both adults and forgave each other for being human, our clumsiness embarrassed us. Marina turned aside and smoothed out her wrinkled hauberk for a resting place. This delay also confused us, but we embraced again and eased our naked bodies together—eased ourselves backward onto Marina's garment until our slow passion had deafened us to both our own breathing and the easy lapping of water against wood.

Without even thinking to be so, I was slow and easefully rhythmic; Marina ran a silken hand over the small of my back while her seawing—her ash-given seawing—clasped my flank. When I came, we were not together; but Marina held me as if I were part of her, and we lay without uncoupling for the duration of the afternoon's pale light.

The vulva smell of the sea intensified as the light failed, and soon we slept in each other's arms in a bed partaking of (as it necessarily must) the smells of the sea's basins.

The next day was Christmas. We saw the white otters cavorting on the sand.

II

There is no life which does not violate the injunction "Be not anxious." That is the tragedy of human sin. It is the tragedy of man who is dependent upon God, but seeks to make himself independent and self-sufficing.

—REINHOLD NIEBUHR

We were married on the first day of the new century.

The ceremony took place on the bay of Pretty Coal Sack, and the sky pulsed with the blue-white urgency of an adder's eyes. The breezes blew soft; the sails of the vessels in the harbor puffed out with their airy pregnancies.

And although the Navarch was present among the guests, he did not preside over our brief nuptials as we had asked him to do. Instead, after the recitation of vows, he spoke with me in an abstracted manner for a few minutes and then kissed Marina on the cheek and wished her happiness. Marina tried to draw him out; she told him of the white otters we had seen and teased him about his overdone wedding-day solemnity. "This isn't a wake," she said. "You're permitted to smile." "Oh, I smile, Marina, I smile in my own inward way." Then he bowed and left us. For the next twenty minutes he conferred with two elderly council members who happened to be standing on the periphery of the circle of our guests.

Between sips of rum and perfunctory exchanges of banter, I could not help glancing at him. His presence compelled attention. Moreover, Serenos had made a point of not speaking to Yves Prendick at all; that fact, along with his conspiratorial conference with my two former colleagues, cast a shadow over everything. I could not convince myself that these three venerable men were discussing only Windfall Last's innumerable social problems.

As a consequence, the seven riflemen who had come for the purpose of protecting the Navarch began to look like hired assassins. Positioned on two sections of the stone wall that partially enclosed the bayside altar, these men guarded all of us from assault with hunched, seemingly stupid backs. One or two of them stared down with set mouths. For that year had been notable for the number of bloody confrontations between the Navarch's Gendarmerie and the disorganized but sometimes murderous packs of prol-fauves that had taken to roaming the harbor area. When Serenos left, however, he designated only two of these riflemen to remain behind as our protection against the prol-fauves. I did not greatly fear these debased human creatures, but the Navarch's parsimonious allotment of gendarmes amounted to a not-to-be-ignored expression of displeasure. And the displeasure of Fearing Serenos frightened me more than any rampant horde of prol-fauves.

I had not expected such curtness from the Navarch. On the day after Christmas I had gone to him and reminded him of his promise of releasing me from formal government service. He had acknowledged both his promise and his unaltered intent to honor that promise.

"When, m'Lord?" I had asked.

"Immediately. But for a single lapse, Markcrier, you have served me well for more than twenty years—twice among the mongrel Parfects. You deserve whatever I can grant you: pension, comfort, access to my person, permanent status as a member of the Navarchy."

"And marriage if I wish?"

"Marriage," he said slowly, the hair on his cheek planes rippling with an involuntary grimace, "if you wish." He looked at me. "I can tell that you've settled on someone, that you're asking my permission. Isn't that so, Markcrier?"

"Yes, m'Lord."

"And the woman is Marina Prendick. That's so, too, isn't it?"

I admitted what he had already guessed.

Serenos paced the chamber, his brutal hands clasped in front of him. I realized that the delicate brindle fur on the man's face, the fur concealing everything but his hard rat's eyes, made it impossible to determine his age. How old was he? How long had he ruled in Windfall Last before I became a member of his privileged council?

Serenos stopped pacing. He made an unhappy gesture with one of those brutal hands. "You have my permission, Markcrier—but only because it is you who have asked. I set one condition. Will you hear it?"

No alternative existed. "I will hear it, Navarch."

"You are still a young man. One day I will call upon you to perform an additional service to Windfall Last. When that day comes, you will do as I ask."

"A legitimate service to the people, Navarch?" My question very nearly violated propriety, the distance between servant and lord. But I did not wish to be trapped by a man whose motives I did not trust.

"I would ask you no other kind," he said sharply. "A legitimate service to your people. Agreed?"

"Yes, Navarch."

And at that, Fearing Serenos had smiled like a water spaniel lolling its tongue. My fears were put to rest, for the Navarch smiled only when genuinely pleased, never as a means of expressing contempt or sarcasm. Therefore, I believed that no stigma would attach to my marriage with Marina, that the dangers we had imagined were indeed wholly imaginary ones. It is true that Serenos declined my invitation to preside at the wedding, but he had done so with self-effacing charm, pleading that he had long since forgotten the sequence of the rites and arguing that he did not choose to embarrass us with his clumsiness. I had expected this explanation and departed from his chambers a happy man.

Then, on the day of the wedding, the first day of the new century, I stood on the harbor flagstones and watched Serenos climb the stone steps that would lead him to the administrative cluster of Windfall Last and the hilltop battlements of the Palace of the Navarchy. Five brightly uniformed riflemen accompanied him; two remained behind.

Although no one but Marina's father and I seemed to realize it, we had been reprimanded. I knew that a reckoning would come. I walked among our many guests, sipped rum, ate orange slices, talked—but all the while I tried to anticipate the outward form that the Navarch's displeasure would take. No man, I supposed, deserved to live out his life in complete freedom from anxiety (nature did not ordain man for insouciance), but neither should a man have to contend daily with arbitrary and featureless threats to his sanity. The two riflemen on the harbor parapet became symbols of a doom over which neither Yves Prendick nor I had any control. At that moment, an attack by the prolfauves would have been preferable to the uncertainty that Serenos had bred in us—even with only two members of the Gendarmerie on the wall as our defenders.

In my distraction I began staring out to sea, wondering in which waters the rapacious sharks had attempted to slake their eternal hunger. I must have appeared forbidding company, for no one disturbed me.

That afternoon Marina and I returned to the *Galleon of the Hesperides*. We remained there a week. We did not see the white otters again, but no one came out from Windfall Last to summon us back. Still, I expected a messenger from the Navarch to arrive at any moment (sometimes I imagined an entire contingent of armed guards) to escort us, under arrest, back to the city. The white Carib sun could not burn away these fears, and Marina became aware of my uneasiness. I had to tell her what I feared. She accepted my account with a sort of facetious stoicism and kissed me. Our week drew to an end. Much to my surprise, no one murdered us in our sleep.

We returned to Windfall Last and took up residence in a climbing free-form structure on Dr. Prendick's estate, The Orchard. Grass and trees surrounded us, and our white dwelling, shaped from a plastic foam that had dried to the graininess of stucco, surrounded the bole of a giant magnolia palm. The Parfects had created both tree and house long before mankind's enforced removal to the island, just as they had built almost everything else on Guardian's Loop.

Like the tentacled devilfish that take over the shelters of other departed sea creatures, Marina and I moved into this sinuously magnificent dwelling. Her father called it Python's Keep. In our five years there, we seldom used that name, but the house did sheathe us as comfortably as its latest unshedded skin contains a serpent.

I continued to wait. We were left alone. Marina sketched, painted watercolors, worked at planting a vegetable garden in a sunlit section of the lawn. I made excursions to the Sunken Library. There I gathered material for a comparative literary history of the most interesting periods prior to Holocaust A. In the evenings we sometimes visited with Marina's parents. Yves told me a little of what was going on in the council sessions; Melantha gossiped with her daughter as if there were no difference in age at all. I also wrote poetry, much of it as good as any I had ever written. And, of course, Marina and I fell into the not entirely unpleasant routines of people who are married. No children came from our love, but we had expected none.

Nevertheless, I continued to wait. Not for children, but for the reckoning I was sure must come.

Occasionally I saw the Navarch. He inquired about my work, gave his best to Marina, scrupulously avoided mentioning the affairs of Windfall Last. Although I continued to wait for the inevitable reckoning, my memory fogged. I could not explain to myself the source of my nagging, subliminal anxiety. Where had it come from?

The years went by. Nothing occurred to suggest that Fearing Serenos had worked out his delayed wrath against us. Had Marina and I been spared? Did the Navarch possess both a conscience and a forgiving nature?

Other occurrences led me to discard these hopes as vain ones.

In 5306 the Gendarmerie went into the streets on administrative command. On the first day they slaughtered a pack of prol-fauves; the fighting (riflemen against rock throwers, bottle wielders, and slingshot artists) lasted three hours and resulted in the deaths of eighty-two illiterate, shambling yahoos, not one of whom died understanding his predicament. There was blood from this engagement on the harbor flagstones for nearly a year, red-brown stains that gradually faded under the natural corrosiveness of sea water and pigeon crap. On the following days the Gendarmerie killed at a less spectacular rate; but riding horseback along the waterfront and shooting any adult male who had the twin credentials of raggedness and glassy-eyed idiocy, they managed to bag thirty or forty more. Eventually, even the most cretinous of the prol-fauves learned to stay away from the areas of patrol; and the once-vicious packs, never truly cohesive except in situations of unthinking rampage, disintegrated into a scattering of frightened, pitiable half-men. Taking pity, the Gendarmerie apprehended these stragglers instead of shooting them.

Public executions took place. In order to conserve rifle and small-arms ammunition (which the government manufactured on a limited scale for its own use), Serenos decreed that the captured prol-fauves would suffer decapitation. On several scaffolds erected at bayside, the blade fell more times than anyone but the sadists on the Navarch's council desired to count. Crowds oohed at each new delicious dramatization, while the resultant gore drew another sort of devotee—carrion flies that iridesced in blue-green clusters over the damp scaffolds.

The majority of the population of Windfall Last accepted these tactics with delight and approval. Had not the Navarch dealt decisively with a troublesome social menace? This delight and approval continued unabated even when the Gendarmerie began mounting the severed heads on spikes and positioning the spikes at four-meter intervals along the harbor wall.

I recalled that I had once mentioned to Serenos the Elizabethan practice of ornamenting London Bridge in a like manner. How often I discovered that I had indirectly abetted the man's barbarism. This knowledge made me suffer uncannily.

Marina and I spent almost all our time at The Orchard. Python's Keep was secure, removed, isolated. Neither of us wished to go into Windfall Last and witness the grotesque reality of men's heads impaled on iron stakes, staring inland with hideous incomprehension. Too, I did not care to be reminded of my own failure to intervene in some way—or of the possible consequences of any such intervention. After all, the Navarch no doubt continued to believe that I had a debt outstanding, a debt he had consciously deferred the collection of. My anxiety was already too great to risk incurring another debt. In these ways I rationalized my refusals to act.

In 5307 the only word I had of the Navarch came to me

hrough Yves Prendick, who had maintained his status both
as Serenos's physician and as a member of the council of
he Navarchy. Prendick said that Serenos never mentioned
either Marina or me and that the old headchopper's health
could be characterized by the single word *excellent*. Like
me, Prendick did not know how old the Navarch was: it
seemed that he had ruled Windfall Last forever and that we
would we foolish to count on his dying very soon.

About this time Marina and I noted a strange thing
about her father. Though he frequently marveled at the
physical condition of his principal patient, he began to
spend an untoward amount of time either tending to him
or working in the theater of surgery where he (Prendick)
had trained as a young man. Prendick did not talk about
these long sessions away from The Orchard, except to deny
that Serenos was ill. "I'm engaged in some difficult experimentation which I've undertaken upon the Navarch's orders. I can't say any more. I won't." Having said this, he
would invariably fall into silence or stride out of the room.
In three months' time he grew irritable, whey-faced, and
abstracted. And I, in turn, grew as suspicious of Marina's
father as a man may be of someone he still respects and
loves. What had happened to Prendick? What was he
about? What did he mean by "difficult experimentation"?

Obsessed with these questions and a nebulous fear almost
eight years old, I concluded that Prendick would be the
Navarch's instrument of revenge. Fearing Serenos had
forced Marina's father to an insidious betrayal. By what
means he had done so, I could not even guess.

But I was wrong. The Navarch required no helpmates
beyond his own cunning and faithlessness. Although I did
not then understand this fact, the day of reckoning was fast
approaching.

On the anniversary of my wedding, New Year's Day,
5308, I received word at Python's Keep that His Excel-
lency Fearing Serenos desired my presence in the chambers of the Navarchy in the newly renovated administrative
palace. At once. Without delay. This rococo complex of
turrets and arches overlooked the entire city of Windfall
Last from a hill that the Parfects had raised inland from
the bay, and I knew that it would take me almost twenty
minutes to reach the palace from Dr. Prendick's outlying
estate. By then it would be noon, the precise hour that
Marina and I had exchanged our vows.

Now that the anticipated moment had actually come, found myself oddly composed: numbness and resignation resignation and numbness. Not even Marina's tears coul penetrate the shell of plastic indifference into which I with drew. We had had seven complete years together, Marin and I. How much more could two ephemeral, parasiti creatures expect? The earth was not made for man, but w had fooled it for seven fruitful years.

I should have taken Prendick's autocart, but I did not Knowing that my journey would take nearly an hour lon ger, I saddled Hector, now a tired, plodding beast, and lef The Orchard on horseback. The white sun shimmere overhead, and in my numbness I almost forgot that I car ried neither pistol nor rifle. What for? To be torn apart b renegade prol-fauves before reaching the Navarch's cham bers would have been an exquisite irony.

And Serenos did not appreciate irony.

Then let it befall, I prayed to no one in particular.

The Navarch's private chambers breathed with the vege table moistness of a garden. Ushered into this closed hot house over a thick scarlet carpet, I was made giddy wit the richness of the air. Vines tumbled down the walls rough stone showed behind the vines, the upper portion o a tree grew through the floor in one leafy corner. I saw tapestries hanging free from two interior doorways. I sav also a large glass aquarium occupying a third of the wal opposite me. Golden fish swam through the fern-crowde waters there—golden fish, all of them golden. *(But wher were the silver-gray sharks: the stupid dogfish with thei evil porcine eyes?)* And then I saw the gleaming mahogany red surface of the Navarch's desk and, behind it, the illus trious person of Fearing Serenos himself. I had not see him face to face in over two years.

"You're late, Markcrier," he said. "Approach."

I approached. There was not a chair other than th Navarch's in the room. I stood before the man and waite for some word from him. In no hurry to satisfy my num curiosity, he leaned back and extended his arms inside th loose sleeves of the silken canary-yellow robe that bore th emblem of his office—a stylized ship in scarlet thread— over his left breast. Then he interlaced his fingers, droppe his hands to his lap, and examined me as if I were a exotic artifact washed ashore from Azteca Nueva. Th image of a mischievous baboon who has just raided th

wardrobe of a prince played before my eyes. I had to fight
the image down.

"It's good to see you, Markcrier. It's good to know that
you're a man who honors his commitments—even if he
does so tardily."

"I obey my Navarch, m'Lord." ·

"In everything?"

"In everything that a man can reasonably be expected
to obey."

His voice took on a husky resonance. "You equivocate."

I held my tongue.

"You do remember, don't you, M. Rains, the commitment that you made to me seven years ago? The promise
that you gave me virtually on the eve of your wedding?"

"I've been unable to forget."

"Yes, I know. The strain has aged you, Markcrier."

I told him what his appearance told me. "You, m'Lord,
have not changed. You've borne the troubles of these last
several years without alteration."

The Navarch nodded. "Quite true." He looked directly
at me. "But even though you've aged, Markcrier, you've
not suffered. Your existence on Guardian's Loop has been
an idyllic one. Leisure in which to write. A home well removed from two million citizens less fortunate than yourself. And"—he paused for a moment—"a beautiful wife."

I wanted to sit down. My hands had begun to sweat, and
this allusion to Marina chipped a little of the enamel off
my shell of indifference. I said, "No, I've not suffered."

"Indeed you haven't. But, M. Rains, you have earned all
the things I've just mentioned, and no one begrudges you."

"That pleases me, Navarch."

"However, one cannot expect to live out his entire lifetime on exhausted past earnings. Don't you agree?"

"I'm afraid I don't understand," I said, not understanding.

"Just as I told you to expect. I now want you to perform
another service for Windfall Last."

"I want to sit down," I said. It took three or four awkward minutes, during which time Serenos studied me with
arrogant dispassion, but someone finally brought in a chair.
I sat down. The fish in the aquarium hovered seemingly
just out of reach; I felt that I was swimming among them.

"What is it you want me to do?" I asked when we were
again alone.

"Go among the Parfects again. They no longer wish to wait a decade between visits from our envoys. Some urgency compels them."

I gripped the sides of my chair, digging my nails into the wood.

"I ask you," Fearing Serenos continued, "because you are still not an old man and because your knowledge of the Parfects is so much more complete than that possessed by any of the rest of us." The voice was insultingly oily, as if the Navarch already knew what my answer would be.

"No," I said. "You have no right to ask that of me."

"I may ask of you anything I like. Further, I may compel you to perform whatever I ask. Do you understand that, M. Rains?"

I spoke out of a profound numbness, a numbness entirely independent of the words that fell from my mouth. "No, m'Lord. You may not compel me in this."

"Indeed?"

"No, m'Lord."

"But I could, Markcrier. I could do so quite easily." His jowls reminded me of those of a large brindle dog. "Do you know how?"

"I have seen the heads on the spikes."

"Prol-fauves, every one. They have nothing to do with you, Markcrier."

"Nevertheless, I have something to do with them. Even should you threaten me with tortures, Navarch, I will not go among the Parfects again. You yourself pledged to spare me from that possibility seven years ago."

"*No* is your final answer, then?"

"I have no hesitation in refusing to perform a service that you have no right to ask of me."

"You insist on an extremely limited construction of what my rights consist of, M. Rains. In reality, no limits exist. At this very moment I could kill you without qualm or compunction, simply for refusing me. But I won't. You've already failed the major test of your loyalty to me—when I have given you everything that a man requires for his comfort."

Fearing Serenos stood up and walked in his sweeping, yellow robes over the scarlet carpet to the tree that grew up through the floor. His hand touched something on the wall, and the ceiling opened like a giant Venetian blind—a blind with invisible louvers. White light sifted down through the skylight and paled the climbing foliage.

Serenos said, "I will give you the opportunity of performing a humbler mission so that you may both keep your word and repay me for maintaining you in your present comfort. Will you undertake this second mission, as humble as it is, without asking me another question?"

"Will it benefit Windfall Last?"

"Not another question!" he roared, shaking a fist. He paced for a full minute, enraged. Then he calmed and stared at me again. "Answer me, Markcrier: Will you do what I ask of you or not? Be quick."

I stood up. I no longer had the bravado to deny one of the Navarch's commands. Even if the trap were about to snap shut on me, the trap I had anticipated for so long, I could say nothing but what he expected. "Yes, I'll accomplish your *humble* mission for you. What is it?"

"A visit to some old friends."

Once again, the specter of exile. I had an instantaneous understanding of who my "old friends" were. My hands trembled.

"The fishermen on Marigold," Serenos said by way of needless explanation. "The ones you lived with for fourteen months."

"How long will I visit them this time?"

Serenos laughed. "Don't fear me, Markcrier. As I said, this is a humble mission, and it will require you to be away from your home and wife only a very brief time. A humble mission. You earn it by your forfeiture of the more important one." He laughed again, darkly.

"Who, then, will you send to the Parfects?"

"Now, now, M. Rains, don't begin to worry about the opportunity you've rejected. I imagine I can put the Parfects off a bit."

"Well, then, what am I to accomplish on Marigold Island?"

"There is an old man there whom you know quite well, I should think. An old fisherman. His name is Huerta." Serenos paused for my response.

"I know him," I said.

"Very good. Greet this man for me, tell him that I am lifting the interdict on his colony so that those who wish to return to Windfall Last may do so. Then bring him back with you. If it's possible, I will speak to him as one ruler to

another." The Navarch crossed the carpet and stood direct
ly in front of me. I had forgotten how tall the man was. He
was of a height with the Parfects of smaller stature. "Can
you accomplish this humble task for me, Markcrier?"

"Yes, m'Lord."

"Then do so. A ship will be waiting for you in the morn
ing. Go to the Navarch's quay at sunrise." He turned his
back on me and looked at the monstrously magnified fish
in his aquarium.

"Yes, m'Lord."

And with his back still to me he said, "I'll never ask
anything of you again, Markcrier."

On that cryptic note I went out.

In the morning I sailed to the fishermen's colony of
Barbos on Marigold Island. Mankind still owned ships, still
went out on the waters in slim vessels whose narrow bodies
imaged the form of woman. Marina was such a vessel,
bearing the burdens of our shared nights and loving with
me against death. A ship was love, a woman was love. And
it may be that the Parfects' knowledge of this fact had per-
suaded them to grant us movement on the seas, for they
had denied us land vehicles and flying machines (with the
exception of small balsa wood gliders and battery-powered
carts). In the early days of the Navarchy on Guardian's
Loop, many sailors had hoped to use their ships as means
of escaping the power of men such as Fearing Serenos. But
there was no place to go. The Parfects would not permit
these ships to make harbor anywhere in the world but at
Windfall Last. Therefore, every vessel that departed port
either returned home again or died the pelagic death of
creatures infinitely older than man. Still, the sea continued
to exist for our love, and ships moved over it, ships that
imaged the form of woman.

Huerta greeted me warmly. He remembered my fourteen
months' exile on Marigold Island. And I remembered him.

He was an incredibly ugly old man with bandy legs and
a chin that was joined by both bone and flesh to his sternum.
He had virtually no neck and walked with his shoulders
thrown exaggeratedly back in order to compensate for the
earth-locked angle of his head and eyes. His rib cage
jutted. His heavy mouth had been pressed into an obligatory
pout. Fortunately, he smelled only of salt water and fish
oil, not of the bile and sulfur of an imbalanced body
chemistry.

Standing on the beach with Huerta triggered a series of remarkable memories, pictures of Huerta's people fifteen years ago and of a bewildered young council member dirtying his hands with physical labor, suffering the stench and closeness of a variety of man he had not entirely believed in. Now I was back. But this time for only three days.

After entertaining me with clumsy feasts and sentimental trips to other encampments, Huerta at last delegated his authority to a one-eyed man of twenty or so (where there should have been another eye, there was not even a socket —only smooth unblemished flesh); and we departed Marigold Island on the afternoon of the third day.

At dusk on the homeward voyage I looked over the starboard railing and thought I saw the triangular caudal fins of four or five small sharks. But the turquoise glinting of the sea made perception difficult, and no one stood beside me to corroborate what I had seen. The last time I had sighted sharks which was also the first and only time they had performed their cruel ballet for me), Huerta and I had been out together in his wooden skiff. Fifteen years ago. Could it be that these sleek fishes were returning to the waters of man? For no reason at all I thought of Fearing Serenos. When the sun finally set, bloodying the sea with its last light, I suffered a profound depression and went belowdecks to seek company.

We reached Windfall Last between midnight and dawn —I had no notion of the exact time. Huerta was taken from me by three uniformed men in cloaks. They had been waiting since the previous noon, they said, and assured me that Huerta would reach the Palace of the Navarchy safely. A bed awaited him, and the old man would have an audience with Serenos in the morning. I said goodbye to my old friend and declined the gendarmes' invitation to go with them to the Palace. I had decided to sleep in my own bed, beside Marina.

Since we had arrived at such an awkward hour, however, I had no transportation back to Python's Keep. Nevertheless, I did not go aboard again, but paced beside the ship's black impassive hull. The stars scoured fuzzy halos into the face of the night, and my feet, as I walked, made echoing *laks* on the flagstones.

Grotesque in the starlight, the impaled heads of the latest batch of slaughtered prol-fauves stretched away from

me down both directions of the habor wall. I tried not t
look at them.

I had almost resolved to wake somebody up (perhap
even the Navarch himself, although that would have re
quired a long walk and I had already declined one invita
tion to stay in the Palace) when a horse-drawn wagon cam
rattling down the street. This wagon, as it happened, be
longed to the shipmaster, a taciturn man who had refuse
to say more than four words to me on our entire voyage
He came down the plank from his vessel at almost the sam
moment that the wagon ceased its wooden moanings; an
I asked, then importuned, and then reluctantly ordered th
man to give me passage home. Python's Keep was som
distance out of his way, and he refused to behave as if h
were not annoyed. He disapproved of the Navarch's liftin
of the interdict, he resented me, and he thought Huerta (i
I correctly interpreted his avoidance of the fisherma
aboard ship) the vilest and most stomach-souring creatur
he had ever encountered. Strangely enough, the shij
master's own wagoner looked himself to be a kind of livin
abortion—he had no arms and no tongue and smelled c
dried excrement. He drove the wagon by manipulating th
reins with his bare feet.

When Dr. Prendick's estate, The Orchard, at last cam
into view, green-black trees tangled against a lightening sky
I got down with relish and left my two charming comrade
without a word.

Python's Keep was not dark. A light burned behind th
stained-glass port in the sculptured module at the base o
the palm. A light for the returning voyager? My hea
quickened; I did not think so. The stillness on the lawn wa
not the stillness of the tender hours before sunrise. It wa
another kind of stillness entirely.

I ran to Python's Keep, the taste of copper, like th
grease from old coins, poisonous in my mouth.

Seated on the driftwood chair in the receiving chamber
Yves Prendick stared up at me with scoured eyes when
came in. His thinning gray hair stuck out comically on al
sides as if he had just risen from bed. But because his hea
was tilted back a little, I could see his exposed throat an
the angry lip of a long cut just above his Adam's apple. Fo
a moment—so still did Marina's father seem—I thought h
was dead. But the cut was a shallow one, and Prendicl

blinked at me, pulled himself erect, and raised an unsteady hand.

His voice seemed almost to come out of the wound in his throat. "Markcrier, Markcrier." He looked at me imploringly. "Don't go upstairs, she won't know you for a while anyway, so don't go up there, please, Markcrier."

"Prendick!" I grabbed his shoulders. "What do you mean 'won't know me'? Why the hell won't she know me?"

I turned to go up the stairs, but Prendick leaned forward, clutched the bottom of my tunic, and pulled me down to my knees with surprising strength. His eyes shimmered behind a wild provocative film. "No," he said. "Don't do that. Her mother's with her now, Melantha's up there with her, and she'll be all right if you control yourself."

"Prendick! Prendick, tell me what's happened!"

And restraining me with both hands, holding me on my knees before him like a supplicant before a priest, Marina's father told me what had happened. I continued to stare at the wound in his throat, the crimson lip that wrinkled as he talked. I thought: *The story you're telling me is an unpleasant story, I don't like it, it must be coming out of the angry half-developed mouth under your chin, a small malicious mouth, a story that has nothing to do with the sea and ships, a murderous narrative from an evil mouth, like the ravening undercut mouth of a shark, even though the sea has nothing to do, I don't think, with the malicious words that wrinkle under your chin.* On my knees before Prendick, I listened.

"Early yesterday afternoon Fearing Serenos raped your wife, Markcrier," my wife's father said.

"He came to The Orchard with three soldiers of the Gendarmerie, found me in the main house, and invited me to accompany him to Python's Keep. He was extremely cordial, he talked of the work I've been doing for him, he said Marina deserved some word of explanation in regard to his disruption of your anniversary. He wanted to apologize, to explain. He thought highly of Marina. He said, 'You know how much I think of your daughter, Yves. You've always known, I think. You both deserve some evidence of my esteem for you,' or something very much like that. We went together to Python's Keep; the cloaked gendarmes followed, laughing with each other as soldiers do, as if they shared a joke. I thought that Serenos would order them to wait for us on the lawn. He did not; he asked them to enter Python's Keep with their dirty boots and their greasy rifles.

"Marina came down the stairs from the third-level module. The Navarch continued to chat amiably with me, the soldiers to whisper. I suspected nothing—even though the presence of the gendarmes bothered me.

"When Marina reached him and extended her arm in greeting, Serenos pulled her to him, kissed her violently, and then slapped her, once with each hand. 'This is for your father,' he said. 'And this is for your husband.' The soldiers laughed.

"I lurched forward, but one of the gendarmes slammed the butt of his rifle on my instep. Another pushed me into the wall and leaned against me with his forearm, choking off my breath. Marina screamed, but Serenos covered her mouth with his hand and raked her cheek with his nails. I could see blood, Markcrier, in the openings between his fingers, and the sight of it made me lurch forward again. Again, the rifle butt. Again, the gendarme shoving me to the wall. This time he put the blade of a long crescent-shaped knife under my chin and held it so that I could not move my head.

" 'Make a sound,' he said, 'and I will slice your jugular.'

"The third soldier ripped Marina's gown away from her, tore it straight down her body, uncovered her for their greedy eyes. Then the Navarch grabbed the hem and tore it up to her waist. He put his knee between her legs. When she screamed, her mouth uncovered again, he struck her with the flat of his hand. I strained forward, but the gendarme who held me lifted the blade of his knife against my throat; I felt its edge slice into me.

"I was helpless, Markcrier. I could have died, I suppose, but I didn't have the courage to die. They made me watch as Serenos beat my daughter insensible; they made me watch him rape her, viciously rape her as the soldiers laughed. He lifted her like a puppet, again and again with his hands and body, biting her on the lips until they bled. I shut my eyes, Markcrier, I couldn't stand it. But by the laughter and the noise I know that Serenos raped her twice, once for her father, once for her husband.

"I wished that I could force my head forward, slice open my throat on the gendarme's knife. But I couldn't, I just couldn't, my body wouldn't move, and after a while it was over."

The story was over, the shark's undercut mouth ceased its wrinklings, the evil mouth resolved into a wound, and I found my strength coming back into me—just as if a soul-tormented priest had granted me absolution for the sin of doubting him. I stood up. Prendick's hands fell away from me.

"What about the gendarmes?" I said.

"No. He wouldn't let them touch her. They wanted to, but he wouldn't let them. They were afraid of him."

"Everyone's afraid of him."

Prendick sobbed.

"I'm going upstairs to my wife," he said.

As the stained-glass windows began to color with the translucent coming of dawn, I climbed the winding stairs to the room where Marina lay.

III

Thou talkest of harvest when the corn is green:
The end is crown of every work well done;
The sickle comes not, till the corn be ripe.

—THOMAS KYD

Strange as it may seem to the unscientific reader, there can be no denying that, whatever amount of credibility attaches to . . . this story, the manufacture of monsters . . . is within the possibilities of vivisection.

—H. G. WELLS

I contemplated revenge, even if it meant the abrogation of many things that I believed in and perhaps even my own death. I discussed revenge with Prendick, but his work in the theater of surgery kept him occupied seemingly day and night now, and he was too weary upon returning to The Orchard each evening to listen to the ignorant schemes I had concocted during his absences. His mysterious work—the work he would not talk about—drained him; it continued with more urgency than before Marina's rape. When he was home, however, I badgered him.

Once he told me pointedly that I should shut up. "If we fail," he said, "I'm afraid of what will happen to our family, to Marina and Melantha. You haven't thought

about that, have you?" Still, the idea nagged. Only whe
Marina began to recover and became aware of what I wa
contemplating did the idea finally die. Marina helped it t
its death.

"Markcrier," she said, "think about the way you've con
ducted your life. You're a genuinely good man—one of th
few who live in Windfall Last."

"That's a rankly sentimental judgment."

"But a fair one. Now you wish to comport yourself in
way wholly out of keeping with the way you've lived."

"I want what's right."

"It isn't right to take a life when one hasn't been los
I'm alive, Markcrier, I'm with you at this very moment."

And so I did nothing. Having been given a lesson in th
morality of post-Holocaust B (a morality that Serenos di
not subscribe to), I kissed Marina, tended to her durin
the long days of her recuperation, achieved a strange inne
peacefulness, and wrote two sections of a long poem tha
I called *Archipelagoes*. My doing nothing about Serenos
Marina convinced me, was in reality an active reaffirmatio
of the ethos that made us who we were. Three week
lapsed.

We discovered that Marina was pregnant.

My own sterility mocked me, the fierce chagrin of th
seedless. But too much philosophy ruled me, and I fough
down both my chagrin and my incipient rage—with self
administered doses of temperance. I could see that Marin
wanted the child. I did not tell her that I would never b
able to love it. How could I tell her? We had resolved t
live as intelligent human beings, we had determined not t
seek revenge, we had committed ourselves to affirmatio
and love. My inner peacefulness dissolved, but I would dis
simulate if Marina's happiness depended on thinking m
happy. Unfortunately, it did. It always had. However, a
diplomat learns how to role-play early in his career, an
for the first time in our married lives I role-played fo
Marina. But God! how my own sterility mocked me, how
my cancerous chagrin gnawed!

I acted my role well. The only clue I gave Marina to my
real feelings was the fact that I did not resume work o
Archipelagoes. This failure of discipline I attributed t
excitement; there were too many other things to do. Th
mother in her aroused, the wife in her less perceptive
Marina believed me.

And for the final six months of her pregnancy I kept up the deception. I very nearly convinced myself that nothing was wrong, that we were indeed happy. But at night in bed I lay awake, knowing the truth. Before it became uncomfortable for her, I often turned to Marina in the early morning and kissed her half-awake and entered her with inarticulate desperation. She responded as best she could. She imagined that I had grown amorous with the psychological aphrodisiac of a new image of her—the image of her as a fertile, child-carrying woman. My amorousness derived instead from my intense need to believe that the child she carried had sprung from my own flesh: there was no love inside me on these mornings, only the sickness of my need and the mechanical impulse to fuck away the nightmares that pursued me through every waking moment. But in our shared waking hours I kept up the deception. I am certain that she never knew. And she had either forgotten or forced herself not to think of the possibility of the child's being deformed.

Her time came upon her early. An hour before midnight.

We had expected her father to deliver the baby, but Prendick was busy in Windfall Last, occupied as always in the performance of his duty. Fearing Serenos ruled him, but Serenos ruled us all. Even when locked behind his own bedchamber doors, the Navarch manipulated the strings of our lives. Sometimes he could not have known in what pernicious ways.

Marina's contractions were frequent and long in duration; they caused intense pain in her lower back. We had made no provisions for the child's coming so early, and I did not know what to do. My wife's pain frightened me. After making Marina as comfortable as I could on our disheveled bed, I told her that I was going to the main house to fetch her mother. She understood, she told me that she would be all right, she winced involuntarily, piteously, at the onset of a new contraction. I left her and went to the main house.

When Melantha and I returned, Marina was screaming. She lay with her good arm and hand behind her head, clutching a rail in the headboard. Her seawing was twisted at a level with her shoulder, flattened awkwardly against the gray sheet. The linen under her hips was wet, her knees up and apart. Melantha straightened Marina's deformed arm, smoothed back the hair plastered against her brow, and helped her remove the underclothes that her amniotic fluid had soaked in breaking.

"I think this is going too fast," Marina's mother said. She was a tall woman with thin lips and eyes the color of bleached shells. "Much too fast."

"What can I do?"

"Get some fresh linen, Markcrier."

"Shouldn't I try to reach Yves? Can't we get him here somehow?"

"I don't see how. Just bring fresh linen, Mark. If you try to reach Yves, you'll only leave me alone for the delivery, everything's happening so quickly." Her thin mouth was Marina's mouth. She said, "You should be beside her—not on your way to Windfall Last."

Marina cried out, turned her head, stared with filmed-over eyes at the ceiling. Something was wrong. Something other than simple prematurity. I went out of the room and crossed an enclosed section of scaffolding to the utility module. Through the window of clear glass I could see the moon-projected shadow of Python's Keep on the lawn, an entanglement as tortuous as death itself. I found clean fragrant linen and returned to the bedroom.

Melantha had eased Marina forward along the bed so that she could squat between her daughter's legs and receive the infant as it was born. Marina lay on the fluid-drenched bedding that I had been sent to replace. Like a serving man at one of the Navarch's dinner parties, I stood with the sheets draped over my forearm.

"Put those down. There isn't time. Hold your wife's arms."

I obeyed. I smelled blood and salt. Leaning over Marina, I could tell that she did not see me; she squinted into a limbo somewhere beyond my head, her face was purpled with the agony of labor. "It's going to be all right," I said, knowing that it wouldn't. Something was wrong. Something other than early parturition.

Marina's mother spoke to her over the glistening mound of her belly, told her to concentrate, to push as if she were having a bowel movement. And I held Marina's shoulders and kissed away the salt on her furrowed forehead, saying, "It's going to be all right, it's going to be all right."

The first thing that came out of her womb came within

ive minutes of my return to the bedroom, so quickly did
ier labor progress. It was a sluggish, slowly flailing thing
with a down of amber hair all over its body and tiny
flippers where hands should have been. I looked at Me-
antha. Her thin mouth was set. She refused to acknowledge me. She placed the whelp, umbilical cord still trail-
ng, on the bed beside Marina and told me to wrap it in
he clean linen. The thing was alive. And very small. It did
iot cry. Perhaps twenty minutes had passed since my
iummoning of Mrs. Prendick from the main house—but
Marina's contractions continued. She did not open her
eyes; she still had not seen the product of her agony.

"There's another child, darling," Melantha said. "I want
you to do what you did before, push when the contractions
come."

"No," Marina said. "Oh, please, not another one, no,
no."

"What the hell is this? What's going on? What is it?"
The smell of blood and salt turned the room into a nightmarish slaughterhouse. I was powerless to control or influence events. Mrs. Prendick ignored me.

"Oh, lord," Melantha said after a while, talking in a
whisper to herself. "This one has presented me its buttocks."

"What does that mean?" I demanded.

"A breech delivery," she said, finally showing a fissure in
her apparent invincibility. Her voice broke. She held up
her bloodied hands. "I don't know, I just don't know."

And she didn't know, for Marina's labor went into its
second hour, then its third, with no progress. Melantha had
no instruments; she would not have known how to use
them if she had.

When the second thing at last permitted itself to be born,
we had both exhausted our repertoire of hysterics. Marina
was dead, the tiny creature out of her womb was dead,
and Mrs. Prendick, her tall body twisted around upon itself, sat slumped on the floor where she had tried to play
midwife. She was not asleep, she was not awake. I covered
Marina. Then I picked up Melantha, carried her to another
module, and placed her on a long brocaded divan. The
night smelled of distant azaleas.

With that odor in my nostrils, I climbed back through
the dark labyrinth of Python's Keep. As if hypnotized, I
found my wife's deathbed. It had about it the ancient still-

ness of an archaeological dig. The corpses were remarkably
well preserved, one small mummified form feigning life
with shallow breaths. I picked it up and covered its mouth
and nostrils with the heel and palm of my hand. It scarcely
struggled. Then I lifted the other small corpse from its
resting place and withdrew from the ancient tranquillity
in which Marina slept. She was too far removed from me
to elicit my grief.

Not grieving, merely sleepwalking, I carried the animal
things from her womb downstairs to the lawn. I walked
through the entangled shadow of Python's Keep.

In Marina's garden I dug shallow depressions with my
bare hands and buried the things she had grown. For a
long while I continued to dig; I tore at the soil with my
bruised nails. At last I stopped and sat on my haunches
in the dirt—almost comprehending how little free will a
free man has.

For I was indeed free.

I resolved, as the tree-entangled dawn came back, to
make Fearing Serenos regret the day of his own birthing.
I resolved this with all the ruthlessness of incorruptible
natural phenomena, the ruthlessness of sunlight and tide.
Serenos would burn in a candle of gas; he would drown
in the waters of a malignant moon. I resolved these things
freely and knew that the Navarch would not escape my
vengeance.

On the day of Marina's cremation, Prendick and I went
down to the quay to scatter her ashes on the water. We had
just come from the official crematory of the Navarchy,
several rows of terra-cotta houses away from Prendick's
waterfront hospital. We were alone. Marina's mother had
remained in the main house at The Orchard, fatigued,
uncommunicative, ill.

I carried an amphora—a narrow-mouthed jar—tenderly
before me. This contained the final, soot-flavored residue
of a human being, and I had to make a concerted mental
and physical effort not to raise the jar to my lips and drink
of my wife's ashes. Unlike the ashes, the jar was cool.

Together Yves and I descended the stone stairs to the
flagstones on the quay. No ship was docked in the place
we had chosen, and no sinister trunkless heads adorned
the spikes along the harbor wall. The sky was the color
of milk.

I began the ritual. I poured the ashes into my hand,

waited for the wind to blow away from me, and scattered the ashes over the water on this gentle wind. Silently, Prendick followed my example. As we scattered Marina's ashes on the bay, I realized that her ashes, metaphorically, were those of Holocaust C, the fallout of a miniature Armageddon. On the rainbowed water she floated like sentient dust.

God no longer prophesied doom, he was through with us, nor did the Parfects truly concern themselves with our petty murders. Dust on the water Marina was, ash on the sea.

"Yves?"

He looked at me—not with a great deal of responsiveness, his hand feebly emptying its contents on the wind. In seven months he had grown slow and morosely sullen. How often he had been forced to change.

"Yves, we're going to do something about Marina's death."

"What?" He stared. "What will we do?"

"Kill Serenos. Or cripple him. Make him experience, in a similar species of coin, some part of the pain he's caused others."

"With what chance of success?" the doctor said. "And how?"

"You have a head, you have a heart, you once had a daughter. Whatever you decide or fail to decide, I'm going to do something, something to unburden my soul." I paused. "As the Navarch's personal physician, you have access to him."

Prendick stared. "What do you mean? What're you implying?"

"That you should use your head to determine how your access to Serenos will most benefit us. A very simple thing, Yves, very simple."

He stared at me for a long moment. Then he turned back to the water and cast a last meager handful of ash into the sea. Our conversation was over, but Prendick had begun to think. I saw inside his head, I saw his emotions running into little wells of intellection, I saw his mind turned into a bleached brain coral and from the brain coral into an ambiguous living thing, confined but free. Soon the wind blew across the empty mouth of the amphora, and the low bass notes of emptiness arose.

We left the quay.

Three days later Prendick invited me to visit him at the theater of surgery for an entire afternoon. Never before had he extended to me or anyone else in his immediate family such an invitation. I knew that the significance of this invitation lay in its following so obviously on our brief exchange on the quay.

Ordinarily Prendick spent two hours every morning in the Palace of the Navarchy, whether Serenos demanded his attention or not. Then he went by carriage down the cobbled streets, past dwellings of rose-red terra-cotta, to the waterfront and the only major building that the Parfects had erected among the salt-drenched quays. The theater of surgery was located in this structure, which everyone called Hospitaler House.

A monument of aluminum and glass, its windows polarized against the sun, Hospitaler House rose fifteen stories over the bay of Pretty Coal Sack on an immense round platform that seemed to float on the waters of the bay. Deep in the great cylindrical column upon which the Parfects had long ago erected this symbol of mercy, one might find the submerged, echoing, antiseptic chambers of the theater of surgery—if one were lucky enough to receive an invitation. Once inside the central chamber, the visitor encountered a window of gargantuan proportions facing toward the open sea. A window on a submerged world. When the waters of the Carib lay unruffled under the refracted sky, one could almost swear that the rippling dome of the Sunken Library, farther out in the bay, was visible.

A man in a frock escorted me into the central chamber of the column and departed.

I stood alone in the copper-bright vastness, the smells of alcohol and of something oddly zoolike preeminent among the odors that clamored there. Looking up, I saw that a kind of tier went around half the cylinder and that Prendick was standing on this level, his hands on the railing, looking down at me. He said nothing.

I navigated a path through the surgical equipment on the main floor until I was almost directly below him. His face sang with the madness of one who communes with the sea and with sea anemones, one who eats the hallucinogens of shipwreck and death. In fact, he looked like a poet—the way Markcrier Rains ought to have looked so soon after "personal tragedy." But he said nothing. Finally,

o provoke some sort of response, I spat on my hands and
did a mocking toe-tap dance on the sleek floor.

"Stop that," Prendick said, "and come up here. The stairs
are over there."

I found the stairs and climbed up to him. Doors with
metal sliding panels for windows made a circuit around the
inside of the tier—ten or twelve such doors in all. They
were all closed and tightly sealed, but on this level the
zoolike smell overrode that of the alcohol; I knew that
behind the closed doors was the distinctly animal source
of this smell. But the thought did not disturb me. Out-
wardly, I was loose and cheerful. Prendick, after all, was
coming round and we would soon have a plan.

"What is this?" I said. "A cellblock for the dogs that
the prol-fauves haven't eaten yet?"

"Let's not waste any time, Markcrier. I'll show you what
it is."

He selected one of the doors and slid back its window
panel as if he were a medieval gaoler in the dungeon of
his lord, which, to some extent, he in fact was. The copper
panel slid smoothly aside. Unctuous as dead fish, the
stench assailed me anew. Immediately upon the panel's
opening, it coated the membranes of my mouth and nose
like a rancid oil. I stepped back from the window.

"My God, Yves!"

"Look, damn you, turn about and look!"

My mood declined from cheerfulness into apprehension.
I examined Prendick's face, then forced myself to stare into
the gleaming cell. The cell was clean, the walls gleaming,
the floor an immaculate gray—so that the stench had to
originate with the hoary creature that sat in the cell's far
right-hand corner. An absurdly squat animal.

Propped in the angle of two walls, it appeared to be
asleep, its paws draped decorously over its middle. A
mantle of white fur, somewhat mangy and sparse, gave the
beast the look of a worldly gentleman fallen on difficult
times. Although fairly long through the torso, the animal
had short deformed hind legs that canted outward from
its body so that its sex lay exposed in a thin lawn of pubic
white. Turgid and intricately veined, the organ had no apparent relevance to the body structure of the creature
possessing it. But in spite of the piscine stench that had
nearly overwhelmed me a moment before, I judged the
animal to be anything but a predator.

I turned away from the window again. "It looks a little like a sea otter." *The memorable scent of hard flesh, intimate and pelagic, on Christmas day.* "Except for the size of its limbs and head. And the primatelike genitals. You've been carving on him pretty viciously, Yves, from what I can see."

"You don't see very much. Look again."

"Please," I said with some exasperation. "What for?"

"Look again, Markcrier. This time I'll wake him up so that you can make a more accurate judgment—although I'm glad that you think it looks like a sea otter, that being what I was striving for." He slid the copper panel back and forth across the window, causing it to clank against its frame. "Now look again!' he commanded me.

Exasperated, uncertain, afraid of what I was being shown, I looked. The animal had not moved, but now its eyes were open and luminous with fear. It remembered Prendick's knife, no doubt, the eventide eternities when the anesthetic had not taken hold.

Then the anomaly of its posture there in the corner struck me—the languidly hanging paws and the tight uncertain eyes. What was it in the creature's lineaments that so unsettled and mocked us? Since its head remained down, only its eyes—looking up under a shaggy misshapen brow—could be responsible for the shame I felt in spying on it: its eyes were the eyes of a human being, trapped but intelligent. The creature seemed unable to lift its head from its breast, but its frightened eyes flickered over our prying faces and showed us, beneath each upward-straining eyeball, a thin crescent of eloquent white.

I turned again to Prendick. Horrified, I shrugged noncommittally.

"That otter used to be a man, Mark. And the man he used to be was your friend from Marigold Island, I've forgotten his name. Do you understand what I'm saying?"

"Huerta?" I said incredulously.

"That's right. Huerta. I'd forgotten the name, it's been so long that Serenos has had me doing this one."

"Doing this one," I echoed. I stared at Prendick. The madness singing in his tortured face had softened into an expression of professional distance; he had no concept of the awesome disparity between his words "doing this one" and the gut-rending fact of converting a human being into an animal. His face registered a hysterical calm, his puffy eyes a smug aloofness from reality. Prendick, I realized, was grown into the archetypal mad scientist—with the telling qualification that his madness had seeped into him from the ubiquitous distillation of the Navarch's evil. I was touched by that madness myself. How could I upbraid a madman for the enormities his madness had perpetrated? How could I condemn Marina's father for succumbing to the evil that had begun to drive me? I turned back to the cell window. Ignoring the stench, I shouted at the incomplete thing slouched against the wall, "Huerta! Huerta, it's Markcrier, I'm going to let you out, I'm going to try to help you!"

Huerta did not move, but the eyes—the eyes fixed on me reproachfully.

"I've decerebrated it," Prendick said. "It doesn't understand."

"Why? Why have you done this to him?"

"Because Serenos wanted me to. He said I could restore creatures like this one—and specimens of the prolfauves—to a condition more suited to their natures or I could condemn my family to death by refusing to do so. Do you understand me, Markcrier? I'm not supposed to be telling you this."

"I understand," I said, going to the railing and looking across the operating hall at the huge window there. The sea pressed against the glass like a woman embracing her lover: crystalline ambiguity.

"At the turn of this century Serenos ordered me to perform experimental work on cadavers, simple work that never required me to be away from home. But about two years ago, perhaps more, he demanded that I 'create' things for him out of living human beings—things that would be demonstrably less than human. I was to use animals for models, both living animals and extinct ones." Prendick pointed at a door several meters down the tier. "There's a kind of protoman in there. A dawn creature, aeons before either of the Holocausts: the books sometimes call it *Homo habilis*. I did it very well, I think—at least in regard to its outward anatomy."

Prendick joined me at the railing. "Of course, after the cadavers the work was more difficult. The Navarch set deadlines. I had to be away from The Orchard for longer periods. After Marina's rape, he provided me with the old man who was your friend, the old man who became the raw material for the sea otter you've just looked at. Serenos said he wanted a sea otter this time. He specified a white one. But the old man was so old that he almost died while I was working on him. . . ."

I folded my hands on the railing and put my head down.

Consolingly, Prendick put his arm around my shoulders; he whispered in my ear so that I could feel his breath. "Don't be upset, Mark. It wasn't a personal thing, what I did to your friend." He tapped my shoulder. "Besides, I have a plan."

I looked into the mutely singing eyes of my dead wife's father.

"You see," he said, "I can do the same thing to Fearing Serenos; I can do the *same thing* to the Navarch."

Long ago, in a very old book, I had read about a man who had attempted to turn animals into men through vivisection. What Marina's father was doing embodied the opposite notion; and although innately more repugnant than "humanizing" dumb beasts, it was a simpler task than the other. After all, the insidiously rational Dr. Moreau had failed because he could not instill a lasting human intelligence in his brutish subjects: the nebulous quality of humankind's "soul" invariably faded with time. But insofar as Prendick had succeeded in carrying out the Navarch's will, he had succeeded precisely because it is easier to destroy than to build, to demolish than to create.

Huerta (if one could forget his eyes) was an animal in every respect. The human being in him had departed with each successive incision of Prendick's scalpel, with each expert deletion of brain tissue, with each cruel alteration of his hands and feet. My rage grew. My heart pounded *ven-geance, ven-geance*. I knew that I did in fact wish to do the same thing to Serenos, to reduce him completely to the animal he already was.

Understanding that Prendick approached the world from the perspective of a madman enabled me to work with him. We were madmen together. I drew energy from his insanity as surely as if I were a psychic vampire. Prendick's plan had no more brilliance than the recommendation of a bactericide for a sore throat, but we sought to effect his remedy with all the insane zeal we could muster, and our very zealousness made the plan work.

It was two months after Marina's death in childbirth that we put this awkward strategy to the test, two months

the day. The first torrential rainfall of October scoured
the streets outside the Palace of the Navarchy, scoured the
rained terra-cotta dwellings, caused the rabid sea to foam
against the quaystones under the force of the October
deluge. We had waited, Prendick and I, for just such a
morning.

We left The Orchard in Prendick's battery-powered
autocart and arrived together at the Palace perhaps an
hour before the breaking of a thin winterish light. We had
informed not a single other person of our intentions; and
because Serenos would have suspected some sort of under-
handedness if he had seen me, I remained in the hot,
breath-fogged cockpit of Prendick's autocart while he ran
up the seemingly varnished steps of the main administrative building. I looked around, prepared to hide if a
gendarme in a poncho should approach. Since not a single
member of the Gendarmerie came forward to check Prendick's vehicle and since it would be better for us if his
autocart were not so brazenly conspicuous at the beginning
of our ruse, I dared to expose myself for a moment and
drove the autocart out of the way. I drove it into a high-
walled shelter between the Palace itself and the eastern
wall of the "imperial" stables. Because of the rain, no one
challenged me.

Bitter cleansing rains of incredible ferocity conspired
with us against the Navarch. It was fitting. Had not one of
my ancestors washed his sullied body in such torrents and
taken their name for his own?

All I had to do was wait. Prendick knew where I would
be. I crawled into the autocart's backseat—in reality, a
storage well—and covered myself with a heavy tarpaulin.
Immediately drenched in my own sweat, I listened to the
roar of the world.

In time, Prendick would emerge into the rain with
Serenos and the Navarch's inevitable uniformed riflemen—Molinier, his favorite, among them. The pretext
for getting the Navarch to take a jaunt in the rain would
be Prendick's avowal of a genuine miracle of vivisection
at Hospitaler House. For several weeks Serenos had been
pressuring my mad friend about his progress with Huerta,
but Yves had put him off with clumsy excuses—so that
we might take advantage of the beginning of the rainy
season.

Now it had come. At no other time would the Navarch

have even considered riding from the Palace to any other part of Windfall Last in a vehicle other than his ornate open carriage, a conveyance drawn by four identical Percherons. But like many men who place no value on the lives of human beings, he did not choose to let valuable animals suffer; therefore, we had assumed that Serenos would not require his beautifully groomed horses to brave this inclement October morning. And we assumed correctly.

I heard footfalls on the flagstones. The door of the autocart opened, turning up the volume on the rain and allowing a gust of muggy wind to lift a corner of my tarpaulin. Then the slamming of the door and a return of the storage well's stifling humidity. Crouched under the tarp, I waited for some word from Prendick.

Finally he said, "He's going to ride with us, Markcrier—or with me, that is, so far as he knows. I'm driving over to the entrance to pick him up."

I said nothing. Moving through the rain, the autocart whined softly.

"Did you hear me?" Prendick said. "And it may be that his personal gendarmes will follow in another vehicle. Perhaps even on horseback, since their horses aren't his own coddled Percherons. Do you hear me?"

"Yes," I said. "I was just wondering what Serenos smells like when he's wet. Have you ever wondered about that?"

"No. Why would I wonder about something like that?"

I did not reply, and the tires of the autocart sloughed through the runoff from the Palace's rain gutters. Then the gentle whine of the batteries ceased altogether.

We were at rest.

There were voices and footfalls. The door opposite Prendick roared open, then kicked shut with a violent *thwump!* We rocked a little. Even from beneath my concealing canvas I could feel another body adjusting to the narrow confines of our autocart, a body of no small proportions.

Then again the amplified crackling of the rain and Prendick shouting out his window at someone: "Hell, no, I won't carry you in here! You're already sopping wet, your capes and jodhpurs all sopping! And this thing wasn't made to transport armies, it wasn't made to—"

A voice shouted back an indistinct response.

Then I heard the Navarch's voice (it was the first time

had heard it since he had told me, *I'll never ask anything of you again, Markcrier*). Now he was leaning over Prendick and shouting at the undoubtedly miserable gendarme in the rain, in a voice that sounded both annoyed and authoritative, "Just follow us, Molinier, you and the others! Get in another goddamn vehicle and follow us closely. Dr. Prendick can be counted on to see me safely to Hospitaler House!"

Molinier or someone else responded unintelligibly. The window went up again, but I thought for a moment about Molinier. He was a handsome man in his late forties, with vestigial gill slits—unfunctioning, of course—just behind his jawbones on the upper part of his neck. I had known him relatively well in the final period of my service to Windfall Last. For a murderer, he was an amiable enough fellow. We had once worked together with a complete absence of either recrimination or jealousy.

Then the tires began whirring through water once more and the engine whining like a swarm of summer mosquitoes. The rain pounded the fiberglass hull of the autocart with barbaric tattoos, the patterns of which altered in intensity and rhythm every few minutes. I waited. I suffered the oppressive humidity of my closed-in hiding place.

But when Prendick said, "Your gatemen weren't very conscientious today, Navarch," I uncovered and stuck a pistol in the intimate depression at the base of Fearing Serenos's skull. The pistol had belonged to Marina.

"If you move," I said, "I won't hesitate to let this nasty little machine take a core sample of your gray matter."

There was a momentary silence. Then, "That could only be Markcrier Rains, Dr. Prendick. Such a nasty day for him to get out."

"Shut up," I said. I pushed the barrel deeper into the depression at the back of his head. I was enjoying myself: the rough language, the gun butt cradled in my palm, this conspiracy of dark rains and lofty madness. Moreover, Serenos shut up.

Because Prendick allowed the autocart to career down the cobbled streets, rocking back and forth over its wheels, it took us very little time to reach Hospitaler House. Several unmasted boats pitched in their moorings beside the quays. A few fishermen huddled together on various decks, pointing and gesturing with heads and hands as if they were demigods attempting to calm the sea. But except for some children we had passed beneath the Palace of the Navarchy, no other people had ventured outdoors.

We halted on the perimeter of the great platform on which the hospital seemed to float.

As soon as Prendick got out and went around to the Navarch's door, Serenos slammed it open, knocked Prendick down, and hurled his lithe muscular body into the downpour. I pursued. Bruising my upper thighs in the process, I lurched out of the autocart's backseat.

With rain slashing out of the sky into my face, I shot the Navarch in the calf. I shot him again in the buttocks. His royal vestments fluttering about him like the wings of a manta ray, he toppled and rolled onto his belly. The rain, like so many fluid needles, pinioned him to the concrete.

In a moment Prendick was up from his back, and the two of us lifted Serenos, held him erect between us, and stumbled with him toward the building's nearest entrance.

We went in.

Prendick found his keys and admitted us to the elevator that would drop us into the submerged operating hall of the theater of surgery. Down we went. In the closed quarters of the elevator, supporting Serenos as he bled, I realized that the man smelled exactly like a wet dog.

I grew angry. Why were we taking Serenos to the cloistered vivisection area to which only Prendick had access? We could end things quickly if we wished: I could shoot the bastard in the head at point-blank range and so conclude eight years of needless suffering. But we were down. We were on the floor of the operating hall.

Molinier and the other gendarmes were not long in arriving. On a closed-circuit television unit we watched them enter Hospitaler House. Prendick went upstairs and told them a remarkable story, one he had devised over two weeks ago especially for this critical confrontation: The Navarch had had a sudden and acute attack of stigmata in his hands and side, an unpredictable infirmity to which men in high positions had been mysteriously subject throughout all recorded history. Because of this attack of stigmata, Prendick went on, he had placed the Navarch in a private room in one of the lower levels of Hospitaler House, where Serenos was now resting comfortably.

Meticulously observant, Molinier had seen evidence of blood on the streaming pavement outside Hospitaler House and in the upper hallway as well. He did not choose to take Marina's father at his word. Therefore, Prendick came back down to me and prepared to give Molinier the assurance that he wanted. Only when I forced the Navarch, at gunpoint, to announce over the hospital's intercom system the nature of his injuries, the extent of his loss of blood, and the fact that he would be staying with us for three or four more days, only then did the gendarmes accept the lies we had fed them. Molinier and the others left.

We drugged the Navarch. He lay unconscious on his stomach on one of the metallic operating tables, and we sat on stools and talked like two medical students above his inert form. We had stripped him, and the finely haired body of the man fascinated us. Ageless and heretofore invincible, Fearing Serenos had the animal vibrancy of a jaguar. The bullet holes in his calf and buttock actually hurt my heart; they were crimson insults to an otherwise perfect physique. But, seeing him naked, I hated Fearing Serenos even more than I had hated him after Marina's rape, or after her pregnancy, or after her preternatural labor. Beast creatures slept in the seed of the Navarch's loins.

"Well, what shall we do with him?" Prendick asked. "What sort of thing shall we turn him into? After I've removed the bullets?"

Turning toward the hall's immense window, I looked at the surprisingly calm waters beyond. Faint undulations swept against the glass, a stirring of unknown powers and unwritten poems.

"Well, Mark, what do you want to do?" Prendick came back into my line of vision; his mad eyes were upon me, opaque with dull expectancy.

"I want you to turn Serenos into a shark," I said. "I want you to give him the shape and the hairlessness and the blunt stupid nose of a shark. That's what I want you to do with him."

The mad eyes stared, they glinted. And without a single flicker of outrage, these same eyes acquiesced in the irrationality of my proposal.

And so we began.

No one truly knew what had befallen the Navarch, although Molinier demanded that Dr. Prendick provide him with tangible evidence that Serenos still lived. This ulti-

matum came on the second day of the Navarch's captivity,
and Prendick, acting upon no stratagem but the intuition
of his madness, simply replied that he could offer no such
evidence because in a paroxysm of nocturnal spiritual
ecstasy the Navarch had cast his eyes up to heaven and
died! For some reason, Prendick filigreed this unlikely
"official report" with the observation that the Navarch's
ecstasy had followed closely upon his viewing a new marvel
of vivisection, the Otter Man.

Although no word of Serenos's "death" reached the
general public, Prendick's report went out to every member and past member of the Council of the Navarchy, including myself. Everyone believed. Inherent in this bizarre
account of our leader's dying was a drama that no one
could ignore. Had the multitudinous sins of Fearing
Serenos at last run him to ground and figuratively torn
away the flesh at his throat? If so, the punishment was
just.

I had to laugh—at my coconspirator's inventive fantasy
and at the sanctimonious reaction of the council members.

Because no one had seen me on the morning of the
Navarch's journey to Hospitaler House, I was above suspicion. Therefore, on the fourth day of Serenos's confine-
ment (the third day after the announcement of his death),
I joined my former colleagues in the Palace of the Navarchy. They treated me with deference and respect. As
the only man in Guardian's Loop's history ever to have
lived twice in Azteca Nueva among the enigmatic Parfects,
I had an enigmatic position all my own. Eight years in
retirement had heightened for these men the illusion of
my venerableness. And, finally, their quietly held knowledge that my wife had died as a result of Serenos's cruelty
secured for me the status of a living martyr.

Desperate for direction, they turned to me. Even
Molinier, who had expressed serious doubts about the
complete accuracy of Prendick's report, accepted my as-
surances that no foul play had occurred. After all, I knew
the doctor. He had suffered more than most of us at the
Navarch's hands (quietly knowledgeable looks passed between the council members when I said this), but no man
had been so diligent as my father-in-law in the impartial
execution of his duty. Swarthy, keen-eyed, gill-scarred
Molinier listened to my word and believed me.

Without seeking the office, I had become the interregnal Navarch. I had not anticipated this outcome, had not been prescient enough to understand the impact of my own reputation. How could I have hoped to understand? My reputation and I shared nothing in common but those two amazingly complex words, Markcrier Rains.

Nevertheless, I assumed the pilot's role almost without thinking.

Although Molinier supported me in this capacity and rallied more than three-quarters of the Gendarmerie in my behalf, a small segment of our official police force chose to support an aging bureaucrat who had never quite acceded to the prefecture of the organization. Even while Serenos had ruled, this man—Duvalier—had openly criticized the policies and methods of his immediate superior, Molinier (perhaps with some justification, considering our relatively effortless capture of the Navarch); but Duvalier had not been removed from his position, primarily because he understood the delicate business of bodyguarding as no one else and because he had made fast friends with several of the more elderly council members. On the second day of my "reign," it became apparent that the faction supporting this man would not go quietly away of its own volition. Molinier approached me; he asked for permission to deal with these reprehensible few. I listened. Not yet aware of the power that resided in my simplest word, I told Molinier to do what had to be done.

The following day I discovered that twenty freshly severed heads decorated the spikes along the harbor wall. The faces were masks of hard black blood, and the sea gulls dived upon them with the impunity of falling sunlight.

Once again I had indirectly precipitated an atrocity. How many times would I be responsible for other people's deaths?

Although this question genuinely pained me, tortured me in the long midnights, I sublimated its painfulness and tried to glory in the newfound security of my position. I had become the Navarch. I hoped that I had not become Fearing Serenos.

A rumor started that the sea gulls near the harbor had gone mad and that they copulated in the air as they fell in screaming torrents on the impaled heads of the slaughtered gendarmes. I half believed the rumor and expected the heads to have been devoured the next time I ventured to the quays. The appetites of animals, sexual and otherwise, haunted my thoughts.

Sea gulls copulating in the air?

IV

May no one die till he has loved!

—SAINT-JOHN PERSE

Nevertheless, the disembodied heads of the rebel gendarmes greeted me when I finally found the time to visit Prendick at Hospitaler House. The libidinous gulls had not completely ravished them or themselves.

Trembling, I sought out Marina's father and came upon him in the sunken chamber of surgery. In the last several days he had taken the first strides toward effecting the metamorphosis of our drugged former leader. I wanted to halt this madness, but I could not. I convinced myself that the process had already gone beyond the point of legitimate reversal. If we stopped now, I argued to myself, Serenos would be a thing, a grotesque parody of his former self. Since we could not restore him, it was best to proceed. Moreover, I realized that under no circumstances would Prendick be likely to permit an interruption of his first tender modifications of our patient's anatomy. He pursued the animalization of Fearing Serenos with too much innocent enthusiasm to be put off by my sober moral concern. He had worked too hard already. Therefore, inertia ruled me—inertia and my own persistent desire to see the Navarch suffer. I delighted in Prendick's malicious skill.

"Markcrier," he said when I came into the hall. "Have you come to see how our experiment progresses?"

I ignored the question; I had other matters on my mind.

"We must give the council a body, Yves. Molinier demands a body. Before we can announce Serenos's death to the populace of Windfall Last, there must be some evidence that he is, in fact, dead. Everyone wants a funeral."

"Give them a sealed casket and a cremation ceremony," Prendick said curtly. "Tell them that will suffice."

"And if Molinier should wish to examine the body?"

"I have *already* examined the body! I am the physician to the Navarch, and no one has the right to question my competence or loyalty." As if I had questioned both, he looked at me accusingly. "All you need do, Markcrier, is tell them that no one views the Navarch's body once it has been prepared for cremation. Tradition dictates this procedure. You're the new Navarch. Who'll not believe you?"

"What tradition, Yves?"

"None. But say it anyway. No one remembers the occasion of the previous Navarch's death; consequently, no one will challenge you about the funeral procedures. The history of Windfall Last," Prendick said in a faraway voice, "is not so well documented as that of several pre-Holocaust civilizations. How very odd that is."

"Yes. Odd."

"Come with me and see how your shark progresses, Markcrier. It's slow, it's very slow—but you'll be proud of me." In his eyes: the images of tangled seaweed and the minute tentacles of an old obsession, one we shared.

I followed him onto the tier above the chamber's main floor, the tier where I had come face to face with Emmanuel Huerta in his new incarnation. This thought I put in a far corner of my mind, but the odor of fish and fur recalled it to me with punishing vividness at brief unpredictable moments in my conversation with Prendick. The tier still reeked. I refused, however, to let these moments rule me.

We looked down on a large round tank that had not been in the theater of surgery on the day of Serenos's capture. A thin milk-colored solution swirled in the tank— a solution that apparently flowed through an assemblage of swan-necked glass tubing into the adjacent cleansing unit and then back into the barbarously foaming tank, endlessly recirculating, like pale blood. So evil did this apparatus look that I had the ridiculous idea that Prendick had created it solely for its appearance.

Fearing Serenos lay at full length in this milky whirlpool, his head held out of the water by means of a metal brace that forced his chin to point at the ceiling. And his face was naked. I would not have recognized the Navarch had I not already known what to expect—primal nudity, the hairlessness of reptiles, flesh the color of burnt rubber.

Looking down at the open tank, at the milky solution

laving Serenos's body, I asked, "Does he know what's going on? Have you . . . decerebrated him?"

"No. I'm not going to. We decided not to, didn't we?"

"Then he *does* know what's going on?"

"No, he doesn't. Look at him, Markcrier. He's on a heavy dose of slightly modified pentobarbital sodium. The drug serves two purposes. It keeps him anesthetized against the maceration process of the whirlpool, which is more frightening than painful, I should imagine; and it produced in his own metabolism the first evidences of a condition approaching that of poikilothermal animals: cold-bloodedness. Once we remove him from the tank, a partial severing of his spinal cord will insure that he continues in this cold-blooded state, just like all good mantas and sharks."

"And what does the whirlpool do?"

Prendick stared not at the tank, but at the gently heaving waters of Pretty Coal Sack. "It also does two things. The solution in the tank consists in part of a depilatory agent to remove the Navarch's hair by inactivating the follicles themselves. I removed his facial hair by shaving and electrolysis. What's especially interesting, though, is that the solution contains another agent to soften his skeletal system and then reverse the ossificaiton process altogether so that his bones turn back into pliant cartilage, the cartilage of the womb. At this very moment calcium and phosphorus are being leached from his bones, Markcrier. When his skeleton consists entirely of cartilage and when the poikilothermal condition has been firmly established, I can begin to use the knife." Prendick looked at me with a weary innocence. "Two or three months' work will remain even after I've removed him from the whirlpool. Perhaps for a Christmas gift I can deliver into your hands this predatory thing we have sired together. A shark will be born."

"Perhaps," I said.

And I left Yves Prendick to his work and returned, under guard, to the Palace of the Navarchy. I did not go back to Hospitaler House for nearly two weeks—although Yves came to the Palace almost every morning to see me. I made use of this time away from the sunken surgical hall to strengthen my grip on the levers of power and to woo a population that could remember no Navarch but Fearing Serenos. Most of this courting took place during

he public cremation ceremony, over which I presided from
beginning to end.

I delivered an impassioned address about the right of
men to govern their own lives within the limitations of law;
I read to the clustering crowd, flamboyant in their yellow
and scarlet mourning dress, a small section of my uncom-
pleted poem *Archipelagoes*.

The casket remained closed throughout the ceremonies,
even when on brief display in the outer courtyard of the
crematorium. When the casket was burned, consumed at
incredible temperatures, it yielded royal ashes—though
they were not those of Serenos at all, but instead the charred
dust of a misbegotten sea otter that had once been Emmanuel Huerta.

I had ordered Prendick to kill Huerta in the least painful way he could devise; and on the morning before the
requiem rites for Serenos, Yves had given the old fisherman a fatal anodyne. His body we had later concealed in
the Navarch's casket for the purpose of the state funeral.
No one doubted our story; no one wept for a last look
at the late ruler's corpse.

All went well in the weeks immediately following the
funeral. The people accepted me, the council supported
my every recommendation, Molinier and his gendarmes
dogged my footsteps with an assiduousness beyond re-
proach.

I did not go back to Python's Keep. I did not leave the
city. Prendick returned to The Orchard every night to
walk among the trees with Melantha, to keep her company, to calm her fears about his long sessions at Hospi-
aler House. But I would not return to Python's Keep. Too
many mementos of another time crowded upon me when
I stepped over the threshold, a fragrance as of ancient
perfumes and constantly rejuvenating seas. I experienced
again the powerful intercourse of two hearts, and the
experience always hurt me.

Nevertheless, I saw Prendick often. I visited him in the
submerged operating hall where he continued to mold
Serenos into the ichthyoid form of something resembling
a shark. He cut. He performed skin grafts. He removed
the former Navarch's genitals and sculptured his bifurcated
lower body into the smooth, resilient muselage of a fish.
Working with the macerated bones of Serenos's skull,
Prendick shaped a neckless head; he flattened the strong

human nose; he moved the brutal eyes out of their forward-looking sockets and placed them on opposite sides
of the streamlined sharkish snout.

Where a man had once existed, Marina's father saw to
it that a knife-born member of the order *Selachii* came
into being. I began to believe that no such man as Fearing
Serenos had ever lived in Windfall Last, for the creature
on Prendick's operating table bore no resemblance to any
human being I had ever encountered. Its moist gray flesh
was marbled with intimations of blue, its face grinned with
the livid sewn-up grin of a museum horror. Things
progressed nicely. But even though it was by then the
middle of November, a great deal of delicate vivisecting
and grafting remained to be done.

And by the middle of November I had begun to make
enemies.

Molinier could not understand my refusal to permit
bodyguards to descend with me into the sunken chamber
of surgery. I argued that the intricacy of my friend's
experiments demanded a silent surgical environment.

Why, then, did the Navarch go so frequently to the
operating area? Was his interest in vivisection so profound?

I argued that Prendick was engaged in activity that might
one day free the population of Windfall Last from its
biological heritage. One day the Parfects might choose to
readmit us to the world we had twice repudiated, and they
would do so because of my friend's work. I went to him so
frequently because my presence steadied his hand, my encouragement made him aware of our trust in his skill.
These lies I told Molinier on several occasions, but he held
his skepticism in check and continued as my friend.

He did not become my enemy until I had made a severe
tactical error by attempting to formulate policy on the basis
of moral conviction. The poet ruled where the bureaucrat
ought to have prevailed.

I decided that the Gendarmerie (even after Molinier's
October purge) was at a strength incommensurate with its
duties—that too many of its members were callous self-
seeking men who used their position as a carte blanche to
insult, intimidate, bludgeon, and kill. I ordered Molinier to
discover the identities of these men and to remove them
from the police force.

At that moment, Molinier became my enemy.

Perfunctorily, he did what I asked—but the men whom he removed went down to the quays and destroyed the vessels, the nets, and the cargoes of a council member's private fishing fleet. None of the remaining gendarmes would make an arrest; not a single marauder came to justice.

While Prendick's knife made careful incisions in the flesh of the former Navarch, my idealism gouged jagged rents in my own, the current Navarch's, credibility. But now I had power. I persisted. I refused to toady to the old men and the fiery youths who encircled me with their own peculiar brands of avarice and who gave me immoral advice. Because of what Prendick and I had done, the position of Navarch belonged to me.

Let its use be worthy, I prayed. For I intended to use it.

Then one night as I lay in my canopied bed, the ghost of Emmanuel Huerta came to me in the form of a white otter and sang to me in my dream. On the next day I took action to lift the interdict on the fishermen of Marigold Island, just as Fearing Serenos had once falsely told me he had done. I decreed that all who wished to do so could return to Guardian's Loop; the day of enforced exile was done.

I sent a vessel to Barbos to deliver this happy news, but few of the fishermen there believed. They knew that Huerta had never returned to them.

The vessel I had dispatched eventually came home— gliding over the waters of Pretty Coal Sack, its sails as lewd as soiled linen, its prow dull and stupid-looking above the spitlike froth through which it cut. I waited on the quay. Not one of the members of the colony of exiles disembarked, however, and the shipmaster insisted that my lifting of the interdict had meant nothing to the people at Barbos, so wanting in discernment and gratitude were they all.

Several nights later a crewman from this vessel, whom I had granted a clandestine audience, told me that three fishermen from the colony had come aboard ship, but that they had been murdered and cast into the sea not more than an hour out from Marigold. I believed this sailor, but could do nothing.

The heavy rains continued to fall, drowning us with their vehemence and their unremitting noise. A biblical deluge for the world's last men, a deluge of tall rains striding over the earth.

As the rains fell, Prendick brought Serenos further along. He amputated his arms, smoothed the shoulders into his tough symmetrical body, began shaping dorsal fins from the skin he had cut away from the amputated arms—skin he had also treated in a chemical brine. Now when I visited Prendick, the smell of the surgical chamber drove me onto the tier above the main floor; I watched everything from a distance, literally and metaphorically aloof.

Exercising my power as Navarch, however, I tried to remain aloof from the evil that existed in Windfall Last. I proceeded with my catch-as-catch-can program of reform. Strangers and aliens seemed to surround me; they looked on as I ordered that all the iron spikes jutting skyward from the harbor wall be pried from their sockets and scrapped, never again to receive upon their cold lance-tips the heads of dismembered human beings. Even in this, unthinking men opposed me.

A work force of impressed prol-fauves removed the spikes from the wall, but the gendarmes whom I had sent to supervise this labor made bets among themselves and instigated bloody little combats among the individual work crews—so that prol-fauves used the dislodged spikes to maim and disembowel one another while their supervisors sat horse on the streets above them and cheered them on. Only the sudden onset of great winds and torrential rains prevented this casually provoked slaughter from developing into a small insurrection. Before the coming of the streaming torrents, the gendarmes had had to shoot several workmen for turning away from the quays and threatening to mob into the city with their crude weapons. On this same afternoon two horses with ripped bellies, having thrown their riders, bolted through the rain toward the Palace; slime-coated intestines gleamed with crimson intensity on the cobbles. Just as in Prendick's theater of surgery, I watched everything from a distance.

Again I had failed. Eight years of isolation from the ways of men had not prepared me for the frustrations of thwarted authority. How had my Marina come to me from such a milieu of contradictory impulses? What sort of animal inhabited Guardian's Loop? Indeed, what sort of ambiguous animal ravened in my own breast, devouring both the bitter and the sweet?

At the beginning of December an unexpected thing happened.

Seemingly materializing from nowhere, a tall silver-eyed Parfect presented herself at the gate of the Palace of the Navarchy and told the gendarmes on duty that she would see the new ruler of our island. As a concession to our sensibilities, she wore a white linen robe with Grecian fretwork at the sleeves and hem. The guards fell back at once and found a council member to usher the Parfect into my chambers on the topmost floor.

When the Parfect entered, I was sitting beneath the open skylight looking at the fish in my aquarium and trying to decide if I should attempt sleep. Dusk had sifted down on me; my head ached. But startled by the twilight apparition of the Parfect, I stood up and discovered with shame that I was weeping. Inexplicably. I did not recognize this alien sister from either of my two stays in Azteca Nueva, but I embraced her as a friend.

We conversed in the fading light. She ignored the salt tears on the tilted planes of my cheeks and moved about the room as she spoke, gracefully gesturing with her hands. Her voice dealt with our human words—our pragmatic Franglais—with a precision born of unfamiliarity. My own voice faltered, faltered in attempting to reach her heart; but neither of us, in reality, said a great deal. The message of this visitor from Azteca Nueva consisted not so much of words as of a perfectly communicated *tone.*

Disappointment.

The Parfects felt disappointment. For centuries they had waited for us, delaying an inevitable decision. It was not enough that we merely struggled. Her voice smoothed out this last suggestion and played with another tone—although that of disappointment continued to undulate gently beneath the surface. The inevitable decision would be delayed again, this time for the purpose of receiving a final representative of mankind in Azteca Nueva. Serenos had put them off. Very well, then, the beginning of the new decade (still more than a year away) would suffice, and they desired the Markcrier Rains once again be that emissary—

—Markcrier Rains, he who no longer slept beside a woman sharing the sea-smell of her womb; he who held the poison-tipped scepter of a mysteriously fallen prince; he who on past occasions had walked haltingly among the Parfects of the luxuriantly flowered mainland, in the shadow of Popocatepetl.

No other could come in my stead, they had settled upon me. Windfall Last would find a ruler more suited to her disposition during my absence, and upon my return that new ruler would step aside for me. Then the decision would be withheld no longer; it would come down to us, out of either disappointment or forgiveness. And the world would be changed.

"Do not think us unfeeling, Markcrier," the Parfect said before leaving me. "It may be that we feel too deeply."

When she had gone, the twilight departing on the trailing hem of her Grecian robe, the room still contained something of her presence. Even in the resultant dark this intangible balm hung in the air, like the fragrance of foreign evergreens. The idea of living again in Azteca Nueva did not seem completely unpleasant.

Only in the morning, when sunlight cascaded in like harp music, did I realize that going once more among the Parfects would signal for me a private doom, a living suicide. I refused to see anyone that morning; I failed to visit Hospitaler House. Nearly thirteen months remained to me before the advent of the new decade, and in that time I might be able to devise an alternative acceptable to the Parfects. But I would not go, I would not. Still, it was almost a week before the lingering suggestion of the messenger's presence disappeared utterly from my council room.

On the ninth day of the month I went to Prendick again and found that his work was nearly done. He had given Serenos the crescentic underslung mouth of a shark. He had also given him an armoring of artificially cultivated placoid scales and teeth to occupy the predatory mouth.

As I watched from the tier of copper cages, Prendick went about the one task that he had purposely postponed until every other procedure of the metamorphosis lay behind him. Once again the tank came into play, but this time without all the paraphernalia of recirculation and cleansing. Marina's father had submerged himself in the tank, which now murmured with stinging salt water; and he was working on the snout of the creature suspended in traction over the water's surface.

I watched for almost three hours. During all this time Prendick and I exchanged not a single word; of late we had had less and less to say to each other, as if the surgeon's scalpel had split our tongues. We communed in other ways,

nowing that only two of us—in all the world—knew of
is ultimate degradation of Fearing Serenos. Prendick was
ad, of course, and I . . . It was too late to concern my-
lf.

The last step was taking place, the creation of the shark's
ouverlike system of gills: the fluttering blood-blue bran-
hiae through which Serenos would breathe. Prendick had
reserved this moment in order not to have to work in the
ater until he absolutely must. But the moment was upon
im; and occasionally lowering his suspended patient into
e tank and then raising him out again, he cut and cau-
rized, severed and tied. Sometimes he worked through
e monster's cruel mouth.

At the end of the third hour, Prendick collapsed Serenos's
seless lungs, administered a stimulant, and dropped him
ut of traction into the water—where his new respiratory
stem began to function. Then Prendick climbed out of
e tank and grinned up at me, his face more cadaverous
nd his trunk and limbs more wanly etiolated than I had
ver seen them. He looked ill.

But I grinned, too, and marveled at the drugged pseudo-
ark stirring its body and tail with lethargic gracelessness.
Ve had done what we had set out to accomplish. If our
pecimen was not a perfect representative of order *Selachii*,
approached that ideal and nevertheless did us honor.

Still, we knew it would be impossible to release Serenos
to the bay before he had recovered from the gill opera-
on and gained the necessary stamina to compete with the
a creatures who would challenge him for prey. Prendick
id, "Give him until Christmas, Markcrier," and those
ere the first words either of us had spoken since my arriv-
l in the early morning. I had no doubt that even in the
ody of a lower animal Serenos would compete quite well.
s a man, he had possessed a gift for tenacious survival;
d although his brain had been cut into seperate lobes and
attened into the narrow brain casing of a shark, Prednick
lieved that Serenos still had at least a portion of his
rmer intelligence. He would not be ready for the open
a, however, for well over two weeks. An eternity.

In Windfall Last I received word of a plot against my
fe. Informers came to my gates nightly with fantastic
ories of treason and rebellion. All pled for my ear, all
xpected reward.

A week before Christmas a man came to me with letters

bearing the signatures of Molinier and a young lieutenan
in the Gendarmerie. The contents of these letters pointe
without hope of any error, at the desire of these two me
to kill me. The next day I ordered Molinier to send me th
reports of the Gendarmerie's activities for the last tw
months. When they came, I compared the signatures on th
reports with the handwriting and signatures of the assass
nation letters supposedly written by Molinier. No noticeab
differences existed. I paid the informer, himself a membe
of the force, and told him to find at least five other ge
darmes who shared his active loyalty to the Navarch. Wit
less difficulty than I had expected, he did so.

These six men I dispatched at a predawn hour to Mo
linier's quarters in the lower courtyard; they took him fro
his bed and returned with him to a vacant section of th
stables where I awaited their coming, two of the olde
council members at my side. We showed Molinier th
documents, and I confronted him with the damning simila
ity of the signatures, studying his impassive face for thos
involuntary tics and crawls that of themselves confess th
man. But he said simply, "I would never have put my nam
to a letter so crassly seditious, Navarch," and glared at m
with unrepentant eyes.

My heart was torn. I did not believe him. I said, "Yo
will die as quickly and as painlessly as a man may di
Molinier, because until now you refused to lie to me—eve
when you disagreed with my executive mandates."

He looked at me coldly. Soul-sick, I waved my hand an
left.

The informant and his five companions took Molinier t
the ivied wall between the stables. There they shot him
The rifle reports echoed over the flagstones like polyps ex
ploding in their shells; a sea dream died with each report.

The repercussions of these shots were felt from th
Palace to the quays. Because the force might have depose
me if properly unified, I left the Gendarmerie directorless
As a result, I could not leave my own sleeping chambe
and conference rooms for fear that a fanatic worse tha
Molinier would slay me in the streets. In the Palace, th
younger council members treated me with borderline cour
tesy and whispered among themselves.

But Prendick, who was now free of our self-impose
labor, stayed with me during the afternoons and "monitore
my health." While every other bureaucrat in the govern

ment engaged in intrigue, he kept me informed of our
patient's progress. He seemed entirely unaware of the pre-
cariousness of my hold on the Navarchy. He thought only
of Serenos, of our magnificent pseudoshark.

"He doesn't eat," Prendick said one afternoon in the
administrative suite. "I'm afraid he's losing strength rather
than gaining it."

"Why doesn't he eat?"

But Prendick responded, "To deny us our revenge,
Markcrier. Some part of his conscious mind is operating to
bring all our efforts to naught. He's *willing* himself to death.
But to combat his will I drug him and feed him intravenously."

"He'll finally grow stronger, then?"

"I don't know, he's a preternatural creature. Do you
know what I heard a simple fisherman once say of him?"

"No. What?"

"That Serenos and the Adam of Genesis are the same
person. The fisherman claimed that Adam never really died
but wandered through the earth cursing his fall and his own
meekness before God after the expulsion from Eden. Since
no one can remember when Serenos was born, the old fisherman believed the story. He believed that Serenos was
Adam."

"A legend," I said. "The legend of the unregenerate
Adam. It has great antiquity, Yves, but not a great deal
of respectability."

"Well, if it's true," Yves said, "we've finally ended it."

"Yes, I suppose we have. Or else the unregenerate
Adam is in the process of ending it himself. Forever. By
foiling our plans for him. An extremely unregenerate Adam
is Serenos."

"I don't want to lose him, Mark, not after all the work
I've done. If he dies, I'd have to create another like him—
only more detailed and less flawed than this one. My
hands know what to do now."

To that I answered nothing. Marina's father had regained a little of his former color with several successive
nights of uninterrupted and heavy sleep, but he still spoke
from a nightmarish, topsy-turvy point of view. Had he
transferred his love for the memory of his daughter to another of his children? Locked inside the Palace of the
dominion that I ostensibly ruled, I did not understand how
one could develop an affection for sharks, even man-made

ones. Pride in accomplishment, perhaps, but never abiding affection. Spontaneous awe, perhaps, but never love.

When Christmas came, the old residual festivities took place, and everyone silently acknowledged the existence of a general truce.

Men and women danced in the streets. The ships in the harbor flew brilliant handmade banners of gold and scarlet. The officers of the Gendarmerie wore their blue dress uniforms and organized a parade of horses and men from the Palace to the quays, a parade in which drums, flutes, and teakwood mandolins (these last played by the only Orientals on Guardian's Loop) provided a gay and stately accompaniment to the clatter of horses' hooves. Sea gulls, screeching and wheeling, rode the updrafts above the Christmas festivities like animated diacritical marks on a parchment of pale blue.

At nine o'clock in the morning I went out on the balcony and told the gendarmes and the footmen in the courtyard that they too could join the merrymaking. The truce was both general and genuine.

Then I put on a cape with a hood, and Prendick and I left the Palace. We walked down the several levels of narrow rose-tinged houses to the hospital. There was a smell of rum on the morning breeze, and children ran down the cobbles and darted in and out of doorways, shouting. Most of them paid no heed at all to the deformities with which they had been born—unless of course their legs or feet had been affected, in which cases they sat on stoops and windowsills where their parents had placed them and shouted as insistently as the others. The children with untouched bodies seemed to have the grimmest faces; they played with the quiet determination of soldiers.

Prendick and I said nothing to either the children or the adults.

At Hospitaler House we got immediately to business.

The day had come to release Serenos into the waters of Pretty Coal Sack. For five days Prendick had refrained from administering any sort of sedative or stimulant to his creation. He believed that a further delay in this final test would serve only to prolong our anxiety. I said, "It's now very much a question of sink or swim, isn't it?" but Prendick was either too distracted or too tactful to respond. In any case, we had no more opportunities for humor, how-

ver feeble or strained, for the duration of that protracted
Christmas day.

The long experiment failed.

We placed the tank of sea water containing Serenos in a
pressure chamber that was sometimes used by divers. We
closed the weighted inner door and introduced enough
water to fill the chamber completely—so that our pseudoshark could swim effortlessly out of the tank, free of all
artificial restraints but the iron-gray walls of the pressure
chamber itself. Then we opened the outer door and waited
for the former Navarch to swim with measured slowness
into the still, cathedral-solemn depths of Pretty Coal Sack.
We felt our heartbeats echoing in the conches of our ears.
We waited for our patchwork ichthyoid to float free of the
shadow of the pressure chamber and into the soundless
sun-warmed sea. We waited by the cold glass. We waited
for the appearance of the thing we loved and hated, our
hands clammy with salt sweat.

At last, the misbegotten body of the pseudoshark dropped
laterally through the waters toward us. It moved its tail
and fins with no apparent enthusiasm or purpose. Then it
turned its sleek gray-and-blue marbled flank to the glass
behind which we stood and slid down this transparent wall
until it was level with our eyes. Here the creature hung,
one piggish unblinking eye staring without hope or love into
our sanctuary. The seas of the world stretched away behind it, but only the perfunctory movement of the raw
pectoral fin betrayed that Serenos was still alive.

Then even that movement ceased, and Serenos died.

Created without an air bladder, as all sharks are necessarily created, the pseudoshark canted to one side, suffered
a spasm through the length of its trunk, and drifted away
toward the bottom of Pretty Coal Sack, spiraling down in
dreamy slow motion.

When Serenos had disappeared, Prendick and I looked
at each other in silence and then turned away from the
window. Three months of our lives we had spent in this
enterprise, no inconsequential portion of the time a man
has allotted to him. Prendick sat down and wept.

I thought, *And is it thus that we have finally avenged the
death of a daughter and a wife? What manner of beast are
we?*

*   *   *

It is the Year of Our Lost Lord 5309. Or so we believe. From the sea we came, and to the sea we eventually return. There is very little more to tell in this account of our exile in the terra-cotta city of Windfall Last.

On the day after our failure with Serenos, I abdicated my position as Navarch and thereby forestalled the inevitable assassination attempt. I did not take this action out of cowardice. Too many other factors influenced me.

The first of these was the knowledge that no emissary to the Parfects, no matter who he was, would alter their ultimate judgment upon mankind. Under no circumstances would I go again to Azteca Nueva; under no circumstances would I offer myself up as the ritual scapegoat of a species doomed from the very moment of its prehistoric inception, particularly when my own sacrifice—just like that of another long before me—would signify nothing, would mark the waste of still another spirit yearning toward the unattainable. For that reason and others, I abdicated. How could I face the Parfects after my part in Serenos's mutilation and murder?

Instead, I have settled upon another course of action, one that appeals to the tenets of my aesthetic and moral feelings.

Tomorrow morning in the sunken theater of surgery, I am to go under Prendick's knife. He has already agreed to my plan, and his insane dedication to the rationale behind it will see him through the disconcerting early stages of my metamorphosis. Later, when my resemblance to shark has grown more and more faithful, he will forget altogether that inside the tapered head resides the essence and the intellect of his own son-in-law. He will not fail with me as we failed with Serenos—from that failure Prendick learned too much, his hands derived too many unconscious skills.

And three months hence I will go with supple zeal into the waters of the Atlantic, no more a man.

I am convinced that we are the freaks of the universe we were never meant to be. In our natures there is an improper balance of stardust and dross, too much of one, too little of the other—but not enough of either to give us the perfection of the extreme.

My entire life has been a struggle to achieve that which the universe long ago decreed we might not achieve. I have been living with the delusions of the evolutionary mistake

of which I am a product. But no more. Tomorrow morning
am tacking about into the indifferent winds of the cosmos
and altering my course. Though perfection is denied me in
the direction of the westward seas, I will attain it by swinging toward the dawn. God! even now the salt is in my blood
and the power of a shark's primordial lust surges through
my heart and loins!

I will swim against the current.

I will seek out the channel that cuts beneath the *Galleon
of the Hesperides* and beach myself among the flowers.
There I will die, knowing that the white otters will observe
my death and scramble into the sea—aghast at so much un-
principled might.

And my death will be more honest than any single instance of a good man's piety.

FOR THE LADY OF A PHYSICIST

*Although Bekenstein's hypothesis that black holes have a
finite entropy requires for its consistency that black holes
should radiate thermally, at first it seems a complete
miracle that the detailed quantum-mechanical calculations
of particle creation should give rise to emission with a
thermal spectrum. The explanation is that the emitted
particles tunnel out of the black hole from a region which
an external observer has no knowledge other than its mass,
angular momentum, and electric charge. This means that
all combinations or configurations of emitted particles that
have the same energy, angular momentum, and electric
charge are equally probable. Indeed, it is possible that the
black hole could emit a television set or the works of
Proust in ten leather-bound volumes. . . .*

> "The Quantum Mechanics of Black Holes,"
> —S. W. HAWKING
> *Scientific American* (January 1977), p. 40.

If I with her could only join
In rapturous dance, loin to loin,
Deep space itself would soon discern
Galactic rhythm in our burn.
Our bodies stars, our debts all void,
Then would we waltz and, thus employed,
Inflate with megacosmic thrust
Through night and death and sifting dust.
Godlike lovers, we would hang
Beyond the cosmos whose Big Bang,
All the mad millennia past,

Was but a popgun to our slow blast.
And as we reeled with raw élan,
Pulsing plasma in vast pavane,
We would shame the Pleiades,
Relume the Magellanic Seas,
Deliver all our Milky Way,
Ionic flux too fierce to stay,
In supernova, and so rehearse
Our own expanding universe.

But my small body is no star,
Albeit something similar:
A blind pool vacuuming into it
All the lambency it's not fit
To redirect and render rife.
The woman I would take to wife
Sees only blackness in my eyes,
Rapacious ebon, hungry skies,
An O-gape gravid with desire
To aggrandize itself in fire;
And so her light sweeps down the hole
That is the maelstrom of my soul.

Therefore, I have become for her
A dark entropic murderer,
Whose chiefest virtue is his pull.
Then, while my strength is at its full,
Let me draw her to my embrace,
Collapse her will and show my face.
With her my Beatrician guide,
We'd tunnel with the thermal tide
Into the arms of Betelgeuse—
With Quasar sets and Marcel Proust
Emergent with us, glory-bound,
Detritus of God's Lost & Found.
Thus, though we cannot create light
From love, yet we will vanquish night.